THE IMAGE OF WOMEN IN CONTEMPORARY SOVIET FICTION

Also by Sigrid McLaughlin

SCHOPENHAUER IN RUSSLAND: Zur Literarischen Rezeption
bei Turgenev

The Image of Women in Contemporary Soviet Fiction

Selected Short Stories from the USSR

Edited and translated by
SIGRID McLAUGHLIN
Lecturer in Modern Society and Social Thought
Stevenson College
University of California at Santa Cruz

St. Martin's Press   New York

Published by arrangement with
the Copyright Agency of the
USSR, Moscow

First published in the United States of America in 1989

Printed in the People's Republic of China

ISBN 0–312–02823–7 cloth
ISBN 0–312–02824–5 paper

Library of Congress Cataloging-in-Publication Data
The image of women in contemporary Soviet
fiction: selected short stories from the USSR/edited
and translated by Sigrid McLaughlin.
    p.   cm.
    Bibliography: p.
    ISBN 0–312–02823–7.—ISBN 0–312–02824–5 (pbk.)
    1. Short stories, Russian—Translations into
English. 2. Short stories, Soviet—Translations into
English. 3. Short stories, English—Translations
from foreign languages. 4. Women—Soviet
Union—Fiction. 5. Soviet fiction—Bio-
bibliography. 6. Russian fiction—Bio-
bibliography. I. McLaughlin, Sigrid.
PG3286.144   1989
891.73′01′08352042—dc19   88–33335
                                            CIP

Nepostizhimy
Tainy perevoda:
Byla parodiya,
A stala oda.

Unfathomable are
The secrets of translation:
There was a parody –
An ode's the new creation.

Byt' zhenshchinoi – chto eto znachit?
Kakoyu tainoyu vladet'?
Vot zhenshchina. No ty nezryachii.
Ni v chem ne vinovat, nezryach!
A zhenshchina sebya naznachit,
Naznachit kak lekarstvo – vrach.
I esli zhenshchina prikhodit,
Sebe edinstvenno verna,
Ona prikhodit – kak prokhodit
Chuma, blokada i voina.
I esli zhenshchina prikhodit
I o sebe zavodit rech',
Ona, kak provod, tok provodit,
Chtob nad toboyu svet zazhet'.
           Rimma Kazakova, 1987

What does it mean to be a woman?
What is the secret one must know?
Here is a woman. But you're blind.
And blind, you're innocent, alas!
And she prescribes herself,
Like medicine a doctor.
And when a woman comes,
True to herself alone,
She comes, like pestilence, a blockade,
Or like a war that passes through.
And when a woman comes,
Begins to speak about herself,
She's like a wire, bringing current,
To turn on light above your head.

Contents

Contents

Acknowledgements

I wish to thank Gail Warshofsky Lapidus and Bettina Aptheker for their encouragement with this anthology. Numerous individuals have helped to give it its present shape: Alexander Podossinov, Tatyana Patera, Boris Keyser and Roza Sakwa helped clarify Russian meanings, and Merike Beecher, Carol Chittenden, Karen Johnson and Janice Robinson read drafts of the translations and commented on the English. Barbara Heldt helped with the Introduction.

I am grateful to Alma Law for letting me use her translation of Lyudmila Petrushevskaya's 'Nets and Traps', and to Tracy Kuehn for her translation of Irina Raksha's 'Lambushki'. The Committee on Research of the University of California, Santa Cruz, provided generous financial support for typing, xeroxing and editorial help.

Valentin Rasputin's 'Vasily and Vasilissa' was first published, in a slightly different form, in *Soviet Literature*, no. 3 (1980), translated by Susan Henderson.

The Translation of Russian Names

Most Russian names have been left in their Russian form in order to convey to the reader the variety of emotional relationships the speaker expresses through the variations of the basic form of a Russian name. Formally, Russian names consist of first name, patronymic* and last name. The patronymic is the only part of the name that deviates from the Western pattern. It is based on the father's name, to which the ending -*ovna* for a woman, or -*ovich* for a man, is appended, meaning 'daughter of' or 'son of'. For example, Valentina Stepanovna of Grekova's story is the daughter of Stepan.

The use of first name and patronymic implies a polite and friendly relationship of strangers and acquaintances. Referring to a person by the patronymic alone reflects a casual, even impolite attitude. If only the last name is employed, distance or formality is implied. The use of the first name alone indicates closeness. Trifonov establishes a subtle hierarchy in his story 'Vera and Zoyka' when he has his narrator refer to the two women of the title exclusively by their first names, and to their employer more formally by first name and patronymic.

Various forms of the first name reveal the emotional relationship of the speaker to the addressed person. The name Valentina allows the endearing abbreviation 'Valya', from which further endearing variations, 'Valyunchik', 'Valyusha' or 'Valechka', are derived that indicate fondness, tenderness and warmth. The ending -*ka* or -*ik* indicates familiarity. At times an endearing form is not obvious, because it sounds very different from the original name: 'Shura', for 'Aleksandra', is an example.

Preface

This collection of stories grew from an interest in the situation of women in the Soviet Union and from a concern over our inadequate information about the heterogeneity of Soviet life. Animosity to Soviet ideology and government, and outdated notions of Soviet 'totalitarian' society and of the artistic inferiority of its literature have made us focus on dissident and émigré writers whose works are eagerly translated into English, often because of their political agenda. Thus, the moderate number of Soviet literary works that have reached the West in the last decade or two fail to get the publicity a work on camp or prison experiences might muster. But much of the literature published in the USSR has been not only of good quality, but also of general human interest. If we continue to avoid encounters with current Soviet literature, we shut out a major path toward understanding a major *other* society.

This collection expands the scope of information about Soviet society by offering a variety of stories, all published in the USSR, that touch on a wide range of themes relating to women: work, the family, customs and beliefs, generational problems, leisure, urbanization, rural life, education, social mobility. Offering literary works for extra-literary purposes is not to imply that literary art is an unproblematical means of knowing the world, nor is it to suggest that simple 'mirror' theories of art are valid. The point is simply that official fiction, at its best, is vital and challenging and provides valuable glimpses of the lives lived in a vastly different country.

The collection focuses on the lives of women, because a growing number of English-speaking women are eager to compare their experiences with those of their counterparts in other countries. Such comparison enhances their self-understanding and helps to set off their own achievements and goals. A focus on women also allows the reader to witness the lives of women in a country that has legislated political and social equality since 1917. Has this legislation led to real equality? Are Soviet women emancipated? What does the concept mean to them? How do they juggle career, family and self? What are their needs, their aspirations? How do they see themselves?

The heroines of the stories are women of various ages, educational backgrounds and careers, and they are caught up in a wide range of situations and activities. They search for their identity and independence, try to cope with their dual roles or with single motherhood, experience love and loneliness, adultery and physical hardship, undergo abortions and divorce, rear their children or refuse to have any, and interact with their parents and in-laws. In the process, the stories reveal a number of circumstances mostly unfamiliar to people in the West, but important for an understanding of the contemporary Soviet mentality: the material and demographic consequences of the Second World War (poverty, hunger, single-mother families); the closeness of family ties; the material difficulties of daily life.

While the literary scholar will be offered a sampling of aesthetically interesting works, the sociologist, political scientist and historian will find material that illustrates some of the attitudes and values, thought patterns and expectations of the Soviet people. It is noteworthy that, in the USSR itself, literature is studied for sociological purposes, as the publication in 1984 of a collection entitled *Literature and Sociology* (ed. Vladimir Kantorovich and Yuri Kuz'menko) indicates; and many sociological studies, in turn, appear in literary weeklies and monthlies: *Literaturnaya gazeta* and *Novy mir*, *Voprosy literatury* and *Literaturnoe obozrenie*. In the United States Vera Dunham has pioneered such a use of literature in her pathbreaking book *In Stalin's Time*.

The stories chosen for this anthology are representative of both men and women authors, so that the reader can ponder whether the stories reflect a female or male consciousness and rhetoric, and in what that might consist. Such selection also raises the question of the different images women and men might create of women. Furthermore, the authors belong to different generations and schools of writing. Some, at around fifty years, are by Soviet standards relatively young: Belov, Kim, Petrushevskaya, Raksha, Rasputin, Tokareva. Two are even younger: Sidorenko and Tolstaya. Of older writers, Trifonov (who died in 1981), Baranskaya, Grekova and Zalygin are represented. The male writers are considered well-established major literary figures. Of the women, Grekova and Baranskaya, now in their late seventies, are widely known as the doyennes of women's writing. Petrushevskaya, mostly famous as a playwright, is beginning to get her hitherto unpublishable stories into print. Tolstaya is the latest rave of

Moscow literary critics and, with Petrushevskaya, the most original writer.

Some of the authors – Belov, Rasputin – belong to the school of 'village prose', whose followers are preoccupied with the spiritual impact of urbanization. Others – Trifonov and most women writers – deal with everyday life in urban settings. Some writers – Kim, Sidorenko – elude classification. The writers also come from different regions of the Russian Federal Socialist Soviet Republic, although most of them have moved to Moscow. As a result, the settings of the stories vary.

Several criteria influenced the selection of the stories: accessibility to an English-speaking readership, quality, and representativeness (age and orientation of authors, chronology, thematics). The stories are realistic and cover the last twenty years of Soviet experience. Their changing thematic preoccupations and perceptions reflect changes in Soviet society at large, changes in consciousness which go hand in hand with political changes.

Each writer is introduced by a biographical sketch and a list of works and secondary literature in English. The Glossary helps readers to familiarize themselves with idiosyncratic facts about Soviet society that enhance comprehension of the stories, and the list of Suggestions for Further Reading is intended to assist readers to explore the book's topics on their own. Words for which there is an entry in the Glossary are signalled in the text by an asterisk.

Santa Cruz   S. McL.
California

Introduction

I

The stories in this collection, all of them written between the mid-1960s and mid-1980s, trace social and moral developments in Soviet society through the image of women. By 1965, when the first story in this collection appeared, Soviet literature had begun to recover from the mandatory optimism, the stereotypical characters, the schematic plots and the moral didacticism which Socialist Realism under Stalin had imposed on the writer. This doctrine demanded that art must be true to life, yet imply the social and ethical ideal of communism. As a result, literary works offered prettified versions of reality, in which the good – i.e. socially progressive and 'humane' – was victorious. Literary methods other than traditional realism were shunned.[1]

In those years, the 1930s, millions of women entered the labor force and gender equality was said to have been achieved. For the readers' emulation, Soviet women were portrayed as superwomen. Perfect and happy housewives and mothers, they were submissive and subordinate in their domestic role, and at the same time distinguished workers, fanatically loyal to their government and country. Love culminated in marriage, was presumed to be permanent, based on trust, free of jealousy, and cemented by shared social and cultural interests. Premarital and extramarital sex was non-existent or restricted to female villains and class enemies. The new Soviet constitution of 1936 supported these values, proclaiming the family as the foundation of society, and female endurance and hard work for family and state the central values. By 1936, divorce was almost unobtainable, abortion was illegal, and common-law marriages were invalid.

The Victorianism of the Stalin era reflected a many-faceted retreat from the promises of the Revolution. The emancipatory

---

1. For a further discussion of the excesses of Socialist Realism see A. Tertz (A. Sinyavsky), *On Socialist Realism* (New York: Pantheon, 1960).

government decrees of 1917 had granted women full equality in all spheres of public life. Theoretically, all educational opportunities and careers were open to them. Economic independence was legally guaranteed, work a right and a duty. Divorce laws were easy and equitable, abortions legal. Of course, implementation in a largely illiterate, economically backward and adamantly patriarchal society was a Herculean task, unachievable in the decade and a half before Stalin turned back the clock.

The Second World War had a profound impact on the lives of women. Even more than before, in life and literature women were heroic, self-sacrificing figures without private lives. Having maintained industry and agriculture and assured the survival of children and the aged, women emerged from the war years masculinized and psychologically devastated. A majority of them were widows or had no chance of ever marrying. No wonder that the demographic imbalance, which has repercussions into the present, led, after the war, to the pampering and adulation of men, and to women happily accepting their traditional role of submissive homemaker or mistress, while paradoxically continuing to carry the burdens of wage-earner and, frequently, even head of household. Often the men who returned from the war were crippled or had trouble readjusting to daily life. This situation had a lasting influence on traditional morals, too. Unable to marry, women had illegitimate children, whom they raised under psychological duress and the enormous economic hardships of post-war devastation and hunger. The literary works of those years depict these solitary women as strong and persevering, heroines not made of feminist convictions but of tragic circumstances.

After Stalin's death in 1953, when the brief episode of militant liberalism and the longer period of conservative 'backlash', as well as the greatest miseries of the war, had passed, the pendulum slowly began to swing. The private lives and concerns of individuals moved into the focus of attention, and the details of the real Soviet social and individual landscape began to emerge. Introspective self-examination, traditional love-triangles, the nature of happiness and fulfilment, and the broken family were recognized as legitimate and socially important themes, even though officially writers were admonished to integrate the thoughts and feelings of the individual into the larger social context of labor and the technological revolution. The mundane conditions of Soviet life – injustices, bribery, the dearth of good housing, the inadequacy of services and the shortages of consumer goods – entered these analyses as formative factors of individual psychology. The prevalent literary form became the story which best captured the turn toward intimate individual themes.

II

The 'thaw' period of unprecedented frankness which had culminated in the publication of Aleksandr Solzhenitsyn's *One Day in the Life of Ivan Denisovich*, about life in a labor camp, was beginning to decline after the fall of Khrushchev in 1964. **I. Grekova's** 'A Summer in the City' (1965) is typical of its time in its attention to individual problems and treatment of a subject that had for a long time been taboo, abortion. Legalized in a decree of 23 November, 1955, abortion has since become the primary means of birth control – with an average of nine per woman – and is no longer a problem for the heroine's daughter. But Grekova's story is about more than the heroine's unsuccessful illegal abortion. It is about attitudes, values and the self-perception of a middle-aged single woman and her female friends, about how men treat these women and how the women respond. It is also about the relations between a mother and a daughter, whose values clash because they were young at different times.

Valentina's divorce does not signify her rejection of the traditional woman's role. While married, she cooked, washed, ironed, shopped and mended for her beloved husband. When she sees him more than two decades later, she wonders about his second wife, 'doesn't she take care of him?' The assumption that these are womanly tasks is so deeply entrenched and so widely shared by Soviet men and women that Valentina feels no insult when her ex-husband wistfully describes these services as 'the eternally feminine something' which his younger wife lacks. Thus, Valentina's resignation and bitterness are not the effects of feeling trapped in a sex role, but the result of freshly realizing that this man has always and still is entirely self-centered, banal and totally uncomprehending of her. But it is hard to miss the authorial irony.

The stories by Trifonov and Rasputin complement Grekova's images. **Yury Trifonov's** two protagonists in 'Vera and Zoyka' (1966) are also city-dwellers and single working women. But a third woman, Vera and Zoyka's employer, is better off. Married to a scientist, she lives in a separate apartment and owns a summer cottage. The difference in the women's status is subtly expressed through the way they address each other, by first name or by name and patronymic.

The story is almost an 'environmental impact' study, if we take environment sociologically. It captures the brutalizing circumstances of the daily grind which destroy Zoyka's self-confidence and make her mean, manipulative, submissive and calculating. Her friend, Vera, however, is slightly better off and has managed to retain compassion and a love of life. Vera's viewpoint dominates. Combining third-person narration with interior monologue, Trifonov's narrative meanders in and out of her consciousness, capturing her speech habits and intonations. Trifonov's women have little education and self-awareness. Unlike the heroine of his later short novel *Another Life*, they are not introspective. Preoccupied with meeting their basic needs, they are virtually devoid of 'self'.

The dismal situation of the women is mediated from the outside, from a compassionate, non-ironic male point of view. Women's own experiences – for instance, what Vera felt about giving her illegitimate son to a boarding school under pressure from her boyfriend, or about having an abortion, or how Lidiya experienced herself in her all-male domestic environment – remain unexplored. The women think and act automatically in terms of conventional sex-role conceptions. For Trifonov, general ethical probing precludes a gender-specific analysis of moral problems.

The village, and in this context also its female population, is the topic of a number of well-established male authors who rose to fame in the provinces during the 1960s. **Valentin Rasputin** is the best of them. His story 'Vasily and Vasilissa' (1967), about a village couple in his native Angara region, is characteristic of the village prose of the 1960s. Life, and in this case a woman's lot, in those distant places is portrayed without embellishment. An image of peasant endurance and native moral strength, Vasilissa echoes her noble nineteenth-century predecessors. Although she accepts her husband's patriarchal rights, she refuses to tolerate his abuses. The mainstay of her family, she shoulders all responsibility for house, animals, garden and children, ignoring her husband, who comes and goes as he pleases. This sober village portrait is clearly a man's. The virtues Rasputin emphasizes are those that keep the heroine in bonds. He puts her on a pedestal, so that her sacrifices, which age-old tradition and specific circumstances necessitate, almost become an image of the fullness of life, and her conduct a model to imitate.

III

If the 1960s initiated a 'thawing' of taboo topics, the 1970s and early 1980s under party-leader Brezhnev and his brief successors Andropov and Chernenko were a time of retrenchment, of social stagnation and conservatism. Certain topics – for example, negative aspects of Soviet history or the present and Stalin's time – became taboo again. At the same time, however, this decade witnessed a detailed and thorough exploration of some of the themes broached in the 1960s, and the expansion of the limits of the permissible – at first by means of indirect reference and allusion, and later by limited direct reference.

It is in this decade that a generation of writers brought up entirely under the new literary and social conditions produced its best writing. Since women are often the protagonists of works by authors of both sexes, some critics have spoken of 'women's novels' gaining ascendance in the 1970s. Natalya Baranskaya's pioneering short novel *A Week Like Any Other* outlined the themes of the 'stocktaking' – the title of one of Trifonov's novellas published early in the decade – that preoccupied most writers: the conflicts between professional and domestic demands, strained relations between spouses and between different generations, and the various contexts of motherhood.

The portrayal of women during the 1970s and early 1980s continued earlier trends, but new motifs and attitudes appeared. Among male images, those of the conservative 'village prose' writers, who together with writers of a Russian nationalist orientation dominate contemporary Soviet fiction, stand out from the rest. Their heroines are longsuffering traditional women who accept their age-old sex roles and sacrifice their lives in service of the family, whereas 'emancipated women' are the negative and unhappy foils.

The dissolution of the patriarchal family resulting from modernization, as well as from the mass migration of about two thirds of the population from the country to the cities, is one of their major themes. These social developments have undermined traditional village culture and its central institution, the patriarchal family, with the 'village prose' writers see as the only counter-force to the moral vacuity of Soviet urban society. Fixed sex roles, they feel give men and women a well-defined place in society, a sense of what is expected of them, and a sense of being an important part of a whole. The patriarchal family provides something like a natural order that guarantees stability. Women's emancipation, an urban development, is seen as professional and personal insubordination of women in relation to men and as sexual licentiousness, and, thus, as a major cause of the disintegration of the family.

These are the views expressed in **Vasily Belov's** 'Morning Meetings' (1977), one of a sequence of four stories with common protagonists, in which Belov looks at ex-villagers after they have spent some time in the city. With Kostya Zorin, Belov creates what is meant to be a positive male character: hardworking, ambitious, reliable, faithful and compassionate. If he drinks, it is his wife's fault. Belov, through his narrators, is highly critical of Tonya, the female protagonist, who has acquired qualities Zorin identifies with becoming emancipated. Zorin resents his ex-wife's assertiveness, her independence, her abortions. But, ironically, some of Zorin's character traits and ideological positions vindicate Tonya's irritability.

If Rasputin and Belov define female being in terms of ideologically colored opposites, other male authors portray women from varying perspectives. In his story 'Cage with a Color TV' (1981) **Anatoly Kim** uses a first-person female narrator to re-create a woman's consciousness. The central theme is women's betrayal of men and its consequences for the perpetrators: the narrator, her young friend Mara, and – by way of ironic contrast – the heroine of Pushkin's 'Count Nulin', the tale the narrator reads. The femaleness that Kim transmits is, however, so stereotypical that it comes across as a sentimental male projection. The physical context in which Kim places the women, the topics they discuss and the content of their observations are banally gender-specific: there are observations about a playground, zoo animals, children's clothing; an old woman watches young people date and kiss; a young woman starts a conversation to share an emotion and goes on to talk about herself; the women discuss feelings and personal matters, though with a certain tentativeness, and become attached.

Yet on several occasions a male perspective can be seen lurking beneath the tritely female. For example, the narrator's New Year vision of her golden-haired, fragrant, angelic young friend rings more true for a fantasizing man; or the old woman's values – condemning abortion, and living a life of sacrifice in repentance for one understandable act of weakness – are values conservative men would like women to live by. Thus, the woman narrator is a man's advocate, upholding what seems to be an authorial notion of women's guilt, weakness and justified self-blaming. The narrator's defense of her young friend's unborn baby is only partly plausible as the view of a woman who has no children and experienced the human losses of the war. It smacks just as much of a sentimental male glorification of motherhood. Mara's decision to leave her husband – that is, her attempt to break away from the pattern of repentance and self-denial in order to search for her own happiness – is condemned by her older friend, whom the author seems to support, even though the portrait of Mara's husband is by no means very positive. The story's latent focus on the victimization of men by women suggests the author's negative evaluation of women as weak, unself-conscious, deceptive, selfish and guilt-ridden, and perhaps manifests his fear of their predatoriness. A woman writer would have told the story differently. Did Kim then choose a female narrator in order to have a woman tell on her gender?

Sergei Zalygin's story 'Women and the NTR' (1986) is very cerebral. Like his other stories and articles, and especially his controversial novel *The South American Variant* (1973), it reflects a philosophy of Woman as the Other, symbolizing immediacy, concreteness, closeness to nature and things living, and of Man as embodying technology and abstract thinking. Women are the upholders of humanistic ideals which contemporary society has lost because the male principle, i.e. technology, has been dominant and produced harmful results in society and nature. Yet, paradoxically, by forcing everything, including women, into their mold, men have become effeminate, thus preventing women from being genuinely feminine. This sorry state of affairs can only be mended, according to Zalygin, if men turn around and reintegrate the female principle to regain a lost balance and wholeness. Zalygin's women thus are historical beings measured against a fictional construct of womanhood.

The heroine Nadezhda craves simply to be an embodiment of the Other, of Woman; but the men of her environment and the circumstances of her life push her into a contradictory role that prevent her from being a Woman. This role gives her power and self-respect – a fact she likes, yet it is shown to alienate her from her 'female essence', a fact she dislikes. More concretely, Nadezhda is a successful employee who loves her work and feels undervalued. At the same time she fulfills the traditional role of a housewife, which she resents for the burden it imposes but clings to for the power it confers. As a result of these contradictions she is internally disjointed, frustrated and constantly on edge. Subservient to a number of men who see her as nothing but a chum and helpmate, she feels desexed as a female and devalued as a human being. Contradictory feelings of superiority over men and dependence on them tear her apart. At the same time, the author endows her with the worst traits and behaviour patterns men attribute to the opposite sex: arbitrariness, emotionalism, lack of focus. The result is the portrait of a fragmented, disharmonious character, far from amiable or admirable.

However, Zalygin's male characters explain and even justify the heroine's obstinacy and capriciousness. Their self-satisfied superiority, their harping on abstractions, their condescending treatment of Nadezhda make them equally unattractive. The emerging picture is confusing, yet it captures very well the vicious cycle of non-comprehension in male–female relations and the contradictions in the roles each sex plays.

Zalygin renders this lack of understanding by linguistic means. As he argued in a discussion of the story in April 1986,[2] the sexes do not communicate with each other. Thus, the men of his story talk in a manner exaggeratedly typical for 'the objective gender': in abstract words, hackneyed phrases, and complicated sentences that lack genuine meaning and parody the bureaucratic jargon of official statements. Their style is authoritative and declarative and implicitly excludes the woman, Nadezhda, whom they invited to participate in a discussion on women and the NTR. In contrast, Nadezhda's speech is concrete and specific, emotional and inquisitive.

The male images offered in this collection display major tendencies of recent Soviet fiction. Rasputin and Belov are representative of a sizable group of 'village prose' writers and Russian nationalists

2. A tape of the discussion and helpful bibliographical information were supplied to me by David Wilson, who is writing his dissertation on Zalygin at the University of Kansas.

who impose their philosophy on womanhood, part of which is idolized as upholder of the family and source of spiritual and ethical strength, and part of which rejected as source of domestic and moral instability. Most other writers – represented by Trifonov and Kim – draw more varied portraits of women in different professions, age groups and locales, and show them confronting personal problems ranging from ethical issues (e.g. responsibility) to situational and general human ones (e.g. aging and loneliness). The women they portray as admirable are usually meek, self-sacrificing, forgiving, compassionate, and ethically unbending, like the nineteenth-century heroines of the works of Pushkin, Turgenev and Goncharov. To think of self-realization or personal happiness is at best suspect. Professional success in women – but not only in women – is often linked with negative traits, such as being selfish, materialistic and calculating. The images tend to be more negative than positive, and the variety of women's internal and external experience is limited. Irony is mostly absent in these portraits.

IV

Are the images women writers have created of members of their own sex different from those created by their male colleagues? And how do women see themselves as writers? The two questions are related. A male writer would never worry about being reprimanded for writing about issues that concern himself: development of self and relations between self and society. Doing so they would follow the ma(i)nstream, the literary tradition, defined by male writing of fiction.

The situation is different for women. One can hardly speak of a women's tradition in Russian fiction. The pressure to adhere to limiting roles and unachievable standards made disclosure of self in a mode other than autobiography and poetry virtually impossible during the nineteenth century, as a recent book has shown.[3] Few women wrote fiction then, and their topics were uninteresting to the mainstream. The prose of Anastasiya Verbitskaya at the turn of the century made the term 'women's prose' derogatory, as it became associated with sensationalism, sexual libertinism, femin-

3. Barbara Heldt, *Terrible Perfection: Women and Russian Literature* (Bloomington: Indiana University Press 1987).

ism, and with writing prettily about domestic themes.

Apart from what one might thus call a problematic women's prose tradition, Soviet women writers have undoubtedly internalized the consequences of being a small minority in the male-dominated Soviet literary establishment. Their self-presentation and declarations about their role as women writers cannot be understood correctly if this context is forgotten. This is, of course, not meant as a reproach, or as an attempt to fit them into or measure them in terms of Western categories. When asked about their themes or about admired predecessors and influences on them, they usually place themselves in the tradition of nineteenth- and twentieth-century Russian and Western prose and emphasize the universality and humanistic orientation of their themes. Focusing on women's problems would be too narrow ('men suffer too'), and so would writing primarily for a female audience. They also insist that they are not feminists and do not want to further the cause of emancipation. Feminism, to most of them, is the outlook of extremists, unhappy outsiders, trouble-makers or ethical nihilists. Emancipation – defined as the right to equal opportunity in education and employment – is considered to have been achieved, and found of doubtful merit: it has brought women a double burden, they argue, and masculinized them. Baranskaya, for example, declares that her widely translated 'A Week Like Any Other', which has been interpreted as a feminist work in the West, was not meant to be a social critique but simply intended to be the description of a 'full-blooded, remarkable, though difficult, woman's life'.[4] And Grekova has recently spoken of the 'harmful, oppressive influence of women in technical institutes', because demanding 'equal rights in this area is a catastrophe'.[5]

The images women create of their gender are made with a male tradition in mind. Understatement and irony are major methods for communicating pain or social criticism. It is not surprising that many of the women writers refer to Chekhov as their model.[6]

---

4. Interview with Baranskaya in *Moscow News*, 1986, No. 49, p. 11. Again, we have to ask for what audiences these statements are made.
5. I. Grekova, cited in Zoya Boguslavskaya, 'Kakie my zhenshchiny?', *Literaturnaya gazeta*, 5 Aug 1987, p. 12.
6. Chekhov broke with the stereotypical images of women and the judgemental approach to them that dominated male fiction for much of the nineteenth century. With his matter-of-fact, all-accepting attitude to what he observed, Chekhov illustrated the falseness of all categories and divisions, be they based on gender or class, profession or world-view. Simon Karlinsky, a prominent

Capturing hidden psychological mechanisms and social forces that shape women's sense of self, women writers produce portraits that are diverse, subtle, sympathetic, often self-indulgent, hardly self-critical and increasingly introspective. The ideological coloring so characteristic of major male writers is absent. Women writers present their readers with a varied menu of female being, mostly in an urban environment. Representations range from traditional women, inclined to accept the double burden as their fate, to professionals who are less willing to compromise, have expectations and demands of their own, challenge their men, or choose to remain unmarried and do so happily with an occasional lover. They reveal, in a muted form, much about the psychological, social and economic constraints of female existence in the Soviet Union.

In **Natalya Baranskaya's** 'The Spell' (1976) the context is village life close to Moscow. The protagonist is a young mother, jilted by her seducer at the age of seventeen. Life in this provincial setting is humdrum: the pressure of old customs and mores is strong; gossip turns on men's betrayals and women's jealousies; life is still divided into male and female spheres. The third-person narrative is colloquial. The narrator acquires a distinct linguistic personality, which is female.

Irina Raksha's 'Lambushki' (1976) offers a portrait of a woman superior to her male counterpart. The woman, who has achieved personal inner liberation, is juxtaposed to a man who is in bondage to mother, wife and the values of the petit bourgeois. An urban professional, she is a descendant of the nineteenth-century heroines of Pushkin, Turgenev and Goncharov; like them, she possesses a native strength of will and character that enables her to act according to her emotions and beliefs. Independent and proud of her professional achievements, she can live happily without a man. The man reveals his indecisiveness and philistinism, which he shares with his nineteenth-century precedessor, the 'superflous man'. Having grown up without a father, Raksha's male protagonist is dominated and manipulated by a lonely, longsuffering mother, whose total dedication has deprived him of his freedom and independence. Thus, Raksha offers a modern version of the

Western Chekhov scholar, has commented, 'Had the work of Anton Chekhov been read in the West as it is written, rather than through the prism of inherited Russian critical distortions, many of his stories would surely be in the canon of the women's liberation movement' – *Anton Chekhov's Life and Thought* (Berkeley, Calif.: University of California Press, 1975) p. 18.

traditional male nineteenth-century portrayal of a male–female relationship.

Valentina Sidorenko is not an urban writer. Her stories are about small towns beyond the Ural mountains, in Siberia. Her portrait of three women from different generations in 'Marka' (1984) has a timelessly gloomy quality. The adult women have been widowed and struggle alone, betrayed or discarded by lovers, unhappy and bitter about their fate, resigned to doing their duty. They cannot win: in the struggle for the man, the loser forfeits her happiness, the winner her self-respect. The unique feature of this story is that it is related primarily from a little girl's point of view.

Other stories by Sidorenko present even gloomier portraits of single women, with or without children. Loneliness and poverty, betrayal and even violence – a topic so far largely shunned in Soviet literature – extinguish all hope for change. Sidorenko's fine ear for the language of Siberian villagers, her gift of psychological insight and observation, her skills as a narrator, and her eye for her native environment give her stories their authentic ring and their power to involve.

Viktoriya Tokareva is a prolific contemporary writer of urban Moscow life. Her women are predominantly Moscovite professionals, usually well-educated and often very introspective. They may fantasize or search for new experiences, be self-critical or explore who they are as they go through a mid-life crisis. In 'The Happiest Day of My Life' (1980) Tokareva captures the mentality of a young teenage girl, confronted with a small but difficult moral decision. The first-person stream-of-consciousness re-creation of her thoughts moves the reader by its authenticity. The girl's concerns are partly universal, partly very Soviet. Should she write what will get her a good grade, or should she write what she sincerely feels? With this issue, Tokareva takes up a subject that has agonized Soviet citizens until recently: should they say and do what is demanded and rewarded, while thinking and believing something else, or should they stick to their guns and live with the consequences?

Tokareva's more recent 'Between Heaven and Earth' (1985) again displays her gift for acute psychological observation and for apt comparison and simile (with one exception: the moralising tree allegory at the end). The story reflects some shifts in the image of women in the course of the two decades the anthology covers. Heroines are with increasing frequency no longer wronged wives, divorcees or lonely war widows, but self-confident, independent women with demands and expectations, trying to understand themselves. This does not necessarily make them positive characters. They can be quite shallow, soulless, selfish, or even tough and pushy in their pursuit of a pleasant life. But this does make them more complex than some of their predecessors.

The attitude of Tokareva's protagonist reflects the rather calculating, unromantic and often cynical approach to life, which is on the increase. The yearning for romance, of course, has not disappeared, but the disillusionment is quick. The heroine has no children and does not seem to miss them. The readiness to take on the double burden is diminishing, probably an adaptive response to men's reluctance to enter long-term commitments and to participate in domestic affairs.[7] The woman is self-assertive and clear about her own needs and no longer eager to sacrifice herself to be helpful: she rejects the basketball-player's needy pleading, as well as the chance to have a quick affair. That is, untraditional and de-heroized images of women in literature begin to reflect new social developments. Moreover, she is well off financially. A weekend flight is a material possibility. New and unusual in this story is also the explicit description of erotic attraction, a topic until recently taboo for Soviet writers, male and female.

Of the women writers represented in this volume, the most distinctive and outstanding are Lyudmila Petrushevskaya and Tatyana Tolstaya. The detachment or critical distancing which their contemporary female colleagues tend to produce by means of understatement or other varieties of irony results, in their case, from a condensed naturalism (Petrushevskaya) or an aestheticizing parody (Tolstaya).

Petrushevskaya's condensed naturalism consists in a laconic and detached recounting of psychological abuses, creating an atmosphere of such gloom and hopelessness that until recently most of her stories were unpublishable. Such blunt and unmitigated pessimism did not fall within the parameters of Socialist Realism during the 1970s. 'Nets and Traps' (1974) made it into print by a fluke. One could call this dramatic monologue a requiem to lost trust, openness and vitality. It is colloquial, terse, matter-of-fact.

---

7. Cf. 'The Militant Bachelor – a New Problem?', *Current Digest of the Soviet Press*, xxxi, no. 32 (5 Sept 1979) 1, an abstract of an article by Larisa Kuznetsova. Cf. also *Current Digest*, xxxii, no. 10 (26 Mar 1980) 9–11.

Only essentials are transmitted. Circumstantial details – looks, dress, place – are cut to a minimum. The effect is one of blow following blow. The clumsy syntax reflects the consciousness of a moderately educated woman, struggling to give expression to a harrowing experience. Although the speaker writes with hindsight, her distance from the described past, and the psychological insight which the passage of time and greater maturity might have brought, are minimal.

The 'nets and traps', which nobody sets intentionally, are external and internal in origin, and interdependent. The speaker is a victim of specific circumstances, her own character and attitudes, and of a society in which life as a single mother means extreme physical and emotional hardship and in which most women pursue marriage fiercely as the source of material security, emotional stability and ultimate happiness.

Tolstaya, the youngest of the writers represented in this collection, made her literary debut in 1983 and is the most artistically innovative Soviet woman writing at present. Her works appear to fit perfectly into the category of 'women's prose'. She seems to re-create the stereotypical male and female characters and situations, but she undermines the genre or the tradition by ridiculing and trivializing its stock characters and themes. Instead of mimesis, there is a conscious toying with the conventions of traditional realism. She draws attention to the medium, and her metaphors defamiliarize and transform the world. Destroying sterile canons, she offers a fresh perception of reality. Unreliable narration, dehumanizing comparisons, realized metaphors, a suspension of logical–causal plot and character development are some of her devices.

The idea for writing 'Dear Shura' (1985) came to the author when her nephew brought home from a garbage dump an old woman's letters and photographs. Tolstaya's sister's compassionate preoccupation with old women provided the larger context of the story. Related in impressionistic bits and pieces by a curious young female narrator, the story focuses on an old woman dedicated to looking pretty and to enticing men.[8] For the heroine, Shura, life seemed endless, holding many promises of love. But there was only one, as it turned out, and she missed it. While she was waiting for

---

8. For this information and my interpretation of the story I am indebted to the author, whom I interviewed in January 1988.

these promises, her beauty vanished, and so did her many admirers. Nothing but memory and fantasy is left. Lonely and isolated from people around her, Shura lives in the past, dreaming about what would have happened if. . . . Her sudden death shocks the narrator too. Like Shura, she had not realized the fraility of existence. Thus, their attitudes intersect, until the narrator is jolted into a new awareness.

But no pity or reproach mars this beautiful cameo of a story. Unlike Kim, whose tale also centers on two women two generations apart, Tolstaya uses a poetically inclined, curious, non-judgemental young woman as a first-person narrator who delights in Shura's life as something exotic and out-of-reach for herself and her Soviet contemporaries. A few selected details and scraps of conversation, thought and commentary, presented in terms of encounters that become more intimate, suffice to evoke the essence of this life. The details are often made unfamiliar. Persons are treated as inanimate objects, abstract concepts made concrete. The passage of time, for example, is poetically realized: 'Thousands of years, thousands of days, thousands of transparent, impenetrable curtains fell from the sky, condensed, congealed into solid walls, blocked up the roads, and wouldn't let Aleksandra reach her beloved, lost in the centuries'. Time thus becomes something materially tangible. The ability of memory to conjure up the past is made palpable by treating the past as if it were present, as if it were contained, shadow-like, in the now, and as if the past were reversible through later interference. Human life then appears as a *nunc stans*, with all of its moments accessible at all times, as the simultaneously displayed four seasons on Shura's hat.

Tolstaya jolts the reader's customary conceptualizations and perceptions by stepping outside the conventions. Dresses, for example, can 'tuck their knees', Shura's ex-lover is 'stretched into four cardboard slots', and the narrator can intercede for old Shura with her deceased lover, as if he were alive, as if it mattered. The effect is the crystalline purity, the *objet d'art* quality of the heroine, an effect quite distinct from putting her on a pedestal for admiration or making her the object of compassion.

V

How representative are these stories relative to what we know of the larger picture of life in the USSR's biggest republic?

Following Gorbachev's pleas for openness about the problems of Soviet society, a writer of plays and long fiction, Zoya Boguslavskaya, addressed this topic with provocative frankness. Not only does she speak of the 'false optimism in the portrayal of our heroines' and the use of old stereotypes – the hospitable woman, the perfect mother, the beautiful wife always smiling and fresh – but she also complains that 'literature reflects the multifariousness of female existence only to a limited degree' and notes that 'writers have to turn to the enormous layers of entirely uninvestigated, unpronounced truths about the lives of women'.[9] Why is this so? 'The first reason', she says,

> is the traditionally closed nature of Russian society, where any information about women, the family and the relations between the sexes was considered 'washing our dirty linen before strangers'. The second is the lack of any relevant statistics about women (some numbers would horrify us today). The third is the usual ridicule if 'the woman's problem' is as much as mentioned. 'There the feminists go again!' our serious male will say, forestalling any further discussion.

Boguslavskaya also offers examples of areas in women's lives which Soviet literature has failed to represent: female aggressiveness, prostitution, alcoholism, child abandonment, and the health problems of women. But more can be added: crime, rape and violence, the nature of female and male sexuality, homosexuality, drug addiction, the experiences of childbirth, of having delinquent children and of undergoing an abortion, and the life of women in prisons and labor camps. Nor have women in fiction begun to explore their own responsibility for their predicament. Only recently, the sociologist Larisa Vasilieva, after blaming men – 'How can you permit yourselves to burden women with demands and expectations that are beyond their power and strength?' – pointed to women's failings, suggesting, 'But perhaps it is us, women, who are responsible for this state of affairs. We allowed it to take hold. We looked the other way when men treated us indifferently,

---

9. Zoya Boguslavskaya, *Literaturnaya gazeta*, 5 Aug 1987, p. 12.

arrogantly, disdainfully and rudely. Where is our women's dignity?'[10]

Sociologists have meanwhile begun to address these taboo topics, offering new and depressing statistics.[11] Petrushevskaya captures some of the female victims of the living conditions in her plays, pointing in the direction for further explorations, which soon should yield a gallery of new images of women in Soviet literature in the decade to come.

10. Larisa Vasilieva, 'The Sparkling Feminine Soul', *Pravda*, 4 Mar 1987, p. 3. Cf. also V. V. Tereshkova's speech at the All-Union Conference of Women (*Izvestiya*, 1 Feb 1987, p. 3); Larisa Kuznetsova, 'The Paradoxes of Emancipation', *Soviet Life*, Mar 1987; and the account of the All-Union Conference of Women in *Station Relay*, 2, no. 5 (May 1987) 2–9.
11. See Larisa Aganbegjan, 'Plan erfüllt: Siebenmal abgetrieben', *Tageszeitung* (Berlin), 1 Sept 1988, p. 12 (a discussion of hygiene, medical care, birth-control, and abortion); Andrei Popov, *Ogonyok*, 33 (Aug 1988) (which offers statistics about abortions); Tatyana Zaslavskaya, 'Soliciting Public Opinion', *Moscow News*, 35 (4–11 Sept 1988) pp. 10–11 (a discussion of divorce and social policy); Natalya Kraminova, 'The Angry Woman Wants Change', *ibid.*, 24 (19–26 June 1988) (about the law for women, discrimination, high divorce and low birth rates). Cf. also current issues of *Soviet Woman*.

1

I. Grekova

Grekova is the pseudonym of the Soviet mathematician Elena Sergeevna Ventsel. The letter Y, *i grec* in French, is the symbol of the mathematical unknown, making her *nom de plume* something like Miss X. Born on 8 March 1907 in Tallinn, she studied mathematics at Leningrad University, received a Ph.D. in Technical Sciences in 1954, and has worked in applied mathematics since 1955. Her publications *Probability Theory, Introduction to Operational Research, Elements of Dynamic Optimalization* and *Elements of Play Theory* have been translated into other languages and are textbooks at Soviet universities.

A mother of three and a widow who never remarried, Grekova suffered alone through war and evacuation, bringing up her children while employed full time. After they left home, writing became her major activity. Her first story, 'Beyond the Entryway' ('Za prokhodnoi'), about a scientist's way of seeing as compared to an artist's came out in 1962, when she was over fifty. Since then, her stories have found their way into a number of Soviet literary journals, including the most prestigious, *Novy mir*. One of her best stories, 'The Ladies' Hairdresser' ('Damski master', 1965), is about a gifted hairdresser, Vitaly, who gives up his job in frustration over the state bureaucracy that controls his trade. This story established Grekova as a master at reproducing linguistic idiosyncrasies and jargon, as well as the fragmentariness of interior monologue and dialogue. A first collection, *Under the Streetlight* (*Pod fonarem*, 1966), firmly established her as a writer with a voice of her own. Her unusual story 'Maneuvres' or 'Testing Ground' ('Na ispytaniyakh', 1967), subsequently published in a revised version in her collection *Thresholds* (*Porogi*, 1986), deserves special mention. It deals with a woman engineer's observations during military exercises in a remote desert area in 1952. Grekova captures with great subtlety the hidden dangers of the last years of Stalin and the difficulties of conducting human relations under extreme circumstances.

Grekova's works reflect the lot of women, such as she, who lived through the deprivations of the Second World War and its aftermath: poverty, hunger, overcrowding, the problems of bringing up children single-handed. But the aspirations and grievances of her heroines also strike a familiar chord: woman's futile struggle to juggle her obligations at home, to her children and herself, and to her work.

In a recent interview Grekova revealed that she herself resolved the conflict between home and profession in favor of the latter, and so do many of her heroines. Asked about 'feminine literature' and about equality of the sexes, she responded that women showed fewer creative achievements because of their 'special emotional and neurological make-up, . . . and their enslavement to the problems of love, marriage, and the family'. She felt that 'complete equality between men and women is hardly possible. . . . There . . . cannot be equality in physiology, in the emotional sphere, or in raising children.' She even questions the desirability of such equality.

Grekova's heroines are often career women, who confront human and professional problems in an academic or research setting. A good example is the semi-autobiographical character of Nina Astashova, a successful scientist, in Grekova's novel *The Department* (*Kafedra*, 1978). But Grekova has presented her readers with a gallery of women from all walks of life. Thus, in the novella *The Hotel Manager* (*Khozyaika gostinnitsy*, 1975), she shows us how a cheerful, submissive provincial girl married to a Soviet military man evolves from being an appendage to her husband to a confident hotel administrator. Or she captures the humdrum lives of four widows – a former operetta singer, a former concert pianist, a religious peasant, and a worker – in a communal apartment in post-war Moscow in a novel called *Ship of Widows* (*Vdovy parokhod*, 1981). Brought up exclusively by women, the illegitimate son of one of the widows is shown to develop into a cynical, egoistic thug. A play based on this novel, which she wrote together with the playwright Pavel Lungin, has proved a great success at Moscow theaters.

Her most recent collection, *Thresholds*, contains old and new works. The title work, first published in 1984, has a male protagonist and is set in a cybernetics laboratory. But her strength is the portrayal of women, and her recent works – 'Tales of a Wild Grandmother' ('Skazki dikoi babushki') and other sketches which have appeared in a variety of literary dailies and weeklies – have been weaker than her earlier stories, which depended more on dialogue, on 'showing' rather than telling.

The story translated below as 'A Summer in the City' was published as 'Letom v gorode' in *Novy mir*, 1965, no. 4.

WORKS AND SECONDARY LITERATURE IN ENGLISH

'A Summer in the City', *Russian Literature Triquarterly*, 11 (1975) 146–67, translated by L. Leighton, repr. in *The Barsukov Triangle* (Ann Arbor, Mich.: Ardis, 1984).

'Ladies' Hairdresser', *Russian Literature Triquarterly*, 5 (1973) 223–65, translated by L. Gregg.

'Ladies' Hairdresser' and 'The Hotel Manager', in I. Grekova, *Two Stories: Russian Women*, intro. Maurice Friedburg (New York: Harcourt Brace Jovanovich, 1983).

'The Faculty', *Soviet Literature*, 1979, no. 12.

A Ship of Widows (London: Virago, 1984). Review by P. Meyer, 'Growing up Soulless', in *New York Times Book Review*, 8 Feb 1987, p. 35.

Nazarov, Nikolai, 'About Grekova's Work' (interview), *Soviet Literature*, 1986, no. 5, pp. 137–41.

A Summer in the City
(1965)

When the lime-trees bloom, the fragrance spreads through the entire city, filling the street-cars, the shops, the stairways.

The large hall of the library was filled with it, too. The windows were open, and, when a slight breeze floated in, everyone sensed the presence of the trees.

A readers' conference was in progress. Everything was as it should be. The table was covered with green cloth, and there were water pitchers, potted flowers, and a microphone. A large crowd had gathered, at least a hundred people. The writer Aleksandr

Chilimov sat at the rostrum, his face sullen and aged, its lower half slightly swollen, a deep wrinkle engraved between his eyebrows. His large crude hands rested on the green cloth, and he was staring straight ahead at the portrait of Turgenev.

At the other end of the table, at the very edge of her chair, sat Valentina Stepanovna, the library director. She was anxious, her throat felt hoarse, and her eyes were burning. Whenever one of the speakers got confused or halted, her lips would move in distress.

Misha Vakhnin, the metalworker from the instrument factory, had just left the microphone. How well he had spoken yesterday, and now he had got all mixed up. He had called Heinrich Böll* Heinrich Buckle, and he just couldn't manage to pronounce 'existentialism'. There was laughter in the hall. It was annoying! They should know him . . . . He was a man with ideas of his own, a fresh viewpoint – something quite rare, after all.

And the writer was bored. How many speeches like this must he have sat through . . . .

Valentina Stepanovna's favorite, the lab technician Verochka from the neighboring Scientific Research Institute, came up to the microphone. She was a mature, intelligent girl, a real jewel! No need to worry about her. And the writer kept staring at Turgenev. The silly fellow! He should be staring at Verochka! Her eyes alone were worth it, and she herself was as gentle and delicate as a church candle. Verochka was agitated as she spoke, 'agonizing over each word', one might say, twisting and straightening her lecture notes. Finally she dropped them on the table, seized the microphone shaft with one hand, and talked and talked, her cheek pressed against the microphone. And her cheek turned red as if the microphone were burning hot.

'Verochka, dear; do you really have to get so excited?' Valentina Stepanovna thought to herself. 'But what a wonderful girl! There's something classical about her, something of the Renaissance perhaps. A girl with a lily in her hand, exactly like Verochka and the microphone. Where have I seen such a picture before?'

So as not to disconcert Verochka, Valentina Stepanovna turned away and started looking out the window. The street outside had a life of its own. A boy in a sailor's suit was chasing a small red ball, baby carriages rolled past, people were feeding pigeons, and a large dark cloud hovered above everything. It was sultry. It would certainly rain.

Verochka finished. Applause filled the room. She let go of the microphone and returned to her seat, weaving gracefully through the chairs. Passing Valentina Stepanovna, she bent down and breathed in a whisper, 'Well, was it very bad?'

'No, Verochka, it was very good.'

'Oh, you're always trying to make me feel good . . .'; and she slipped away.

The writer sat as motionless as before, the wrinkle between his eyebrows. He could at least have smiled.

'Now Marya Mikhailovna Lozhnikova has the floor. She's a pensioner and a senior member of the Library Soviet.'

A tiny old woman with curly hair stepped forward, a stocking slipping down one leg. A hearing-aid hung on a chain around her neck like a hunter's horn. She spread her notes on the green cloth. The writer shuddered. Marya Mikhailovna moved to the microphone and, standing on tiptoe, shouted in a metallic voice, 'Comrades! Now, as never before . . .'

'Not so loud!' voices called from the audience.

'What?' Marya Mikhailovna asked. She looked like a little siskin: her nodding resembled the bird's pecking.

'Not so loud! Softer!' strained voices came from the hall.

'I can't hear!' Marya Mikhailovna yelled into the microphone, sure of herself.

Well, everyone was laughing again. Valentina Stepanovna stepped forward: 'Marya Mikhailovna, my dear, just step away from the microphone a little and don't shout so much!'

Taking the old woman by the shoulder, she moved her to a different position. How light she was!

'Stay this way and don't strain your voice, please.'

Birdlike, Marya Mikhailovna peered over the rims of her glasses and brought the horn to her ear.

'Not so loud!' Valentina Stepanovna shouted into the ear trumpet. This was getting to be too much like a circus; she was greatly distressed.

'Oh, you mean not so loud'; the old woman finally understood. She clutched her notes again and stood on tiptoe: 'Comrades, now as never before the educational role of literature is coming to the fore. Today we are discussing the works of our venerable Aleksandr Petrovich. [Oh Lord! The writer's name was Aleksandr Aleksandrovich!] These are fine works of high quality. In these works, we can see with our own eyes the progressive features of the heroes of our time, of the generation of the builders of communism. Our venerable Aleksandr Petrovich [again!] is particularly successful in portraying our struggle to over-fulfill the plan and our fight against bureaucracy and red tape. But we cannot agree with all his images. There is, for example, the character Vadim, who in the pages of the novel behaves poorly, allows himself a whole series of amoral actions; plainly speaking, he drinks. As an old teacher I ask you, Aleksandr Petrovich, what can this Vadim teach and to whom? Can we raise our young people on such models, I ask you, Aleksandr Petrovich?'

She turned to the writer.

'Aleksandr Aleksandrovich,' Valentina Stepanovna whispered imploringly.

'I can't hear!'

'Aleksandr Aleksandrovich!!' Valentina Stepanovna shouted into the horn.

'Oh, I understand,' the old woman nodded. 'Can we bring up our young people on such models, I ask you, Aleksandr Aleksandrovich?'

The writer shook his head. Now, finally, he smiled.

'Excellent!' Marya Mikhailovna rejoiced. 'You see, he's already admitting his mistakes. Well, I'll go on then.' She clutched her notes again. 'Examples such as Vadim can only disorient our young people, drive them onto the wrong path, the path of moral degradation. We have to give our young generation genuine examples of heroism, the imitation of which . . . imitating them . . . .' Looking for her place, the old woman started to get flustered.

'Her general line's obvious,' said a heavy-set fellow in the first row.

'Let her finish,' snapped a worn-out woman in overalls.

The old woman still shuffled through her notes, quite flustered by now.

'He will not wait until his time . . . . No, that's not it. . . . Ah, here it is: with his hero he portrays. . . . No, again that's not it. . . . Here, I think I've found it: "In a human being everything must be beautiful – face and dress, soul and thoughts", as the great Russian writer Anton Pavlovich Chekhov taught us.'

'We know,' said the heavy-set fellow.

'Shhhh!' the woman in overalls hissed at him.

'It continues on another page,' Marya Mikhailovna said, starting to hurry. 'I'll find it in a minute.'

Her hands were trembling. The notes got scattered, and some fell to the floor. The writer jumped up and rushed to collect them.

'Why in the world are you doing this? Why?' Marya Mikhailovna repeated. 'You're a famous writer, and here you are, picking up pages from the floor. . . . Let me do it, let me!'

Several heads of the Presidium disappeared under the table. The writer re-emerged first, his large face flushed from the exertion. He shuffled the pages together and handed them to Marya Mikhailovna. She was beaming and nodding her head: 'Thank you, but it's not worth the trouble. I'd better say it without the notes. It won't be on the same level, but it's from my heart. The main thing is: I've read your works and I had to cry. And it's not all that easy to make me cry. My neighbor in the apartment can offend me – but I won't cry. I turn deaf, I won't cry. But when I read your works I have to cry. Do you remember how your Vadim goes home after his mother's funeral? You don't remember? Well, it doesn't matter. I'll read it to you right now. I copied it down here for myself. . . . All right, it's not necessary. I'll just tell you, I cried. Here and at nine other places. I've stuck in bookmarks where I cried. And for these tears I thank you and bow deeply to you, Aleksandr Petrovich.'

She stepped away from the microphone and bowed deeply before the writer, all the way down to her waist, like a nun. There was thundering applause. Aleksandr Aleksandrovich rose, clumsily stepped out from behind the table and kissed Marya Mikhailovna's hand.

She gave him a peck on his forehead and burst into tears. The clamor in the hall increased. People rose, applauding and shouting: 'Thank you, thank you!' The heavy-set fellow in the first row clapped particularly loudly, sounding like cannon fire. Marya Mikhailovna returned to her seat in confusion and hid her face in a handkerchief. The writer stood there, his eyes lowered, clapping hesitantly and softly. The grey tuft of hair on his forehead trembled. Finally he sat down, and the audience, too, took their places again. Valentina Stepanovna tapped the microphone, and the hall became quiet.

'Comrades, ten people have spoken already. Nobody else has signed up. Would anyone else care to add a word? Or shall we give the floor to Aleksandr Aleksandrovich?'

'Yes, let him speak! Let him speak!' the hall buzzed.

The writer rose, big, embarrassed, his arms hanging at his sides.

Immediately the audience fell silent. The microphone hummed faintly.

'What should I tell you? In the lives of us writers anything can happen – both good and bad. And generally it's more bad than good, to tell you the truth. You write – and tear it up, and you write again – and tear it up again, and so on. And you feel so untalented, so vile, all emptied out and squeezed dry. . . . I won't deny it. And sometimes you feel like a scoundrel – why hide it? – it does happen. But good things happen too sometimes. If they don't praise you in the newspapers, so what? They praise you, they abuse you, it's all a matter of chance. But when you understand that somebody needs you – not everybody, but just somebody – that's a great thing. You thanked me here today. It's not you who should thank me. I should say thank you, dear friends. God bless you with happiness, as the saying goes.'

Oh, what a commotion arose in the audience! Valentina Stepanovna quickly rapped the microphone: 'Quiet! Quiet! Aleksandr Aleksandrovich hasn't finished. Please continue.'

'Why continue? I think that's all I have to say.'

'Did you hear, comrades? Unfortunately, that's all. Allow me, comrades, to thank Aleksandr Aleksandrovich in your name – in the name of the entire collective of library workers, in the name of the group of reader activists, and in the name of the entire mass of readers . . . .'

Applause, clatter of chairs, shuffling of feet. The crowd began moving, people started getting up to leave, dispersing in various directions. Eddies formed in the stream of people. A crowd gathered around the writer: some asked questions, some shoved books at him to autograph, some snapped pictures. It became hot and densely packed. Valentina Stepanovna knew that this was the most important part, the part when the most frank and the most urgent conversations would begin. First, here, at the door to the hall, then in the cloakroom, then in the street, under the pale eyes of the street lights, on the embankment, on moist park benches. . . . And the evening would go on and on, and nobody would be able to leave. They were all good, and they were all intelligent, and they all loved each other . . . .

But it was absolutely impossible for her to stay today. Lyalka would come home, and there wouldn't be any dinner.

'Aleksandr Aleksandrovich, thank you! I'm so sorry, but I've got to go.'

'That's all right, Valentina Stepanovna. Don't worry. I'll chat with your young people for a while. They are certainly marvellous.'

'Yes, that's true. Our young generation is really wonderful.'

'Come back to visit us again!' shouted a shaggy-haired girl with lots of freckles.

'Yes, I'll come back.'

It had rained. The street was full of big puddles. It's true, our young people are marvellous. After the rain the fragrance of the lime-trees was even more powerful. But, actually, it was a disgusting smell. Sweet, obtrusive, cloying – no, it was even rotten. It was a rotten smell; that was it, exactly. The lime-trees had smelled the same way then. . . . Interesting how tenacious memories were, how indestructible. So many years had gone by; the wounds had healed; but suddenly it smelled of lime-trees, and it was as if everything had happened yesterday.

Valentina Stepanovna walked along the street. Pensioners were sitting under the lime-trees. Old men with white haloes around their bald spots played cards. Old women sat on the benches their swollen legs clumsily parted. They held their handbags upright on their knees, hiding their round stomachs. Pigeons strutted about, children played in the sand.

In front of her walked a man in a loose check jacket, apparently another pensioner. He was plodding along dejectedly, his head tilted to the right, his hair, a motley grey, carelessly cut. There was something familiar about the gait, a subdued dance. Could it be true? The man turned around. It was true. It was Volodya. But how he had aged!

'Valyusha, is it you?' Volodya said.

'As you see, it is.'

'We haven't seen each other for such a long time,' Volodya mumbled. 'About three years, ah? To tell the truth, I've been hanging around here waiting for you for several days already. Do you still work over there?'

'Yes, I'm still there.'

'Still there. . . . And you're still the same. You don't change. You've even grown younger.'

'That's a familiar trick: tell a woman she's grown younger, and you can't go wrong.'

'No, I'm not joking. I've been dreaming of meeting you for a long time. You know, when you approach the end of your life, you're drawn to all those who were particularly dear to you. Haven't you noticed?'

'No,' Valentina Stepanovna said. 'I'm not approaching the end of my life. You may be, but I'm not.'

'Well, you always were a stickler. I recognize the old Valya, I sure do!' Volodya laughed, momentarily displaying his large, closely set teeth. They were still beautiful, those teeth; they hadn't changed. Yet, everything was past, everything.

'Let's at least sit down for a while,' Volodya suggested. 'I'd like to talk with you. Especially with you. I'm lonely. You don't believe it? I give you my word.'

'All right,' Valentina Stepanovna agreed wearily.

They sat down on one of the pensioners' benches. A tall old woman with biblical eyes who had been feeding pigeons at the other end of the bench rose, glanced at them severely, and went away.

Volodya sat down, rubbing his hands. His jacket was baggy and made his shoulders look uneven. His fingernails were not entirely clean. Wasn't she looking after him?

'Well, a lot of water's gone under the bridge,' Volodya said. 'Nowadays I think of the past a lot and I see that maybe we, you and I, made a mistake.'

'Speak for yourself. I didn't make any mistake'

'Prickly!' Volodya said and smiled again.

'All I need now is to fall apart over those teeth,' Valentina Stepanovna thought to herself.

'No, joking aside, I've always missed you. And now, when I see you looking so young, interesting, and smart. . . . My word of honor, something starts to stir in me . . . .'

'So you've turned vulgar and banal too,' Valentina Stepanovna said sadly, drawing in the sand with her heel. 'Or perhaps you've always been vulgar and banal, and I just didn't notice?'

'Vulgar and banal, exactly, that's right,' Volodya rejoiced. 'Right to the point. I have to admit that without you I've degenerated a bit, morally and maybe even physically. Manya is a beautiful woman, a good doctor, but she doesn't have that something – that eternal feminine. Imagine, sometimes I have to wash my own underwear. Of course it's not difficult: our apartment is in a new building, there's hot and cold water, a garbage chute – it's all there. But a man even feels awkward doing housework, don't you think so? Just take literature. Where do you find a man doing housework? It's unnatural. It wasn't that way with you. I remember what a

charming housekeeper you were in our little room on the sixth
floor – in our garret. Do you remember?'

'No, I've forgotten.'

'I don't believe it.' Volodya started laughing. 'Women never
forget.'

'Good Lord!' Valentina Stepanovna thought. 'I used to love this
face, these very cheeks. And how I used to love them! I would
wake up: I love you, I would fall asleep: I love you. All the time: I
love you.'

'The limes are so fragrant, did you notice?' she asked him.

'Yes, a wonderful smell.'

'Well, I've got to go now. Lyalka's waiting,' Valentina Stepanovna
said.

'Yes, and how is Lyalka by the way?' asked Volodya with a
hungry look on his face. 'Is she all grown up? Finishing the
Institute?'

'She's in her third year.'

'She's probably a beautiful girl.'

'To me she's very beautiful.'

'Whom does she look like?'

'Like you.'

'And would you believe it,' he said pensively, 'that's what I live
for. Of course you don't believe me, but it's a fact. I live for you,
for you and Lyalka.'

'Well, what of it?' said Valentina Stepanovna and got up. 'You
can do what you like. I've got to go.'

He also rose.

'Valyusha, won't you perhaps allow me, an old man, to drop in
on you now and then? We could have a cup of tea, talk . . . have
a couple of laughs . . . .'

'What's the point of it?'

'I'm still her father.'

'She doesn't know you and doesn't want to know you.'

'It's sad,' Volodya said.

The old Volodya. She felt sorry for him in spite of everything
and asked, 'How's your health?'

'It's fine.'

They said goodbye. His hand was weak, wilted, almost lifeless.
When she got to the end of the avenue she turned around. Volodya
was sitting there, his hands hanging down. His gray check jacket
seemed greenish in the distance.

Valentina Stepanovna climbed the stairs slowly. 'Don't rush, and count to a hundred on each landing,' the doctor had told her. There was nothing she could do about it. Now she had to count to a hundred, count to her very death.

In her bag she had early spring vegetables: radishes, parsley, carrots and lettuce. They were all moist, fresh and light green. She hadn't bought them in a state store, but at a market. Expensive, but good quality. Lyalka needed special nurturing; she was very pale.

On the sixth and last landing, she only counted to fifty and then opened the door. The lock clicked. She was home.

'Is it you, Stepanovna?' her neighbor Polya called out to her from the kitchen.

'It's me. Isn't Lyalya home yet?'

'No, she didn't show up. Got up at ten, did her hair and ran off. Had no tea, nothing. Always in a rush. If she didn't stay in bed till ten, she'd get around to everything. I . . .'

'Didn't she call?'

'Don't think so. It's none of my business. I beat out the rugs. You should've seen the dust! Enough to blind your eyes. Maybe she did call. It's none of my business. I've got nobody to call me, so I don't listen.'

It was always like this with Polya: you said a word to her, and she answered you with twenty. Valentina Stepanovna took off her coat and went to her room. It was cool there. The window was open, the white curtain billowing in the wind.

She sat down at the table to think, as always before starting her housework. She didn't reflect at length, just for about three minutes, to sort out her chores – planning them carefully to avoid wasting time, so that she would have time for everything without rushing.

First, sort and clean the vegetables; second, put on the soup; third, rinse the laundry while the soup's simmering.

She counted, bending back her fingers.

Lyalka would always tease her: 'First column stand, second column march . . . a real battle commander!'

'But you've got to work out what you want to do when. That's why I have enough time, but you don't.'

'Just the same, I can't do it that way. I just can't plan.'

'You can do everything if you want to, Lyalka.'

And that was true. Lyalka could do anything she set her mind to, but only in fits and starts. There was the sewing phase, when she sewed herself an evening dress. Her girlfriends came and gasped. And the dress was nothing! She even sewed trousers for Oleg! Then she had a cooking spell. Somewhere she turned up a cookbook from the eighteenth century. A colorful apron, so stiff it could stand by itself, her slender arms in flour up to the elbow . . . .

Polya had stood beside her, stomach protruding. 'Is that the way to bake? Who does it that way? Unleavened dough's unleavened dough, and yeast dough's yeast dough. And you throw everything in one pot. Here you got yeast, and here you got baking soda, and you want to add fancy bread dough, too. It's ridiculous! And everything by the book! As if you couldn't ask people. Well, I say yeast dough's yeast dough, and unleavened dough's unleavened dough . . . .'

'Listen Polya, have you ever been wrong in your life?' Lyalka asked.

'No. What do you mean "wrong"?'

'Very simple. Has it ever happened that you were wrong?'

After seriously pondering for a while Polya answered modestly, 'I don't remember. I don't think so.'

And the pie turned out well: it was high, plump and had a golden crust. Even Polya said, after she had tasted it, 'Not bad.' But she added right away, 'But it's better our way.'

Lyalka's studies went the same way, in spurts. She had a spurt of 'A's, her portrait on the roll of honor, and Valentina Stepanovna was happy. The next exam period started with a 'D'. Lyalka lay around smoking: 'I don't want a student's life, I just want to be a wife.'[1]

'You should be ashamed of yourself, Lyalka! You, with your abilities . . . .'

'Who knows what my abilities are? Maybe I could have been a great singer.'

And there it was: the music phase. She bought a guitar and taught herself to play by a teach-yourself book. She sang along – zealously, but off-key. She had no ear.

'Lyalka really, you won't make a great singer.'

'How come? Am I very bad?'

'Yes, dear.'

---

1. Lyalka quotes a famous rhymed line from Denis Fonvizin's comedy *The Minor* (1782) which has entered general usage in Russia.

'But how come Borka fell in love with me when I did Carmen for him? It was because of my singing.'

'Not because of your singing but in spite of your singing.'

'And you're supposed to be a mother! You're no mother, you're a beast! A real mother has to adore her child blindly, you understand? Blindly. She has to create a golden childhood for her child. You understand? And now let's try it. Mama-mouse, do I sing well?'

'No, badly.'

'Oh, your honesty will be your ruin. Still, I do love you . . . .'

Tilting her head sideways, she looked at her, gave a little squeal and started kissing her: 'How good you are! how lovely you are! How sweet you are!'

. . . Well, all right. It was time to get going: first, clean the vegetables; second, put on the soup. Valentina Stepanovna went into the kitchen, took a little bowl from the shelf, and a cutting-board off its nail. Everything had its own place, each item its own nail. It wasn't pedantry, just time-saving.

She began to pick through the vegetables. Next to her Polya was washing clothes. She was bent low over a zinc tub that had seen better days. The back of her jacket was dark with sweat.

'Polya, you should use my washing machine. It's much faster. I did a big load yesterday in just an hour.'

She shouldn't have started talking. With Polya it was always the same: you pull the chain and get a flood.

'A machine! I know your machines. A machine for everything. You want to blow your nose or just relieve yourself, and pretty soon you'll think up a machine for it.'

In Polya's eyes Valentina Stepanovna was the embodiment of the intelligentsia with all its sins and weaknesses.

'No, Valentina Stepanovna, I don't need no machine. I wouldn't take one for nothing, never mind paying thousands for it. It turns and turns and you never know what it's turning out. And you gotta watch it by the clock. Four minutes for everything. Dirt or no dirt, white stuff or black, the machine don't care. Four minutes. Do you see me washing four minutes by hand? I take a look at every little spot against the light. Maruska from downstairs used the machine the other day – we couldn't stop laughing. She stuffed everything in there and turned it on. And what d'you think came out? Miserable stuff, god-awful.' (Maruska from downstairs was the eternal object of Polya's censure.)

'But it's hard by hand,' sighed Valentina Stepanovna.

'Everything's hard for you, lady. You ain't no spring chicken no more, and you gotta heart condition. I'm your age, but I'm a lot tougher. Got myself in shape with work. I bet my laundry's whiter than yours with the machine.'

'Well, it's up to you.'

Polya bent over her trough again and started to wash, swaying back and forth angrily. Valentina Stepanovna cut the vegetables into small pieces. It was quiet except for the laundry splashing in the tub and the knife tapping against the wooden cutting-board.

'Good thing she's quiet,' Valentina Stepanovna thought. 'After all, everyone has a right to a little peace and quiet.'

But this peace and quiet didn't last. Polya hadn't talked herself out yet.

'Listen, Stepanovna, I got something to tell you. Duska Savrasova has a nephew. He's young but cultured – oh my, so cultured, it's just a joy to see. He finished the Technical Institute. He'd go out – all dressed up and ironed smooth, chubby and rosy like a cherub – a transistor radio over his shoulder. Well, that was all right. Duska and me just had to look at him and we were happy. He got a room and moved out of Duska's. Lived pretty well, except he started losing his hair. And he lost more and more, you know, and all of a sudden he wanted to get married. Duska wasn't against it. What did she care? He wasn't living with her anyway. So he got registered with some girl. At first everything was just fine, but then she started acting up. She boiled white and grey and pink stuff all together – can you believe it? First he didn't say nothing, but then he started making demands. She got even worse, hung up her bra with a string! That's how brazen she got, you know. Well, he won't stay with her, for sure; he'll leave her.'

(Polya was never able to praise anybody without condemning someone else first. And most of the time it was herself she praised.)

'I wouldn't allow such brazenness – I mean, hanging up your bra with a string! I work as an ordinary old nightwatchman, and I didn't go to none of your fancy institutes; but I know what culture is, all right. My late husband drank, but I stuck it out. If he threw up I wiped it up, so I wouldn't have to be ashamed in front of the neighbors. I did his laundry, the mending and ironing – spic and span, neat as a pin. . . .'

She fell silent. It was quiet except for the swishing of the laundry.

'Valentina Stepanovna, there's something else I want to ask you,' Polya said suddenly. 'Is that fellow of yours sick or ain't he coming no more?'

'Who are you talking about, Polya?' Valentina Stepanovna asked hypocritically.

'Come on! You mean you don't know?' Polya said, squinting her eyes. 'That Oleg of yours, of course! Who else do you think? I ain't blind. With those thin walls it's hard not to notice. First he comes running all the time, your fellow, and then, what d'you know, he's gone with the wind, like flushed down the "to'lit". And you know, your Lariska, she looks god-awful. You think I've got no eyes in my head? Paints herself and puts on creams, but looks like death warmed over.'

Valentina Stepanovna said nothing.

'You're just hiding it from me, I know. But why? That's life for you – ordinary stuff, women's business. You know I don't wish nothing bad on you and Lariska. She grew up under my nose! She came running into the kitchen when she couldn't even look over the table: Auntie Polya this, Auntie Polya that. Didn't I wipe her nose? You just ran off to your work, showed your face, and off you were. But old Polya was there; so where was she going to go? Lariska was a child after all, not a cat. And I even feel sorry for cats and feed 'em. But you treat me like a leper!'

'Polya, dear, don't feel hurt! I'm not hiding anything from you, honestly. I don't know anything myself.'

'Hide it or don't, it's obvious anyway. Can't hide a needle in a cloth bag: it'll poke through. The fellow used to come round and now he ain't showing his face. And the girl ain't herself no more. Any chance she's got something in the oven?'

'Good Lord, Polya! What in the world are you saying? And what language you use! I just can't get used to your jargon!'

Valentina took a knife and pushed the vegetables off the board and into the boiling, thickening soup.

'And now she's cross again!' Polya said. 'Some ja'gon. You ain't gonna move me with such words. Your sort's awfully dainty, lady, daintier than a hair. How about yourself, didn't you have a baby and didn't you run around? You had a baby, and you ran around too, but you don't let me say nothing. You'd better keep an eye on Lariska's laundry. The girl's a slob, throws her stuff all over the place. Just take a look at it.'

'Excuse me, Polya, but I have a headache,' Valentina Stepanovna said, slipping off to her room, as if going underground.

. . . Third, rinse the laundry. It would be better to rinse it in her room. Polya was in the kitchen. How talkative she was! Probably because she didn't read. Instead of reading she talked. Should I perhaps introduce her to books? No, it wouldn't work. She'd cure me of books first.

So as not to waste time, Valentina Stepanovna set about dusting. A soothing occupation: your hands were busy, your head was free, nobody fussing in your ear, and you could think about whatever you liked – for instance, today's conference. No, she couldn't think about the conference. The thoughts swirling in her head were quite different: Lyalya and Oleg.

A photograph on the wall showed Lyalya and Oleg in the woods on skis. Oleg, dark blond, stood erect and stately, a tight sweater over his broad chest. He had a handsome face of milky-waxy ripeness. His black eyebrows had grown together above the nose. Next to him was Lyalya, bent over as if hanging on her ski-poles one leg splayed; laughing, and with snow in her hair . . . .

The telephone rang. Valentina went out into the hall and picked up the receiver.

'Mama-mouse, is it you?' the beloved, indistinct and rather low voice said in the distance.

'It's me, my dear. Where are you calling from? I'm waiting for you. I've made a salad.'

'A salad! That's perfect, I love salad. Mama-mouse, can you hear me? I love you, understand?'

'I understand. But when are you going to be home?'

'I don't know. Pretty soon. Did anyone call?'

'No, not while I was here. Do you want me to check with Polya?'

'No, no need to.'

'All right. So I'll wait for you.'

'Right.'

Valentina Stepanovna hung up the receiver. She hadn't moved away when the phone rang again. If only it were Oleg!

'Valyunchik, it's me.'

'Zhanna! Where in the world have you been?'

'Ah, that's a long story. Imagine, I fell in love again.'

'Lord have mercy!'

'Yes. Be disgusted if you like, you model of virtue, but you have to accept me for what I am. Tralala. Are you going to condemn me, Valentina Stepanovna?'

'What do you mean? Condemn you! I'm happy for you.'

'You know what? Most of all he liked my calves! "Those calves," he told me, "embody the elegance of the century."'

'And he's not an idiot?'

'Mmm . . . I don't know. But I'm not so bright myself, right?'

'Maybe.'

'I love you for your sincerity. You're always such an honest little schoolgirl.'

'What do you mean "girl"? Soon I'll be an honest old grandma.'

'How so? Already! Lyalka?'

'No, what are you thinking of? I just mean I'll soon be old enough.'

'Oh – as far as getting old is concerned. That's our nightmare, don't you think? Still, you don't want to give up your illusions, right?'

'Well, you know I gave mine up long ago.'

'So did I. But from time to time they come up again. You know last year I had given up on love for good. I decided I had had enough. But then it swept me off my feet like a hurricane. I feel as if something's swirling and churning inside me. . . . No, I can't express it over the phone, Valyunchik. I'll drop by, all right? What are you doing?'

'I'm getting dinner ready, and I'm waiting for Lyalka.'

'Well, I'll drop in for just a second. I'll sit down, smoke a cigarette, and be gone. All right?'

'Of course it's all right.'

'Love you!'

'I'll be waiting.'

. . . Oh, Zhanna. Always laughter and tears, but I love her. A whole life together: that's no joke. A whole life. We went to school together, worked together, suffered through the war together. If it hadn't been for Zhanna, both Lyalka and I would have died. The baby was getting scurvy. And who saved her? Zhanna. With fruits and lemons. And that during the war! And where did she get them? If you asked her she just laughed and said, 'I earned

them with honest labor.' She had some sort of warehouse administrator then. Who'd condemn her? Not I.

And how beautiful Lyalka had been when she was small! Enough
to make you ache. Even people in the street stopped when they
noticed her. What a girl! Black hair, green eyes, a serious gaze,
and those eyelashes. . . . Actually, it's been a long time since I
saw Lyalka black-haired. Every week her hair has a new color –
ripe rye, or mahogany. And not long ago she came back all gray,
with a lilac tint. It was very simple: silver dye, a little bit of ink,
and that was it.

'Lyalka! Another color? Take pity on me. I've got a heart
condition, you know.'

'You got to go with the times, Mama-mouse. Brace yourself and
catch up! And, besides, what are you talking about? My hair? It's
mine. My lips? They're mine. If I want to, I paint them. You don't
like it? Oh my dear, my treasure! That's the nineteenth century
coming out in you.'

'But Lyalka, I didn't even live in the nineteenth century. You
know that perfectly well.'

'It doesn't matter. Your heart's in the nineteenth century. It's
such a cosy century; everything clear-cut, like with Polya: white's
white, and black's black. You'd like to see me pure, white, like a
heroine from Turgenev, with a fishing-rod in my hand by an old
pond. A copy of Liza Kalitina from *A Nest of Gentlefolk*.'

'That's a lie.'

'All right, it's a lie. But you are so young, so beautiful! And what
ears you've got, what ears! Like two cameos. And your hair?
There's almost no gray in it. Oh, I'll squeeze you to death!'

'Lyalya, you're mad, let me go . . . .'

And Lyalka in front of the mirror was another picture. It was
interesting to watch how she 'put on a face'. Serious, agonized
lips, black pencil in the corners of her green eyes. Two, three
strokes and her eyes came to life: oblong, enigmatic, and slanting.
And, then, the finishing touches for her eyelashes. In her hand a
blunt penknife. With this knife she patiently curled up her lashes,
one by one. And it definitely had to be blunt. Once Oleg,
conscientious Oleg, had found this knife and sharpened it; wanted
to do her a favor, so how could you object? But Lyalka almost

clipped off her eyelashes. Then they blunted the knife intentionally, rubbing it against a flowerpot. . . .

Oh, Oleg! What made him dissatisfied with Lyalka?

The bell rang. Zhanna had probably arrived; yes, it was her. Polya opened the door and went back into the kitchen grumbling. She didn't like Zhanna.

'Valyunchik, hello sunshine!' Zhanna kissed Valentina Stepanovna on the cheek. 'Did I get lipstick on you?'

'I don't think so. Come in.'

From behind the kitchen door you could hear Polya's monologue: 'Empty-headed old hag, useless bitch. Goes traipsing off here, and running off there, but what's the point of being so fancy! It's time she thought about her soul! Over forty ain't twenty! But she's got to doll herself up. And Lariska right in her footsteps. Same way . . . .'

'What's that? Is it Polya talking? Who's with her?'

'She's all by herself. That's just how she is. Don't pay any attention.'

'And there she goes on knocking herself out and puffing herself up,' the voice behind the door said loudly. 'Going on fifty, but runs around with bare knees, all fixed up. And what's under them knees? Nothing but veins, bluer than the ocean. And what for? It's all the same – you can't jump over your own shadow, can't be smarter than Mom and Dad. Old she is, and old she stays. Time don't flow backwards . . . .'

'Is she talking about me?'

'No, she's talking about herself. Let's go.'

Zhanna sat down in an armchair, wrapping one leg around the other, snake-like. Indeed, she had amazing, eternally young legs. She took out a cigarette and began to smoke.

'Well, that's how things are, Valyusha. Once again love has come my way.'

Zhanna always talked in such ready-made expressions. Strange that it wasn't unpleasant, coming from her; in fact, it even suited her.

'And who's the lucky fellow?' Valentina Stepanovna asked.

'A sailor; really nice, cultured too. You know, I've always had a weakness for gold or silver braid. There's good reason why women through the ages have loved military men: all the gold, the shakos, the fur-lined hussar cloaks, the dolmans . . . .'

'Do you actually know what dolmans are?'

Zhanna gave it some thought.

'Some sort of saber?' she asked.

'Not quite. A kind of military jacket.'

'Yeah, I thought so, some sort of jacket. Ah, nowadays everything's so colorless, nothing but khaki and more khaki. A sailor's uniform has always excited me, believe it or not.'

'I well believe it.'

'You're always laughing at me. Of course I'm laughable. I'm perfectly well aware of this trait of mine, my weakness for a quick fling. When love comes my way, I forget everything and catch fire straight off.'

'Where did you dig him up?'

'Oh, that's a whole novel. We met in a ticket line. I was buying tickets for Sochi, he for Minvody. We got into a conversation, laughed, and he sang to me "Oh, those black eyes . . .". One word led to another. "Do you really have to go to Sochi?" he asked me. "I really do." "Is someone waiting for you?" "Nobody's waiting for me, I'm free as the wind." "If that's true, why can't we go to Minvody together?" Well, it was as if a tornado had swept me off my feet. The room was spinning around me. And I went off to Minvody.'

'Just like that? Right away?'

'No, two days later. Well, of course I had to do myself up: I plucked my eyebrows, colored my hair – can you tell? I used the Gammut brand, chestnut tint. Don't look at the parting, it's grown out already. Look here: a wonderful shade! Anna Markovna fixed up the suit for me: she lowered the armholes and pleated the skirt softly. I got myself a matching handbag, and Hungarian shoes with high heels, you know. Off I went like a queen, looking absolutely smashing. Wouldn't have given myself more than thirty-eight years, and you know what an eye I have for age. Altogether, it was a beautiful dream . . . .'

'And how long did it last?'

'Two weeks. The money ran out.'

'His?'

'No mine.'

'And he?'

'He stayed there. When we parted, he even shed a few tears. Gave his word he'd call me as soon as he got back.'

'Is he married?'

'Seems like it. So what? Valyusha, do you condemn me?'
'No, honestly.'
Suddenly Zhanna buried her face in the back of the armchair, bursting into sobs. Not just tears, but sobs.
'Zhanna, my dear, what's the matter? Did I hurt you?'
'I hurt myself.'
'For God's sake, don't cry. I'm not Polya. I understand everything.'
Zhanna shook her head. Her glossy chestnut-colored locks parted, and at the roots touches of gray showed through the dark hair.
'Valyusha, today I thought of Leonty Ivanych.' (Leonty Ivanych was Zhanna's late husband, a general.) 'With him I was secure as if a stone wall protected me. If he were alive, nothing would have happened. He kissed the air around me. This damned loneliness! Well, you can't understand.'
'But I'm alone too.'
'You have Lyalka.'
'That's true, I do have Lyalka.'
Suddenly, out of the blue, Zhanna calmed down. She sat down, wiped away her tears and smiled.
'You know I'm lucky that I didn't get fat. From behind you could even take me for a girl, right?'
'It's true.'
'Well, I'd better be off. I've sat and had my smoke and my cry. . . . It's so good to have a place to cry!'
'Come over any time.'
'To cry?'
'And to laugh too.'
'Friendship is such a blessing! Valyusha, you're a true friend.'
'Yes, you and I are old friends.'
'Old? I'd say ancient! Come to the door with me, I'm afraid of Polya.'
Valentina Stepanovna took Zhanna to the door.
'Parasite,' a loud voice said from behind the kitchen door.
Zhanna bravely pulled on her gloves.
'So long, Valyunchik. Take care and give Lyalka a hug from me.'
'Come back soon.'
The door slammed, and her high heels clattered down the stairway. Behind the kitchen door Polya's monologue continued: 'But I don't need no man. What do I want a man for? He brings

home nothing but dirt. And you just keep doing the laundry for him, always the laundry. . . . And men also smell. Is that you behind the door, Stepanovna, or what? Come in, don't be shy! Ain't I telling the truth, eh? Thinking of men at her age, that's the last straw! When I was young, I was hot stuff! But now I've got no use for a man. Wouldn't take one for free. Men drag in dirt, bring in a smell, and they won't come home without their half-liter of vodka. I'm better off going to church. I don't need no man.'

Quietly Valentina Stepanovna slipped off to her room. She should get the soup finished. But it would be impossible: Polya was there. Amazing how someone who's always right can enslave everyone else.

All she had left was the dusting. It was true, Lyalka was messy! Just look at all the stuff on her table: a handbag, lecture notes, eyebrow pencils, an elastic belt, one stocking! It had a run that needed mending.

Valentina Stepanovna picked up Lyalka's bag, but she was a little clumsy, and various odds and ends came spilling out: a lipstick, a powder box, crumpled-up roubles, some papers. Kneeling down, she started to pick up what was scattered on the floor, just as the writer today had picked up the papers. Catching sight of an unfolded piece of paper, she read, against her will, 'Larisa Vladimirovna Savchenko . . . born 1940 . . . is assigned to the Gynecological Section of Maternity Home No. 35 . . . for the interruption* of a pregnancy . . . six or seven weeks . . . .'

For a moment the bright sky outside flashed just as if it had winked at her. On her knees, Valentina Stepanovna collected the odds and ends; then she rose, holding on to the edge of the table. She put everything back into the handbag. It made no sense; it was impossible, absolutely impossible. She reread the paper with the same result. Well, all right. Terrible, but all right. One has to get over it. Terrible that Lyalka kept it from me. And I thought that she had no secrets from me.

Valentina Stepanovna went out to the kitchen and turned off the gas under the soup. Thank God Polya wasn't around. Then she returned to her room and sat in the armchair. She couldn't get comfortable in it. She tucked her legs under and put her head on the armrest, which felt comfortable for some reason. It was almost painless to sit this way. She closed her eyes. Children shouted in the street. The breeze blew the curtain aside and swept in the fragrance of the limes.

The lime-tree had smelled exactly the same way during that cursed summer. I remember, I was standing here, facing the window; and he was over there, with his back to it.

'Valyusha, you can't really be serious. Do you really want me to leave?'

'I'm absolutely serious.'

'You're a fool. Try to understand that this doesn't mean a thing! Only a fit of passion. I got carried away. It does happen.'

'Why did you lie to me?'

'Lie? What should I have done? Told you everything, every detail? Merci! You would have made a scandal, broken off everything. Our relationship was too valuable for me to tell you.'

It was Volodya who had said this. Impossible. It couldn't be him, not really him.

'Valuysha, you're making a mountain out of a molehill. Just understand: I love you. That other woman means nothing to me, absolutely nothing. If you want me to, I'll break off everything with her, all right?'

How could he not understand that it wasn't a matter of the other woman, but of the lie? I said, 'It's not a matter of the other woman.'

'What then?'

'It's me. I don't love you any more. Just leave.'

'Just wait. You'll be sorry.'

And he left. I remember the feeling. The whole world turned upside-down, fell to pieces. And at the same time I felt it wasn't too late yet, too late to run after him and bring him back. His cigarette was in the ashtray – still lit, still smouldering. Why am I standing here? Run after him, bring him back! And then the door slammed downstairs. That was it.

No, there was no more Volodya: he had split in two, divided, fallen into two pieces. One was the former, beloved Volodya, familiar as your own hand. The other was new, deaf and cruel: a stranger. And then I thought, how does this new one dare enter the body of my very own dear Volodya? The murderer!

When the world falls into pieces, you're stunned. Something inconceivable has happened. It seems impossible, yet that's how it is. The contradiction seems insurmountable, you seem to die, but that's nonsense. You're alive and keep on living even as you're dying. You live, forget, and get well again.

That's how it happened that I didn't tell him about Lyalka. Why? He might feel sorry. . . . Another lie. Besides, at that point there wasn't any Lyalka yet. I thought it would be a boy, another Volodya. The boy had only just begun to exist, and there was no absolute certainty. I thought I'd tell him later. And so I didn't tell him at all. He only found out about Lyalka's existence two years later, and then by chance.

But I didn't think about Lyalka then. I thought about Volodya all the time, just about him. When had it begun? Had there been snow or was it already spring? And, for some reason, the most important thing: when did the old Volodya stop existing and the new one appear? It was important to find this line in the past and to cut things off somewhere along it.

None the less I went to work that day. Zhanna sat in the library, chatting with readers. There was always a line at her desk. She saw me and was startled: 'Valyusha, what's the matter? You look almost green.'

And I became ill. She took me to the bathroom. Some buckets of lye were standing there, a big brush in one of them. And most important, the floor was of colored tiles – yellow with red – I see them as if they were in front of me this minute. That floor came straight at me. Zhanna held my head. Then I felt better.

'Valyusha, dear, tell me, is this . . .'

I nodded.

'God, how wonderful. You're going to have a baby!'

At that time Zhanna was infatuated with Hollywood and would say 'baby' and 'darling' in English.

'And Volodya's all excited, of course?'

'Volodya doesn't know.'

'What do you mean?'

'Zhanna, you'll find out anyway, so I'd better tell you right away. There's no Volodya. We've separated.'

There were tears in Zhanna's dark eyes. What are words? It's tears that count.

'Valechka, can I ask you just a single question? A tiny little question?'

'No.'

'I don't want to ask about Volodya. If I can't, I can't. I want to ask about "that". Are you going to keep it or are you going to get rid of it?'

The 'it' was Lyalka.

'I don't know, Zhanna, I don't know anything.'

And then a strange life began – a kind of delirium. I would lie around, thinking. I would leave work on the dot and rush home to lie down. I would get home, lie on the sofa, facing the back, thinking. The phone would ring, and I wouldn't answer. But with every ring my heart would start pounding, hammering in my ears. The neighbor would knock at the door: 'Telephone!'

I wouldn't make a sound. The neighbor would shout in the hall, 'She's not home! Or maybe she's asleep!'

My heart would keep on pounding, but it gradually calmed down. Half an hour later, another ring, and again my heart would start. I didn't answer once. I just keep repeating one single odd sentence over and over again: 'If it's you, go to hell.'

And I started thinking again, always about the same thing: where should I draw the line? On one side was the former Volodya whom I loved. On the other side was the new one, whom I had to hate. But the line kept shifting in one direction or the other, and at times the new Volodya would flow into the old one. For minutes at a time the old Volodya seemed never even to have existed. And then I would shout at this new Volodya as if he were really alive, 'What are you after? Do you really want to rob me of everything?' And sometimes the opposite would happen: the former Volodya would begin growing into the new one. That was the worst. Then I was almost ready to forgive him and call him back. . . . A piece of lint on the back of the sofa remained in my memory. It would always move back and forth with my breath, sort of swaying. I almost stopped eating and cleaning my room. I couldn't bear seeing anyone except Zhanna. She was the only one I could stand. It's very important to have someone who doesn't get on your nerves, and Zhanna never did. She wandered about the room, humming something, swept up the floor, dusted, went up to the mirror – doing her curls, her eyelashes, this and that, winking at herself in a funny way. She was as imitative as a monkey: she'd raise an eyebrow, and – became a new person. Or she talked about clothes in a mysterious throaty whisper, Hollywood movie-star style: 'The cut is verrry nice. . . . Puffy sleeves, shoulders raised, not too much, but just like this. This way you get a soft square, understand? A knee-length skirt in six gores, belled a little at the bottom. Some trim around the collar . . . .'

You listened to her, and you almost started feeling a bit better, as if looking past your grief at a colorful, pretty, carefree bird. That's how Zhanna was. You looked at her, and she was entirely made up of bits and pieces, every one of them borrowed from somewhere and every one, generally, mediocre. But all of them taken together were Zhanna – sentimental, generous, crazy, dear Zhanna.

We never spoke about Volodya. That's what we agreed on. Zhanna kept her word. And one has to know her to understand how hard that must have been! It is difficult for her to keep quiet about anything. But one time she actually prepared herself for a conversation, even put on lavender lipstick.

'Valyunchik,' she began talking, 'please allow me to say a word . . . or else I'm going to have a heart attack. You know I love you. I'm not trying to persuade you to return to Volodya . . . .'

'No.'

'But you've got to look at the future, right? You know I only want the best for you. You can count on that, it's as solid as a rock. If you've decided to get rid of it, you must do it now or it'll be too late.'

I knew nothing about those things, and I didn't want to know anything. Never before had I had to deal with such a thing. These were some kind of criminal dealings: making appointments, hiding, sneaking – I had read of incidents in the newspaper. The doctor and the woman both had to go to court. Become a criminal, a defendant. And still I had to do it. What else was I to do with this new Volodya? Even without him I had enough trouble with the two old ones.

Zhanna arranged everything. She took me to a doctor, to Vladimir Kazimirovich, a fellow in an imported suit. He had a greasy voice, like cracklings frying, a dark complexion, was well groomed, and looked intelligent. Zhanna assured me that Vladimir Kazimirovich was gentle. 'You'll see, he'll do it so that it'll be a real pleasure even.' And I gave in, I simply didn't exist . . . .

'There's no doubt about the pregnancy; it's obvious, Vladimir Kazimirovich said. 'As far as a surgical intervention is concerned, it might not be necessary, if the proper measures are undertaken in time.'

He spoke in this complicated fashion, with long and intricate sentences. He would circle around and around the meaning, in loops like figure eights . . . .

He suggested 'an easy, painless sequence of injections', 25

roubles a shot. The stuff was imported direct. He wouldn't guarantee anything, but it could help. So I started going for injections. He lived in a dacha in Karpovka. The dacha was a mansion: two storys, built of stone, with all the conveniences – gas, bath, telephone – and the garden had a silly Cupid. There were bird-droppings on its head, and the Cupid cried. That cursed dacha! A small shady street all overgrown with lime-trees went up to it. The branches, thickly covered with blossoms, bent low over the fences. That's when I understood how mean the fragrance of lime-trees could be.

The injections didn't help. Vladimir Kazimirovich said every time, 'It won't be today or tomorrow, just wait.' But I had stopped believing in those injections. I felt that he had hooked me like an experienced fisherman and was reeling me in slowly, taking 25 roubles each time in order to get his thousand with greater certainty. I didn't have any thousand; I borrowed from Zhanna. But he was charming, this Vladimir Kazimirovich. Every time we said goodbye he would hold my hand in his, but it felt as if I were holding a toad. And there I was . . . .

'Well, young lady,' Vladimir Kazimirovich said, wiping his hands, 'our injection treatment is finished, but unfortunately it didn't produce any positive results. As you know, I honestly warned you beforehand that I could not give a 100 per cent guarantee of success, right?'

'And what now?'

'If you still don't feel a burning desire . . . eh . . . to keep the fetus, we shall have to meet another time in order to apply a less pleasant but more reliable method.'

That was Vladimir Kazimirovich's complicated way of speaking.

What should I have done? I agreed. He demanded the money in advance: 'You must know, some young ladies with weak nerves have run away from me, right off the operating-table, one could say . . . .'

The appointment was set for Friday evening after ten, when it would be dark. Nobody was to accompany me, and nobody was to meet me afterwards; it was an outright conspiracy. I was to bring two sheets, two towels, boiled and ironed on both sides. 'I warn you, the laundry will not be returned,' he had said. I was not supposed to bring any documents. After the operation I was not allowed to remain at the dacha for more than ten minutes, because all sorts of things might happen, after all. 'The responsibility is immense, but I'm not shying away from it,' Vladimir Kazimirovich said. 'I want to emphasize again: no accompaniment, and no meetings afterwards.'

Then Friday evening came. Dusk fell, and then it grew dark. I was in the tram again, on my way. The pain and the danger before me were hardly a concern. Throughout the trip the two Volodyas were tormenting me. Even worse, I felt as if I, too, had divided into two. I couldn't make out where 'I' was and where 'I' ceased to be; everything seemed completely lost. Everything around me seemed rotten, I felt in the power of rottenness. . . . I approached the dacha. It was already dark. I recognized it by its Cupid. I went up to the gate and reached through the fence to undo the latch. Suddenly somebody stood next to me, as if sprung from the ground. The beam of a flashlight . . . .

'Citizen, your documents!' . . .

Someone was coming. No, that wasn't Lyalka's kind of ring. Lyalka always rang loudly, insistently and gaily, while this ring was short and weak. Valentina Stepanovna was still sitting in the armchair, her head settled on the rough armrest. No problem, Polya would open up.

The door opened, and Lyalka came into the room.

'Mama-mouse, you're here? What are you doing here? Why in the dark?'

'Nothing, I'm just sitting here. I don't feel well.'

'What's the matter? Let me feel your head. It's cold! Mama-mouse, you're just pretending! I'll turn on the light, all right? There, that's better. I want something to eat, I'm starved. Where's the salad?'

'I didn't make the salad,' Valentina Stepanovna said. 'Come, sit down here.'

Lyalka settled down on the sofa. Thin, tall, leggy as a grasshopper, she even had a grayish-green dress on, quite short, above knee length. A grasshopper, indeed. When she sat down, her knees rose above chin level. She was pale; the blue circles under her eyes reached halfway down her cheeks.

'Lyalka, listen . . . .'

Lyalka removed a hairclip and started chewing on it: 'Now what? Do you want to have a talk with me?'

'No, I just want to tell you a story.'

'All right.'

. . . 'Well, and what happened then?'

'Then I ran away. Never in my life did I run like that. They whistled, but I ran. My legs were young and strong. Even now my legs aren't bad, they do their job well.'

'And you got away?'

'Just imagine, I did. I heard the whistles get weaker, and then they disappeared entirely. But I still kept running. I'd thrown away my bundle right at the beginning, so I was running without anything, no money, nothing. And you know, it felt great to run. . . . I felt I'd got away from all of them, the police, the doctor, the courts . . . .'

'They took you to court for it in those days?'

'They took you to court for everything then.'

'Well, and then what?'

'Nothing else. I ran to the station; the tram was standing at the platform. It was dark, but the tram windows were large and bright. It was a beautiful tram, and it seemed to be waiting just for me. I ran into the car, and everybody looked at me, red, dishevelled, and happy as I was. The minute I got on, the tram started. The conductor came through, and I was without a ticket. He didn't fine me, I don't know why. We arrived in the city. I immediately ran to a phone booth and called Vladimir Kazimirovich. I was afraid they'd arrested him because of me. But he was fine, not even particularly frightened. He said, "Don't worry, I am used to fulfilling my obligations." He invited me to come on Tuesday. Friday's a hard day, he said. And then I swore and cursed at him.'

'Don't tell me! I can't believe it. What in the world did you tell him?'

'I'll never come back to you, you scum.'

'You really said that? What a heroine! And you didn't die of a bad conscience on the spot?'

'No. And I also told him, just to spite you I'll have ten children.'

'An obvious exaggeration. Well, and what happened then?'

'Then? You were born.'

'A cheerful little story.'

. . . Something fell in the hall, and Polya's whiny voice said, 'That's parasite manners for you! No peace and quiet, even at night. Thump and bump. Sacking up during the day and making a row at night. Not like decent folks. I'm going to change apartments. I am.'

2

Yury Trifonov

Of the writers represented in this anthology, Yury Valentinovich Trifonov is the only one who, as the book goes to press, is no longer alive. Born in Moscow on 28 August 1925, he died unexpectedly early on 28 March 1981, of complications following an operation. Trifonov's work has an international reputation and has been translated into numerous languages. In the Soviet Union he was the leading author of the 1970s, which are known among Moscow literati as the Trifonov decade. The event that determined much of his thinking and writing and motivated his preoccupation with the past was the execution of his father – a revolutionary and Civil War hero – and the exile of his mother in 1937. He began his literary training as a factory delegate to the Gorky Literary Institute during the Second World War.

His literary debut in the 1950s gave no indication that he would become a controversial writer. A Stalin Prize for his novel *Students* (*Studenty*, 1950) seemed to place him firmly among the orthodox. A good example of Socialist Realism, the official literary doctrine, the novel depicts the conflict between an honest, hardworking student and a self-centred opportunist, who is exposed and defeated. The characters and action are flat; the positive, as defined by the political context, is victorious; and the style is straightforward.

A number of well-received books followed in a phase (1959–65) that Trifonov himself described as the second stage of his development as a writer. In addition to short stories, sport sketches and film scripts, which reflected travels within the Soviet Union and abroad, he published the novel *Quenching of Thirst* (*Utolenie zhazhdy*, 1962), which was well received and is the major work of this phase. Its action takes place right after Khrushchev's de-Stalinization speech at the Twentieth Party Congress. The title refers both to the construction of the Kara Kum Canal in Turkmenistan, the objective of which is to secure water for the desert, and to the thirst for justice to redress the wrongs done in Stalin's time. The conflict is one between unselfish devotion to a common

49

cause and careerism. During this phase Trifonov also completed a documentary historical work, a biography of his father, called *Reflection of the Fire* (*Otblesk kostra*, 1965), which was little discussed in the press and was not reprinted until 1988 because of its controversial political content.

A marked qualitative change characterizes his third and mature creative phase. To the beginning of it belong such transitional works as the story printed here, 'Vera and Zoyka', and its twin, 'Summer Noon' ('Byl letnii polden'), both published in *Novy Mir*, 1966, no. 12. However, the qualitative shift became more manifest in the novellas of Trifonov's Moscow cycle.

These works – *The Exchange* (*Obmen*, 1969), *Preliminary Stocktaking* (*Predvaritel'nye itogi*, 1970), *The Long Goodbye* (*Dolgoe proshchanie*, 1971) and *Another Life* (*Drugaya zhizn'*, 1975), all of them serialized in *Novy mir* – were avidly read and widely reviewed in the Soviet press. Many criticized Trifonov for showing only the negative side of reality, for attacking the intelligentsia, and for withholding his own judgement. Indeed, the moral failures of the Moscow intelligentsia, their intrigues, deceptions, manipulations, cowardice, fraud and status-seeking, and the pangs of conscience of the better among them, are the dominant themes. Their families are intact only in name. Wives and husbands live together without love and respect, in-laws cause daily agonies, and children cheat and exploit. Pressured by his wife, the protagonist of *The Exchange* betrays his family's humanistic values for the sake of enlarging their living-space. Reminiscences of his recent past unmask the middle-aged protagonist of *Preliminary Stocktaking* as a pharisee who finds fault with the ethics of the people around him, but fails to attend to his own. The intrigues, deceptions and moral compromises of Moscow literati are recounted in *The Long Goodbye*. The heroine's self-incriminating examination of her relationship with her husband and of her guilt at his premature death evokes a harrowing picture of searches for 'another life' in the novella of that title.

The House on the Embankment (*Dom na naberezhnoi*, 1976), almost a rewrite of Trifonov's first novel, impresses by its artistic density, its boldness and the candor with which it alludes to banned topics. Much that is easily understandable to the Soviet reader who shared Trifonov's experience of the 1930s and 1940s will be missed by Western audiences. This book is the first in which Trifonov draws more openly on his own and his family's experiences. The 'house' of the title, for example, was the domicile of numerous party functionaries and government officials, including Trifonov's own family. The central topic again is betrayal, the protagonist a careerist. Trifonov's anatomy of the protagonist's moral conduct has an almost scientific exactitude, showing the character as so firmly embedded in his particular milieu that his moral failings become understandable, even if they cannot be condoned. But he is not evil, and a victim as well as a villain. All of Trifonov's characters are human – some better, some worse – painted in the gray hues of empathy. Nor does Trifonov provide solutions or conclusions, although the ideal moral conduct is implicit. Narrative density and complexity – different points of view and narration on several chronological planes – are inseparable from the subtlety of meanings conveyed by the text. These traits are characteristic of Trifonov's last literary works.

With his historical novel *Impatience* (*Neterpenie*, 1973) about the revolutionary party 'People's Will' and its acts of terrorism (1878–81) Trifonov returned to a historical subject that had contemporary relevance: the relationship of ends and means, the causes and consequences of wanting to rush history, and the circumstances of betrayal.

This characterization also fits Trifonov's subsequent works. In the novel *The Old Man* (*Starik*, 1978), the search for the truth about the Soviet past and its effect in the present are central. The old protagonist tries to uncover the truth about events during the Civil War while he is simultaneously drawn into the petty wrangles of his family at a Moscow dacha settlement during the 1970s. Again, the opportunists and speculators are successful, and the righteous lose.

Trifonov's last work, *Time and Place* (*Vremya i mesto*, 1981), sums up his major themes – memory, history and ethics. The novel's plots evolve against the background of events from the 1930s to the present, capturing the suffering and alluding to the crimes of the Stalin era and the repercussions of those years even in the present. An autobiographical figure, the novel's protagonist is a writer, parts of whose own novel enter the work. The fate of the Soviet writer born and raised entirely after the Revolution is the central theme.

Two other posthumously published works are 'Topsy-Turvy House' ('*Oprokinuty dom*', 1981) and *Disappearance* (*Ischeznovenie*, 1987). 'Topsy-Turvy House' is a comprehensive statement about

Trifonov's sense of the fluidity and transforming power of time, which turns tragedy into farce; *Disappearance* is an unfinished, largely autobiographical account of an adolescent's perceptions of Stalin's purges, recalled five years later. This work captures the atmosphere of chaos and loss in 1937–8, the desolation of wartime Moscow, the hardships of evacuation in Siberia, and the adolescent's nostalgia for the lost ideals of the old revolutionaries.

WORKS AND SECONDARY LITERATURE IN ENGLISH

The Students (Moscow: Progress Publishers, 1953).
The Impatient Ones (Moscow: Progress Publishers, 1978).
The Long Goodbye (Ann Arbor, Mich.: Ardis, 1978).
The Old Man (New York: Simon and Schuster, 1983).
The House on the Embankment and Another Life (New York: Simon and Schuster, 1984).

Bjørling, Fiona, 'Jurij Trifonov's *Dom na nabereẑnoj*: Fiction or Autobiography?', *Biografi og Vaerk*, Svantevit IX, no. 1 (Aarhus, 1983) pp. 9–30.
De Maegd-Soep, Caroline, 'The Theme of "byt" – Everyday Life in the Stories of Iurii Trifonov', in Evelyn Bristol (ed.), *Russian Literature and Criticism*, Selected Papers from the Second World Congress for Soviet and East European Studies 1980 (Berkeley, Calif.: Berkeley Slavic Specialties, 1982) pp. 49–62.
Hosking, Geoffrey, 'Trifonov', *Beyond Socialist Realism: Soviet Fiction since 'Ivan Denisovich'* (London, 1980) pp. 183–7.
——, 'The Search for an Image of Man in Contemporary Soviet Fiction', in C. J. Barnes (ed.) *Studies in Twentieth Century Russian Literature* (Edinburgh: Scottish Academic Press, 1976) pp. 61–77.
Hughes, Ann C., '*Bol'shoi mir* or *zamknutyi mirok*: Departure from Literary Convention in Iurii Trifonov's Recent Fiction', *Canadian Slavonic Papers*, XXII, no. 4 (Winter 1980) 470–80.
Kolesnikoff, Nina, 'Jurij Trifonov as a Novella Writer', *Russian Literature Journal*, XXXIV, no. 118 (1980) 137–43.
Kustanovich, Constantine, review of *The Old Man*, in *Ulbandus Review*, 1, no. 2 (Spring 1978) 169–72.
McLaughlin, Sigrid, 'Jurij Trifonov's *House on the Embankment*: Narration and Meaning', *Slavic and East European Journal*, XXVI, no. 4 (Winter 1982) 419–33.
——, 'Iurii Trifonov's *Dom na naberezhnoj* and Dostoevskii's *Prestuplenie i nakazanie*', *Canadian Slavonic Papers*, XXV, no. 2 (Summer 1983) 275–83.
——, 'Literary Allusions in Trifonov's *Preliminary Stocktaking*', *Russian Review*, Winter 1987, 19–34.
——, 'Antipov's *Nikiforov Syndrome*: The Embedded Novel in Trifonov's *Time and Place*', *Slavonic and East European Journal*, 32, no. 2 (Summer 1988) 237–50.

——, 'A Moment in the History of Consciousness of the Soviet Intelligentsia: Trifonov's Novel *Disappearance*', *Studies in Comparative Communism*, XXI, nos 3–4 (Winter 1988) 303–11.

Shneidman, Norman N., 'Iurii Trifonov and the Ethics of Contemporary City Life', *Canadian Slavonic Papers*, XIX, no. 3 (Fall 1977); also in revised form in his book *Soviet Literature in the 1970s: Artistic Diversity and Ideological Conformity* (Toronto: Toronto University Press, Toronto, 1979).

——, 'The New Dimensions of Time and Place in Iurii Trifonov's Prose of the 1980's', *Canadian Slavonic Papers*, XXVII, no. 2 (Summer 1985) 188–95.

Szenfeld, Ignacy, 'Yurii Trifonov's New Novel *Starik*', *Radio Liberty Research*, 183/78 (23 Aug 1978).

Woll, Josephine, 'Trifonov's *Starik*: The Truth of the Past', *Russian Literature Triquarterly*, 19 (1986) 243–58.

Vera and Zoyka
(1966)

Just before lunch an old customer, 52–80, came by – a very proper and neat lady in her Bologna raincoat, who always brought in the laundry neat and proper, with a lot of men's clothing among it – and asked if Vera could come to clean up a dacha outside Moscow on Saturday and Sunday. Vera inquired if there would be a lot of work. She didn't let on that she was pleased. But, in fact, she was extremely pleased, because she needed the money badly, and it was only this morning that she had realized how desperately she needed it. Up to this point, Vera hadn't had any time to get hold of herself. She kept tripping over an uneven floorboard as she ran back and forth between the counter and the shelves. It almost seemed to have become a law: as soon as she got a little nervous, she tripped over this damn floorboard.

Her customer explained that the dacha had to be swept up, the floors washed in four rooms – three downstairs, one upstairs – and the storm windows taken down, all the things that usually have to be done after the winter. She spoke rapidly and carelessly, as if she were talking of something simple and trivial that wasn't worth going into in great detail. But Vera understood that she was being sly, that getting Vera's consent was important, and that actually there were, of course, mountains of work, and heavy work too, especially as nobody had lived in the house all winter, and nothing had been cleaned up. But Vera did not shy away from any work, and therefore she thought, quite happily, that it was fine there was so much work: they'd pay more. She needed the money desperately. In the morning one customer, an old lady with the hideous number 48–44 – all those fours! – had made a great fuss over a blanket: they had given her the wrong one. In place of her six-rouble blanket, she said, they had palmed off on her someone else's cheap one. The old lady was right, but she had caught on too late – after she had already signed two receipts. The mix-up was the fault of the packing women. Vera was guilty only in that she had not carefully checked each item as she handed things out, but only the package. She'd always done it that way, and nothing had ever happened. For a long time they had all searched for the six-rouble blanket, but couldn't find it anywhere. They offered the old lady a replacement, but she rejected it and demanded her own. At this point Vera got angry, because the packers kept blaming it all on her. She told them that the old lady had already signed and that it was no longer her, Vera's, business. The old lady had gone to the manager, Raisa Vasilyevna. Vera and the packers were called out, they screamed and yelled – the packers at Vera and she at them. When it came to screaming, Vera could outshout everybody because she had a piercing, shrill voice, even though it was rather hoarse – and, above all, she resented that she alone was being blamed, as if the packers had had no part in it at all. How often had Vera saved their skins? How often had she handed over things that actually belonged to other people? Here, take it, in God's name, I don't need someone else's stuff. Now they didn't want to hear of it, didn't remember anything. They just wanted her to pay the six roubles and that was it. And six roubles was no mean amount. Vera had to slave three days for it. The packers should have been able to put themselves in her position. Both had husbands who earned money; they could have thrown in one rouble, and it would have made things easier. But no! And Yevdokiya, the oldest packer, even made fun of her: 'What's the problem?' she said. 'Your Seryozha will just have to do without his two half-liters, that's all there is to it.' The viper, the beast! What business of hers was it how Vera spent her money! She herself was a parasite, lived on her husband's money and didn't have the slightest idea how hard others had to work.

'Well, what do you say, Vera? Are you going to come?' asked 52–80 (Vera managed to decipher her last name on the receipt:

Sinitsyna). 'Otherwise I'll have to arrange things with someone else.'

'You don't need to. I'll take the job. I've done all sorts of work!'

'Perhaps you can find someone to help? You're so . . . well, so small . . . .'

'Don't you worry about me being small. I'm not afraid of any kind of work. In the factory I've worked with men, dragging around castings.' (Vera lisped a little, so it sounded like 'Dragging around cashtingth.') 'And I can also get some help. No problem!'

Vera had thought instantly of Zoyka. She always thought instantly of Zoyka: when some extra job turned up, or when she did something in her free time, or when the food co-op threw salted perch or buckwheat on the counter. But Zoyka never thought of her. Vera wasn't offended though. She knew Zoyka wasn't well. Something was wrong with her liver, and that's why she was always grumpy and dissatisfied. And she had other worries, too: she had two children on her hands and an old grandmother. Vera also was well aware that she and Zoyka weren't real friends. Vera had never had a true girlfriend, except maybe Nastenka from ages ago, who had gone to second grade with her. She and Zoyka were nothing but neighbors, both without husbands. Vera had never had a husband, and Zoyka's had left five years ago and was paying alimony.

The woman told Vera she would expect her on Saturday around four o'clock. On a piece of paper she jotted down her address, her telephone number and her name: Lidia Aleksandrovna Sinitsyna.

At lunchtime Vera rushed home as fast as she could, hoping to find Zoyka there to ask her about Saturday. Zoyka worked as a janitor in a school. On Sunday she'd certainly be free, but, as to Saturday, Vera would have to find out, and, if Zoyka couldn't do it, she'd have to find someone else. Vera lived in the 'barracks', across the court from the laundry. Hers was a great job, and convenient too: a two-minute walk and she was home.

'Barracks' was the name the inhabitants of the Peschanye Streets had given to the five wooden two-story houses that were oddly tucked into the thicket of high-rises built after the war, at the beginning of the 1950s, in an area where there had been vacant land, garbage dumps, gardens, and the cottages of seasonal workers. Nobody knew why these five barracks had remained unscathed. Most likely the builders had made some mistake. Ten years ago the barrack-dwellers were still trying to change their fate, demanding demolition and resettlement; they pointed out that these 'ugly structures spoiled the splendid overall look of the district'; they were offended that the inhabitants of the remaining barracks had been given apartments in new buildings long ago. In what way were they more deserving? But it was evidently not easy to correct the mistake. The construction enterprise disappeared from the district, the accounts were closed, and the unlucky ones had to accept their fate. From four sides six-story high-rises pressed down on the barracks. They reminded you of a little village in a mountain valley. And life there had a character of its own, like in the country: there were tiny front gardens, and onion beds, and lilacs in the windows.

As always, Zoyka's grandmother, Granny Lyuba, an old woman of about ninety, sat on the bench next to the entrance, a black kerchief pulled all the way down to her eyes. Vera asked if Zoyka was at home. Granny Lyuba nodded, lowering her sallow face covered with deep wrinkles (her mouth, lips sucked in and tightly closed, looked like another wrinkle). Suddenly her lips drew apart: Granny Lyuba had decided to say something. But Vera didn't hear, she was already running up the stairs. She felt sorry for Granny Lyuba and had defended her more than once before Zoyka. But she didn't like standing there and talking to her. An unpleasant grave-like smell seemed to exude from Granny Lyuba.

Zoyka was standing in their communal kitchen in her long cotton dressing-gown, her bare feet in rubber slippers, cooking porridge for the children. When she heard about the cleaning job at the dacha, her immediate response was rude: evidently there weren't any other fools, she said, ready to go outside the city for a job; there were plenty of cleaning jobs in Moscow too. Vera had got used to the fact that Zoyka met all her suggestions with hostility. Apparently Zoyka suspected some hidden design that would be disadvantageous to her and highly advantageous to Vera. So Vera answered calmly, 'All right, I can manage by myself just as well.'

Zoyka started warming up the potatoes that she had roasted the day before. She filled the whole frying-pan, poured in some sunflower oil, cracked an egg over it, chopped in the remainder of some sausage, about 50 grams of meat, and lunch was ready – the envy of anyone! Vera knew that in a minute, after some thought, Zoyka would show up and ask for the details and how much they would get for the job. And she was right. Vera told her so far they hadn't discussed the pay, but that the work was more or less such

and such. They could probably ask for 20 roubles. For some reason
Vera had got this sum into her head.

'All right then. We'll see tomorrow,' growled Zoyka, and left
the kitchen angrily, the pan in her hand. After she had disappeared,
she suddenly shouted back from the hall, 'Did Grandma tell you?
Nikolai was here.'

'Nikolai?' Vera gasped. 'And what did he say?' What a person
Zoyka was, not to tell her right away! Vera dashed into the hall.
Zoyka kept on going to her room and answered, without turning
around, 'How should I know? He talked to Granny, go and ask
her.'

Head over heels, Vera ran down to Granny Lyuba, who confirmed it. Nikolai had come, had been disappointed that Vera
wasn't at home, and had asked them to tell her that he definitely
would be back on Sunday evening. Vera was all excited and, in
her joy, even gave Granny a kiss on the cheek. She hadn't seen
Nikolai for about five months and thought she'd never see him
again. She had last seen him in the street, after the movies. They
had seen a film in the Friendship Theater. Vera had wanted to run
to the shop to get something to drink, but he suddenly said, 'No
thanks, I don't need anything. Let's say goodbye on good terms,
as friends, because I'm going to get married.' That's how people
who had gone together for four years separated: in the middle of
the street! They shook hands and went in different directions. For
a whole month afterwards, Vera felt ill and wanted to poison
herself, but Zoyka talked her out of it.

On Saturday at 4 p.m., as agreed, Vera and Zoyka appeared at
Sinitsyna's apartment in an eight-story building across from the
delicatessen. Zoyka had brought along her son Mishka, an eleven-
year-old, who had finished school the week before and was loafing
around with nothing to do, waiting to go to summer camp.

Sinitsyna gave them a friendly welcome and asked them to come
in, but there was no time for a visit because she was already
dressed in her Bologna raincoat. Vera managed to look around the
entrance hall. It was very nice and had a big oval mirror hanging
next to the coat-rack, just like in the theater. Vera liked the entrance
hall, and she said immediately, 'What a nice place you have. I
clean for an actress on Chapayevsky Boulevard, and her apartment
is also decorated just beautifully. Except her hall isn't like yours,

it's like . . . .' And Vera started describing it with her hands.

'Does the boy come along too?' Sinitsyna asked.

'If you don't mind,' said Zoyka, smiling ingratiatingly, her long thin face tilting to the side like a supplicant's. 'He's very shy, you know! And he can help too!'

Misha stood there looking at the floor. In his right hand he held a butterfly net.

'Yes, he is a good boy, a very good boy,' confirmed Vera. 'Lida Aleksandrovna, there's just one thing you should know. On Sunday I definitely have to be back about six o'clock, no matter what.'

'That depends on you, girls. If we finish early, you might be back for lunch.'

'Well, and did you ask about the pay, Vera?' Zoyka asked timidly.

'Not yet. We'll see about it when we're there. It depends on the work, right Lida Aleksandrovna? You won't take advantage of us, I hope, and we won't of you. But bring along plenty of money!' and Vera began to laugh in her peculiar way, resoundingly and in fits and starts.

A dark-haired lad in glasses and a white shirt stepped into the entrance hall. He nodded politely to Vera and Zoyka and said, 'Well, are you ready to go?'

'Kirill, I'd like you to come tomorrow,' said Mrs Sinitsyna.

'I don't know yet. We'll see later. And I beg you not to overdo it, Mother, d'you hear? I know you're going to work like a horse, until you're blue in the face, and who needs it?'

'I won't, really. You see what excellent helpers I have, but I do expect you tomorrow, do you hear, Kirill? Anatoly Vladimirovich will come by car and pick you up. You must get some rest and you've got to get some fresh air.'

The son went up to her and she took his hand. He was taller and looked down on her, smiling vaguely.

'And I hope . . .'

'Everything will be fine, Mother. But I have a lot to do, as you know.'

'Anatoly Vladimirovich will come for you in the morning.'

'All right. We'll make it there somehow.'

'Goodbye, then!' Vera said, and smiled at the young fellow in the glasses as she had become accustomed to smiling at men: she closed her lips tightly, because two of her front teeth were missing. This contributed to her lisp.

Vera took two brooms and a bucket with soap boxes for washing the windows, and started down the stairs. Zoyka followed her with two bags: one was full of food, the other, large and checkered, was stuffed to the brim with curtains, rugs, a kettle, an electric hotplate and, balanced on the very top, a black table lamp. Mishka hobbled after his mother, bent down by the weight of a bale of blankets he was dragging. Mrs Sinitsyna followed last. She carried another bag, a small handbag, and a big roll of green paper which she held very carefully because she was afraid of getting it crumpled. When she had gone down several steps Mrs Sinitsyna said, 'As to the pay, I really don't know. . . . Last year I paid 15 roubles for about the same work.'

'Don't compare this year with last, Lida Aleksandrovna!' Vera shouted from below.

'I'm not comparing it, I just wanted to let you know what I paid last year. But you shouldn't argue at this point; you haven't seen the job yet.'

'Of course, of course,' Zoyka said judiciously. 'We'll have to see first and then we'll come to an agreement. You're strange, Verka . . . .'

'Your son is really dark. Takes after his father, does he?' Vera shouted.

'That's right, he does,' said Mrs Sinitsyna.

'That's what I thought, seeing that you're fair and he's really quite dark.'

At the delicatessen they got in a taxi. Mrs Sinitsyna sat next to the driver; the others sat in the back, Vera by the window. They put their odds and ends in the trunk and drove off.

The day was clear and warm. It was the middle of June, and the city park was radiant with fresh green. Crowds of people milled around everywhere as they always do on Saturdays about this time: at the bus stop where they drove by, and at the entrance to the grocer's, and also at old Moiseich's tobacco stand. Vera was all eyes; joyfully she looked out the window as if she was seeing her neighborhood – which she had actually seen a thousand times and knew inside out, down to the last window and the last brick – for the first time.

'Look at that long line in front of Moiseich's! That's some crowd of men for you! And they're lining up for ice-cream at Klavka's. . . . And there's a client of mine, 58–10! There! There!' Vera suddenly cried so passionately that Mrs Sinitsyna flinched and turned around and the driver swore quietly. 'Lida Aleksandrovna, look, there goes a customer of mine! Over there, it's the one with the brief-case! There he goes, there! 58–10! A very nice person. He always comes himself, and his wife hardly ever shows up. But she's also very nice. I know her. She works here in the Institute, right by the Sokol subway station.'

They turned onto Leningradsky Prospekt. Vera continued to chatter. She was in a splendid mood, as if she had forgotten yesterday's tribulations, her tears over the blanket, the six roubles she had to pay for absolutely nothing, and the two days of hard work ahead of her instead of some rest. It was as if she were going off on a vacation to a dacha, to the woods where birds were singing; and tomorrow evening Nikolai would come to see her. Whatever she said, whatever she thought about, there was always one thing on her mind: tomorrow Nikolai would come.

At Begovaya Street they turned off to the right, crossed a bridge, passed by the Vagankovskoe Cemetery, and Vera remembered that an aunt of hers was buried there – may she rest in peace. She should visit her grave and take some flowers; she hadn't been there since last summer. Along the Krasnaya Presnya old houses were being torn down. Some were just burnt down, like trash in spring. On the right side black flat mounds were still smoldering here and there, and behind this belt of ash heaps, about 200 steps from the road, loomed new five-story housing-blocks.

'Their misery's over. Lucky them,' Zoyka said.

'But I'm sorry for these little houses. It is old Moscow, after all, historical old Moscow: the Krasnaya Presnya,' said Mrs Sinitsyna. 'And they're getting burnt down mercilessly.'

'And that's just as it should be! Why feel sorry for these dumps and flea-traps!' the driver said with unexpected irritation. 'People live there on top of each other, ten people on seven square meters. What's history to them? At least they're getting some decent housing.'

Mrs Sinitsyna looked out of the window and said nothing.

'But you know, these new houses aren't exactly what you'd call an ornament,' she said. 'They're ugly enough, and they don't have elevators.'

'And so what? So they are without elevators,' said the driver. 'We're working people, we're not spoiled. We can walk.'

'That's right!' Zoyka said. 'How many years have we been petitioning to get our barracks torn down?'

'But what for? I like our barracks,' said Vera. 'Our barracks are great. First of all, they're warm. Second, it's green all around – we don't even need dachas, right Mish?' She gave Mishka a shove with her shoulder and burst out laughing.

Zoyka waved her hand: 'Just go ahead and jabber.'

'I'm not jabbering, I'm telling the truth: our barracks are even quite remarkable. They're built solidly, and they're going to last another hundred years.' And Vera burst out laughing again, even more loudly than before. She virtually exploded, shooting off salvoes of laughter, and in between she screamed with her thin voice, 'Oh, I can't go on! Oh, they're going to last another hundred years for sure!' Nobody else laughed. Zoyka grumbled angrily, and then asked the driver for a cigarette and started smoking. Gradually Vera calmed down, repeating in a hoarse whisper, absolutely exhausted, 'Oh, I can't go on!' and wiped the tears from her eyes with the back of her hand.

They turned onto the Tryokhgorka, the embankment, and across the big bridge to Leninprospekt. Soon wooden houses appeared on both sides. Behind them towered cranes and the brick walls of new buildings. Then the new buildings disappeared and only the little houses remained, and then the houses disappeared and only fields were left, undulating and soft green in the late afternoon sun.

Lidia Aleksandrovna rolled down the window; the heavy, bracingly fresh air from the fields filled the car, and for some reason everyone fell silent, inhaling this air. Mishka began to doze.

As always when silence set in or when Vera was alone with no one to talk to, unpleasant thoughts came to her mind. Again she remembered the six-rouble blanket. She would have to pay, the devil take them; she wasn't going to split hairs. But she was going to keep her eyes open in the future; any slip and she'd have them. If they were going to be like that, she could be the same way. Now she wouldn't let those parasites get away with anything. There, take the money, choke on it! She'd throw it in Raisa Vasilyevna's face: you aren't going to get rich on my six roubles, and I won't get poor. Lucky that Lidia Aleksandrovna turned up: if Lidia paid a tenner each, she could pay up right away, throwing the six roubles into Raisa's face. And she'd have four roubles left to welcome Nikolai.

Vera began to think about Nikolai, and this made her feel warm and happy; but at the same time an inner anxiety weighed her down. And, the longer she thought, the heavier this anxiety became. Why in the world should he show up again, the miserable wretch? Why upset her? For five months now Vera had been going with the Tatar Seryozhka, a good person, a locksmith at the Institute. He earned a decent salary, he drank a little, and in general he was a very good person, only sickly: he had some heart problem. And Vera had begun to forget Nikolai and to imagine how she and Seryozhka would get married. Seryozhka was much more suitable for her: he was her age, thirty-six, whereas Nikolai was three years younger and had repeatedly reproached her with 'You're too old for me.' Too old, yes, too old, but for four years they had gone together and he had never paid attention to younger women. How come this idiot showed up now? Maybe he had turned sour on his new woman, and had begun to think that maybe the old one wasn't so bad. Oh Kolya, oh Nikolai, you won't have such a bed of roses again . . . .

And much else crossed Vera's mind: she thought of how she had sent her little son Yurka to boarding-school – Nikolai had demanded it – and how hard it had been at the beginning, and how she finally got used to it. And she thought of how ill she had been after the abortion, lying in the hospital, when all the other women had visits from their men, who brought them food and letters, while for two weeks she had received neither food nor letters. She was the only dupe in the whole big ward, and the women felt sorry for her, but she hadn't given herself away. She had only bawled at night. On the fourteenth day, though, Nikolai suddenly turned up, knocked at the window from the outside, face beaming, a bouquet of flowers in his hand. He said they'd whisked him off for some business trip far away – maybe it was even true. And much else crossed her mind, all sorts of other things: offenses, happy days, conversations and kindnesses, and she did not notice how the car turned off the main road into a lane, passed some summer cottages, birch-trees, fences, crossed a wooden bridge over a stream, climbed uphill, turned right (Lidia Aleksandrovna directed the driver) – turned right once more and stopped by a small gate in a rickety fence.

The dacha turned out to be a large wooden building, but it was old and neglected. Windows were missing on the porch, and a board was nailed across the door. The garden, too, had gone to seed. Thick elderbushes, some small spruce and an aspen were growing between tall firs.

'What sort of work-horse managed to get this little dacha pieced together?' the driver mumbled laughingly in his beard. He was helping to carry the baggage from the car into the house.

Lidia Aleksandrovan did not hear him; she was looking for the keys in her handbag, but Vera exclaimed, 'Whoever put it up is a fine fellow, right, Lida Aleksandrovna? And he'll get on all right in life! Don't you agree?'

All four of them worked until dark. They sorted through and carried out the rubbish, wiped off the furniture that had become damp during the winter, shook out and beat the dusty, musty-smelling old rugs and mats; they swept, washed and scoured. Lidia Aleksandrovna wrapped a scarf around her head, put on coarse blue canvass pants and a sleeveless sports shirt, and worked away non-stop like Zoyka and Vera, without falling behind. Even Zoyka gave herself more breaks. She'd sit down a minute, saying, 'My back hurts', or she'd go into the garden to have a smoke. After eleven they decided to stop. On the following day only the windows in the upper floor needed washing.

They put Mishka, who tired faster than the others, to bed upstairs in the warmest room and he dozed off instantly. The adults sat in the porch to eat supper. It turned out that there was no tea. They had forgotten to bring it from Moscow. Lida Aleksandrovna went off to some neighbors. Meanwhile Vera and Zoyka sat on the porch and ate noodle soup which Vera had brought along in a pot. The windows were closed because of the mosquitoes, and it had grown chilly too; but the cold and the mosquitoes crept in through the broken glass.

'How old do you think Lida Aleksandrovna is?' Zoyka asked.

'About thirty-five I think. My age. The noodle soup is delicious! I didn't bring enough, though, did I? Lida Aleksandrovna is a very nice woman, really, and she is a hard worker, too.'

'Of course she's nice. That's easy if life's nice to you,' Zoyka said, and her long thin face assumed that expression of hidden resentment Vera knew so well, an expression that usually ended in a nasty remark. Zoyka looked at the ceiling of the porch, at the yellow lampshade made of wax paper and at its reflection on the black glass. 'And I think she's going on fifty. What a healthy son she's got.'

When Lidia Aleksandrovna returned with some tea, Vera asked her how old she was. Lidia Aleksandrovna answered, 'Forty-four.'

Kirill was eighteen. He was enrolled in his first year at the Institute. Vera was absolutely astounded.

'You'd never guess it, Lida Aleksandrovna, never! Beside you I'm an old woman, I even have teeth missing, and I've got wrinkles everywhere, but I'm actually eight years younger. How's that possible? You probably have a really calm disposition. With me, everything hits home very hard.'

Silently, and with the same expression of hidden resentment, Zoyka poured the tea.

'I think you're just putting yourself down, Vera. You're very likable, and nice and plump. Like a round loaf of bread,' Lidia Aleksandrovna said and burst out laughing. 'And men probably like you, right?'

Vera also burst into a laugh, feeling flattered.

'Well, Lida Aleksandrovna, that's how it is: when I go to the movies, someone is definitely going to be after me to take me home. They even call me Miss. In the dark you can't tell the difference!'

'Of course they like her, because she feeds them on her money,' said Zoyka.

'Who do I feed?'

'Everyone. Do you think I don't know?'

'Who do I feed? Who? Who?'

'Didn't you feed Kolka all the time? You did. And Arkasha, the policeman? Do you deny it? And now it's Seryozhka.'

'You're probably much too good-hearted, Vera, don't you agree?'

'Don't you listen to her, Lida Aleksandrovna! She's lying. She's just envious in general.'

'The question is, envious of what?'

'Of course she's envious, because I have a lot of company, and she has visitors only once a year, I swear. Men hold me in respect, Lida Aleksandrovna; they respect me a great deal. I'm like a comrade to them. I can drink – of course, just a little bit, why should you drink a lot, right? – and eat a snack and even lend them some money before pay day. Of course, the problem is how much to lend them. Well, most of the time it's a rouble and a half or three. I'm like a comrade to them Lida Aleksandrovna, I swear.'

'You fool, you've got a room of your own!' Zoyka said. 'But, in my case, there's four of us living in 12 square meters.'

Vera was about to answer, but instead she suddenly started hiccuping. For a minute or two she fought it, then she gave up with a wave of her hand which meant: what's the point of talking to you anyway? Continuing to hiccup, she put her old-fashioned round handbag on her lap, a gift of the actress, once a beautiful dark green, but now badly worn and with a loose lock. Hastily she began to rummage in it, placing various objects from it on the table: a comb, a mirror, some pieces of paper, pencil stubs which she used to write out receipts in the laundry, and, finally a warped photograph on shiny paper.

'Read it, Lida Aleksandrovna. Kolya gave it to me on Navy Day.' She hiccupped once more and whispered, 'Lord in Heaven, help me and take pity on me.'

Lidia Aleksandrovna took the photograph and read aloud, 'In memory of Navy Day from Nikolai Z.' 'Well,' said Lidia Aleksandrovna. 'A very nice dedication. But, girls, how about turning off the light and opening the windows? The air in the garden is so wonderful.'

'And imagine, Lida Aleksandrovna,' Vera said, getting up to turn off the light, 'we were together for four years and now all I have is one picture. If I had at least a ring or some earrings. . . . Well, actually I don't need anything.'

As soon as the light under the yellow lampshade was switched off, you could see that the sky was still quite light, as it always was in June. Along with the chill, the pure humid night air from the woods poured into the room, fragrant with conifer and grass.

Vera took the kettle and went to the kitchen to boil some water on the hotplate. She loved to have her tea at night, three glasses at least. While Vera was gone, Zoyka seized the opportunity to tell Lidia Aleksandrovna that Vera wasn't at all as simple as it seemed, that she 'giggled' and 'cackled', but was quite clever at managing her affairs, had got her son into a boarding-school with the help of a lady customer from the District Executive Committee. She would never have been able to arrange it by herself, but the customer had helped her. She just knew how to twist someone's arm. Of course, it was a thousand times easier to live alone. All she had to do was to cook noodle soup for three days, and that was it. She could manage to go to the movies as well as to the GUM,* and she could receive guests, whereas she, Zoyka, had three people on her hands, young and old, and had to sweat and slave no end.

Vera returned with the kettle and Zoyka fell silent. Lidia Aleksandrovna started talking about her life: her first husband had died eight years ago of tuberculosis. He had been a very good-hearted person, a scientist, and Lidia Aleksandrovna had had a hard life after his death. She was poor and ill, and her son was small. They had wanted to sell this dacha, because they had no money to pay into the Co-op,* but somehow they had got over the hump by starting to rent it out during the summer. And then Lidia Aleksandrovna had met a wonderful man, also a scientist, who had married her and taken in her son so that now she was doing very well. And she had already given up the hope of ever living well again! But a woman should never lose hope. She had an acquaintance, a fifty-year-old artist who had recently married a man eight years her junior, also an artist, who just adored her. Her situation had also been desperate. Her husband, an important military man, had suddenly jilted her after twenty years of married life, because he had fallen in love with a ballerina from the Kirov Ballet in Leningrad and had decided to move there. And this woman, the artist, now had a splendid, happy life. Her new husband was a very gifted interior decorator who arranged exhibits abroad, traveled all the time, and brought home lots of things for her.

Vera and Zoyka listened greedily without interrupting. Both were tired and took turns yawning. They wanted to go to bed, and at the same time they wanted to listen. The life about which Lidia Aleksandrovna was telling them was so different from their own, yet in some strange way it resembled theirs. They were particularly struck by Lidia Aleksandrovna's comment that a woman should never lose hope. That was exactly what they had always vaguely sensed, but would never have been able to express as clearly and distinctly. And gradually both stopped listening to Lidia Aleksandrovna and began thinking about themselves and their hopes. They had many hopes, and they never lost hope. They had retained all their hopes, even the earliest, silly ones of their youth.

Then it got cold. Lidia Aleksandrovna closed the windows and they went to sleep. They slept badly, because the house was damp and they froze, even though Vera and Zoyka covered themselves with their coats and piled rugs and mats on top.

In the morning it was warm and sunny, and the birds were singing. Mishka and Vera ran all over the garden, through the wet grass, catching butterflies with a net. From the distance both looked small and blond, like a boy and a girl.

Unwashed and with a grey, puffy face, Zoyka stood on the stairs combing her hair.

'That's enough messing about! Mishka, go and get some water!' she shouted angrily. 'Let's finish quickly and get home. No need to mess around here.'

Early in the morning, Lidia Aleksandrovna went to the railway station to call Moscow, and she returned pleased and happy: husband and son, both of them, would come around twelve. According to Lidia Aleksandrovna, her second husband was good-natured though not very practical, and liked peace and quiet above all. Therefore Lidia Aleksandrovna was eager to finish all the housework in his absence. Around eleven o'clock the windows upstairs were washed, but the barn still needed to be cleaned up and a broken couch had to be brought down from the second floor into the garden, all the way to the fence.

Nobody came at twelve nor at one o'clock. Vera and Zoyka had finished everything and were just waiting for the arrival of the husband, who was supposed to bring the money. Lidia Aleksandrovna had brought only seven roubles.

Around midday it turned very hot. After Vera and Zoyka had washed at the well they sat on a bench in front of the porch and discussed in subdued voices whether they should ask for more. Vera was unsure, but Zoyka felt they should definitely ask, because nothing had been said about the barn or the porch. Lidia Aleksandrovna should pay 26 roubles – that would be just right. And Zoyka also prodded Vera to ask Lidia Aleksandrovna if they could take the empty wine-bottles from behind the barn, sixteen of them; they seemed to have just been dumped. You could make one and a half roubles if you rinsed them out and returned them to the store. You could put them in a shopping-bag and take them to Moscow.

'Go ahead and ask,' Vera said. 'Just ask, ask yourself.'

'Why should I? You ask: you set everything up.'

'What would I do with them?' Vera waved her hand carelessly. 'It's a lot to carry.'

Zoyka turned pale with venom.

'Of course, the fine lady doesn't need to carry a load,' she hissed. 'You're free, you've given up your boy, so you don't need to carry anything. But what about me? What am I going to live on?'

'But I told you: go ahead and ask.'

Mishka came up to them, holding a strange oval thing in a straw case in his hands. 'Mother, look, a water-bottle!' Mishka said quietly and happily. 'I found it in the corner, by the trash-can. It's like new. Let's take it!

'Don't you dare take anything without asking!' Zoyka snatched the bottle from his hands and put it on the bench. 'You put it back where you found it.'

'But it was thrown away.'

'That means it's garbage, and we don't collect garbage. You stay here now; we'll be leaving in fifteen minutes.'

'But, Mother, in camp we'll take field trips and I'll need a water-bottle,' Mishka whined.

'Put it in the bag and that's all there is to it.' Vera said. 'If they threw it away, it means they don't need it. Just think, such a fuss about it.'

Mishka made a shy movement toward the water-bottle and stretched out his hand, but Zoyka slapped it fiercely.

'What did I tell you? And you, fool that you are, don't you tell him what to do.'

Mishka sulked and moved off. A little later, he suddenly walked to the gate decisively.

'Don't you go far away – we're leaving soon!' Zoyka shouted.

'But when can we go swimming?'

'Don't you dare go to the river without me, do you hear? I forbid it!'

'But you promised . . . .' Mishka's whining voice sounded more and more distant.

'Don't you dare go to the river! Mikhail! Do you hear?'

The gate banged. Lidia Aleksandrovna leaned from a window in the second floor and shouted joyfully, 'Have they come?' Vera answered, 'No, Misha's just left.' And Zoyka growled angrily, 'They'll come, just keep waiting. We've lost a whole Sunday. . . . Don't employ people if you have no money.'

But, when Lidia Aleksandrovna came down, Zoyka started talking to her in an ingratiating, sugary voice, her head tilted sideways: 'Lida Aleksandrovna, I wanted to ask you about something, about those bottles over there . . . .'

It turned three, and still nobody had arrived.

Zoyka demanded the seven roubles, took the empty bottles and left with Mishka, but Vera stayed and waited. For a long time she and Lidia Aleksandrovna sat on the porch, drank tea and ate bread – they had nothing else left, and there was no money to buy anything – and Vera asked for advice about life: how should she behave when Nikolai came? Should she agree to go with him again if he wanted to, or should she send him packing. Seryozhka, the Tatar, was a very nice person, very good-natured, but his mother was always interfering. His mother dreamt of finding him a Tatar girl, and Tatars listen to their mothers a lot. He would never go against his mother's will. He wouldn't even stay overnight at Vera's that often: he'd always try to get home, no matter how late it was. 'I don't want mother to worry,' he'd say. But why should she worry? His mother knew Vera perfectly well. How often had Vera dropped in on them, brought them potatoes from the market; and she always took the clean linen from the laundry back to them herself; and on Saturdays she washed the floors in all their rooms. They were a big family occupying three rooms in a wooden house on the Volokolamka. Once it was so late – about 2 a.m. – that the last trolley-bus had gone. So Seryozhka had walked all the way to the Volokolamka. 'If it weren't for my mother, I'd marry you right away,' he had told her. So it was a very complicated situation, difficult to sort out.

Lidia Aleksandrovna couldn't really advise anything, and, besides, her thoughts were elsewhere. She only said, 'The main thing is that you remember your dignity as a woman, Vera.'

Vera nodded in agreement: 'Absolutely, Lida Aleksandrovna! Absolutely. That's a must!'

Vera also talked about her former life, about her childhood in the village of Bogorodskoe, about being orphaned, about the war and how she had studied at the trade school, how her aunt had died and Vera had got the room all to herself, how a sixty-five year old man from Kamyshin had wanted to marry her and how she had chased him away, because she had guessed that he had his eyes on her room. But, while Vera was doing all the talking, Nikolai was constantly on her mind, and suddenly she decided that nothing good would come of today's meeting with him. No, nothing good would come of it. He would want to borrow five roubles until pay day – that was all. Five or ten roubles. And, when this simple thought suddenly occurred to her, she fell silent immediately. Lidia Aleksandrovna was also silent, sitting lost in thought.

Vera sighed.

'Perhaps there's been an accident, Lida Aleksandrovna?'

Lidia Aleksandrovna shook her head.

'No, Vera. I don't think so.'

Towards five it rained for a while, and after the rain had stopped Vera got ready to leave right away. She had one rouble and 20 kopeck of her own. 60 kopecks she lent to Lidia Aleksandrovna, who would otherwise have had no way of getting back to the city.

Vera took the path across the meadow to the train station. On both sides of the path the high grass was ready to be cut. It breathed and swayed barely perceptibly, stirred by the steamy air rising from below. Vera took her shoes off and went barefoot. For many years she had not walked barefoot on a warm path in the summer. She walked slowly, quite alone in the big meadow, in no rush to get anywhere.

3
Valentin Rasputin

The most famous of the 'village prose' writers and, to many, the best living Soviet writer, Valentin Grigor'evich Rasputin was born on 15 March 1937 in a village on the Angara river, 300 miles from the Siberian city of Irkutsk. After finishing his studies at the history and philosophy departments of Irkutsk University in 1959, Rasputin worked as a journalist.

He appeared in print in 1961 with stories that romanticized the taiga and strong characters living in it in unity with nature. Gradually, the inner world of his characters and their relations to family and friends absorbed him more and more. 'Vasily and Vasilissa' (*Literaturnaya Rossiya*, 1967, no. 5) represents these new preoccupations.

His real literary debut came in the same year with a collection of stories, *A Man from This World* (*Chelovek s ètogo sveta*), and his short novel *Money for Maria* (*Den'gi dlya Marii*), in which a farm store-manager discovers a 1000-rouble shortage for which she cannot be responsible, as everyone knows. Yet, unless she finds the money in five days, she will go to prison. The outcome remains open. Both works immediately confirmed Rasputin's artistic mastery – his ability to re-create individual personalities of his native district with psychological and linguistic truth. These works also show his interest in the effects of a materialistic outlook on people and on the rural environment. The subtlety with which he uses dreams, recurrent symbolic images, temporal shifts between the present and the recent past reveals a craftsman with a sure hand and an unerring aesthetic sensibility. Furthermore, juxtapositions of the manners and mores of the city and the country, of the young and the old, betray a keen moralist and traditionalist. The village and the older generation, and often women too, appear most often to have the moral advantage.

As in *Money for Maria*, the innocent victim in *Live and Remember* (*Zhivi i pomni*, 1974) is a pure, uneducated, hardworking, strong woman, who unquestioningly accepts her age-old sex role as supporter of her husband, faithful to him rather than the law. The story is doubly unique because this husband is a Red Army deserter, who ran away under most extenuating circumstances. Her tragic death by drowning in the Angara while on the way to a secret meeting with her husband, by whom she is pregnant, can be seen as accident or as suicide. Her submissive yet unquestioning devotion and sacrifice stand out against his selfishness.

Rasputin's subsequent works are variations on the same set of themes. *The Final Term* (*Posledni srok*, 1970) illustrates the moral superiority of an eighty-year-old Siberian woman who is keeping death at bay in the hope that all her children will come to take their farewells. Her depth and spirituality are contrasted with the selfishness and shallowness of her children, who have lost their roots, their closeness to the land and their affinity to family unity and warmth. As in *Money for Maria*, Rasputin is an observer who leaves it to the reader to derive the implied conclusions.

In many works a new element enters: concern over the ruthless destruction of nature for the sake of its resources. This exploitation, carried out in the name of progress and supposedly to improve people's lives, is unmasked as motivated by greed and as impairing the quality of life. The theme of environmental and cultural destruction dominates Rasputin's best novel, *Goodbye to Matyora* (*Proshchanie s Matyoroi*, 1976). New technology in the form of a hydroelectric project spells the end of an island in the Angara river, inhabited since ancient times: it is to be flooded. But forces discounted by the modern engineers prove unexpected obstacles: an enormous larch that lumberjacks cannot fell, the villagers' belief in the ancestral spirits that seem to arise from graves, and the impenetrable Angara fog, which in the end symbolically veils the shore from the last men to leave the island. They are lost and adrift, endangered by an impending flood. As nature, traditions and old values are tampered with, Rasputin urges his readers to consider what are the gains, if any, and what are the losses. His fictional answer implies that men are acting blindly, mute to the consequences of what they are doing.

The novella *The Fire* (*Pozhar*), published in *Nash sovremennik*, 1985, no. 7, similarly investigates the moral degeneration of a Siberian logging town in which drink and personal gain prevent the protagonist from upholding higher values. The work was widely discussed on its appearance, and Rasputin was repeatedly reproached for becoming too journalistic in his writing.

Rasputin's concern was the thoughtless exploitation of the

natural riches of the Soviet Union have, indeed, led him to become one of the most outspoken activists on environmental issues, fighting for the survival of Lake Baikal and against the project to reverse the flow of the Siberian rivers. He has even voiced his worries in interviews abroad. With his fellow writers Zalygin and Aitmatov, he leads the group of writers who bring these issues to public attention and put pressure on the responsible government agencies to act.

Some of Rasputin's recent works reflect a search for new directions of a philosophical, metaphysical or even religious nature. In five stories published in *Nash sovremennik*, 1982, no. 7, he probes – with irony – a higher reality behind everyday human existence, harking back to such predecessors as Dostoevsky and Andrei Platonov.

Unfortunately, the publication of his best works in English has not brought him the renown he deserves among English speakers, even though many of them share his environmental concerns.

WORKS AND SECONDARY LITERATURE IN ENGLISH

Money for Maria, Soviet Literature, 1969, no. 4.
'French Lesson', *Soviet Literature*, 1975, no. 1. This story is also reprinted in *Soviet Russian Stories of the 1960s and 1970s* (Moscow: Progress Publishers, 1977).
Live and Remember (New York: Macmillan, 1978).
Farewell to Matyora (New York: Macmillan, 1979).
'Vasily and Vasilissa', *Soviet Literature*, 1980, no. 3.
Money for Maria and Borrowed Time (New York: Quartet, 1981).
'Downstream', *Contemporary Russian Prose*, ed. Carl and Ellendea Proffer (Ann Arbor, Mich.: Ardis, 1982).
You Live and Love and Other Stories (London: Granada, 1985).
'The Fire', *Soviet Literature*, 1986, no. 7.
'What Shall I Tell the Crow?', *Soviet Literature*, 1987, no. 2.

Afanas'ev, Aleksandr, 'V. Rasputin: The Human Race is not Accidental', *Soviet Literature*, 1983, no. 7, pp. 159–64.
Brown, Deming, 'V. Rasputin: A General View', in Evelyn Bristol (ed.), *Russian Literature and Criticism*, Selected Papers from the Second World Congress for Soviet and East European Studies, 1980 (Berkeley, Calif.: Berkeley Slavic Specialties, 1982) pp. 27–35.
Dunlop, John, 'V. Rasputin's *Proshchanie s Matyoroi*', in Bristol (ed.), *Russian Literature and Criticism*, pp. 63–8.
Gillespie, David, 'Childhood and the Adult World in the Writing of V. Rasputin', *Modern Language Review*, 1985, no. 2, pp. 387–95.

Mikkelson, Gerald, 'Religious Symbolism in V. Rasputin's Tale "Live and Remember"', in L. Leighton (ed.), *Studies in Honor of Xenia Gasiorowska* (Columbus, Ohio: Slavica, 1982) pp. 172–87.
Pankin, Boris, 'Matyora – Farewells and Encounters', *Soviet Studies in Literature*, 1981, no. 3, pp. 46–75.
Shneidman, Norman N., *Soviet Literature in the 1970s: Artistic Diversity and Ideological Conformity* (Toronto: Toronto University Press, 1979). Includes a chapter on Rasputin.

Vasily and Vasilissa
(1967)

Vasilissa usually wakes up early. In the summer the cocks rouse her. But in winter she does not trust them. They might oversleep because of the cold, and that is something she couldn't allow herself. For a while she remains in bed thinking about the different things she will have to do, appraising the day so as to see whether it will weigh heavy on her or not. With a sigh she lowers her feet from the wooden bed onto the painted floor. The bed also sighs, following her example, and after that they both calm down. Vasilissa gets dressed and, looking at the wall across from her, thinks that, thank goodness, she has finally managed to get rid of all the cockroaches: she can't discover a single one.

This state of half-waking and half-sleeping only lasts a short time. In fact, she herself is barely aware of it. For her, it is only one step from sleep to work, and no more. As soon as she is dressed, Vasilissa starts bustling about, running here and there. She lights the Russian stove, climbs into the cellar for potatoes, dashes across the barn for some flour, sets various iron pots on the stove, prepares the swill for the calf, feeds the cows, pigs and chickens, milks the cow, strains the milk through a piece of muslin, and pours it into all sorts of jars and glasses – a thousand different little jobs. Then she puts on the samovar.

She loves doing that. The first wave of work has receded, the early morning has passed, and by this time Vasilissa usually feels thirsty. Her day is divided not into hours, but into samovars – that is, into how many times she puts on the samovar: one, two, three times . . . . In her old age, drinking tea has taken the place of virtually all other pleasures.

She continues to bustle, fusses with the iron pots, yet keeps an eye on the samovar. It begins to snuffle, then to puff, to murmur and finally to gurgle. Vasilissa carries it over to the table, sits down close to it, and sighs. She always sighs, and these sighs express a whole range of emotions, from joy and surprise to pain and suffering.

Vasily gets up late. There is no reason for him to rise early. The only window in his barn, tiny like a bathroom window, is curtained for the night. Vasily dislikes moonlight. He believes that it makes everything cold. His bed stands with the head toward the window, and at its other end is a small table. Various items of hunting and fishing gear hang on nails next to the door, and on top of them are sheepskin coats and padded jackets. After he wakes up, Vasily pulls open the curtains, squints at the daylight that streams in, and, as soon as he is used to it, peeks out of the window to see what it is like outside: snow, rain or sun. He dresses in complete silence, no panting, grunting or groaning.

When he enters the hut, Vasilissa does not turn around. He sits down at the other end of the table and waits. Without saying a word, Vasilissa pours him a glass of tea and puts it in the middle of the table. He moves the glass toward him and takes a first sip that scalds his throat and goes down like a solid lump.

Vasilissa drinks her tea through a piece of sugar held in her mouth. He takes it without. He dislikes sugar. He believes that everything must be used in its pure, natural form – vodka without admixtures, tea unsweetened. After finishing his tea he puts the glass back into the middle of the table. Vasilissa takes it, fills it again, and returns it to the middle.

Silence reigns. Curled up in the bed by the wall sleeps Pyotr, Vasily and Vasilissa's youngest son. As always, summer or winter, his bare knees poke out from under the blanket.

Vasilissa sighs and pours herself another glass of tea. Vasily puts his glass in the middle, gets up and leaves. Vasilissa does not turn.

'Hey, you lazy good-for-nothing,' she says to Pyotr, 'get up or you'll get bedsores.'

Disgruntled, Pyotr opens his eyes and hides his knees under the blanket.

'Get up, you good-for-nothing,' Vasilissa repeats without malice. 'You aren't on a fishing-trip! Drink your tea and get going.'

Pyotr's wife, Tanya, also wakes up, but she doesn't have to go to work. She is pregnant.

'You stay put,' Vasilissa says to her. 'You don't have to rush anywhere. I've just got to get this good-for-nothing up.'

For her, lazy people come in three categories: simple dawdlers or people who have trouble getting going in the morning; born loafers with experience and a long record of lazing about; and real good-for-nothings, who are incorrigible. Pyotr doesn't deserve to be included in the third category, and Vasilissa knows that she's unfair to him. But she has to have her grumble.

'He's a lazy good-for-nothing, no getting round it,' she mumbles.

She is back in the kitchen again, finishing some cooking and frying. The day has only begun, and the rest is still ahead. Vasilissa sighes.

For almost thirty years Vasily has been living in the barn, in the middle one of three barns standing under one roof. The barn is small and clean, without flour-bins, has a nicely finished floor, like that in the hut, and a well-fitted ceiling. The children used to sleep in it in the summer, but that was very long ago, when Vasily still lived in the hut.

In the winter he brings in an iron stove. Five years ago Pyotr laid a cable to give him electric light, but after that the swallows stopped building their nests under the eaves and moved elsewhere. This upset Vasily terribly at first, because he had liked to watch them. But then he got used to being without them.

Only once a day, when the young people are still asleep, does Vasily go into the hut, and it is then that Vasilissa pours him a glass of strong, hot tea. She sits at one end of the table, he at the other, and they are silent. Not a single word is said, and it is as if they don't see each other. Each knows of the other's presence only by the glass which is placed and replaced in the middle. They are silent, but there is no tension in this silence; in fact it is no silence at all but a normal physical state of wordlessness, when no one expects words and they are unnecessary.

Vasily eats his lunch and supper in the barn. He has a few odd dishes, and he learned how to cook long ago. His cooking is primitive, of course – mostly buckwheat groats and macaroni mixed with something from cans. But sometimes, when he is lucky hunting, he has some fresh meat too. On such days, Pyotr comes over to get his allowance; in fact, he keeps running back into the hut for a frying-pan, some salt, an extra fork, an extra glass, which means they have opened a bottle to celebrate the hunter's luck.

'If you are going to get drunk over there, you don't need to come home!' Vasilissa shouts after him. 'There's a good-for-nothing for you!'

She says 'good-for-nothing' in a sort of singsong voice, with obvious satisfaction.

The children usually hang around the barn – Pyotr's Vaska, so called after his granddad, and Nastya's three. Nastya, Vasily and Vasilissa's middle daughter, lives in the same house, but its other half: the house is divided, and Nastya lives in the smaller part. Three houses away lives their eldest daughter, Anna, who is married to a schoolteacher.

Vasily is not greedy. He always retains only a small portion of his take for himself; he needs very little. The largest portion goes to Nastya. She is worse off than the others, with three children on her hands and no husband. Pyotr chops off a piece for himself and immediately carries it to his own barn, so that it won't make someone else's mouth water. Vasily divides the rest of the meat in half, and tells the children to take one part to Anna. The whole gang takes off. It is now that the frying-pan is procured with the fresh meat still sizzling from the heat, the fat spitting and crackling, the sides of the big pieces fried to a crust. They close the door and open the bottle.

Vasily cannot live without the taiga.* He knows it and loves it as if he had created it himself, laying it out with his own hands, and filling it with all the riches it contains. In September he goes off to gather cedar-nuts and continues to knock down cedar-cones until the first snow. That is when the hunting-season begins. Vasily goes off twice on long hunting-expeditions for squirrel and sable, once before and once after the New Year. In spring he looks for nuts again: after the snow has gone, the fallen cones virtually lie at your feet waiting to be picked up. In May you can pick bird-cherries; in June it would be a sin not to fish for the red-and-black graylings, and in July the berries are ripe – and that's how it is, year in, year out.

The men in the village come to Vasily to ask advice: 'What do you think, Vasily, are we going to have any nuts this year or not?'

'If the nutcrackers don't eat them, we will,' he replies slyly.

'That makes sense,' the man mumbles uncertainly.

'In a week I'm going off to scout. I'll take a look myself,' Vasily says unable to hold out any longer. 'Then I'll tell you. As you see, at the moment I'm sitting in the barn, and from here you can't tell anything.'

He does not work anywhere. The taiga feeds and clothes him. He brings more furs and skins to the depot than anyone else, and in good years he can fill up to five or eight large sacks with nuts. As early as winter he receives letters from the Forestry Commission in Lithuania* and from geologists in Moscow or from his own district, asking him to be their guide on summer expeditions. As a rule he prefers the Lithuanians. It is fascinating to him to observe people of a different nationality and to memorize their strange-sounding words. When he gets up after a rest-stop, he says, unable to restrain a smile of sly satisfaction, 'Einam', 'Let's go', and the Lithuanians laugh and follow his steps. Vasily is also particularly fond of forestry people, because they are interested in maintaining and preserving the taiga. They would never set fire to the woods, whereas the geologists are more like casual visitors and liable to make a mess, chop down a precious cedar for the sake of a dozen cones, or fail to stamp out their camp-fire properly.

When he goes off into the taiga, Vasily locks up his barn and Vasilissa, watching him from the window, grumbles, 'That's right, lock 'em up, your treasure-trunks. They might get stolen! Might at least buy himself a decent pair of trousers with all this money. Walks around with his backside half-bare, a laughing-stock to everyone. He's got no shame or conscience.'

They sit opposite each other, Vasily on the bed, Pyotr on a child's low chair, nailed together for him twenty-five years ago, and Vasily, not yet tipsy, complains about the pain in his lower back.

'It's begun to hurt like hell. You bend over and can't straighten up again.'

'It's about time it gave you pain.' Pyotr says reproachfully. 'You want to run around like a youngster at the age of sixty-five, don't you? You're in good shape, as it is; I wish we could all be as healthy as you!'

'I'm even afraid of going alone after the squirrels this year. I've got to find a companion.' Vasily says it almost with pride, as if wanting to stress that only now he needs a companion.

Pyotr prods his fork into the frying-pan with great concentration.

'How about coming with me?' Vasily asks, knowing full well that Pyotr won't go anywhere.

Pyotr lifts his unshaven, snub-nosed face with a jerk: 'I would go, but who's going to let me off work? The collective farm won't let me go.'

'That's true, it won't,' Vasily agrees.

'Well then.'

The question is settled, and Vasily once again fills their glasses.

Meanwhile Vasilissa has got company. The seventy-year-old Avdotya has stopped by.

'I was just walking along and I thought, well, I'll just drop in and see how Vasilissa's doing,' she shouts, loud enough to be heard all over the hut.

Vasilissa takes off her apron – she had been doing some laundry but hasn't finished it – goes over to Avdotya and holds out a hand.

'Let's shake hands, Granny Avdotya.'

Granny Avdotya's hand is as limp as a rag.

'I was just walking along and I thought, well, I'll just drop in and see how Vasilissa's doing,' she shouts again. 'But you don't even have time to sit down for a moment.'

'How can I sit down?' Vasilissa responds readily. 'I'm on my feet all day. It's one thing after another that needs doing.'

'You'll never get it all done, even in a thousand years!' Granny Avdotya shouts. 'Just remember, Vasilissa, it'll be there even after we're dead and gone. Even if you work like a horse, there'll be plenty left.'

'That's true, there's going to be plenty left,' Vasilissa nods. 'You drag it along from one day to the next, and then you have to drag it even further. So you're always trudging like a gipsy with his bag.'

'And you can't get away from it!'

'How could you?'

'No, you couldn't.'

They sit there for a while nodding at each other in agreement. Then Granny Avdotya asks, 'And where's your Pyotr? At work?'

'At work? I'll say he's at work!' Vasilissa snaps angrily. 'He's over there. They shut themselves up in the barn and are probably hitting the bottle for all they're worth.'

'Well, well, well!' Avdotya shouts, delighted. 'It's just the same story with my sons-in-law. One of them's sober, but the other won't leave the bottle alone.'

'And you don't go over there?' Granny Avdotya motions with her head in the direction of the barn.

'Have you gone out of your mind or something, in your old age?' Vasilissa replies, offended. 'I won't even sit next to him in the outhouse. What nonsense are you going to dream up next?'

Granny Avdotya laughs. 'I just got interested, so I asked. I thought maybe in our old age you'd got together again, and I didn't know.'

'You just keep your thoughts to yourself, Avdotya.'

Vasily shakes up the remainder of the vodka and pours it out. Pyotr sits uncomfortably on the child's stool and moves over to sit on the bed.

'It upsets me that you don't show much love and respect for the taiga, Pyotr,' Vasily says. 'All our ancestors were taiga people, loved it, roamed all over it, were part of it. But when I die you'll even sell the gun.'

'I like the taiga too,' Pyotr objects weakly. 'But who will let me off from the collective farm?'

'That's true.'

'No one will give me time off. If I weren't a tractor-driver, it might be another matter. But, since I am, it's like beating your head against a wall.'

'Don't sell the gun,' Vasily suddenly says in a strict voice.

'What you think up! Why should I want to sell it?'

'Just don't sell it. I haven't got much longer to live. Keep it to remember me. And you never know when you might meet a wild animal. It's a good gun.'

'That's enough. I said I won't sell it. That means I won't.'

They become silent. The last bit of vodka in the glasses has not been drunk yet; it trembles slightly, and the electric light from above makes it look as if it is coated with a thin film.

'Pyotr, let's sing a song,' says Vasily.

'All right.'

'Which song?'

'I don't care, just start.'

Vasily doesn't start for a long time. He takes the glass and holds it in his hand. Then, leaning over the table, he makes up his mind: 'All the pear and apple trees are blooming . . . .' He turns towards Pyotr, who joins in. They do not look at each other.

> 'To the shore down goes Katyusha,
> Where the bank is very steep and high.'

Vasilissa raises her head and listens. Granny Avdotya has left.

Vasilissa sighs, but the meaning of this sigh remains hidden even to Vasilissa herself.

It happened two years before the war. Vasily had suddenly started to act up. Every other day or even daily he would come home drunk, and once he even tried to beat up Vasilissa. He chased her onto the Russian stove, from where she couldn't escape, and climbed up after her. At the last second Vasilissa came upon an oven-fork. She grabbed it, thrust it toward Vasily as he was climbing up so that its prongs went either side of his neck, and pushed forward with all her might. Vasily fell on his back and, without letting go of the oven-fork, she jumped down and managed to pin him to the floor with his neck between the prongs. He squirmed around, stretching his neck, like a cock on a chopping-block before its head is cut off, wheezed and swore, but he couldn't tear himself out of the grip of the fork. Vasilissa let him go only after he had promised to leave her alone.

Later, whenever he got drunk, Vasily would remember this occasion, become furious realizing his disgrace, and attack Vasilissa with his fists. Usually she could manage to calm him down. When he was drunk he was easy to handle. But once, when Vasilissa was pregnant again, he seized an axe that was lying under the bench and started wielding it. Vasilissa was frightened to death, began to scream, her voice unrecognizable, and rushed out of the hut. That night she had a miscarriage. When she returned home, she shook the sleeping Vasily and showed him the door.

'Get out!'

Half-awake, Vasily didn't understand anything. She repeated, even more firmly, 'Get out, I'm telling you!'

Vasilissa herself carried Vasily's bundle of clothes out to the porch and he dragged it over to the barn along the narrow wooden walkway which he had built not long before. In the evening he wanted to come back into the house, but Vasilissa stood resolutely in the doorway and said, 'I won't let you in.'

They had been married for twenty years, and they had seven children. The two oldest boys were already at work; the youngest, Pyotr, was only four. When the war broke out, the chair of the Village Council* sent a special messenger around to each house to inform everyone and to warn them not to go off into the taiga. Vasilissa's family was sitting at the table when the messenger came. It was a runny-nosed boy to whom the war was a game for grown-ups. He drummed against the window and shouted merrily, 'Hey, hey! War's broken out! We're at war!'

Vasily came home soon after, and Vasilissa didn't chase him out. She had other things on her mind now. He sat on the bench by the door, his hands on his knees, and said nothing. Obviously being silent alone in the barn was unbearable.

Three days later he came in again with his things packed in a bag. He left the bag by the door and walked into the center of the living-room. Everyone stood up, including Vasilissa. Frowning, Vasily waved his hand vaguely and began awkwardly to poke his face into the children's shoulders, taking leave of them. Then he went up to Vasilissa. The children stood looking at them, waiting in tortured silence.

'Vasilissa,' Vasily said hoarsely, 'don't condemn me any longer. I'll probably be killed. The children here . . . you. . . .'

Vasilissa was the first to offer her hand. Vasily pressed it and left without finishing his sentence. He closed the gate carefully behind him and walked off in big strides to the Village Council office, where carts were waiting to take away the recruits.

Later the carts would leave directly from people's yards. Vasilissa watched her two eldest sons and her daughter Anna go off to the front. Each of them climbed into the sled or cart right in her courtyard, and Vasilissa herself opened the gates, pressing the apron to her lips and making the sign of the cross as she watched the carts coming one after another out of the yards and moving slowly along the street out of the village, as she heard the men sing drunken songs and the women, clutching onto them, wail. Vasilissa did not follow them outside the village to see them off but stood watching from the gate, which she then closed as if trying to shut out more recruiting-carts.

One of her sons did not return from the front at all; the other came back but left immediately for the city, where he still lived. Vasily appeared last of all.

It was already autumn, and the villagers were digging up the potatoes. Vasilissa had just carried home a sackful and was about to pour the potatoes into the cellar when Nastya came running up.

'Mama, Dad's back! He's coming!'

Vasilissa straightened up.

'So he's alive, it turns out,' she said slowly, as if reasoning to herself. 'But Sasha was killed.'

Without untying the bag, she threw it down into the cellar and shuddered when it hit the ground with a thump. Vasilissa went into the living-room and her irritation grew. She did not change her clothes. There was no reason to. When she heard footsteps on the porch she was ready to swear. Vasilissa couldn't decide whether she felt tired or nauseous.

'It's me, Vasilissa,' Vasily said from the doorway, and she again shuddered because she had not heard his voice for a long time. She said nothing, but her face expressed her eagerness to answer, and, unable to restrain herself any longer, she said, giving in to this eagerness, 'They killed Sasha.'

Vasily nodded.

She said nothing else. Fortunately, the children came running, and she was able to go out into the yard and get on with her chores. Later, visitors arrived, men who had also returned from the war, and Vasilissa sat in the kitchen until she got tired. Then she lit a lamp, climbed down to the cellar, and began to sort out the potatoes.

The men sang in unfamiliar voices, which they had acquired somewhere far away, in the war – voices hoarse from shouting 'Hurrah' and from crying for help. To Vasilissa it seemed as if they had gathered only for the purpose of using up these alien voices, shouting them out of their system, and as if after the disappearance of these voices their own would return.

The songs were drunken, but restrained, without any rollicking daredevilry, and it was as though the men while showing off their tuneless voices, were continuously looking around to make sure that nothing was happening behind their backs; it seemed as if each of them kept halting so as not to forget himself or to become confused. And the loud drunken talk was also restrained, interrupted with frequent songs. What went on resembled a dull, gnawing pain that sprang up first in one place, then in another.

Vasilissa felt tired and climbed out of the cellar. She did not feel like doing anything else, called Nastya, and said, 'Go and set up things in the barn for your dad.'

'Mother!' Nastya said, her voice full of reproach.

'Do what I said,' Vasilissa answered. 'It's none of your business.'

Almost immediately Vasily came into the kitchen.

'So I take it you don't want to forgive me?' he asked, standing right in front of Vasilissa. 'I see, you won't. I brought you a little present, Vasilissa, but I just didn't know how to give it to you.'

'You and I don't get on,' Vasilissa said. 'That's the way I'm made, Vasily, and there's no way of changing me.'

'The war changed everyone,' Vasily objected quietly.

'The war, and the war again . . .,' Vasilissa repeated. 'The war means grief, but not a decree. As it stands now, the war has made men out of women anyway. And when are new women going to grow up? The sooner this war of yours is buried, the better.'

She sighed. Vasily tried to embrace her, but she moved away and his arms remained hanging in the air.

'No need for that,' she said, moving away. 'I'm burnt out, Vasily; there's no use trying to warm me up.'

When he had left she was afraid she suddenly might want to cry, but it turned out that she didn't feel like crying at all and was pleased. That night she fell asleep quickly, and her sleep was untroubled. And in the morning, when she got up and saw that everything was covered with an impenetrably thick fog, she felt like climbing back into bed and going back to sleep again.

After the war Vasily did not stay at home for long. He waited until the summer and then took off for the Lena river to go prospecting for gold. As he said goodbye, he gave them to understand that he would not return soon, and perhaps never would. Who knows whether he wanted to try getting rich or whether it had simply become unbearable for him to live next to his family, yet be completely separated from them, like an outcast? Before he left, Vasily gave Pyotr all his decorations and medals and instructed him to guard them with his life. He washed his soldier's shirt the night before his departure and went around the village to say goodbye. That day he was talkative and merry, and promised everyone to send money. But the next morning he fell silent, as if he were about to leave before his time was up.

Nastya and Anna accompanied him to the steamer. Pyotr, who was running about somewhere, was late. When they lowered the gangplank, Vasily suddenly became nervous. He shook his daughters' hands almost distractedly and walked off. A minute later they saw him on the desk, but he was no longer looking at them. The steamer sounded its horn three times and cast off, and Vasily still stood on the deck as before, apparently still not looking anywhere and not seeing anything.

Nastya got married while he was away. Compared to her brothers and sisters, who were all equally sluggish and sober-minded, Nastya stood out by her impulsiveness and remarkable energy. Vasilissa referred to her as an 'early maturer'. At twelve Nastya had been the confidante of almost all the lovers in the village, who gave her notes to carry, and the twenty-year-old girls confided their secrets to her. At fourteen Nastya went to work on the farm, at seventeen she married, and a year later she had twins. She was always in a hurry even when there was no reason to rush. Her womanly happiness evidently could not withstand such haste and collapsed: four years later Nastya's husband was killed felling timber, leaving her with three small children. After that, life slowed down for Nastya.

Vasily returned the summer after he left. He had had no luck prospecting, nor did he bring home any money. He arrived emaciated and infested with lice, wearing only his soldier's shirt, which Nastya steamed and ironed for a long time. Vasily spent a week catching up on sleep in the barn. He went nowhere and spoke to no one. Then he gathered his equipment and left for the taiga.

It is the second half of July. The summer has already begun to decline, but the days are stifling and oppressive. Endless dust rises from the roads and settles on the roofs, making the houses look old and shabby, like last year's haystacks. A cloud of smoke hovers above the Angara river – somewhere forest fires are burning.

The collective farm has finished its mowing, but it is too early to bring in the hay. The farm-workers use this brief respite as well as they can for themselves, cutting hay for their private needs. Each morning the villagers make their way to the river islands or disappear into the taiga, leaving at home only a few people who eagerly, twice a day – in the morning and in the evening – water the vegetable gardens. In spite of the heat, the pleasant fragrance of cucumbers hangs in the air.

Pyotr and Nastya have been allocated haymaking plots in the

same place, 15 kilometers from the village. Going there and back every day is very difficult, so they leave for a week at a time. That way they also can start earlier and finish later. Only Tanya stays behind to take care of the two families with all the children and the housework. Vasily could also remain at home, but he is well used to such excursions and feels obliged to help his son and daughter. This year, for the first time, Vaska, Pyotr's nine-year-old son, is allowed along.

The weather is perfect for haymaking. The hay dries quickly in the heat. But it is difficult to cut: the grass has stood too long and dried up at the root, so you have to struggle keeping the blades whetted. Vasily has a wide sweep, but leaves a short trail behind him. He stops frequently to have a smoke, using his shirtsleeve to wipe the sweat off his forehead and neck.

'Vaska!' he shouts. 'Where's the bucket?'

Vaska comes running with the water, and Vasily drinks it greedily. Then he tilts his head backwards and squints at the sun. The sun, like a ball, seems to have rolled into a hole and got stuck there, so that it will burn for ever now.

'If only some measly little cloud would come and cover it,' Vasily mumbles and picks up his scythe again.

Not far away, Pyotr is working in a T-shirt, a handkerchief tied around his head. His scythe has become blunt and swishes ineffectually as he plunges it into the grass. He lifts it up, dips his whetstone into the water, and begins to run it quickly along the blade. Then he turns around to look at Vasilissa, who for some time had been sitting motionless on a log.

'Mother,' he shouts, 'you should go into the hut! Let the heat drop a little, and then you can do some cutting again.'

Vasilissa doesn't answer.

'Mama!' Nastya calls, having heard Pyotr. 'Go and get the lunch ready. We'll be in in a minute.'

Vasilissa gets up and goes over to Pyotr.

'I've got no energy left,' she says to him sadly and sighs. 'I'm worn out. I thought I could help, but no . . . .'

'What's the matter, Mother?' Pyotr asks.

'I'll go, don't worry. I'll be off and lie down for a while, but tomorrow I'll be my old self again. I'm just not used to mowing any more. Haven't done it for a year.'

Bent over, she goes into the hut, and the three of them, Vasily, Nastya and Pyotr, look after her.

'Let's have a smoke,' Vasily calls to Pyotr.

Pyotr comes over to him and, clutching the bucket, takes a long drink. Then he blows the drops of sweat from his forehead and sits down.

'What's the matter with mother?' Vasily asks.

'She's old,' Pyotr answers in his usual voice. 'What's her age?'

'She's two years younger than I am.'

'She's old,' Pyotr repeats.

Late at night they sit by the camp-fire and drink tea after supper. At times the fire flares up and clearly illuminates their tiredness as if it were a garment. Then it dies down again. Behind the hut, in the darkness, one can hear the dog licking the remains of food from the can. Night descends on the trees and the newly mown grass. It only avoids settling on the fire, as if afraid of getting burnt. Thus, the fire leaps up and down and dashes about.

For a long time they cannot sleep. They have made a start on the haymaking, the first day has passed as it should, and all of the emotions and experiences of this day are fresh and alive in their hearts and minds.

'Time to settle down,' Vasily says finally. 'We've cut down enough for about nine haystacks in one day, and that's not bad at all.'

'No, we've done more than that,' Nastya corrects him quickly (she always spoke quickly). 'I did five stacks by myself.'

'It would be good if it were more,' Pyotr responds.

'Tomorrow we'll have to get a move on,' says Vasily, getting up. 'The weather's going to change.'

'What do you mean, bad weather?' Vasilissa asks alarmed, looking at Pyotr.

'The dog ate grass,' Vasily tells Pyotr. 'That's a sure sign.'

Pyotr does not reply.

Vasily and Pyotr got married the same year, even the same month. Pyotr, who had just turned twenty, brought home Tanya, the smith's daughter from the lower end of the village. Vasily took a woman from outside the village to live in his barn. She had at one point wandered into the village by accident and stayed on, going from one hut to the next, sewing dresses and tunics for the women. She was very good at it and didn't charge much, so the orders kept pouring in. Gossip had it that she had come from the Ukraine looking for her son, from whom she had been separated during the war, and that she had run out of money for the return trip and so had decided to earn some.

No one knew where and how she and Vasily came to their arrangement. The family had already celebrated Pyotr's wedding, at which Nastya of all people sang and danced more than anyone else. The November holidays* had passed, and the first snow, later that year, had fallen. Vasily, who had been getting ready to go off on a hunting-excursion, suddenly dropped his preparations and called in Pyotr.

'Have you seen that woman, I mean the newcomer?' he asked his son without looking at him.

'You mean the one that sews?'

'Yes.'

'Of course I have. She's walking around the village after all.'

'I want her to live with me,' Vasily said, turning to Pyotr.

'You what? Are you serious, Father?' Pyotr said, unable to hide his surprise.

'So what? Is there a law against it?'

'What do you mean, a law against it?' Pyotr mumbled, at a loss as to what he should say. 'I can see. You're not old yet. Who says it's impossible?'

'The point is not whether I'm old or not,' Vasily explained unhappily. 'I am sick and tired of doing my own washing and cooking. I live like a prisoner. I need a woman to keep house, that's the point.'

They were silent for a while.

'Drop in tomorrow, in the late afternoon, we'll share a bottle between the three of us, sort of have a wedding-party. I'll tell Nastya to prepare some food.'

In the house Vasilissa was bustling about the kitchen.

'Mother!' Pyotr shouted excitedly as he came in. 'Father's getting married!'

'I see,' Vasilissa responded indifferently.

'It's true. She's moving in tomorrow.'

'He can get married a thousand times for all I care. I've got nothing to do with him.'

'Aren't you hurt a little?'

'What kind of rubbish are you babbling?' Vasilissa flared up. 'Oh yes, I'm hurt, so hurt that I've fallen apart already! She's got to be out of her mind to move in with him. No normal woman would!'

Vasily's new wife was called Aleksandra, and she was a little older than his eldest daughter, Anna. Vasilissa saw her for the first time out of the window the next morning, when Aleksandra walked across the courtyard to the outhouse, limping slightly.

'Ha, got himself a lame duck,' Vasilissa rejoiced. 'As I said, a normal woman wouldn't have him, and right I was. They'll get on fine now. One devil doesn't break the horns of his kin.'

At first Aleksandra did not show herself anywhere, but stayed in the barn. Vasily made tea himself and went to the shop, but he too avoided going out unnecessarily. For the village his wedding was like a ladle of honey poured on an anthill. It was disputed and analyzed in all ways. It became the most important event since the war, much more important than any of the deaths that had occurred in the last few years. The women suddenly started running out of salt and bread, their washboards and irons disappeared, and they came to borrow all these things from Vasilissa, starting conversations about the 'newlyweds' – implying, of course, that they were asking about Pyotr and Tanya. Only Granny Avdotya, who was hard of hearing, did not have to be cunning.

'They say you've got yourself a new sister, Vasilissa!' she shouted, comfortably settled on the bench.

'You've got nothing better to do than to go around spreading rumors, Avdotya,' Vasilissa answered angrily.

'And does it upset you?'

'I couldn't care less. I don't have to wash their dirty linen.'

Granny Avdotya glanced around the hut with a searching look and shouted again, 'And does she come in here?'

'Just let her turn up! I'll scratch out her eyes!'

'That's right, just scratch 'em out,' Granny Avdotya egged her on. 'You give her an inch, and she's going to squeeze you out of your house. You'd better keep your eyes on her, Vasilissa.'

Soon after this they met. It was impossible to live in the same yard and not to meet. Coming out of the barn, Aleksandra suddenly saw Vasilissa right in front of her and stopped in indecision not knowing what to do. Vasilissa looked her over with interest and waited.

'Hello,' Aleksandra greeted her, almost inaudibly and entirely at a loss.

'That's how it is! "Hello" indeed,' Vasilissa replied in angry astonishment. 'Wouldn't you like to have a glass of tea? Just limp where you were limping to, you lame duck. I'm not made of sugar,

I won't melt from your "hellos". What a polite little bitch!'

For a long time she couldn't calm down, grumbled at Pyotr, yelled at Nastya through the wall, and clanked the dishes so that the noise could be heard all over the house. She felt offended, but was unable to come up with an appropriate response. She kept repeating Aleksandra's ill-starred 'Hello' in all sorts of ways, as if it hadn't ceased stinging her.

Nastya, meanwhile, made friends with Aleksandra and called her Shura, for short, only a month later. And then in Nastya's part of the house the sewing-machine began to rattle. Aleksandra was making shirts and pants for the children, who came naïvely running to Vasilissa to show off their new clothes. Once Tanya stopped by, attracted by the sound of the machine, and after that she became a frequent guest of Nastya's. She cut out patterns, did some sewing and later appeared in a new dressing-gown and a new skirt. Vasilissa frowned, but said nothing. Through the wall she could hear the talking and laughing in the other half of the house. She felt that no one noticed her any more, no one took her into account, that they simply put up with her, thinking to themselves, 'Since you're alive, you may as well go on being here.'

'Why don't you call you new friend "Mother", eh?' she asked Nastya, offended.

'Mother, now don't you pick on me for no good reason,' Nastya replied angrily.

'You can just go ahead for all I care. I'm going to die soon, but she's still young. Whinnies like a mare.'

'You've lived a long life, Mother, but you haven't learned much sense,' Pyotr said, defending Aleksandra. 'You go around angry, but you don't even know yourself why. What has she done to you?'

Vasilissa became more and more silent and withdrawn.

Once after the New Year, when Vasilissa had gone to visit friends, Aleksandra at last plucked up enough courage to enter the house. She wouldn't have crossed the threshold for anything. But Tanya called her to help sort out some sewing-pattern. They were entirely engrossed in their conversation when Aleksandra glanced out of the window and gasped: Vasilissa had just closed the gate behind her. Aleksandra dashed for the door, but did not have time to slip past Vasilissa unnoticed.

'What's this supposed to mean?' Vasilissa began to shout when she saw her. 'You shameless hussy! Wants to get into the house! I'll show you your way, I'll show you . . . . .'

'Tanya called me in,' Aleksandra said, trying to justify herself.

'The barn's too small for her!' Vasilissa thundered, searching the courtyard with her eyes as if looking for a stick. 'Nastya's half isn't enough any more. Wants to come here! I'll get you out!'

'Don't you dare!' Aleksandra cried, as she tried to defend herself.

'I'll give you your "Don't you dare!" I'll make you lame in your other leg!'

'So, you're angry?' Aleksandra suddenly shouted, preparing to attack. 'You want to get rid of me? Well, it won't work! And he won't live with you anyway.' Pushing herself off with one leg, she advanced toward Vasilissa. 'He's mine! He doesn't need you, do you hear, he doesn't need you!'

'What? What?' Vasilissa snarled, taken aback. 'Shut up, you cuckoo, shut up!' she bellowed, and went into the house without turning around.

'Don't you ever let that lame duck come in here!' she reproached Tanya severely. 'I am still the mistress here and not she. My health is ruined even without her, my life hasn't been an easy one. You'll remember when I'm dead.'

She took off her scarf, something she rarely did, and began to comb through her gray hair. Tanya curled up on the bed, too frightened to say a word.

'I wouldn't mind a glass of kvass,' Vasilissa said unexpectedly to Tanya.

'Are there any hops and rye bread?' Tanya asked, relieved. 'I'll put some on. . . .'

'No,' said Vasilissa with a sigh.

In time Vasilissa seemed to get used to Aleksandra. She no longer grumbled or got angry, and whenever she met her she simply looked the other way and walked past in silence. She did not mention what had happened, either because she felt guilty, or simply because she did not want to touch an old wound. She became reserved, thoughtful, and, at night, after she was finished with her housework, she went off to drink tea with other old women and returned home only at bedtime.

'You're not ill, Mother, are you?' Pyotr would ask.

'As if I had time to waste on being ill,' she would answer roughly and walk away.

Then it came out that Vasilissa had written a letter to her middle son, who lived 30 kilometers from the village at a timber-processing plant, asking him to let her live with him. The son had agreed gladly and even prepared to come and pick her up. But she let him know through some people that she was in no hurry, and in the end she was unable to bring herself to move to a new place.

'The grass is always greener on the other side,' she said to Tanya, sighing. 'What's the point of moving now, when I'm going to die soon?'

Vasilissa had recently become very attached to Tanya. In the morning she tried to be considerate and to avoid clattering with the pots and pans. She wouldn't let Tanya do any heavy work. Tanya was often ill, and then she looked at Vasilissa with a sad and apologetic smile.

'Don't worry, you rest and get better,' Vasilissa would console her. 'Later you'll have children and there won't be time to be ill. And life goes on a long time. Your life won't be sweet either. Your husband isn't exactly a gem.'

Then she went to Nastya and said, 'Nastya, how about going over to the barn. They probably have some raspberry jam. Tanya should drink some tea with raspberry jam. Tell your Aleksandra it's for Tanya.'

The winter passed. In March, water from the melted snow began to pour down the mountain, and in the yards the cocks started crowing. At this time Nastya's children had to be chased home with the threat of a good spanking or the promise of a cookie. They would run off and leave the door open, so anyone who felt like it could just walk in and take anything. Their mother was at work. Vasilissa kept an eye on things as best as she could, but it was impossible to keep track of everything.

One day Vasilissa went to see if anyone was home at Nastya's. She opened the unlocked door and suddenly stopped dead. Someone was crying. Stepping cautiously, Vasilissa glanced into the room, like a thief. There, on the bed, her face buried in a pillow, Aleksandra was sobbing pitifully.

'So that's how it is. She's crying,' Vasilissa said in surprise.

She waited a while, but Aleksandra did not calm down. Vasilissa thought for a moment and then went right up to the bed.

'Tears aren't going to wash away your troubles,' she said quietly, just to indicate that she was there.

Aleksandra jumped up in fright and sat on the edge of the bed.

'Perhaps there's nothing really the matter,' Vasilissa continued. 'Women are just like chickens; they live close to the water.'

Without stopping to sob, Aleksandra looked at her with terror, as before.

'Come over to my place,' Vasilissa suddenly suggested. 'I'll put on the samovar and we'll have some tea.'

Aleksandra shook her head.

'Come on, let's go. Don't be pig-headed!' Vasilissa kept on. 'I've got nothing against you, so don't you hold anything against me. We've got nothing to fight over. So?'

She let her into the house and sat down at the table. Aleksandra sobbed and hiccuped, hiccuped and sobbed.

'I can't stand it when women cry,' she explained to Tanya, who was in bed and quite dumbfounded. 'It's like a sharp knife in my heart. Life's like a five kopeck coin. One side is heads and the other tails, and everyone wants it to come up heads. But what they don't realize is that, whichever side comes up, it's only worth five kopecks. Oh, women, women!' she sighed. 'If we cry a lot, everything's going to be damp, and dampness makes for mold. Anyway, who says that if things are bad you have to cry?'

She went out to the kitchen and began rattling with the samovar.

'Well?' she asked Aleksandra when she came back. 'Is it him?' and she motioned in the direction of the barn.

'No,' Aleksandra replied, shaking her head. 'It's because of the boy, because of my son.'

She glanced at Vasilissa and fell silent.

'You tell me everything,' said Vasilissa. 'It'll take a load off your heart.'

'It won't now. I'll wait for the tea; that'll help. I can't talk about it just like that.'

Aleksandra was silent for a while, but then almost immediately, unable to hold back, she started her story: 'He was four years old, and really small. They drafted me into the labor force, and he stayed behind with my mother. When I was away they were evacuated. For a long time I couldn't get into the town, and when I finally did, they were gone.' She sobbed again.

'The tea will be ready soon,' Vasilissa reminded her.

'Mother was wounded on the train and taken off. He stayed on the train and came to your area, they told me.'

'The tea will be ready soon,' Vasilissa said again.

'Now I dream of him. When he turned ten, I saw him as a ten-year-old, and on his fifteenth birthday I dreamt about him as a fifteen-year-old. And now he's entirely grown up. Last night he came and said, "Mom, give my your blessing, I want to get married."'

'And what did you say?' Vasilissa asked, leaning forward intently.

'I told him, "Wait for me, son; I'll find you and then you'll get married." And he said, "Are you going to find me soon?"'

'Oh, my!' gasped Vasilissa.

'"Soon, very soon, I'll find you, my son." And then he went away and called, "Look for me, Mom!"' Vasilissa sat motionless, waiting for the continuation, but Aleksandra was silent.

'And so he just walked away?'

'Yes.'

'And he didn't tell you where to look for him?'

'No.'

'You should have asked him – I mean, put him some questions.'

Aleksandra shrugged her shoulders helplessly.

They drank tea and talked, and then continued talking even after they were done with the tea. Several days later, early in the morning, Aleksandra came in to Vasilissa to say goodbye.

'I'm packed,' she said sadly. 'I'll be on my way.'

'God be with you,' Vasilissa blessed her. 'Go and keep looking, Aleksandra. There's only one earth, and you just walk all over it and look. I'll be praying for you.'

She went out to see her off from the gate and stood for a long time looking after her, as she had done seeing off her children to the front.

That morning was the first time Vasily came into the house for tea. Vasilissa poured him a glass and put it in the middle of the table.

Recently Vasily has been complaining more and more often about his lower back. He sits on his bed and tries to loosen up his back by rocking back and forth. He frowns and grunts, and his tortured face with its reddish stubble is covered with beads of sweat.

'Oh,' he groans, 'it's got me in its clutches, the cursed devil, it's been lying in wait for me! If it only gave me a moment's peace!'

Overcome with exhaustion, Vasily lies down and closes his eyes, but he cannot lie still either, and half raises himself again.

'Vaska!' he shouts through the open door.

No one answers.

'Vaska!'

There is no Vaska.

After work Pyotr comes by to see Vasily.

'You tell Vaska to drop in and see me now and then,' Vasily says. 'Otherwise I'm alone all day. I could die and there'd be no one to close my eyes.'

'How are you feeling?' Pyotr asks.

'What do you mean "how"? You can see for yourself. My whole back feels as if it's dropping out. It's murder.'

'We ought to get a doctor.'

'A doctor!' Vasily says angrily. 'The medical attendant was here yesterday, but how much sense does she have? I tell her that my lower back hurts, and she just bats her eyelids. She didn't even know until then that a person has a lower back.'

'They call it something else.'

'They also call the runs something else, but they've got to treat it; that's what they've been trained to do.'

'What did she tell you?'

'Nothing. She sort of tapped me and left, as if she'd been on an excursion. "I'll come by tomorrow," she said and was off.'

He throws himself back against the wall and groans. A minute later he straightens up again.

'You run along to the shop,' Vasily says. 'A drop inside makes me feel a little better. It doesn't last long, but at least I can catch my breath. Money's above the door. You can help me finish off what's left.'

Pyotr gets up, silently gropes for the money and leaves.

The next day Vaska goes for the vodka.

'I got some sweets as change.' Vaska brags to Vasilissa.

'They've thought up some great medicine,' Vasilissa jeers with pleasure. 'Gulp down a glass of vodka, grunt, and all your pain takes off like it's fleeing the plague.'

After the vodka Vasily calms down and drops off to sleep. But then the pain is even worse, as if angry over its forced retreat, and it rages with renewed strength.

Finally the doctor comes again and says that Vasily has to go to the district center for X-rays. Vasily agrees in silence. He is tired out. He would just like to have a drink and go to sleep. Let them take him wherever they please, even to Moscow – he'll stand everything and do exactly as told. He has had a long life and evidently someone can't get born while he is still on this earth. Or it's just that his turn has come, and he is holding up the traffic.

The doctor leaves, and Vasily quickly pours himself a full glass of vodka and half a glass for Pyotr. They drink, and a moment later Vasily comes to life again.

'You tell me,' he asks, 'why do people get born and die mostly at night?'

'I don't know.' Pyotr shrugs his shoulders.

'There you are. No one knows. But why does man arrive in this world at night and leave it at night? It's not right. I want to die during the day. People are talking, the chickens are flapping their wings, the dogs are barking. At night it's frightening. Everyone's asleep. But here a child just came out of its mother and is crying. And elsewhere an old man cries because life's going out of him. And the people in between are asleep. And that's what's so frightening: that they are asleep. When they wake up, the going and coming's all done with. They do or don't do their work, and then it's night again, and again they sleep, and again everything gets shuffled. Ha! At night nobody's going to help you. Nobody's going to say, "Die in peace, Vasily: don't be afraid. You did everything you could, and what you haven't done others will finish." A person needs to be calmed down, and then he won't be terrified of lying in his coffin.'

'What's all this for, Father?' Pyotr asks, startled. 'What nonsense is this?'

'"Nonsense", you say? But I'm frightened. You'll get up and go and I'll be alone. I've got used to being alone – I mean, to living alone. But it's terrifying to die alone. I'm not used to that.'

He reaches for the bottle.

'Let's have some more, then I'll lie down.'

When Pyotr comes home he says to Vasilissa, 'Father's in bad shape.'

Vasilissa does not answer.

It is day again. The barn door is open once more.

'Vaska!' Vasily calls.

Vaska is not around.

Vasilissa peers cautiously through the door, keeping her hands on her kerchief.

'Vaska isn't around. Don't waste your breath,' she says.

Vasily raises himself a little bit and looks at her.

'Is it you, Vasilissa?' he asks in a weak voice. 'Where's Vaska?'

'He ran off somewhere.'

'Come in, Vasilissa. It doesn't matter now.'

Vasilissa crosses the threshold and stops.

'Come over here, Vasilissa.'

'Are you ill or something?' Vasilissa asks from the door.

'I can tell I'm going to die soon. Come closer and let's say goodbye.'

She goes cautiously over to him and sits down on the edge of the bed.

'We've had a bad life together, Vasilissa,' Vasily whispers. 'And it's all my fault.'

'It hasn't been so bad at all,' Vasilissa says, shaking her head. 'The children have grown up and are working.'

'It was bad, Vasilissa. I'm ashamed now, before my death.'

Vasilissa raises the edge of her scarf to her lips and bends over Vasily. 'How in the world did you get that into your head, Vasily?' she whispers. 'How come you imagine all that?'

'Your tears are dripping on me,' Vasily whispers with great joy. 'There's another one.'

He closes his eyes and smiles.

'How did you get all this into your head, Vasily? Good Lord, what a sin it is!'

She shakes his shoulder, and he opens his eyes and says, 'Let's say goodbye, Vasilissa.'

He offers her his hand; she presses it and, sobbing, gets up.

'Now go,' he says. 'Now I feel better.'

She takes one step, then another, and turns around. Vasily smiles. She bursts into sobs and goes out.

He lies there, smiling and smiling.

It is a mild day with a hint of rain in the air. On such days it is good to sit and eat yoghurt, not too cold and not too warm, and to watch from the window what is going on in the street.

4
Lyudmila Petrushevskaya

Petrushevskaya is at present one of the most controversial authors on the Soviet literary scene. Her dramas provoke the most extreme and opposite reactions, because she ignores existing artistic canons while broaching new subjects and issues. The unmitigated harshness with which she evokes the blatantly ugly and utterly bleak jolts the reader from complacency. Life's trivial yet most debilitating tragedies, which are the substance of her work, produce shudders of recognition and disbelief. Neither causes nor solutions are offered. Her purpose is to shock people into a catharsis. She wants to make them think for themselves and search for alternatives. Her portrayal of the morally ugly veils her deep longing for the realization of an ideal. She writes 'in order to liberate [herself] from grief,' she said in an interview. 'Perhaps there is a grain of salvation in what I have written. . . . Why do people tell things to each other? In order to get rid of a burden. In order to maintain the notion of an ideal, something worth striving for, a sense of how it should be' (*Literaturnaya gazeta*, 23 Nov 1983).

In conversations with me in November 1986 and the summer of 1988, she elaborated on how she wants to be read. 'There are three steps in understanding my works: the first is to realize what miserable creatures these people [in the story or drama] are; the second is to feel sorry for them; and the third is to recognize yourself in them. . . . My stories ask: can one really live that way? And the sensitive reader will answer: no. His task then is to discover how to live differently. . . . The task is to remain humane under all circumstances.'

Petrushevskaya's implied solution to the concentrated suffering she depicts is not social change. Emphasizing the need for a personal ethic, she rejects the label of 'social critic' and feels misunderstood when reproached for 'blackening' reality or writing pathological stories. This is also why she refuses to be considered a feminist, although she has sketched picture after picture of the dismal lives of women in the Soviet Union. 'There is no existential difference between men and women', she argues. 'There are enough unhappy men too, and every person is unhappy in his or her own way.' She insists that her work not be used for ideological purposes. 'While writing, the author ignores his own personality, becomes genderless', she says. 'If he defends his own sex, he's in trouble. An author must be a man, and a woman, and a child and a rooster and the sun, all at the same time.

Born in 1938 and trained as a journalist – she finished her degree at Moscow University in 1961 – Petrushevskaya began to write fiction in her thirties. A voracious reader, she was profoundly impressed by Thomas Mann and Proust, whom she read in translation. This translated prose moved her by its bareness and austerity, and became her model. In fact, she calls her own prose 'translated prose' (*perevodnaya proza*) to underline its terseness, its 'maleness', as she said. Almost doing away with dialogue in her stories – she calls them 'anti-plays' – is part of her artistic asceticism.

Her emphasis on the information value of the story, she feels, is related to having very little time and concentration for writing, since household and children are her main occupation. That explains the 'effect of the rolled-up spring', as she calls it. 'I rarely write,' she says, 'only twice or three times a year. But when I sit down I write with enormous speed, force and concentration, and only the absolutely essential. It works like this: the spring is rolled up very tightly, and then something happens, something sets off this spring. In such a state, an author won't respond to trivia; it must be an immense tragedy.'

Petrushevskaya's first stories were written in 1968. 'Nets and Traps', ('Seti i lovushki') printed below, first appeared in *Avrora*, 1974, no. 4. But until 1982 she tried in vain to get further stories published. They were rejected because of their form and content; and they were genuinely disliked by some. Therefore she turned to plays, and many of them shared the same fate. She was widely attacked for writing 'black stuff' (*chernukha*) and for being ungrammatical – she compares her fascination with Russian, as Muscovites speak it, to that of Shaw's Dr Dolittle with the English of Londoners. *Music Lessons* (*Uroki muzyki*, 1973, first performed 1983) was her first play, followed by *Chinzano, Love,* (*Lyubov'*), *The Apartment of Colombine* (*Kvartira Kolombiny*, consisting of four short pieces) and her most substantial play, *Three Girls in Blue* (*Tri devushki v golubom*). A parody of Chekhov's *Three Sisters* (although she denies this), this play is a black comedy, permeated by bitter humor and irony. Its heroine escapes from the misery of her life –

a non-stop chattering landlady, a sick child, a censorious mother, a room invaded by crude and selfish relatives – into a romance with a married man. Just to be jilted, of course, when she appears at the Crimean resort where he holidays with his family. Meanwhile her son has been deserted at home. Her new play *The Moscow Choir* (*Moskovski Khor*) has not appeared in print yet. It treats family feuds caused by the purges.

Petrushevskaya's first collection of stories, *Immortal Love* (*Bessmertnaya lyubov'*), appeared in 1988. The publication of three stories in *Avrora*, no. 2 (1987), of a novella ('Svoi krug') in *Novy mir*, no. 1 (1988), and a 'dialogue' in *Novy mir*, no. 12 (1988), reflects the increased attention her prose is capturing.

WORKS AND SECONDARY LITERATURE IN ENGLISH

Plays and short stories are available from Theater Research Associates, Apt 733, 1111 Arlington Blvd, Arlington, VA 22209.

Alma Law has translated *Four by Lyudmila Petrushevskaya* (New York: Institute for Contemporary East European Drama and Theater of the Center for Advanced Study in Theater Arts, 1984).

Four of her plays have been performed in the United States.

Nancy Condee's 'Liudmila Petrushevskaia: How the "Lost People" Live', published as a newsletter to the Institute of Current World Affairs (1986) (NPC-14), pp. 1–12 is the first assessment of her work as a dramatist.

Nets and Traps
(1974)

Translated by Alma H. Law

Here's what happened to me when I was twenty years old.

Actually, my being twenty had nothing to do with it – I could as easily have been seventeen or thirty: what's important is that for the first time I acted out such a role and found myself in such a situation. That never happened again. I could sense the possibility of finding myself in that same role again – and then I would immediately dodge and slip out of the nets waiting for me. Though there were never any nets set out and no one ever – even on that first occasion – thought to drive me into any kind of net. To be honest, nobody had any evil intentions or set any traps either that time or later; there wasn't even a simple minimal interest in me as a person. I was interesting and needed in that situation – not for myself, but as my husband's wife, no more.

And so there were absolutely no nets set out at that time when my husband, a future graduate student, was still at his assigned place of work, and I, his wife, expecting a baby, went to his mother's in another city. Before long my husband was supposed to come after me, to legalize our marriage, to celebrate our wedding at last, to pass his exams for graduate school and to start us out on a new life together.

So the near future was clear and cloudless, and the rest was supposed to straighten itself out later on, and that's just what happened.

The situation I found myself in was absolutely clear and simple; or it would have been clear and simple if I had had in my possession a document confirming that I was Georgii's wife. All the rest was fine: I, Georgii's wife, was going to his mother's home to have my child, since he couldn't get away yet; he wanted me to have the baby in his home, because giving birth requires peaceful surroundings and not the atmosphere of that cubbyhole where Georgii and I were living. It's true, I could have gone to have my baby at my parents', who lived rather a long way off; but I wanted to tie my life as closely as possible to Georgii's life, to his family, to his mother, whom I had never seen before and who knew of my existence only from her son's letters.

And so everything looked perfectly normal, unless you consider the fact that I was not yet Georgii's wife. And I wasn't Georgii's wife for the simple reason that he was already married before he met me. He had a five-year-old child, and his first wife lived right in that same city where Georgii's mother was living, and where he himself had spent most of his live. Georgii and his wife had been separated a long time ago, and that wasn't simply the result of a prolonged absence where the husband works in one city and the wife and child live in another, and gradually the ties disintegrate and they grow apart and no longer go to visit each other, although there is no direct reason for a formal divorce or a final settling of accounts. In the case of Georgii, everything was much more convincing: they separated when they were still living in the same city. Georgii's wife took their child and went to live with her family, and after a while Georgii was assigned to work in another city where I had also come from the Far East, and he was now paying his wife support for his son.

There you have the story of my friendship with Georgii, and at the same time the story of why, on a hot summer day, three years after beginning my studies, I was going to my husband's mother's in a strange city with a suitcase, a raincoat and a handbag in which there was a letter from Georgii to his mother.

To be honest, Georgii wasn't too happy that I was going to his mother's to have the baby. However, I managed to stand my ground. Rather, I just did it my own way since I had fears which were normal for my condition – if I went to my parents' in the Far East and Georgii went to study for a graduate degree, we wouldn't be able to get together very soon to start our family life. In the Far East, I would be well off, my child would receive excellent care, I would soon go to work or to school, and the whole shape of my life would then be such that everything would be arranged without Georgii. And that was just what I was most afraid of: peace and security without Georgii. I preferred insecurity and an uncertain existence with Georgii, because I knew that his conscientious, noble character would not allow him to leave me with a child in an uncertain situation. I knew that in such a situation, if it came to pass, he would come to my aid. That meant he would simply come and arrange everything properly.

Insecurity must automatically bring about a striving for security, whereas the sort of security I would find at my mother's in the Far East or in that city where Georgii and I were living – where I could, if necessary, ask for a place in the student dorm – would only delay the achievement of real security, inasmuch as from the very beginning Georgii would be reassured about me and the baby, and with a light heart would begin a new life at the Institute. And to force him to do something – to file for divorce and have me and the baby come to him – would be practically impossible.

However, all that in no way explains the state of blind delight with which at that time I threw myself into the arms of a strange family – or, more precisely, of Georgii's mother, Nina Nikolaevna. She lived in a large, old, well-appointed house, and what a pleasure it was for me, on coming in from the dusty summer street, to go into the bathroom, where the washbasin was an old-fashioned, porcelain one with a blue pattern and a crack, and the bottom of the bathtub had already lost its enamel right down to the iron!

Our first meeting passed, nevertheless, without excessive enthusiasm. I must say that Nina Nikolaevna didn't conceal her doubts. She read the letter carefully, and during that time I stood in readiness at the door, determined to leave immediately if things went wrong. I had left my suitcase at the railway station and had even wasted half a day (I arrived in the morning) finding somewhere near the station where I could spend the night.

At this point, I have to admit I didn't expect to count for much in Georgii's house. Georgii, who was ten years older than I and had already seen and done a lot, had clearly outlined for me the situation with his home and his mother. He had told me that everything would depend on me, and me alone – on the extent to which I proved myself intelligent and independent, especially independent. He repeated this word in various ways, explaining to me its meaning: independent – that's when you stand on your own two feet not depending on anyone, not demanding anything from anybody. Only a person like that, Georgii instructed me, could count on success with his mother; only a person like that, and by no means someone who was weak, grateful for any sympathy, ready to given in, to help, in order to show her goodness and decency. Georgii said this because he didn't like my eagerness to please everybody, to be liked by everybody, my willingness to trust everybody immediately and without reservation; he didn't like my eagerness to open my heart to just anyone in order to meet understanding. Georgii wanted more firmness from me, and he turned to stone inside when I tried to receive guests in the little room where we lived after I left the dormitory. Georgii didn't like the way I tried to please everybody, my readiness to laugh at any joke and to accept any sign of attention at face value, my yearning for friendship and only for friendship. When Georgii's friends left, Georgii might not speak to me for several days, displeased that all his instruction had been for nothing and that I wasn't becoming that staunch, independent person who alone could react properly to coarse jokes and superficial talk. Even the way I reacted to that silence of Georgii's, how I would cry and try to win back his favor – even in that he sensed a clear deviation from the norm, from the behavioral norm of a proud, independent person. 'You could try being proud for at least a minute,' Georgii would say to me as a result, and again fall silent.

Overall, during the last month of our life together it was impossible to get any response out of Georgii: he often disappeared somewhere, didn't talk about his plans, and wouldn't even say how his exam preparations were going, as if I really needed to know all the details of something so insignificant. He seemed to think that I couldn't live without attacking him with questions about how the day had gone and what had happened. He zealously kept from me his books, his notebooks, his files, his small purchases.

And yet he simply sat down and wrote a letter to his mother when I said that I was going to her to have the baby because there was no money to travel to the Far East. He wrote that letter not only because I got down on my knees before him, but also, it seemed to me, because he himself needed me to leave as soon as possible wherever and however I wanted, just as long as I left. In that sense, of course, I had been too hasty with my groveling, with all that bowing and scraping, since (as Georgii told me, again taking up his moralizing) nobody has ever forced anybody to do anything by such means. He began reproaching me that I didn't understand the mood of the moment and, in general, couldn't see further than the tip of my nose, that I was a person lacking independence and that my trip to his mother's wouldn't result in anything anyway, since I wasn't an independent person. Then he gave me his usual lecture about the kind of person he would like me to be. That was a major event in that final month, since he had almost stopped paying me any attention at all, and only protected his inner world, restricting my intrusion into it as much as possible and gradually widening the boundaries of the forbidden zone so that I was spending most of my time in the kitchen. It was summer, and I stayed in the kitchen all the time since I didn't want to miss the moment when Georgii left to take his exams. On top of everything else, he simply could not bring himself to leave me the key and I would have to go out of town to the landlady's house, and the landlady didn't much welcome me since she had quickly guessed the particulars of my condition and frequently said that she had rented the room to a single engineer and now there was a whole gang living there.

And so Georgii sat down and wrote the letter and I didn't say anything to him in return, but simply took this sheet of paper and went back to my kitchen. With that I began putting into action my decision to rebuild our relationship from scratch and to cultivate my self-esteem. And so, without saying a word, I took the letter, waited until Georgii went out, quietly packed my things and left, not even leaving a note.

I pondered why Georgii so unquestioningly let me go to his mother's, but just couldn't reach any conclusion. I knew that relations between him and his mother were complex, that to begin with, his first wife hadn't got along with his mother and only later had done so with Georgii. However, for some reason this didn't frighten me. I thought and thought about it and then stopped, but the train went on and on and finally, after a day and a night, it left me at the station in the city which was Georgii's home, where his legal wife and son lived, where the house stood in which he had spent his childhood, and so forth. All these thoughts deeply disturbed me, and on arrival I didn't immediately look for a place to spend the night as I had planned.

And so, if Georgii's mother didn't give me a very friendly reception, I hadn't expected anything anyway. Nina Nikolaevna read the letter in the entrance hall, not letting me into the apartment. Actually, I looked quite respectable – I had washed at the landlady's where I had taken a bed for the night. I had also sewed a white collar on my dress there, since the charm of a pregnant woman consists mainly in cleanliness and neatness, in the special charm of hygiene, and not at all in following the fashions.

After reading the letter, Nina Nikolaevan didn't behave more cordially, but she did invite me in.

Her room was huge, rather dark, with handsome old furniture, and with an almost black parquet floor. I immediately fell head over heels in love with that room. I was filled with unbounded delight and a yearning to stay there for ever.

However, to the question of where I was staying I answered that I was staying with friends and that in that respect everything was just fine. Asked whether I had some money, I replied that I had and that I had come just to get acquainted with her since I was coming to the city anyway. Asked why I had come, I answered that I was going to wait for Georgii together with the baby. 'And will the baby come soon?' Nina Nikolaevna asked, and I replied that I didn't know exactly, since the doctor had said one thing and I knew another. Nina Nikolaevna asked me what I knew on that subject and I answered that you had to count from the November holidays. Then Nina Nikolaevna asked whether it was Georgii's baby. I answered yes, and burst out crying.

I couldn't contain that terrible crying, into which I evidently poured everything I had gone through in the past months when I hadn't cried, but instead had laughed in response to Georgii's comments about my lack of independence. This idiotic, pointless laughter, by the way, annoyed Georgii more than anything else, but I couldn't do anything about it; it erupted involuntarily, in the same way as I had started crying involuntarily after Nina Nikolaevna has asked me whether the child was Georgii's.

My crying had an effect on Nina Nikolaevna. It was as though she understood with whom she was dealing, because from then on she treated me in such a way that all her actions evoked in me a feeling of incomparable, boundless gratitude, and of such happiness that it was as if I had found my wished-for childhood home. There was only one difference – I had no wish to find my childhood home. And the horror of it all is that since then I have never yearned for any home on earth, not even for my and Georgii's new apartment, as much as I did for that home of Nina Nikolaevna's, that wonderful, dear home where nothing was intended for me, and where every object existed as though on a higher level than I – more noble and more beautiful than I – and at the same time filled me with hope. With what reverence I looked at the pictures in their heavy frames, at the beautiful pillows on the sofa, the rugs on the floor and the table clock in the corner!

Furthermore, even all sorts of tasteless knick-knacks – various little boxes, fancy little shoes from forty years ago all embellished with seashells, empty vials for perfume – aroused a feeling of tenderness in me. I would have lovingly dusted them with a cloth and put them on the shelf under the mirror. Later I tried to do that, but each time Nina Nikolaevna nipped those attempts in the bud, not allowing me to touch a single thing in her room.

Actually, that room really wasn't so beautiful and it really wasn't so carefully kept. However, the special charm of a long life lived there, the charm of durable old objects, was transmitted to me immediately, catching my eye, as food always catches the eye of a hungry person, or a quiet haven that of a vagrant.

I repeat, no nets were set out with the intention of catching and destroying me. Furthermore, I myself blindly went ahead without any expectation that nets would at some time be set out for me. After all, the tenderness and maternal patronage which I sensed in Nina Nikolaevna couldn't be considered a trap! I didn't express myself right: it wasn't maternal – rather, it was higher than that, because a mother doesn't bestow patronage. At the same time, I felt so close to her that once I shouted from the room into the bathroom that I would like to call her 'Mama' for short. She didn't hear and asked me to repeat, but the noise of the water drowned my words, and I never again tried to make such a revolutionary proposition.

I was in seventh heaven. At first I still meant to go and see that lady near the station and arrange with her for a cot sometime in the future, just in case. But later I didn't even breathe a word about that to Nina Nikolaevna (I had very quickly revealed to her my secret about the bed rented in advance).

Nina Nikolaevna didn't let me go anywhere the first day, and with each day she became more and more attached to me. She literally didn't allow a single speck of dust to fall on me. Before leaving for work, she managed to go to the market for vegetables, and she grated carrots for me for breakfast.

As I have already said, Nina Nikolaevna didn't allow me to lift a finger – she herself prepared food for the entire day; all I had to do was warm up the dinner. In the evening, I didn't eat supper, but waited for her, sitting by the window. She would come home, we would eat and go for a walk before going to bed. I slept on a very wide sofa, on linen sheets.

Every now and then Nina Nikolaevna would give me presents: we went to the shop and bought two cotton dresses wide enough for future growth; she also brought me nightgowns, sandals for my feet, which were getting more swollen every day, and so forth.

Absolutely never, neither before nor after, have I felt so happy. The complete unity of our souls was crowned by the fact that she loved funny stories, and I also liked to laugh, and we always laughed, long and sincerely, happy at any excuse to do so. Nina Nikolaevna admitted that without me life would be dull, and that my ringing voice livened up her quiet solitary world.

Meanwhile, there wasn't any news from Georgii. We didn't know how preparations for his exams were going, or even where he was. I wrote him several letters in Nina Nikolaevna's presence, but didn't receive either answers or my letters back stating 'addressee has moved'.

Since we didn't have any new information, Nina Nikolaevna and I spent hours chewing over old news about Georgii. We told each other about his childhood – I knew no less than she, and maybe more. I told Nina Nikolaevna about things she didn't know – about Georgii's fall from the roof when he was ten (he had kept quiet about it, about his first love, then about later times, about Georgii's work, about his friends, about his habits, about his relations with his superiors. Nina Nikolaevna ate up such conversations; she would immediately light up, demanding more and more details about our life together, about the division of responsibilities in our household, about how Georgii took the news of our future child. I told Nina Nikolaevna about how Georgii and I had met at a party at the Institute, and how two fellows had seen me home – he and a friend of mine ('What friend?') right to the dormitory ('And where is this friend now?'). I understood everything; I understood that she was comparing dates – and names and events, in order to make sure that I really was carrying Georgii's baby, her grandson, under my heart, and not the child of some other admirer of mine who had also seen me home one dark night and then disappeared, leaving Georgii to get me out of the mess. To be honest, I was even moved by such naïve interrogations, such unveiled doubts. They showed me even more clearly how afraid she was of having her hopes deceived, how much she cherished and treasured the dream of her future grandson!

Once a week Nina Nikolaevna went out to the dacha to visit her first grandson, taking along presents. I liked that custom, that remembering, that observance of duty to an innocent child. I even asked her several times to take me along, but she would become unusually stern and with a few simple, but merciless, words put me quickly in my place. It was clear that she also had her own special world, separate from the world of her relationship with me – a world of her own, just as Georgii had. This world of hers to which I had no access formed gradually, imperceptibly, but also steadily within her, and she began jealously guarding it from my intrusion, while I, once more having opened up completely, was left with nothing. She carried on long-distance calls with someone and didn't say with whom. She started going out for entire evenings, not leaving me the key. Our evening conversations were now no longer on equal terms – now, I was the one who did the asking, who would talk about this and that. I would praise Nina Nikolaevna's figure, I would serve her sour cream and she would say, 'I'm the mistress, I did the cooking, I'll take it myself, and you help yourself.'

Just how that transformation took place I don't know. I suddenly had the feeling that she was hovering high above me, that she was hanging over me like a mountain, weighing down all my movements. Now I moved around her room with difficulty, spoke to her with difficulty. Everything irritated her, and sometimes she didn't even answer my questions.

However, this situation, which I had already experienced once before, was, for me, a familiar trap, a well-known net – although, I repeat, it was neither a trap nor a net, but an unalterably fatal situation, more fatal than the situation with Georgii, which, hopeless as it was, had still offered a glimmer of hope in Georgii's mother, in her nobility.

I continued to drag out my ambiguous existence in Nina Nikolaevna's home, since I had nowhere to go. The lady near the station, whom I visited, advised me to hang on to what I had because no one would rent me a room once I had a child.

I began going to the so-called 'market' where apartment-owners and prospective tenants gathered. Summer was moving towards autumn and Georgii had long since arrived; I felt, I physically sensed that he was there, although he didn't show up at his mother's and she became more and more hardened. Suddenly, as if she had shed all responsibility whatsoever, she began talking about a friend with daughters who were coming to visit, and afterwards she would be going to visit them and the apartment would be locked up – the neighbors were out of town, they had entrusted the apartment to her and no one would let an outsider who didn't belong to anybody live in the apartment.

I suggested that we have an open and frank talk. She said that everything was already sufficiently and disgustingly open, and that one shouldn't attribute someone else's child to a man who had nothing to do with it physically or morally, in as much as there had been all that going to dances and being seen home right to the gate.

I began to laugh and that ended the conversation. My things were put out in the hall, Nina Nikolaevna locked herself in her room and I spent the night in the kitchen. In the morning, Nina Nikolaevna put my things out on the stairs.

And so my adventure ended. The rest isn't interesting any more – after that I lived with the lady near the station and went to the market, hiding my bulging waistline under my raincoat, and in the end some crazy fellow recruited to work in the North rented me his room for next to nothing. There's no point mentioning that in the room there was an absolutely empty bed with bare springs, and that on my first night in the new place I slept with my coat covering the springs, happy and carefree until, towards morning, it was time to go to the maternity hospital.

So ended this period of my life – a period which will never again be repeated, because I have mastered some simple tools. Never again will that period of my life be repeated, when I believed so much in happiness, loved so strongly, and gave myself so unconditionally to others, lock, stock and barrel, like something that had no value. That period will never be repeated – later came quite different periods and quite different people, later came the life of my daughter, our daughter, whom Georgii and I are raising as best we can and whom Georgii loves with a devotion he never felt for me. But that doesn't bother me much, because now I am in another period of my life, a period that is completely different. Utterly different.

5

Natalya Baranskaya

Like Grekova, Natalya Vladimirovna Baranskaya belongs to the older generation of women writers. Born on 12 December 1908 in St Petersburg, she studied at Moscow State University. Her professional life was spent in museums – the Literary Museum and the Pushkin Museum. A war widow since 1943, she has never remarried and brought up two children on her own, doing postgraduate work on the side. Her career as a serious writer started by accident: 'In those years, in the mid-1960s, Moscow began to spread out to new construction projects on the outskirts. My neighbors received a new apartment and left. Their room remained vacant, and so I rented it. It was an empty room with a big oak table left over for the sole reason that it was no longer in vogue. I took my chair over to that room. What else does a person need for honest work?' (*Moscow News*, 1986, no. 49, p. 11).[1] Friends persuaded her to take her stories to Alexander Tvardovsky, the highly respected editor of *Novy mir*, and her first story was printed in that journal in 1968. She has also published stories in the journals *Yunost'*, *Zvezda*, *Sem'ya i shkola*, and *Sibir'*.

International renown followed the publication of her almost documentary sketch 'A Week Like Any Other' ('Nedelya kak nedelya') in *Novy mir* in 1969. It was soon translated into English (as 'The Alarm Clock in the Cupboard', *Redbook*, 1971) and other languages. A seminal work, widely interpreted in the West as a feminist statement, it describes a week in the life of young scientist, Olya, with a full-time career, a husband (also a scientist) and two children. Although she is happy in all her roles, she almost breaks down from the stress of juggling her duties and becomes increasingly and, enigmatically to herself, resentful of her predicament. Olya's self-recriminations and her uncritical, unassertive attitude to her superiors and her husband illustrate the absence of what we would call 'feminist consciousness'.

---

1. I owe the *Moscow News* article and the information it contains to Colette Shulman.

Asked about her response to Western interpretations of her work, Baranskaya has rejected a feminist stance, arguing that the story is about 'something entirely different, about a full-blooded, bright, though difficult life'. Yet this story prompted Soviet philosophers, sociologists and psychologists to investigate women's working-conditions more critically and to demand better services and childcare.

Baranskaya's first collection of stories and novellas, *A Negative Giselle* (*Otritsatel'naya Zhizel'*), was published in 1977. The psychology of adolescent girls and their problems in the family, at school and at work – problems often quite different from those experienced by Western girls – are of central interest. The teenage protagonist of the story 'Lyubka', for example, faces a Citizens' Court for disturbing the peace of her neighbors. Compared to her women characters, Baranskaya's men are less complex and individualized. Her narrative is uncomplicated, her language simple and clear, reflecting the speech of today's youth, their jargon, colloquialisms and idiomatic words and phrases – censored, however, for decorum and propriety.

In 1977, Baranskaya also published a novella entitled *The Color of Dark Honey* (*Tsvet tyomnogo myodu*) about Pushkin's wife. Written from the wife's point of view, the story describes the first year after her husband's death in a duel, which her flirtatiousness and infidelity had forced upon him.

A second collection of stories, *The Woman with the Umbrella* (*Zhenshina s zontikom*), appeared in 1981. Her topics here are the ethical problems women confront, their loneliness after the Second World War, and conflicts between the sexes and the generations. *A Portrait Given to a Friend* (*Portret podaryonny drugu*, 1982) contains new stories and two pieces about the life of Pushkin.

At this point, her entire output amounts to thirty stories and six novellas. *Remembrance Day*, a novel about the war, memory and women, is due to appear shortly.

The story printed below first was published under the title 'Koldovstvo' in *Yunost'*, 1976, no. 7.

WORKS AND LITERATURE IN ENGLISH

'The Alarm Clock in the Cupboard', *Redbook*, Mar 1971, pp. 179–201, is Beatrice Stillman's translation of 'Nedelya kak nedelya' ('A Week Like Any Other'). This work has appeared also in another American translation (by Emily Lehrman, in the *Massachusetts Review*, 1974, no. 4) and in a British translation (by Pauline Jaray, in *Spare Rib*, 1977, nos 53–9).

'The Retirement Party' ('Provody'), tr. Anatole Forostenko, *Russian Literature Triquarterly*, vol. ix (Spring 1974) 136–44, are reprinted in *The Barsukov Triangle*, ed. Carl Proffer (Mich.: Ardis, 1984).

The Spell
(1976)

It all started when Shura Shatrova's picture was cut out from the honors board of the Zagorev Musical Toy Factory, in the suburbs of Moscow. The exhibit on the board was new, just finished. It stood just across from the church porch (the factory was located in the parish church) – that is, facing the entrance, where lots of people passed by, in a bright spot, directly under a lamp.

Who was the culprit? Who needed Shura's picture? And why hadn't that person just asked Shura herself? For three full days the women in all three work halls wondered and pondered about it.

The chair of the factory trade union,* Pelageia Ivanovna, called Shura in and asked her if she had any idea whose handiwork this was. Shura shrugged her shoulders; she hadn't a clue. Pelageia asked her to get another picture taken. The board couldn't be left with a hole; it would be inappropriate. And Shura, as a shock worker,* simply *had* to be represented.

Shura had worked for five years in the section that produced toy pianos, grand pianos and balalaikas. She painted the keyboards and drew the notes of the song 'May there always be sunshine . . .' on the lids; and she decorated the balalaikas with flowers. It was delicate work that required a light hand and a perfect touch. Shura did it extremely well. But, if it was necessary, she wouldn't refuse other work: she was perfectly at home with all stages of production – from splitting the plywood in the joiner's shop to making the factory imprint 'Zagorev'.

'Why is it that this time I have to pay to have the picture taken?' Shura asked with a frown. She was not greedy, but she had to keep track of her money. She was a single mother and received very little for Vovka.

'What can we do, Shura? The board cost us a lot, and we spent everything we had allotted for it. Pay for the picture now and I'll make it up to you later, but I can't give you money. You'll get time off. And get your hair done, like the first time. And have them take the picture from the front; look right into the camera. It'll be more serious that way, more stern. It's an honors board, a public affair. It's important. There's nothing funny about it.'

Pelageia Ivanova was giving her a hint: the picture that had disappeared had shown her faintly smiling.

Shura promised to do all this, though she didn't feel like it. But, once she had made the promise, she was going to keep it. After all, Shura was an independent woman. And this despite the fact that she was a single mother, and very good-looking, something everyone agreed on. People even thought she looked like the Argentinian actress and beauty queen Lolita Torres. This summer Lolita had visited the Soviet Union, and her photo had been in the papers. And the newspaper display board stood in the corner across from the honors board. Somebody had probably noticed the similarity. One person mentioned it; the others repeated it. Shura had no time to worry about such things; she was swamped with work.

Her son Vovka was seven and had started school that year. Shura had been seventeen when she met a soldier at a dance, fell in love and – as her stepmother put it – danced up a pregnancy. Shura was afraid of her stepmother. Had her own mother been alive, things certainly would have turned out differently. How could she confess to her stepmother? How could she tell her father? So Shura put it off and put it off, until it was too late to discuss anything. And then she gave birth.

They didn't throw her out. They reproached and shamed her, of course, as soon as her pregnancy became visible. And later they did not help her care for the baby. So Vovka was in the nursery from the age of three months, and was entirely Shura's responsibility.

Shura had a tough time, but she got used to living austerely. Rarely would frivolous thoughts enter her mind, and, if they did, she would keep them to herself. That's what happened as she was leaving Pelageia Ivanovna's office: could this be a joke of Sergie Khokhlachev's? she wondered. All the women thought so. They were unanimous. And she liked hearing it. Yet she thought: no, anybody but him. He had made advances more than once, and more than once she had sent him packing. Every independent woman observed the unwritten law of their village: if you are an unwed mother, chase away every man. Shura observed it without any bitterness. She chased them away again and again. Would Serezhka really have snatched her picture? Serezhka, the curly haired, merry joker, the girls' favorite eligible bachelor? No, it wouldn't make sense. But Shura wasn't going to trouble her head about it. However, she soon found out what the others thought.

For two days Shura tried to go to the photographer. Then on the third day she fell ill with a cold. She had dragged her laundry to the river to rinse it, and the water was cold. It was mid-October. She was ill for five days and returned to work worn out and covered with fever blisters.

Aunt Dunya, the oldest of the factory women, broke into moans and groans when she saw her. 'What in the world's the matter with you, girl? First time you've been laid low like this!' Aunt Dunya looked her over from top to bottom, nodding her head, and said significantly, 'There's got to be some reason for it, you bet there is!'

But Shura had no time to ask her what she meant. She had to get to her brushes; a lot of work had piled up.

Pelageia nagged her because she hadn't gone to the photographer right away. Now they'd have to wait until she got her looks back.

But what could be done? They had to wait. Finally the fever blisters were gone. Shura appeared with her hair done – she had gone to the hairdresser the previous day – and was all dressed up.

She managed to calm down Pelageia Ivanovna. Right after work she'd go to have her picture taken. But, as she was setting off for the photographer, she slipped on an apple core and twisted her ankle on the steps. Luckily, Sergei Khokhlachev grabbed her so that she didn't fall. But she couldn't put any weight on the foot. Sergei made her a cane out of a piece of lath, wrapping something around it so that she wouldn't get a splinter in her hand. Then he helped her onto the bus, and accompanied her to the polyclinic. The suburban bus had a circular route, via the train-station, and she had to change. She couldn't have done it alone.

And in the polyclinic he waited for her. There was a long line to see the doctor.

Shura asked Sergei to leave and send her Vovka. But he wouldn't. 'Do you think Vovka can get you home?' Shura kept looking round to check whether anyone had noticed her with Sergei. He understood and said, 'Don't worry. I'll wrap my hand in a handkerchief so it looks as if my finger got bitten off.'

She laughed at the 'bitten off' finger. But she continually looked around to see if anyone were watching them. He took her home, but she didn't allow him beyond the gate and hopped inside alone, on one leg.

Again she had sick leave. Three days later she limped back to the factory. It was better to go to work now, because the next day she had to see the doctor again.

When she arrived, Aunt Dunya beckoned her aside. 'You didn't listen to me, but I told you: there's a reason you got sick again. Someone did it to you. And whoever did it is the person who stole your picture.'

Shura said, 'I don't get it. What do you mean "did it"? And what's my picture got to do with it? Tell me what you mean!'

'Somebody's put a spell on you. And they did it with your picture and sent you bad luck.'

'That's plain nonsense, Aunt Dunya. What do you mean "bad luck"? I had a cold, and I twisted my ankle. More accidents!'

'Accidents? Just look at how out of sorts you've been! You've been healthy your whole life, and now you've got fever blisters all over you.'

'It's true. I've been as sick as a dog. It can happen, though. It happens to others, too. It's cold outside, and I had rubber boots on when I went into the river.'

Aunt Dunya drew Shura's head closer and whispered in her ear, 'Maybe it's Klava Pantyushkina who did it. She's supposed to be having an affair with Sergei, but it's you he's chasing. Everyone knows it.'

Shura stepped back. 'That's none of my business. And Klava's got a husband. People say all sorts of things. Anyway, my ankle hurts and I can't stand up any longer.'

Shura's face turned gloomy, and she knitted her eyebrows. All day she didn't smile or say a word.

Oh, these women's tongues! They put a bug in your ear, and you can't stop thinking for three days. And you don't want to think, but you do it anyway, as if something were driving you. What business of hers was it that there was something going on between Sergei and Klava? Wasn't it all the same to her? Of course it was! But there she was, thinking. Or take what Aunt Dunya had told her, that something had been 'done' to her. Such rot. She even had to laugh. But then she started thinking: for years she hadn't had a single period of sick leave, and now one after another. And then again: who needed her picture? Somebody did take it!

Shura racked her brain for a day or two. But she really didn't have the time to think. She was busy. And the ankle got better. Finally she threw out the cane Serezhka had made her. On her way home from work, she dropped it into the river as she crossed the bridge and said, 'Swim to Moscow little stick, take my sorrow with you, quick.' She laughed: was it really sorrow? She had felt real sorrow when she had walked here eight years ago, wondering whether she should drown herself or not. She hadn't considered it for long: just the time it took to cross the bridge. On that bridge she realized that she wouldn't be able to drown herself. She had grown up on the shore of this river, had swum all over it. She knew all about it. And, though the river had lots of dangers and was quite tricky, and though many people drowned in it, she wouldn't be able to drown in this river of hers. She'd swim out to the shore. Her legs and arms would do it automatically. The river itself would carry her to the shore. So Shura gave up the idea of drowning herself.

But what was there to remember? She had been young and foolish. There was such beauty all around now. On the hill, a willow that hadn't lost its leaves was shining like a ball of gold as it drooped its branches over a spring. And the firs lining the valleys were motionless and silent. The hubbub of the rooks was gone until spring. Absolute stillness hung over the river; there were no more swimmers. And in the swift, clear water little fish were suspended, miraculously unmoving, in spite of the current.

As Shura crossed the bridge with light and even steps, the planks rang out brightly with the clatter of her boots. 'Now I've broken the spell,' she laughed.

But in the middle of the night her tooth started acting up, a molar in the upper gum. It was so bad that it felt as if somebody were driving a nail into her gum and then kept twisting it. Shura tossed and turned, got up, and put the kettle on to see whether a warm rinse would help. But it got worse. She put some valerian drops on cotton, bit on it, and walked back and forth. It didn't help. She became tired, completely exhausted. Suddenly, towards the morning her cheek swelled up. Where had *this* misfortune come from out of the blue? Her teeth were all white and even, and had never hurt. And she had to go to work. Only later, after she had received permission to leave, could she see a dentist.

Shura wrapped herself in a scarf, covering her cheek, and went to the factory. Aunt Dunya moaned when she caught sight of her. 'And you still don't believe what I told you! Somebody's put a spell on you, no doubt about it! What'll be next? You'd better get something done about it and fast!'

'Christ! What spell are you talking about? I've got to get to a dentist as quickly as possible!' Shura said, barely able to open her lips.

'Going to the dentist makes sense, but doing something to break the spell makes sense too. I'll tell you what you've got to do. You've got to get Klava's picture and get all her spells sent back to her, so that *she* gets stuck with all the illnesses.'

Shura only waved her hand. She had had enough of all this nonsense; she didn't feel like hearing it any more. By the time she had finished some work, asked for permission to leave and made her way to the polyclinic, it was far into the afternoon. The doctor on duty, a curly haired girl, was working hard, but the line filled the entire hall. Finally, near the end of the working day, it was Shura's turn. The girl took a look with a mirror, tapped around a bit, which made the pain soar, and said that all the teeth were firm and solid, and that she couldn't tell without an X-ray which one was hurting.

'Come back on Monday between nine and one.'

She gave Shura a prescription for the X-ray.

'But today's Friday . . . .' Shura looked at the doctor and her eyes filled with tears. 'You mean I have to live through another three days with this pain?'

'Then go to the emergency dental clinic in Moscow.' And she called the next person in.

When Shura stepped outside, the street lights were already on. She stopped. Where in the world was this emergency clinic? She had stupidly forgotten to ask.

Suddenly a man rose from the bench nearby, threw away an unfinished cigarette, and came up to her. It was Sergei Khokhlachev!

If she had followed the unwritten conduct rules of the village, she would have said, 'What business do you have here? I didn't ask you to come.' But Shura, who had gone through such suffering in the last twenty-four hours, couldn't stand it any longer. A warm wave rose in her, and whimpering like a puppy she buried her head in Sergei's shoulder.

He hugged her tightly, not letting her get away.

'I had the feeling they wouldn't help you here. I've got you all sorts of medicine.'

And, letting go of Shura, he started digging all sorts of little bags, boxes and packages out of his pockets – all the toothache medicines the drugstore sold. He didn't mention the quarter-liter bottle of vodka he had also picked up. He decided it wasn't worth risking it, since everything had turned out so well so far. Maybe Shura's thoughts would fix on this bottle and turn in a direction where he wouldn't want them to turn. So he said nothing, as silence seemed to him not worse, and maybe even better, than other ways of handling this situation.

He would definitely go to the city with her the next day. They would find the emergency dental clinic. There was an information bureau by the train station. She couldn't go alone after all these tortures and with so little sleep.

They left for Moscow very early, on the six o'clock train. And it was a good thing they went together, because the information bureau was closed, and Sergie had to get two-kopeck pieces for the telephone so that they could call and find the address. It was a great polyclinic, open twenty-four hours a day. It could save you, free you from toothache, at any hour.

They had to wait for two hours. There were lots of young couples watching and, for some reason, it was the women who had all the toothache. Some cried, others moaned, and others just snuggled up to their husbands, who comforted them quietly. And they all, whispering, shared experiences of past suffering with each other.

Shura, her head propped against Sergei's shoulder, listened as he said to a neighbor, 'Her teeth are all fine and healthy, one like the other, and still it hurts. . . . We haven't slept for two nights.'

The X-ray showed the bad tooth. It was pulled out, and a minute later Shura smiled and thanked the bearded young doctor.

They got back at twelve. The train was almost empty, and they were the only people on the seat. Sergei put the pastry they had bought on the way right next to them so that nobody else could sit down. They talked about their wedding. Shura didn't want a wedding. The cruel unwritten rules demanded that, if the bride had a child, there would be no wedding.

'You're a man, you don't understand,' Shura said. 'The women'll tear me to pieces. They'll say: she's caught herself a man two years younger, and she's got to brag about it too.'

'Don't you listen to anyone. Listen to me. These two years I've thought about no one but you.'

Two years? He's known me only for one, Shura thought.

'You thought of me, but went to Klava!'

'What Klava? That's gossip. The women thought it up.'

Those spiteful women; they poked their noses into everything, dug up everything, and then spread it around.

'You mean, you aren't going to run off to her?'

'How can you say that? Do you really think I would? All I want is you . . . .' He put his arm around her and pulled her gently toward him.

And she thought, calmly and affectionately, 'At the beginning you're all nice . . . .'

They resumed their serious conversation and decided she wouldn't have a white dress, or a veil; they wouldn't decorate the car with balloons and ribbons, and, of course, they wouldn't put a doll on the dashboard. But everything else would be done according to custom.

On Sunday Shura finally got her picture for the honors board taken. Because it was such an important matter, the prints were to be ready in three days.

Meanwhile, at the factory Aunt Dunya had been waiting for Shura. She took her aside and, on her outstretched palm, showed her a little document-sized photo.

'There you are. I dug it up for you. Take it and get rid of the spell before some other trouble hits you.'

'Who's that? I don't recognize the person. Is it Klava?'

Aunt Dunya didn't answer. It was evidently very important to her to find out as fast as possible if her power to cast spells still worked.

Whistling through her false teeth, she hissed in a loud voice, 'First of all you poke out her eyes with scissors so that she can't see you, then you scratch her out with a pencil and say, "May your spell turn against yourself. May all my ailments and illnesses leave me and settle on Froska."'

Shura was simply dumbfounded. But when she heard the name Froska she asked, 'What do you mean, Froska?'

Aunt Dunya didn't want to explain. 'Don't concern yourself. . . . "May her legs get broken and her arms twisted; her head split with pain and her lips break out in blisters; may her teeth ache and her liver harden in her chest. May all the illnesses finish her off."'

'Stop it! Stop it right away! That's enough!' Shura shouted. 'You could drive a person batty with your nonsense!' She grabbed Aunt Dunya, shaking her in order to stop the terrible sequence of incantations. 'And who's this Froska you're talking of?'

Aunt Dunya got embarrassed. Froska probably was an old acquaintance with whom Dunya wanted to settle accounts. Shura didn't push her any further. Thank God it wasn't Klava, though. It was terrifying just to hear such words, much less to say them! It should make your tongue wither away.

Aunt Dunya wasn't about to say who Froska was, but started to explain about past times and spells: 'In olden times, when my mother was still a girl, such spells were used to get rid of a competitor. You'd tear out a bunch of hairs, for example, or cut off a piece of material from her skirt and put a spell on it.'

'But, for God's sake, why? For what reason? How can your conscience allow you to wish a person . . .'

'You wonder why. Because people are jealous! Jealousy's a brutish animal, more vicious than love. People get killed because of it, and drowned and poisoned, and cursed and bewitched.'

'Aunt Dunya, stop it! Just stop talking! What's all this got to do with me? I don't believe in spells. Your words just give me goose-pimples. I think you're upset because of your old man. Did he chase girls?'

'My old man was a saint! The girls made him sin.' Aunt Dunya sighed or – did she sob? – evidently remembering those terrible and, at the same time, happy days when such fire burnt in her that even now, in her seventieth year, its sparks remained.

On Thursday Shura presented her new picture to Pelageia. This time she did not look like Lolita Torres. Her cheeks were hollow, her face looked longer, her eyes sunken, her lips pressed together. Pelageia was not satisfied with Shura's new appearance.

'You should have waited until the tooth problem was all over,' she said. 'Now people might think we're wearing our shock workers to shreds.'

'My tooth is fine,' Shura answered, 'and I'm going to get married.'

Pelageia didn't even ask who the bridegroom was. She obviously knew.

'So you've made up your mind after all?'

'I have.'

'Is he going to move in with you?'

'Yes, until my brother gets back from the army. I have half the house, and Sergei's folks have a small apartment. It's tight.

'Well, best wishes, anyway.' And Pelageia sighed.

It was a good thing Shura didn't give in to Aunt Dunya's vicious witchcraft, and it was also a good thing she wasn't jealous of Klava, for Klava herself hadn't thought of being jealous or of using witchcraft. And it was not she who had stolen Shura's picture.

It was Valka Vatrushkin who had, a clever pupil at the middle school. Shura's photograph stood on a little pedestal above his books. On the front of the picture, by the shoulder, one could read something written carefully in ballpoint pen: 'To dear Valentin Vatrushkin in memory of my summer performances in Moscow. Cordially, Lolita Torres.'

So there was a similarity after all.

Shura didn't fall ill again. A year later she gave birth to a little girl. Sergei wanted to call his daughter Lolita, but Shura talked him out of it. They called her Nastya in honor of Shura's mother. Now Nastya has begun school, and her older brother Vorka is about to leave it.

Shura has put on weight and doesn't look at all like her old photographs. But she is pretty in a new way. She has almost forgotten the business about the spell, but sometimes she still remembers how Sergei waited for her outside the polyclinic when she had her toothache. And when she does she forgives him everything. She forgives him that he cures his colds and toothaches with vodka, and that he was seen around Klava's place, and even that he took an axe and hacked her fancy shoes to pieces when they attended some relation's wedding. He had become jealous when she danced in those shoes with a young soldier.

6

Irina Raksha

Irina Evgenyevna Raksha was born in Moscow in 1940. When she was fourteen, she moved to the Altai region of Siberia, where her father had been appointed an agricultural specialist on one of the new state farms in the Virgin Land area. After finishing school she also started work at the state farm, driving tractors and combine harvesters, sowing, and riding horses. Her first poems, essays and stories appeared in Altai newspapers. Her neighbor and friend was Vasily Shukshin, himself to become a famous actor and writer of screenplays and stories, whose literary debut she later immortalized in her story 'Eurasia'.

In 1959 she returned to Moscow to study at the Timiryazev Academy of Agriculture and sat in on Mikhail Svetlov's courses at the Gorky Literary Institute. After publishing a story in a journal with a nationwide readership (1960), she entered the screenplay department of the State Institute of Cinematography (1962). Her contemporaries, 'her clan', as she said in an interview in November 1986, included many writers destined for renown: Shukshin, Gladilin, Aksyonov, Kazakov, Nagibin, Amlinsky, Tokareva. Her first collection of stories, *Arriving by Train* (*Vstrechaite poezdom*), appeared in 1965, followed by *A Meadow Flower* (*Mar'in tsvet*) and *The Gold Ring Slipped from Her Finger* (*Katilos' kolechko*). After graduation she worked with Moscow Central Television until 1970, producing features and documentaries based on her scripts. She was also a correspondent for newspapers and traveled all over the country. While attending higher literary courses at the Gorky Institute of Literature, 1973–5, she returned fully to creative writing. More collections of stories appeared: *The Whole Wide World* (*Ves' bely svet*, 1977) and *How Far Is It to Chukotka?* (*Daleko li do Chukotki?*, 1979). Another collection and an autobiographical novel are in progress.

The protagonists of Raksha's stories are unsophisticated people – hunters, teachers, drivers, engineers, herdsmen, railway workers, soldiers and post-girls – close to nature, often on the move, their lives not well organized. The moral life, the hopes, expectations,

disappointments and compromises of these people are the subject
of her stories. Her narrative structure and style are conventional,
following nineteenth-century models. Her interest is not social–
critical but humanistic. Her major device is irony.

When asked, in an interview in 1986, about her goals as a writer,
she said, quoting Pasternak, that it was 'surrender of self', not
fame or money. She sees herself as a medium transmitting her
own unique perceptions and experiences in life. Being such a
medium, to her, is a God-given gift, and her mission is to make
use of it. She refuses to divide prose into women's and men's,
because the term 'women's prose' is negative in Russian usage. It
implies a childish, excessively lyrical style – like a woman's
knitting – whereas she feels that prose must be 'serious, powerful,
strong'. When a woman writes good prose, she writes like a man
and better, because 'a woman knows much more than a man: she
gives birth, she's a mother, she's a womb, is earth itself. She can
write more subtly.' But she is more easily distracted from work,
because 'she is fussy and fidgety by nature'. Women, she feels,
are also superior to men because their role as producers of life
makes them more compassionate, and their will to sustain that life
makes them more quick-witted.

Raksha does not identify with any women's tradition in writing,
although she is familiar with Russian and Soviet women authors.
Her favorite authors are Bunin, Chekhov and Tolstoy, and, among
women, Vera Panova and the poets Anna Akhmatova and Marina
Tsvetaeva.

Her favorites among her own stories are 'Eurasia', 'Beyond the
Tree Was the Sun', and 'Lambushki'.

WORKS IN ENGLISH

'The Whole Wide World', *Soviet Literature*, 1979, no. 3.
'Is It Far to Chukotka?', *Soviet Literature*, 1981, no. 3.
'Stories' ('What Day Is Today?', 'The Gold Ring Slipped from Her Finger',
'Beyond the Tree Was the Sun', 'Lambushki'), 1984, no. 3. This is the
source of the version of 'Lambushki' printed below.

Lambushki
(1976)

Translated by Tracy Kuehn

Igor Anokhin landed in a dense crowd in the long passageway
into the Byelorussian metro station. He moved slowly along in the
thick stream of people, holding his briefcase up high and listening
to the shuffling of hundreds of feet echoing under the vaulted
ceiling. He didn't like the crush in the metro at rush hour and
usually took the streetcar home from work. It was more convenient.
But that morning he had been called to the main office for a
meeting and had dropped by his mother-in-law's afterward. In
another week he and his wife were going on vacation and he had
to find someone to take care of his dog for about three weeks.
That had turned out to be harder than he thought. Last year his
mother-in-law had taken the animal, but now she categorically
refused. 'I like toy dogs. I'd take care of one of those. But yours is
a small horse, not a dog. And it has to be taken for walks and fed.
No, Igor. Do what you like, but I have high blood pressure and
neighbors.' Anokhin hated toy dogs and his mother-in-law knew
it. He had a pointer, a wonderful three-year-old pointer. There
was a time when Anokhin had dreamed of hunting and had even
bought an expensive gun, but somehow he never had got around
to going.

At the end of the passage, he noticed a blue balloon above his
head. It rose slowly under the white vaulted ceiling and could
probably have risen all the way to the sky, but it reached the
ceiling and could go no further. Behind him someone shouted the
name 'Garik' loudly. Probably calling a lost child.

As he drew near the wide stairs the crowd thinned and it was
easier to breathe. He went down to the platform and again heard
the voice: 'Garik! Garik Anokhin!' He glanced back in surprise
(were they calling him?) and saw a rosy-cheeked woman in glasses
and a light-colored scarf pushing through the crowd toward him.

'Hello, Garik. I wasn't sure it was you,' she said when she
reached him, breathing rapidly. 'It is wonderful to see you! Why
didn't you turn around? I kept calling you.'

He stared, not recognizing her immediately.

'Good Lord, Lilya!' He hadn't seen her in five years – not since they graduated from the Institute. 'Lilya! What a small world!'

'I was afraid I'd lose you in the crowd,' she spoke quickly. 'There is such a commotion here.'

'Let's go over there out of the way,' he suggested, and took her arm, allowing her to go in front of him.

She had really changed! She was heavier. Or maybe that was just the cut of her coat, rather dumpy and provincial. What about her legs? They were still the same. She had beautiful legs.

'That's better. It is quieter here.' She sat down on a marble bench along the wall and shoved her gloves in her handbag. 'Have a seat.'

He had a jar of ground currants from his mother-in-law in his briefcase. He did not like these endless presents – a cake from his mother or jam from his mother-in-law – but he had no choice but to take them. He sat down carefully, balancing his briefcase on his knees.

She couldn't take her eyes off him and stared at his face, his briefcase and his hands.

'You know, I simply can't believe that it is us. You and I. Here we are in the metro again, and on the Circle Line.' She was nervous. 'Remember how we used to ride on the Circle?' Then she interrupted herself. 'But enough of that. Tell me how you are and what are you doing. Tell me the most important things.'

What can I tell her? he thought. Certainly not about the morning meeting.

'I am a big boss now,' he smiled jokingly. 'A new department is being formed and I have been asked to head it. To tell you the truth, I still don't believe it myself.'

She nodded happily.

'Sadovsky had told me that your star was rising. But what about your research work? What about your dissertation? I always thought that you would . . .'

'Which Sadovsky? The red-headed one? From the administration board?'

'Who else? From the bridge department. He is often in Karelia and comes to my institute, to visit.'

Her thin, gold-rimmed glasses set off the softness of her skin and her former, girlish blush. She was just as pretty as before. Maybe those were even the same glasses. He remembered the time he had first kissed her late one night near the dormitory. She had just eaten an apple and he could taste it on her lips. He had listened to her breathing and her soft whisper: 'Garik . . . . Let me go, you're crazy! You'll break my glasses. . . . Garik . . . .'

'And what has happened in your life?' he asked, looking away.

'Guess.' Her eyes were mischievous and playful.

'You won the lottery?'

'I have brought a metronome to the exhibition,' she said proudly.

'Interesting. What kind?'

'My own electronic one, with an electric meter. Impulse seventy.' As before, she was so bright and fresh. 'You know, I was working in the patent office and there wasn't anything similar. I've been told it is a unique instrument.' She glowed and one might have thought that everything came easily and was going well for her. 'And do you know what else it is? It is a new program. It means the reorganization of the entire educational process.'

Igor had barely made it through the fifth semester because of her, and had even lost his grant for five months. She kept getting hold of free passes and series tickets and dragging him to exhibitions and concerts. To Bach and Handel. And he would look at her captivating face under the heavy sounds of the organ which meant nothing to him, and hungrily dream of kissing those cheeks and lips later that evening in the dormitory before her room-mate Bobrova returned. But they usually didn't let strangers in the dorm after eleven, and he was a stranger since he was a Muscovite and lived at home. So he would sit in the yard on the cold ground, leaning against the brown wall of the transformer booth. Among all the numerous shining windows, he saw only hers. And, when the light went out at midnight, he talked to her long and tenderly. He believed that Lilya heard him, lying there in her bed. He had always believed in the power of telepathy.

'The All-Union Exhibition is in September,' she said rapidly. 'I am really nervous. Do you know who is on the jury?' She still had those same puffy, childish lips. How many times had he touched them with his own? 'Professor Komov. Nikolai Ivanovich Komov. Remember what we used to do at his lectures?' and she laughed quietly, rearranging her handbag in her lap.

He had been madly in love with this woman! He had never experienced the same feeling since and never would. From her dormitory he used to walk the entire length of Moscow at night to get to his apartment on the other side of the city. Actually, he didn't walk, he flew. Across streets and squares, along the empty bank of the Moskva river. The water had shown black and thick, like oil, and the clear, cold air had been suffused with the pungent smells of autumn leaves. He often had to stand at the apartment door for a long time, ringing the bell, since his mother had begun to chain the door so she'd know when he got home.

'Ma-a-a!' he shouted one night through the door. 'Ma-a-a, open the door! I'm getting married!'

She opened the door in fright and stood there in a long nightgown, pale, tiny and withered. Then she turned and quickly went to put on the kettle. He sat down merrily in the kitchen and spooned out some jam his mother had just made for the water since he was starving. The sweet, thick fragrance of currants hit his nose. His mother lit the stove and asked quietly, 'Have you decided to give up your studies? Or maybe you plan to leave home?' Her lips trembled. 'Have you decided to destroy your entire future?' She looked at the blue flame through her tears. It flickered. 'And I thought I brought you up right. Now you come home at all hours and yell so that you wake up the whole building. Is that for the neighbors' benefit? Oh, if only your father were alive! It's all my fault.' She was almost crying. 'I gave you too much freedom.'

'Mom, why are you talking like that?' He stood up and hugged her thin shoulders. 'Mom, don't be like that.'

She sobbed bitterly, like a child, burying her head in his shoulder.

'Just remember – you have only one mother. . . . There will be plenty of other girls.' Her voice was hollow and rent with sobs. 'You have your whole life ahead of you.'

He stroked her dry, reddish hair, which was completely gray at the roots. Maybe his mother was partly right, he thought. Yes, she probably was right. Why hurry?

He saw less of Lilya their final year at the institute. She was totally immersed in studying the metronome. Their concerts ended, but she continued to buy expensive records with her grant money and listened to them in the evening. Even when they managed to be alone. Igor was tired of Bach and Handel and couldn't bear to hear them any more. One night, lying in the dark next to her, he listened with pleasure to the record scratching when the music ended. She wanted to get up, but he held her back. 'Leave it.' Nevertheless, she wrenched herself free. 'Garik, we can't leave it. It's an awful noise.' She ran barefoot to the record-player near the window, stopped the machine and paused, looking outside. Large flakes of snow fell in the light from the street lamp like a fairytale.

Passers-by in white capes moved silently, as if to the music, as if on stage. Igor got up angrily and turned on the light, and everything disappeared. The light blinded them. 'It's time for me to go. Bobrova will be back soon,' he said curtly, though he knew that she would be in the lab until nine. He simply did not like classical music and never had. He liked tangos and blues, and lately he had become interested in horse-racing. 'There is something about it,' he had begun to say. 'Beauty, speed and excitement.'

In the metro there was a constant rumble: people came and went and trains moved along the Circle Line. But Lilya didn't seem to hear all that. It was as if they were alone.

'It is a wonderful machine,' she said smiling. 'When I press the keys and look at the lit-up screen and see the figures racing by I feel like I am listening to music.' He looked at her, surprised at how she could have retained her former spontaneity. 'The meeting of the organizational committee is tomorrow at two. On the whole, I am calm, though there is a lot of discussion about it.' Lilya straightened her scarf. There was no ring on her finger and her nails were not manicured. 'I'm only afraid for the selector switch,' she confessed, sighing. 'I should have given it a stronger power unit.'

Listening to her, he suddenly remembered the stormy morning meeting. An engineer from the May First* Mime had made a big fuss about a delay in the delivery of equipment. He had been right, but Anokhin wasn't directly involved, so he had sat quietly, twirling his lighter on the table and thinking about who might take his dog over the vacation. During the break he had joined the engineer in the snack bar and had sympathized, even going so far as to express indignation about all the red tape. But the engineer had interrupted him sharply. 'So why didn't you say something at the meeting?' 'What good would that have done?' Anokhin had responded. 'Nothing would have changed.' The engineer had picked up his plate. 'You take that position and don't say anything, and somebody else. . . . So why are you complaining now?' And he had left. Anokhin had grinned and ordered strong tea with lemon. He liked that engineer. Maybe he really should have supported him?

Lilya suddenly noticed that he wasn't listening.

'Well, to sum up, I defended my dissertation in December. Come if you can. I'd be glad to see you. I'll show you the forests and lakes of Karelia.'

In their final year, on the day she defended her undergraduate thesis, he had wanted to go and see her in the dorm to congratulate her. But he vividly imagined how she would hurriedly change clothes behind the closet door and gaily set him and Bobrova to work chopping vegetables for the salad. She herself would run from the kitchen to the telephone or to the hall to be congratulated by everyone. Then the tiny room where he was used to being with her alone would fill up with people and noise. He imagined Sadovsky giving her a Mozart or Bach record. So he hadn't gone. He had called her from a phone booth so as not to upset his mother. Soon after that Lilya was assigned somewhere in the North (he had even forgotten where), lived close by in Klin. That was all so long ago!

She touched his hand softly.

'What are you thinking about now?'

'Nothing much.' He shrugged his shoulders. 'I was remembering my youth. Our student days.'

'Oh-h-h.' Her look became tender. 'That wasn't so very long ago. In fact, it seems like only yesterday. Remember that autumn in Ostankino? The camp-fires of red leaves. And I lost a glove. You still have the same thin hands.' She grew silent for a time. He could hear the rumble of the trains and the shuffling of feet, and noticed the clock at the end of the hall with its huge, luminous dial. Good lord! They were waiting for him at home for supper.

'Do you know what *lambushki* means?' She raised her eyes. 'We have *lambushki* in Karelia. They are small lakes scattered throughout the forest like blue, northern eyes.'

He smiled. She had been amusing before too. Always found something wonderful in everything and asked funny and unexpected questions. One winter they had stood in a long line, but hadn't been able to get tickets to the play, *The Seagull*. Lilya had been in a light coat and had cried as they walked away along the slippery sidewalk. 'Stop it, stop crying,' he had insisted, embarrassed to think that those walking by might get the impression that he had offended her. And suddenly she had asked through her tears, 'Is it true that there is gold in human blood?' Raising her reddened eyes, she had continued: 'Do I really have gold in me too?'

'I certainly envy you Muscovites,' she said. 'Yesterday I found a book of Akhmatova's poems. I bought five to take to the others at work. Those in our department sometimes organize evening poetry readings.'

It was strange that she wasn't married. She was so pretty. She could have married Sadovsky. He'd been in love with her since their student days.

'Yes, someone got me Akhmatova, too,' he said, and remembered that he hadn't even opened it. He had stuck it somewhere on a shelf. 'By the way, how are you for time?'

'I am free. I am completely free,' she said happily. 'I have three whole days. Can you imagine what that means – three days in Moscow?'

He should invite her home, but he remained silent.

'Where do you live now?' she asked.

'On Begovaya Street. We bought a co-operative apartment. Three rooms.' What was so bad about inviting her? They were just former classmates, friends in their Institute days. He should take her home for supper. To meet his family. But then he imagined his wife's face and all that would follow.

She smiled sadly, 'Well, your dream came true, The race course is probably right under your windows. You loved horses then too.'

'Yes,' he nodded. 'The apartment is a nice one with balconies. We need to do some decorating, but there never seems to be enough time. And I can't find bookshelves. You know, the kind that come apart. They're convenient. I was told they have them in Tallinn and I've been meaning to go there.' He could invite her to a restaurant where they could sit and have a real talk. The Arbat, for instance. She had probably never been there. But he was sure his mother-in-law had already called his wife to tell her that he was on his way. And he had that damn jar of currant jam in his briefcase.

'I have a real problem,' he said worriedly. 'We are going on vacation and need to find someone to take our dog for three weeks. She's a pointer with an excellent pedigree.' He perked up. 'And she is very intelligent. Understands everything you say. We are the best of friends. Can you imagine? The two of us went to the races once and I asked her which horse to bet on. She seemed to think about it and then barked three times. I bet on number three and we won! Can you imagine?' He laughed with genuine pleasure.

'I know,' she nodded. 'Sadovsky told me that she had a good pedigree.' Clicking the clasp on her bag, she took out her gloves and pulled one on.

A train moved loudly out of the tunnel.

'It's time for me to go.'

'So soon?' They stood up. 'Maybe you'll come by or call? Write down my number,' he nevertheless said for good form.

'No, Garik. Thank you. I only have three days and I want to go to Klin* to see my mother.' Her face was still light and young as before, but now it looked a little tired.

Suddenly he realized with panic that he wouldn't see her anymore. That he wouldn't see those lips, those eyes. She was about to leave him for ever. Go out of his life, as did his youth, as did love.

'Listen, Lilya,' he said in agitation. 'When will you come again?'

'When there will be another metronome,' she laughed.

'Don't joke, I'm serious. When will you come?' He took her hand quickly, wanting to tell her something.

'Wait, let me put on my glove,' she said and she pulled her hand away.

People poured from the train and pushed against them.

'Well, that's it. I'm off,' she smiled. 'I hope you find someone to take care of your marvelous pointer. Everyone loves dogs these days.'

She moved into the crowd and waved her hand.

Everyone left, but Anokhin stood next to the bench, feeling empty and lost.

As he walked in measured steps home along Begovaya Street, skirting dirty puddles, he kept repeating the word *lambushki* to himself. He hadn't even known that such a strange word existed. And he didn't know that, from that moment on, it would remain with him, worrying and gnawing at him.

7

Vasily Belov

Vasily Ivanovich Belov achieved fame as a writer following the publication of his short novel *An Ordinary Affair* (*Privychnoe delo*) in 1967, when he was thirty-four. Like Turgenev, who in the nineteenth century acquainted his readers with his native Orel region through his *Hunter's Sketches*, Belov introduced his home region, the Vologda area north of Moscow, into literature. He was born there on 23 October 1932 to a family of farmers. He attended the village school, trained as a joiner and mechanic, became a staff writer on a regional newspaper, and attended the Literary Institute in Moscow from 1959–1964. He still lives in Vologda.

Belov belongs to the 'village prose' group of writers, which includes Fyodor Abramov, Victor Astafyev, Mikhail Alekseev, Sergei Krutilin, Boris Mozhaev, Evgeny Nosov and Valentin Rasputin. They have witnessed and written about the disappearance of old rural customs and values. Belov's central topic is the physical and moral destruction of the village, which has been forcibly transformed by collectivization and by the inroads of modern technology. Simultaneously, its inhabitants have abandoned it in droves in favor of the cities and industrial centers. Life in the country had been so bleak and disadvantaged for so long that in the end the flood of migrants could no longer be stemmed. Old values such as honesty, readiness to help others and individual initiative have all too often, in Belov's view, been supplanted by the values the collective farm rewards: obedience to orders, attention to production figures, egoism, opportunism and materialism.

Many of Belov's works describe, in an elegiac manner, what remains of traditional village life, its customs and relationships. A recent demonstration of his love for his home district is his meticulously illustrated ethnographic study *Harmony* (*Lad*). But Belov is just as concerned with re-creating the authentic atmosphere (including the language) of the country around Vologda as with identifying the causes of the destruction of village life. Thus he touches on two related themes: the beginning of the transformation of the village, and the nature of the new urban setting that has

133

attracted the villagers. His novel *The Eves* (*Kanuny*, 1972), for example, presents a picture of the village in the late 1920s, when collectivization began, while *Carpenter Tales* (*Plotnitskie rasskazy*, 1968) continues the comparative investigation of country and city lifestyles and values.

Childrearing According to Doctor Spock (*Vospitanie po doktoru Spoku*, 1978) collects four stories published previously in journals. The story translated below, 'Morning Meetings' ('Svidaniya po utram'), was reprinted in this collection, and first appeared in *Nash sovremennik*, 1977, no. 1. The central character of all four stories is Kostya Zorin, the protagonist of *Carpenter Tales*, and he is not the only recurring character. But these stories are no longer set in the village; they deal with village migrants to the city, their adoption of city mores, and the conflicts that arise when these mores clash with old village values. Of course, family, marriage and the relations between parents and children are profoundly affected by the individuals' conflicting ways of thinking and living.

In these stories Belov explores, for example, the conflict between an emancipated, urbanized wife and a husband who still lives by the patriarchal values of the village. Is it possible to satisfy one's human needs and to find inner peace and happiness under such conflict-laden circumstances? The dilemmas of women's emancipation, the problems caused by the conflicting demands of old sex-role conceptions and new professional and psychological expectations, and the clash between generations become agonizingly evident in these stories, and no solutions are in sight.

Belov's most recent and controversial work, entitled *Everything is Ahead* (*Vse vperedi*), was published in the nationalist journal *Our Contemporary* (*Nash sovremennik*), 1986, nos. 7–8. It is set in the city, but not surprisingly, is an anti-urban work. The city is blamed for the disintegration of the family, and this – according to a recent interview with the author – 'is the source of his greatest distress as both a writer and a citizen'. The family life of the protagonists Lyuba and Dima Medvedev falls apart because the husband suspects his wife of having seen a pornographic film in Paris! Such 'depravity', the hero and the implied author convey, is the result of women's emancipation, and emancipation is connected with divorce, divorce with alcoholism, and so on. The authorial voice conveys a sense of loss in the face of change, but at the same time it seems to belong to a wise prophet who knows the truth about the evils of scientific progress and materialism, and how to counter them. Such a stance, combined with inadequate psychological analysis, makes the book artistically unconvincing, as critics have pointed out.

WORKS AND SECONDARY LITERATURE IN ENGLISH

'Carpenter Stories' (excerpt), *Russian Literature Triquarterly*, 5 (1973) 197–215.
Morning Rendez-Vous (Stories) (Moscow: Raduga Publishers, 1983).

'Belov, Vasili Ivanovich', in Harry B. Weber (ed.), *Modern Encyclopedia of Russian and Soviet Literature* (New York: Academic International Press, 1978) ii, 181–8.
Hosking, Geoffrey A., 'Vasili Belov – Chronicler of the Soviet Village', *Russian Review*, xxxiv, no. 2 (Apr 1975) 168–85.
Zhegulin, Gleb, 'The Contemporary Countryside in Soviet Literature: A Search for New Values', *The Soviet Rural Community* (Urbana: University of Illinois Press, 1971).
Cf. also an abbreviated version of an interview in *Current Digest of the Soviet Press*, xxxviii, no. 9 (Apr 1986), and the summaries of Soviet discussion of *Childrearing According to Doctor Spock* in *Current Digest* xxix, no. 29 (May 1977) 8–9, 14, and no. 48 (Oct 1977) 14–15.

Morning Meetings
(1977)

Grandma usually got up just after five, when the noise of the early-morning traffic would wake her up. Nowadays she slept lightly, dozing and thinking all night. Outside, the first trolley bus went by, probably still empty. It rattled, and she imagined that something had broken already, though it was only morning. They certainly weren't looking after their machines! There were plenty of them around, but nobody took care of them.

Today was Sunday. Her anxiety about the coming day had already set in the night before, and now it gripped her old heart immediately. Grandma had begun to be afraid of Sundays and of all holidays. Earlier, when she had lived in the village, she had looked forward to them, but now she was apprehensive. Would there be trouble again today? Yesterday her son-in-law had come home late, and her daughter hadn't said a word to him. Again they had slept apart.

Quietly, Grandma fumbled for her slippers. She slid them on, holding back a coughing-spell so as not to wake up her granddaughter, and whispered, 'Sleep, my sweetheart, sleep! Christ be with you. No nursery school today.'

Her granddaughter from *that* one, the child of her first son-in-law, slept with Grandma. Ever since she had been weaned, she'd been sickly. Sometimes the child would have screaming-fits, and her daughter would lose her temper and throw the child on the bed like a doll. And all this because of her *nerves*. People had bad nerves these days, very bad nerves; lots of people had.

All this ran through her head as she tucked in the child's blanket, which had been tossed off.

The most important thing for her now was to get to the bathroom. It was only about four steps, but she'd have to open the doors, two of them, and cross the parquet floor, and the parquet creaked. Not even the carpets she'd brought from the village helped. She had woven the carpets herself, just for them. Her daughter had asked for them in a letter, when village things became fashionable. And it didn't matter anyway, fashion or no fashion, you couldn't have too many rugs.

Cautiously she opened the door to the hall. Cautiously she went step by step along the carpet. But the parquet floor creaked anyway, as if dry birch-bark had been packed under it. Thank God, they hadn't heard anything in their room. All she had to do now was to open the door, with God's help. The door also squeaked, and the light-switch would make a loud click. She decided not to turn on the light. The bathroom had a window into the kitchen. She could manage in the faint light. In fact, it was even better. The new son-in-law had wallpapered the entire bathroom with pictures of naked girls. She always felt ashamed looking at them – almost as their mothers had brought them into the world! To hang up such *hussies*! But what could she do? That was *their* business. Grandma sighed, trying to decide what was the best thing to do. She really should flush the toilet all the way, but it made such a racket, simply awful. Not to flush, though, wasn't right either. Her daughter would scold her because of the noise; her son-in-law would be upset over the smell. You just didn't know whom to listen to and whom to please.

Again she decided to go fifty-fifty: not to flush with all the water, but just part of it, and carefully, so that it wouldn't gurgle. Washing was no problem. She could wait. And just as quietly she returned to her tiny room, six square meters in all, where her granddaughter was still asleep.

From the front door came a sharp, yet brief and almost shy, ring of the doorbell. Holding her breath, Grandma tiptoed to the door. Good Lord! What should she do? She just didn't know. If she didn't open, they'd ring again and wake up everybody. But opening the door was just as wrong. If only the son-in-law would wake up and come out. Maybe it was for him.

She waited tensely; perhaps they'd go away out there. She sneaked up to the door and listened. No, they hadn't gone. You could clearly hear somebody outside. It was better to open.

Carefully she turned the key – she made no noise – and opened the door a fraction.

Cap in hand, a bald old man in boots and a gray cotton jacket stood by the door, hesitating. 'Good health to you!' he bellowed, and Grandma waved her arms at him: 'Quiet, quiet!'

The old man shifted his knapsack and, lowering his voice to a whisper, said, 'I'd like . . . . Well, I mean, Kostya. . . . Isn't Konstantin home?'

'No, he ain't here, he's gone.'

'Where is he then? Maybe on some business trip?'

'I don't know nothing, my dear. I really don't. He don't live here now.'

'You mean, he's moved?'

'Yes, he has, I'm sure he has. And who are you?'

'Well, I, I mean . . . . Tell Kostya that Smolin was here. That is, Olesha. Sorry to disturb you.'

'God be with you.'

Carefully Grandma closed the door. Her luck had held – nobody had awakened. It was good that they slept; Christ be with them. They had worn themselves to shreds during the week. Grandma thought with respect of her daughter, her son-in-law and his sister, who had come from another town to start her studies. Meanwhile the alarm said six. After a prayer she sat at the foot of her granddaughter's bed. It was very bad and even unpleasant to sit around like that, doing nothing. And there was plenty to do. But they wouldn't wake up before nine. She could have knitted, but she had just run out of wool. She should write a letter to her son, but the paper and envelopes were in their room. She could go down to buy bread and milk, but the shop wouldn't be open till ten. For the time being there was nothing she could do. Thoughts came crowding in on her from all sides, uninvited. And they were all about her children. Her sons were far away, but her heart ached for them. The youngest was an army officer serving in Germany. The other lived in Siberia. He had left home as a teenager. One daughter was in Moscow. The other, her eldest, lived in the village. Her husband didn't drink; he was a craftsman. It wasn't too painful to think of them. They were doing well, already had grandchildren of their own. But she felt most sorry for this daughter here, though she lived right under her eyes. It was like living in a railway station. Her daughter had become as thin as a rake, and hardly a day went by without a fight with that husband. She had divorced the first one because of drinking. The second one didn't drink, but he was sort of *ordun'ry*; he just didn't stand on his own two feet. Worse than any woman. They'd fight over flea-bites. But what was there really to fight about? They had money, food and clothes. Thank God, times were better, and the shops were full. Before, if a shop got a delivery of cotton print, you drew lots to buy it. But nowadays they didn't know what to put on first, and they got gifts every holiday. And there were God knows how many holidays. And how did they act with each other? Often they were like dogs. 'Was that the way I brought her up?' Grandma wondered bitterly.

And she began recalling old times. Old times, but they were so clear and near, as if no time had passed. In those days husbands and wives didn't sleep apart, except if the men went to war or left for a job elsewhere. But now? The women were too lazy to have children, and the men had forgotten how to feed their families. Could you really call him a man, if he made less than his wife?

Suddenly she felt ashamed of herself, picking on others like this. In a frantic whisper she scolded herself and remembered yesterday's letter from the village.

She felt really sorry, so sorry for all of them, for those who were suffering right now, and also for those whose pain had ended. In that letter she had read that her next-door neighbor, younger than she, had died. And he'd wanted to live to ninety. She mustn't forget to pray for him in church. And what he had gone through! Wounded and robbed, too! They had just about skinned him alive as a prisoner, even spat in his face.

She also recalled her own husband, killed in the last war. And then she thought of her mother-in-law, and her husband's sisters and brothers. Well, you couldn't say that her mother-in-law had been awfully warm and kind, God be with her! But she had been fair. For example, she'd sit by the samovar, and she'd pour the first cup of tea for her husband, the second for her son, and the third – not for herself or for her younger daughters, but for her, the daughter-in-law. Her father-in-law was the same, but he warmed up to her, and later he wouldn't let anyone pick on her. A tough old man, no doubt about it. It was a sin to remember bad things, but when she first came into their house she worked herself to the bone. Once she was sweeping the room, and, lo and behold, there was a silver rouble under the bench. And she was all alone at home. Silly she hadn't guessed right away that the rouble had been put there on purpose. At any rate, she gave the money to the old man before teatime: 'Here, Dad, I found it under the bench.' How pleased and happy he had been! He had praised her and stroked her head like a little girl's. And, when his oldest daughter couldn't milk the cows well, he made her, the daughter-in-law, the senior mistress of the house. Life was long, oh how long it was, and how much one could get done.

Grandma's thoughts came flowing one after another. Suddenly the parquet floor in the hall creaked and the kettle in the kitchen clattered. They were awake and were getting up. Grandma suddenly remembered that today was Sunday, and she had to take her granddaughter for a walk. Her heart began to ache. Without making a sound, Grandma stepped to the window and sneaked a peek down the street, in the direction of the telephone booth and the vegetable shop. Was he there? Yes, he was. He stood there, the poor fellow, in his grey raincoat, with the collar turned up. Smoking. The child was still asleep, and he was already waiting. That's how it was every Sunday morning. He'd come and wait until Grandma came out to the courtyard with her granddaughter. But sometimes the daughter would take the girl for a walk in the square, and then he'd turn up his collar and hide in the telephone booth, standing behind the glass until they passed.

'Oh, Lord have mercy!' Grandma sighed. She picked up the drowsy girl and took her to *them*. That was how mornings on a day off usually began.

So it was already nine o'clock. Zorin climbed down the short flight of stairs that led to the vegetable shop. Down there it wasn't as embarrassing to stand around. The shop wouldn't open until eleven, and only the most curious people would notice him down there as they passed. The devil only knew what they wanted! Didn't they have enough worries of their own? They looked you over as if you were some prehistoric monster.

From here he could see the windows of his former apartment quite well. In the kitchen the small inset window was already open. That meant that Tonya was lighting the gas and putting on the kettle. Or maybe the new occupant of the apartment was smoking?

Zorin felt bitter that his little daughter Lyalka and this newcomer lived together in one apartment, and particularly this one. His mouth also tasted bitter, from the cigarettes: he hadn't smoked for thirteen months. And he hadn't felt like it either. Smoke irritated him as much as the impudent stares of the passers-by. He recalled the day, or rather the night, when he had had a fresh taste of that junk. After that he had started smoking with even greater ferocity. It had been some regular holiday plus two additional days off. This meant that for a whole week not a single brick was touched at the construction site. Oh, these holidays! Zorin and his wife had gone to visit the Golubyovs. At first it had been quite nice and decent. There was some lady, a relative of the Golubyovs, who would break into nervous giggles, or suddenly fall into a haughty silence. Some featherbrain put on a record of the Beatles, and someone else was trying to deliver a fancy lecture. But very soon it degenerated into a wild orgy of drinking. Someone stomped around with someone else to the blaring of a gramophone; others were singing. Zorin went into the adjacent room and collapsed in an armchair. Golubyov, drunk as he was, followed him, hiccuping. Hugging Zorin clumsily, he stuttered, 'W-w-well old man, there th' three roomth. Those two have shut themselves up in one already. How about us? W-we're no worse th-than they? Here's what I s-suggest. Mine'th f-fed up with me. D'you f-feel like thwapping? Swapping, just temporararar–.'

Zorin sobered up instantly and cringed. Something trembled within him. And the worst of it was that Golubyov's wife would snuggle up much too tightly to her partner when dancing. For a moment Zorin looked at Golubyov, studying his inane smile. And suddenly he jumped up and slugged him on the jawbone with all his strength. Golubyov flew head-first into a chest of drawers. Zorin had a hard time remembering later what happened next: how he had ditched his wife and left the party, how he had continued drinking with someone else, and how he had asked someone in the street for a smoke. Two days later, Golubyov had turned up with a bottle and listened wryly as Tonya caustically instructed Zorin, 'You might at least have the decency to apologize!'

Zorin had remained silent, gritting his teeth. When she had left, Golubyov pulled the cognac he had brought from its hiding-place behind the mirror: 'No need apologizing, old m-m-man. You were right. I'm a pig, but what's our chest of drawers got to do with it? It's in bad shape.'

It had been almost impossible to harbor any grudge against him. For a long time his own disgusting compassion for Golubyov had infuriated Zorin. Once, in the heat of a quarrel, Zorin had told Tonya the entire sickening story, and she suddenly had shown a surge of jealousy. To this day, though, he felt that her jealousy had been insincere. In fact, he was virtually certain now that his wife had been pretending.

Zorin looked at his watch again: twenty past nine already.

Women like Tonya would always at the outset peremptorily attribute their own sins to their husbands, then get used to the idea and start believing quite sincerely in their – the husbands' – unfaithfulness. Good Lord, what sirens, indeed. His life as a bachelor had forced Zorin to hang around restaurants even more than before. There he often would see a group of women sitting without men. Six or eight of these smart ladies would gather, put in three roubles each, and go out for dinner. With great relish they'd talk about their husbands. On those occasions, and especially after a glass of port, they'd forget who was around, lose their inhibitions and vie with one another at being witty. 'You know, it turns out that . . . .' 'No, but do you know . . .?'

Yesterday Zorin had picked up an unusual voice as he was involuntarily eavesdropping on such a get-together: 'You have to make them decent meals.' But the woman who felt that men should be fed well to make them drink less was in such a tiny minority that she fell silent instantly. The others joined forces, attacking her. 'I can just see myself cooking for that idiot!' 'That's all I need.' 'He comes home from work and grabs his newspaper, and you don't know what to do first, ten things at once! The laundry alone's enough.' 'Why listen to her? She's in love with her Slavik!'

In short, it wasn't fashionable to love Slavik – that is, one's own husband – according to this jolly company. Tonya had always accused Zorin of callousness, of insufficient respect for women, and finally, of a medieval *Domostroi** mentality. If no one else was around, he would immediately fly off the handle: '*Domostroi.*' Have you ever read it, this *Domostroi?*' 'I haven't, and I'm not going to.' 'And do you know that this *Domostroi* actually advocates faithfulness in husbands?' But she was incapable of grasping such subtleties. She was genuinely offended by his despotic behavior. That's how all their quarrels began. In the end he just gave in to her and did as she wanted: he learned to agree without argument. But this didn't save them from trouble either. The persistent habit of opposing everything, the expectation of endless dirty tricks from everybody, including her own husband, and her constant alert defensiveness, which would change into aggression – all this made her register her protest on every possible occasion. Once he made an experiment. He decided not to insist on his point of view and do only what she wanted. And the result? Instead of accusations of *Domostroi* mentality and despotism he heard something entirely unexpected: 'What kind of a man are you? You don't even know how to stand up for yourself. You shouldn't have listened to me!' 'But you would have accused me of despotism!' 'Really?' And so on and so forth. He had studied all the details of this remarkable situation. At first he was furious and felt sorry for himself, but little by little he got used to the hopelessness of it all and learned how to program not only his own but also her conduct. And then came that business with Golubyov. Or, rather, with that boy . . . .

Ten o'clock already. Soon the shop would open, and he'd have to pretend that he came to buy eggplant pie. In the house across the street somebody turned on a tape-recorder full blast and put the speaker in the open window. What for? Why was he, Zorin, who longed for peace and quiet, forced to listen to this rubbish? A modern Caucasian–Ukrainian tune with a Russian accent. For Zorin this tune was associated with that shameful – as it seemed to him – period in his life when he was getting divorced from his wife. That pimply fellow had been incredibly persistent for his age. Almost every day he had promenaded before the house, and always with that idiotic transistor radio.

Tonya probably liked that kind of persistence. In fact, he was sure of it. It didn't just amuse her; it also flattered her enormous vanity. So someone had a crush on her! She had the age of Balzac's women, but, all the same, someone had a crush on her – there you are, dear hubby, see how you stomach it. You yell and scream at me, act crude and vulgar, come home drunk, and one can wait

for ever to hear a kind word from you. So here's something for
you to chew on. And how had she got the fellow behaving like
this?

Zorin blushed. He was revolted by his own belated agitation.
Most likely it had been triggered off by a run-of-the-mill flirtation
in the library. Or maybe she had allowed him to sit beside her in
the bus, and maybe she had smiled at him, looking in his eyes.
Does it take much to egg on an inexperienced boy who's burning
with lust? Zorin was convinced that the boy hadn't gone further
than making these visits. And she was sensible. It was enough for
her to know that someone had a crush on her. But what difference
did that make? Only fear and cowardice prevented her from going
any further. Her inconsistency only confirmed her fundamental
depravity. Did vice cease being vice simply because it wasn't acted
on? Zorin had always been faithful to his wife. He loved her. He
always felt repelled by these feminine tricks. He hated those
unconcealed allusions, those glances from strangers whom he'd
met by chance, those squints and half-smiles. Decent women don't
look into the eyes of strange men. They walk down the street
normally. Men's filth and dirt wouldn't cling to them; they'd
remain pure even in the vilest situation. But were there many such
women?

That pimply booby had the nerve to turn up one day at the
sandbox where his daughter was playing. Another time he stole
into the house and went up to the landing. Zorin met him as he
was taking down the garbage and could barely stop himself from
dumping the bucket on his head. 'Listen, man,' Zorin had told
him, 'if you don't stop hanging around here, I'll throw you
downstairs, got it? Head first.' The fellow gave Zorin a provocative
and at the same time desperate look. He also used to come in the
mornings. Zorin had grabbed him by the collar, led him down like
a sheep and quietly shoved him outside: 'Get lost!' The fellow
suddenly got hold of himself and became daring.

How sickening it all was. That day Zorin hadn't been able to
hold out. He had got stuck in the same old bar, the Smeshinka,
had come home late and had subjected his wife to a savage
interrogation and a slap on the face. She had dispatched him to
the medical sobering station. There he had started acting up. They
undressed him completely and tied him to the bedstead. The
nurses made fun of him when he begged to be untied. Never
before had he experienced such humiliation and bitterness. He

started yelling that he'd beat his head against the wall if they didn't untie him and give him his clothes. But they just kept laughing at him. In despair, he started beating his head against the wall. Then they called somebody else and gave him an injection.

Good God. . . . And how was he to know that nothing else had happened between them, that this moron – pah!

Zorin spat, recalling that pimply physiognomy. In his childhood, when he read *The Captain's Daughter**, he detested Shvabrin the same way. But what was this? The same pimples and the same transistor radio, the same nylon jacket; only the reddish sideburns were new. The fellow was standing by the telephone booth, slobbering over his cigarette and staring in Zorin's direction.

Zorin stepped out of his hiding-place: 'Listen, man . . . .'

The fellow looked around in alarm.

'You've lost your game. I feel sorry for you, but you bet on the wrong horse, too. . . .'

The fellow took off quickly. At the same time a heavy-set matron who knew Zorin opened the shop. To avoid being seen by her, Zorin dived back into the telephone booth and looked wearily at the corner of the house. It was eleven already. Could Grandma be sick? They should come down any minute now, they'd have to. . . . He could force his way into the apartment, yes, push Tonya aside and enter his former apartment by force. He hadn't even tried putting in for an exchange,* but had simply moved into a dormitory. He could have had a friendly talk with Tonya's husband and come to an agreement that he could take his daughter to some playground. But he didn't want the girl to cry. And Tonya was still so furious that she even refused to hear of Zorin and didn't want to recognize him as the child's father. She insisted that now she could finally breathe freely, now she was married happily, and that she and her husband were in love. Love? Good Lord – love! How could people fail to understand that love was good and appropriate only in youth? Then, and then only. Yet they waited for love at forty, even fifty, when everything was over, naïvely using the word 'love' for mere lust. But these lovers of both sexes ought to have understood at some point in their lives that after the birth of a child any other 'love' was treachery. And, for that matter, was everyone even capable of love? Most people considered the mere desire to love and mere liking to be genuine love. Incapable of loving, they expected love from their partner. They needed this playing at love even after the birth of children. What were children to them? They couldn't care less about these children's pain! Fathers dodged alimony payments and roamed the country like goats. It was easy: they could find a job any time, any place. And many modern women had more female vanity than maternal love. Tonya was no exception. Zorin knew that more than once she had sacrificed Lyalka's well-being to her own idiotic self-assertion. He had been horrified when he made this discovery. It shook him to the very depth of his already shaken being. From then on he was no longer able to love her as he used to.

And she was in love again. . . . Of course, she was lying; it was nothing but a game, a pathetic, strained game. She had always accused him of being behind the times when he argued with her about love and the family. She felt that a woman should be free and independent. But could one be free of one's conscience, of one's duties as a parent?

Oh, those cheats who traded their children for this so-called 'freedom', a freedom full of drunkenness and misery. He knew those wretches inside-out. They wanted nothing but drunken blather. Women didn't despise them for nothing. Such men didn't care where and with whom they slept, where and with whom they drank, where and how much they worked. Yes, Zorin knew them better than anyone else. Without a second thought, the wife or mistress would send this sort to prison, where he'd sit locked up for about two years and then come back to her as if nothing had happened. He'd start drinking again and eating at her expense until he ended up in the morgue or back in prison. Let's assume that they're sick and nothing can be expected of them, Zorin thought. But Golubyov – where did he get his cynicism, his consumer attitude to the world, to women, and even to himself? And weren't people like him, even we ourselves, infecting our wives, sisters and children with our own irresponsibility? When a woman turned into some sexless being, it somehow wasn't so revolting, because the change turned out sort of feminine anyway – that is, not completely repulsive. Though who knows . . .?

Well, emancipation – that was something somebody had deliberately dreamed up, Zorin thought. Emancipation assumed the existence of inequality from the very outset. But how could one really categorize people by that ghastly scheme: man – woman? It was a crime. People could only be divided into good and evil. And there were just as many wise people and fools among men as there were among women.

Those were Zorin's thoughts as the second-hand on his watch crawled forward.

Lyalka. . . . His heart palpitated as the girl came skipping around the corner. Her mother, Tonya, followed, and Zorin started feeling wretched to the point of tears. Again he wouldn't be able to hug and kiss and hold his daughter tight. No, he couldn't risk a vulgar scene in the courtyard, the child torn from his arms and shrill abuse halting passers-by. Well, he'd watch them from the telephone booth and then leave unnoticed. . . . But, thank God there was Grandma! His former mother-in-law had appeared in the courtyard. She knew where Zorin was waiting; she'd do everything possible to let him see his daughter. But what were Tonya's plans? Apparently she was going to work. Or shopping? Heavily made-up, as always. As always, in a rush. And, as always, in conflict with Lyalka. The two were engaged in a battle of wills: 'Drop that dirty thing this minute!'

But Lyalka didn't want to give up the old can she had just picked up in the courtyard.

'Can't you hear? It's dirty! Drop it!'

Lyalka said nothing. Zorin's heart contracted when Tonya grasped the girl's arm with one hand and gave her several slaps on the behind with the other. Lyalka burst into tears.

'Bad girl! Are you going to do what I tell you? Are you?'

'Mum, Mummy . . . .' Lyalka was already choking. 'Mummy, don't hit me, don't . . . .'

'Are you going to obey or not?'

'Yes, yes, Mum. Mummy! Dear Mummy . . . .'

Oh, these tears of a child, this dear little voice: 'Yes, yes, Mum.' His daughter's tears scorched Zorin even from a distance, and he choked with pity for this helpless, unprotected little creature. He was dumbfounded, crushed by the senseless beating of this human being, his daughter. Loathing and hatred for this cruel woman, his former wife, took hold of him, welling up in his eyes. He couldn't stand it any longer, he'd run out and slap her in the face.

'Such a brat!' Tonya said, almost shoving the crying girl into the arms of Grandma, who had been hovering around them. Without turning back, Tonya walked away and disappeared into a side street.

'No, she doesn't love the child,' flashed through Zorin's burning head. 'She doesn't love her. She wouldn't fly into such a rage if she loved her.'

Gritting his teeth, he left the telephone booth and crossed over to the sandbox. Grandma didn't see him, she was so busy soothing the girl. Three steps away from them he stopped and everything else in the world vanished. Everything, absolutely everything disappeared and was forgotten: the dormitory with its constant noise, the room in the psychiatric clinic and the inane daily planning-sessions. And his exhaustion and bitterness. He was happy.

The girl had evidently sensed her father's presence and noticed Zorin before Grandma saw him. Not knowing what to do first, she just kept looking at him. 'Dad, Daddy,' she breathed through her sobs as she ran up to him. He picked her up and took her in his arms.

'Oh Lyalka, my darling little Lyalka. What are we going to do about you, my little sweetheart? Don't cry. . . . Look, I've brought you a new bunny. A blue one? Yes, there are blue ones, even blue bunnies exist. But we won't cry any more, all right Lyalka?'

Traces of pain, despair and bewilderment vied with a faint smile of joy on her little tear-stained face. He pulled out a handkerchief and wiped it, unable to hold back his own tears. Then, with the other hand, he gratefully hugged Grandma's bony shoulder. 'We aren't going to care about the old folks staring; we aren't going to care about anything, are we, Lyalka?'

Her little body was still trembling.

'Daddy, you won't go away any more, will you?' the girl said, slowly calming down. And again he hugged her firmly, this one dear, true, helpless little bundle of life.

8

Anatoly Kim

Born in Korea in 1939, Kim was adopted by a Russian family and raised on the Far Eastern island of Sakhalin. Since 1957 he has lived in Moscow. After studying art for a while, he earned a living as a construction worker, came to know numerous people and their stories, and began writing. He considered these human encounters his first studies in literature. In 1971 he finished a course at Moscow's Gorky Institute of Literature, and in 1973 his first story, 'Dog-Rose Meko' ('Shipovnik Meko') appeared. Since then he has published seven books: *The Blue Island* (*Goluboi ostrov*, 1976), *Four Confessions* (*Chetyre ispovedi*, 1978), *Nightingale Echo* (*Solov'inoe ekho*, 1980), *The Jade Belt* (*Nefritovy poyas*, 1981), *Herb Collectors* (*Sobirateli trav*, 1983), the novel *The Squirrel* (*Belka*, 1984) and *The Taste of Sloe at Sunrise* (*Vkus terna na rassvete*, 1985).

Many of his works, such as the story selected for this volume, are conventionally realistic. But in his most recent fiction another dimension is added. He portrays the suffering of all creatures in specifically Soviet circumstances, partly from an authorial standpoint of 'enlightenment' in the Eastern sense, that is, he introduces a point of view that transcends temporal and spatial limitations. From this viewpoint, individual being is a brief interruption from endless being, a momentary incarnation for purposes of spiritual growth.

This Eastern spirituality is Kim's response to what he sees as the soullessness of contemporary life. His goal in writing seems to be to infect the reader with his sense of a higher reality, to inspire him to be more humane and compassionate by leading him to recognize his true essence and hence his kinship with all individualized living creatures. This trait is reminiscent of the writings of Sologub and other symbolists. Tolstoy too was influenced by Eastern philosophy, but recast it in a rational, pragmatic, Western form. Kim's writing shares nothing with Tolstoy's. He has found entirely different artistic means for conveying his more comprehensive and intuitive vision.

His novel *The Squirrel*, subtitled 'a fairytale novel', re-creates his spiritual world with startling artistic originality. On the level of traditional realism, the four artist protagonists experience life like the Buddhist squirrel in the cage, purposelessly spinning the wheel until crushed. They perish swallowed by the petty trivia of life or victimized by individuals who, in pursuit of their own goals, both literally and metaphorically become animals. Yet at least one of them is clearly aware of another, timeless, infinite reality, to which Kim draws attention through a variety of devices: folklore motifs, improbabilities, transfigurations, metaphors, narrative fragments interchangeably offered by a polyphony of voices. Although not without artistic flaws, the novel is unique in that it tries to introduce Eastern thinking into the Russian tradition.

Kim's story 'A Cage with a Color TV' appeared as 'Kletka s televizorom' in *Oktybr'*, 1981, no. 11.

Cage with a Color TV
(1981)

I[1] remember I was sitting on that comfortable old bench in the playground, looking at the old pony, who was brown with white spots and had shaggy ears and a long mane that hung down over her eyes. A child ran up to the dozing mare, a boy in a blue coat and a knitted cap as red as a ripe strawberry against green grass. He stretched out his hand, offering something to the pony, but the decrepit mare only lifted her head listlessly, not about to accept the offering. Disappointed and puzzled, the boy turned to his bearded father, who was walking towards them smiling indulgently, a long pipe between his teeth.

It was a warm, uncommonly quiet and sunny Moscow October. Dry, crumpled yellow leaves covered the park and concealed the tree roots. It was getting dark early, and when I returned home, walking along the iron fence of the Suvorov* Military Academy, I no longer saw what I would see in spring and summer.

Normally I would see the Suvorov students, tall, strong boys in black uniforms, dating their girls right at the fence, because they

---

1. The Russian verbal endings indicate that the speaker is a woman.

had no time off. The courting couples would stand here and there along the fence, their faces close together, and the space between the iron bars was wide enough for them to exchange ardent kisses as I slowly walked past, tapping with my walking-stick.

This went on from spring to autumn, but in autumn all the kisses disappeared, like birds of passage that had taken off, and only dried leaves rained upon the deserted iron fence of the Military Academy. But the stillness of the tall trees remained, and so did the two dreamy, pot-bellied ponies who for many years had been standing over there in the park. And, at regular intervals, as if counting the minutes and hours of the quickly vanishing golden autumn, the blue metro trains flashed by, making the same mechanical noise. An overground line passed along the edge of the park.

On one of these autumn days, when melancholy overcame me as I watched the children – and among them a boy with an extraordinarily red cap – run to the old mare again and again, trying to pet her, to offer her some food or to stir her up, she came up to me, a tall blonde about whom everything was harmonious and pleasant: she had shoulder-length curls, light, wide-bottomed slacks and a soft, fluffy sweater that matched the blue of her eyes and hung loosely on her slender, almost excessively tall figure.

The stranger sat down next to me after testing the bench with a finger to make sure it was clean, and, turning to me in the absence of anyone else, said with a quiet chuckle, 'Dear me! And I was so scared . . . .'

'Scared of what?' I asked.

'I thought at first that it was a huge dog,' she said, pointing to the pony.

I looked at the short-legged, pot-bellied Lilliputian, who was peacefully dozing under her long, reddish-yellow mane, and I honestly couldn't see the slightest resemblance to a dog. She was an old pony and nothing but a pony, even though she was small.

'You're here for the first time?' I asked, continuing to observe pony Bee, an old acquaintance of all the children and inhabitants of our district.

'Yes,' was the answer. 'I moved here recently. I got married.'

We introduced ourselves, and my new acquaintance told me her story – not suspecting that the story had only just begun, and allowed no predictions about the future. Mara had come to Moscow in order to study at the University, but she had not passed the entrance exam. Since she had no reason to return to her Baltic home town, where her parents were getting a divorce, she had chosen to stay in Moscow, where she had begun working as an unskilled temporary worker in construction. Soon the superintendent had noticed her and made her a timekeeper. This very same superintendent had recently proposed to her and she had accepted, although he was fifteen years older. No, he had never been married before; his passport turned out to be clean. He had a separate apartment which he had inherited after the death of his mother, and he had remained a bachelor for so long only because he had been waiting for a girl like her, Mara – that is, for the girl of his dreams.

'And you know, he won't allow me to work. He feels that a man his age must be able to support his wife; he's a little ashamed, because he's older than I. You know, he calls himself "old man" – joking, of course! How can you be an old man at thirty-four? Nonsense, isn't it?'

'Of course,' I agreed.

'And now I sit at home, and don't have to get up any more at dawn and race off to work at eight. I don't live in a dormitory but in my own apartment. It's hard to believe.'

'Yes, at your age one wants to sleep a little longer,' I asserted.

'After my husband's gone to work I can stay in bed till noon, if I want to. It's quiet in the apartment; I get up slowly and prepare myself something in the kitchen . . . .'

'Not bad at all,' I remarked. 'You arranged yourself quite nicely.'

Embarrassed, she glanced at me, lowered her eyes, and said quietly, 'You know, it was tough working in construction. My arms hurt, and the barrow with the cement was so heavy I kept dropping it. It was so heavy, and my arms hurt.'

'Good heavens! Don't think I'm condemning you, my dear!' I said, and now it was my turn to be confused. 'I worked in a library for the blind for many years, until my retirement; I didn't need to haul barrows with cement. But you know what I learned through my work? Caution. Before I form an opinion about someone else, I always try to imagine myself in the other person's place. And I also learned to read with my fingers, and gradually I've read that way – I mean by touch – lots of good books which have taught me all sorts of things.'

'But you have normal eyes; why did you have to read with your fingers?' Mara asked, amazed.

'Yes, I do have normal eyes,' I answered. 'And I could have read normal books. But one day I felt ashamed handing out books which weren't real books. I just couldn't accept those fat bricks as genuine books. I felt like a fraud who didn't really hand out Chekhov or, let's say, Dostoevsky. And then I decided to learn braille. It wasn't easy, I tell you, but I have no regrets. I reread everything I'd read before, and, if you read Chekhov with your fingers, he's quite different, at least to me.'

'What's he like? Another Chekhov?'

'He's terribly sad.'

'How interesting! I'd also like to read that way.'

'I can teach you, if you want,' I said, smiling.

I looked at her that moment and admired her face. It was ravishing. Under her delicate skin one could intimate her bright-red blood, which easily blazed up at moments of confusion or joy.

From then on we often met at the playground, took long walks together, visited the brown bear, and the sad monkey and the other poor animals kept in the park's little zoo and fed them through the fence. Soon I knew aspects of Mara's married life.

She complained that her husband, in spite of his goodness, had turned out to be quite attached to his money. He demanded that she keep a book on her expenses into which she even had to enter such trifles as money spent on movies or flowers. Having to account for flowers depressed her particularly.

'Because I bought the flowers for him! So that the apartment would look nice! But he scolded me; he said he could certainly do without this "hay". He said "hay" – can you believe it? Once I asked him, why don't we ever visit your friends? Don't you have any? And he answered, you don't understand life. Be glad we don't have friends with whom we have to drink vodka. Let's go to the Borodino Panorama.* But we've already been there three times. It just happens that it's close to our place.'

And her only entertainment was the movies, Mara complained. 'Well, once we went to see the Ostankino TV Tower,' she added sadly. 'From there you have a view over all of Moscow. And from the top the people and cars are like little insects.'

We approached my favorite meadow, where the two ponies – Bee and Baby, mother and daughter – stood motionless, dozing, far away from each other. On the other side of the fence, on the sports field of the Suvorov Academy, we saw the students, who had taken off their belts and were doing gymnastics with selfless devotion as if they had entirely forgotten their girlfriends behind the iron fence.

Windy, cold November days began. Sometimes it snowed; then it rained. The trees in the park stood black, their trunks wet, and damp leaves clung to the benches. My leg ached and I rarely managed to get to the park. My walks with Mara stopped and I lost track of her for a long time.

It was almost New Year when I ran into her again, as I was leaving a bakery, and Mara walked me home. She took my arm and the shopping-bag with the bread. By her look I could tell that she was very happy about our encounter. Her face was flushed. The beautiful blonde curls that spilled out from under her shaggy cap lay scattered over her collar. She struck me as more grown-up than before.

'Well, how are you doing, Mara?' I asked her gaily (it was such a pleasure for me to look at her). 'What's new?'

'We're quarreling a good deal,' she said, smiling.

'Over what?'

'I'd like to find a good job, and he won't let me.'

'And why not?'

'He's jealous! Can you believe it? At work the men are going to be after me, he thinks.'

'Good gracious, how silly!'

And Mara told me that, to ease her boredom at home, her husband had allowed her to join dressmaking classes. Now every evening he'd pick her up, regular as clockwork, at Taganka Place, in front of the house where the classes were held.

'What about the expense? Didn't he mind about the money?' I teased her.

'No, what do you mean?' Mara said, embarrassed. 'Anyway, we had a talk about it. You know, he told me what's behind it. During the war his mother raised the children by herself – five of them, imagine. My husband was the eldest and he had it tougher than the others. They nearly starved, and he even went begging to the neighboring villages. And the bits of bread which he collected in those days now have this effect. He says that all he wants is to live normally; he has starved enough for a lifetime. And you know, I can understand him very well.'

'It's not hard to understand! I'm glad you had a good talk with each other.'

'And do you know what else he's done?'

In a fit of generosity he had replaced the old television with a color TV, so that his pretty wife wouldn't be bored at home. He had also started to go skating with her to the Fili Park rink and he had turned out to be a great ice-skater.

'So, all in all, we're doing all right.'

'Well thank goodness!' I rejoiced.

'But I'm going to get a job anyway,' Mara declared. 'He won't talk me out of that. I'll break him down!'

Without noticing it, we had walked all the way to my house. There, at the entrance, Mara kissed me goodbye, wished me the very, very best for the New Year, and dashed off to do her own errands.

As usual, I met the New Year* without much fuss. For a long time I have done without a tree, which I would have had to put up in some corner, certainly on some cotton snow, and to decorate with colorful glass trinkets, just to throw it out a little later. Nor do I need the gay company of champagne-drinking friends, among whom I would look like a grandma. No, no, I prefer to imagine that I'm young, and to drink a glass of kefir* when the chimes ring, welcoming the New Year so that I can sleep soundly.

But this year, when I sat in front of the TV waiting for the Government's New Year address, I suddenly felt the invisible presence of the fragrant young being with the golden locks – angel-like – who had kissed me the day before at the entrance, gently embracing my shoulder with one hand and handing me my old reddish-brown shopping-bag with the other.

New Year receded into the past, and in spring I had to go to the hospital. I felt very ill and was away for almost two months. At the beginning of May I was discharged. One day soon after I had returned home, I was limping along the street, carrying a bottle of kefir* in my shopping-bag, when Mara caught up with me. She wore an elegant leather coat and a large flat cloth cap with a peak.

May was still cool, the buds on the poplars along the street had just burst open, and the branches had plumed themselves with small glossy, reddish-green leaves. Mara's hair, shining in the sun, her red cheeks, and even her silly cap were in perfect harmony with the dizzy enchantment of spring, but her eyes were gloomy, something I had never noticed before.

'I think I'm trapped, and I have no idea what I should do,' she told me when I asked if anything was wrong. 'You know, I'm pregnant.'

'What's wrong with that?' I exclaimed, astonished. 'You're married, so what's wrong? You'll have a baby! A boy or a girl!'

'No, I can't!' she said quietly, and her big blue eyes, as they looked at the tops of the poplars, filled with tears.

'Mara, dear, please tell me exactly what happened!' I said, disturbed.

'I can't have a baby,' she answered, 'because I want to leave him. He's so primitive; I can't live with him any longer. Imagine, once when I was ironing I looked away for a moment and singed his shirt. For a whole week afterwards he didn't say a word to me, as if I had mortally insulted him. The other day I said to him, "What do you actually want? Do you expect me to stay with you, locked up in this cage until the end of my days, watching your possessions?" You know what he answered? "That's how it's going to be. But it's a cage with a TV, a color TV!" That shows you what he's like.' Mara ended her story. 'And I wanted to ask you. . . . I don't really have any good friends here apart from you. Don't you know a private doctor? I'm already over the limit; I think I'm probably in my third month.'

'I don't know such a doctor,' I answered. 'And you shouldn't do it, Mara. You loved your husband. You must keep your baby.'

'You're a good person, but you're trying in vain. You've thought too well of me,' Mara conjectured sadly. 'For a long time I tried to convince myself that I had married him out of love. But there's a limit to every lie. And you're a clever woman, you understand everything. And you understood it from the outset.'

'No, I didn't,' I objected quietly. 'I still think that you did love him.'

'You're wrong,' she almost whispered, trying hard not to break into tears. Then she recovered her composure, and more firmly she said, 'The problem is not whether he's a good or a bad person. The problem is me, the problem is that I am the way I am, and my life had such a beginning, and now it's too late to make any changes. What am I to do?' she cried out quietly. 'Just what? When I dream . . . . You know, in my dreams I'm always beating him with my fists or with sticks. Can something like this be called love?'

I suddenly felt very bad. My heart started beating violently, like never before, as if it wanted to blow me up from inside. Prickly fireflies flitted before my eyes. But Mara didn't notice anything. She stood before me, quietly crying and wiping her eyes with a kerchief.

'Excuse me please,' I said with difficulty. 'I feel awful. I have to go home. Let's meet tomorrow in the park, all right?' With these words I took my leave, and headed for home.

In my room I closed the curtains tightly, took my medicine and lay down. My heart calmed, but I didn't feel better. And soon, with relentless force, the truth struck which I feared more than anything else.

I took the heavy book of firm yellow paper from the night stand, a volume of Pushkin in braille, closed my eyes and began to read 'Count Nulin',* groping with my fingers: 'It's time, it's time! The horns are sounding . . . .' Slowly and arduously the familiar brisk line penetrated to me from a terrible distance, as if the poet's voice was sounding from behind a mountain. My fingers, as if seized by cramp, were unable to move on along the lines. No, I couldn't read. With a heavy thud the book fell to the floor. The moment of merciless truth would not pass me by.

And then it seemed to me that *nothing had ever happened*. Not my brief marriage, nor the oath I swore to my husband to wait for him after the war – nothing.

And in order to come to terms with my trouble I began to recall mercilessly and carefully what indeed *had* happened.

I had married at eighteen; my husband was nineteen. He was a daredevil and rode a motorcycle. We had been married a little over a month and everything was fine until one day we quarreled. I had started it because I was jealous about something. He turned pale and, hot-headed as he was, he jumped on his motorcycle and tore off. At the first turn he crashed. In the hospital I saw him unconscious, stretched on a board – the spine was injured. The doctor, an older woman, told me there was little chance he'd live, and, if he lived, he would be a cripple. My relatives, in chorus, fell upon me, urging me to leave him, and I, deeply frightened, allowed myself to be convinced. I kept remembering the contortions of his face, when he moaned without opening his eyes. Frightened, I returned to my parents. But he was young and strong and wanted to live. Not only did he live, but after a few months he was well enough to be discharged from the hospital. One arm dangled at his side, lifeless – I saw him from a distance. After a year the arm was fine too, and again he started whizzing past my house on his motorcycle.

Soon came 22 June 1941.* My husband was found fit for the service and was enlisted the very first week of the war. On the day of his departure he came by to take leave. My family were away, and we met as if nothing had happened. In the evening I accompanied him to his meeting-point. And then and there I swore to him that I would wait for him for ever, whatever might happen to him.

And now, at this moment of truth, I ask myself, which feeling predominated during our last meeting – compassion, grief, repentance, presentiment of his imminent death or enormous self-deception? He didn't return from the war, and I remained faithful to my oath. But is that so? Was it faithfulness or constant remorse and pain over my guilt, for which I had been unable to atone? And, if there had been no war, would he have come to me, forgiving everything? And had he really forgiven?

There are no clear answers now to these questions. The war has buried them for ever, and the fate meted out to me is holy faithfulness unto death. I don't know how many such young widows are left with nothing but this faithfulness in their hearts, but I do know that at this point all of them are old women, like me.

Although there are no right answers to these questions, I have my life, as I have lived it, and this very life can be considered an answer. And tomorrow I will tell Mara that for a woman a cage with a TV or disappointment in love isn't the worst fate. Often we invent such 'cages'. Once we've flipped love over to hate in our burning heart, like a pancake on a griddle, we are able to make up things even worse. But the saddest and most terrible fate is when you want to repay a debt, but are unable to. And there comes an age, a time, when some secret dread grips you when you find yourself among children, because not one of them has ever touched your breast with his little hand.

And I will tell Mara about a good woman who never saw a glimmer of light, but married another good, blind man, and both wanted a child but were afraid that it might be blind. And this woman told me, her pockmarked face blushing, that she could *see* this future baby of hers.

And I will also offer her my one-room den – it also has a TV – as a hideaway, if she wants to use it to lie low and find herself.

The next day I went to the park, to my favorite place. But Mara didn't show up on that day nor on any of the following.

The dwarf ponies were at their place, eagerly cropping the fresh May grass with their soft mouths, their muzzles stretched to the ground. And the children kept running up to them.

The Military Academy was evidently getting ready to celebrate the Day of Victory:* through the fence you could see the Suvorov students march, column after column, harmoniously, with uniform strides.

I sit on the warm bench, my hands resting on the knob of my walking-stick, and dream, listening to the monotonous rattle of the passing metro trains. I doze and imagine that time will pass and one day a boy in a red knitted cap will run up to sleepy Bee, and his cap will be as red as a ripe strawberry against green grass. And it will turn out that this boy is Mara's little son to whom she gave birth after having overcome her fear of life. And the three of us will go to the little zoo to look at the unfortunate animals in their cages, and I will take the boy by his hand.

9
Viktoriya Tokareva

Born in Leningrad on 20 November 1937 Viktoriya Samoilovna Tokareva attended the Moscow Institute of Cinematography and graduated from the script department in 1969. As a second-year student in 1964, she published her first story, entitled 'A Day without Lies' ('Den' bez lzhi'). This story made her instantly famous, and marked the beginning of a very successful career. Her stories and novellas, which, as one critic has said, form one big book, have appeared in the following collections: *Stories about What Did Not Happen* (*O tom, chego ne bylo*, 1969), *When It Turned Warmer* (*Kogda stalo nemnozhko teplee*, 1972), *The Swings that Fly* (*Letayushchie kacheli*, 1978) and *Nothing Special* (*Nichego osobennogo*, 1983). Her most recent novella, *A Long Day* (*Dlinnyi den'*), was published in the prestigious literary journal *Novy mir* (1986), no. 2, pp. 79–114).

Tokareva is known not only for her stories and novellas, but also for her thirteen films and the TV adaptations of her works based on her own scripts. Three of her films have won international prizes. Her play *Fantasy-Impromptu* (*Fantaziya èksprompt*), based on motifs from her story 'Raraka', has enjoyed great success on the Moscow stage.

Her stories deal with women searching for happiness – which often means a man to love – and for their identity. Or they portray women as they come to terms with misfortunes, such as losing a husband, or experience an affair and confront tough choices. But tragedy is absent; humor and lightness prevail. In an interview in November 1986 she said that she sees herself as a follower of Chekhov in themes and methods, and builds her stories on the telling details of ordinary life.

Most of Tokareva's stories are realistic, some fantastic, many full of irony. Life-experiences do not crush her heroines, who have the indestructible buoyancy of Chekhov's Dushechka – especially the heroine of the story 'Nothing Particular' (1981) – or the tenaciousness of a dog whose jaws are locked over a juicy bone. They struggle actively; they hang on, whatever happens; and they are able to have some fun on the way. Her stories breathe moderation and optimism, even though lasting love between the sexes seems elusive and a resigned and, at times, cynical accommodation is the norm.

Tokareva does not see herself as belonging to a category called 'woman writers'; to her, the term 'woman's prose' is derogatory, implying absence of focus, triviality, and decorative, over-descriptive prose. She considers herself emancipated – 'unfortunately': 'emancipation has many negative sides, . . . it destroys the family because the woman takes on burdens a man should shoulder'; she equates it with material independence, which she sees as the precondition of further independence. Her purpose in writing is not social criticism, even though it may enter inadvertently, but communicating experiences – many of them personal – in an artistic manner. Her favorites among her own stories are 'The Happiest Day of My Life' and 'The Old Dog' (1979).

Her latest novella, which could only be published, she feels, because of Gorbachev's *glasnost*, is more serious than most of her preceding work. It raises the question of personal ethical responsibility in a context of human and institutional inadequacies, and captures the effect of the double burden and the harsh living conditions on a woman's character and morals. A successful journalist by profession, the heroine is a dominant and pushy, and at the same time attractive and manipulative, female – a 'tank sprinkled with flowers', Botticelli's 'Spring' with 'iron armor showing under fragile green and rosiness'. These traits are mustered against the male world: the inaccessible surgeon whom she wants to treat her sick child, her helpless and boring husband and her preoccupied boss. Using her profession to gain entry to the doctor, she craftily provokes his male interest in her, uses it for her own purposes – typically, her child comes first – and leaves him cheated, and herself too: he is one of the few men she comes to admire and feels drawn towards. She is not an attractive character: purposeful role-playing and manipulation have extinguished genuineness and altruism. Nor is the doctor a conventional 'male chauvinist'. Her only genuine feelings are her love for her daughter, and her guilt at neglecting her to carry on an affair. Her life is filled with the pursuit of material necessities. The ending is happy, yet the aftertaste of sordidness is strong.

'The Happiest Day of My Life' ('Samy schastlivy den') appeared in *Novy mir*, 1980, no. 2, and 'Between Heaven and Earth' ('Mezhdu nebom i zemlyoi') in *Novy mir*, 1985, no. 3.

WORKS IN ENGLISH

'Sidesteps', *Soviet Literature*, 1986, no. 6, pp. 184–8.

There is no secondary literature in English.

The Happiest Day of My Life
(The Story of a Precocious Girl)
(1980)

We had to write an essay in class on the topic 'The Happiest Day of My Life'.

I opened my notebook and started thinking. What *was* the happiest day of my life? A Sunday four months ago came to my mind, when Dad and I saw a matinee and then went to visit Grandma – two fun things on the same day. But our teacher, Maria Yefremovna, says that a person is truly happy only when helping others. And how had I helped others by going to the movies and visiting Grandma? I could simply have ignored Maria Yefremovna's opinion, but I needed to improve my grade for the term. If I got a 'C', they wouldn't let me go on to the next year and I'd be sent to a vocational school. Maria Yefremovna warned us that our country has a big surplus of intelligentsia and a deficit of the working class, and that therefore we would be made into a reserve of qualified labor.

I glanced at my neighbor Lenka's notebook. She was scribbling away with unbelievable speed and energy. Her happiest day was when she was made a Young Pioneer.

I thought about the day when we became Pioneers. We were in the Border Guards' Museum, and I didn't get a Pioneer's badge. Our sponsors and the leaders ran around looking for badges, but they couldn't find any. I told them that it didn't matter, that it was quite all right, but my mood was spoiled and my mind started wandering. They took us around the Museum and told us about its history, but I don't remember anything except that at one point we were dividing some river with the Japanese and got into a fight. But it didn't come to war. Or maybe I'm mixed up. I have a hard time remembering that sort of thing. It's totally boring.

Once Mom and I helped a drunk home. He'd lost a boot and was sitting in the snow with just his sock on. Mom said we couldn't leave him in the street, because maybe something terrible had happened to him. We asked him where he lived and took him home. This was obviously helping others, because the man ended up sleeping at home and not in a snowdrift, and his family didn't have to worry. But I wouldn't call that my happiest day. We took him home, and that was that.

I turned to my right and glanced at Mashka's notebook. She sits in front of me. I couldn't make anything out, but she was probably writing that her happiest day was when they got a replacement for their defective particle-accelerator, which had exploded. Mashka's crazy about diagrams and formulas. She has a knack for math, and already knows where she's going to study later. She's found a meaning in life. But all I've got is an enormous vocabulary, as Maria Yefremovna says, and I am good at using it. That's why in music school I get chosen to read out reports about the life and work of composers. The music-teacher writes them, and I read them aloud. For example: 'Beethoven was a plebeian, but everything he achieved in his life was due to his own labor . . . .' And at concerts I make announcements. For example: 'Katya Shubina from Mr Rossolovsky's class will perform a sonatina by Clementi.' This sounds very impressive because I'm tall, look pale like a true intellectual, and wear brand-name clothes. The clothes and complexion I get from Mom, and the height from who knows where. I read somewhere that the walls of the modern prefab apartments don't allow the air to circulate; so they're like greenhouses and that's why children grow like greenhouse cucumbers.

Mashka Gvozdeva will certainly become a member of the intelligentsia, because her brains are more helpful to society than her hands. But I don't have brains or skilled hands, just my big vocabulary. That's not even literary ability. I just know lots of words because I read a lot. I get this from my Dad. But you don't need to know a lot of words. The boys in our class get along perfectly well with six: cool, mellow, right on, dynamite, O.K., man. And Lenka Konovalova supports any conversation with two phrases: 'That's true in general . . .' and 'Well, in general of course . . .'. And this is perfectly adequate. First of all, she gives the other person a chance to speak, which is always pleasant. Second, she supports the other person's opinion: 'That's true in general . . .', 'Well, in general of course . . .'.

Last week I listened to a radio program on happiness. It said that happiness is when you want something and get it. And great happiness is when you really want something and get it. Of course, once you've got it your happiness is gone, because happiness comes from trying to realize your wish, and not from actually realizing it.

What do I want? I want to get into ninth grade, and I want a real suede coat instead of my fur coat. It's too big for me, and it makes me feel boxed in. In our cloakroom, though, the boys slash holes in our coat sleeves with razor-blades and cut the buttons off. So it's risky to wear a suede coat to school, but where else do I go?

And what do I really want? I really want to stay on for another year, go to Moscow State University and study humanities, and meet K.K. the actor. Mom says that at my age girls usually fall in love with actors. Twenty years ago she was also in love with an actor, insanely in love – the entire class was crazy about him. And now he's as fat as a pig. It boggles the mind to think what time does to people.

But Mom doesn't understand me. I'm not in love with K.K. at all. It's just that he plays d'Artagnan, and he plays him so outrageously that K.K. seems to *be* d'Artagnan: talented, unpredictable, romantic. Not like our boys, who are two centimeters shorter than I and eternally repeat their 'exactly', 'that's normal'.

I've seen *The Three Musketeers* six times. Rita Pogosyan has seen it ten. Her mother works at the Hotel Minsk and can always get tickets, not like my parents. They can't get anything: they don't have any special privileges; they just live on their income.

Once Rita and I waited for K.K. after the show. We followed him into the metro and started to look him up and down. When he looked in our direction, we immediately glanced away and giggled. Rita found out through friends that K.K. is married and has a little son. I'm glad that it's a son and not a daughter because girls get more love; less affection is wasted on boys, and that way a part of their soul remains free for some other love. Of course, there's a big age difference between K.K. and me – twenty years. In five years I'll be eighteen, and he'll be thirty-eight. But that's his problem. Youth has never stopped anyone.

Rita said that K.K. is a careerist. In America people shoot

presidents to make careers. So what? Of course, I don't mean 'so what'; but at least people here don't yet do such things to make a career. I'm not sure if this is a good thing or a bad thing. My Dad, for example, isn't a careerist, but I've never seen anything like great happiness in his face. He has no ambition and gets just a small salary. But what you earn shows how much adults value you. Recently I gave a report about the political situation in Honduras to our class. I mean, really, what do I care about Honduras, and Honduras about me? But Maria Yefremovna said that apolitical students won't make it into the ninth grade. So I prepared like a good girl and 'carried out politinformation'. Why should I take any risks because of Honduras?

Lenka Konovalova turned the page. She had already filled up half her notebook. And I was still sitting there, sifting through my memory for my happiest day.

I remembered a phrase from the radio program on happiness: 'The prospect of sleepless nights behind the steering-control of the combine . . . .'' Maybe the combine-operator was also a careerist.

If I were honest, my happiest days are, on the whole, when I come home from school and nobody's home. I love my Mom. She doesn't pressure me; she doesn't force me to take music lessons and always have bread with everything I eat.[1] When she's around I can do just what I do when she's not. But it still isn't the same. For example, she's terribly careless when she puts the needle on the record and it makes a deafening crackle. It feels like a needle's scraping my heart. When I ask her, 'Can't you put the needle on properly?' she answers, 'I put it on properly.' This happens every time.

When she isn't at home, there's a note on the door: 'The key's under the mat, food's on the stove. I'll be back at six, you little nut. Love, Mom.'

I read in the paper that Moscow has the lowest crime rates in the world. That's true. My own experience has brought me to the same conclusion. If the most stupid, amateurish thief or even just a curious person with bad inclinations happened to pass by our door and read Mom's note, he'd get exact instructions: the key's

---

1. This is a reference to the bad times after the Second World War, when it was a blessing just to have bread, let alone anything to put on it. Often people who remember those years consider it sinful to eat something you normally put on bread – ham, cheese, etc. – without bread itself.

under the mat. Open the door and go in. The food's on the stove. Heat it up and eat. The owners will return at six. He wouldn't need to hurry and he could even take a rest in the armchair, with the newspaper. And around six he could leave, with Dad's jeans and leather jacket and with Mom's suede coat, trimmed with Alaskan wolf. There aren't any other valuables in the house, because we're members of the intelligentsia and only have our salaries to live on.

Mom said that, when a person is afraid of being robbed, he will definitely be robbed. Whatever you fear most is bound to happen – that's how it is in life. Therefore one should never be afraid. It's true. If I'm afraid of being called on, I will definitely be called on.

When I step out of the elevator and see the note I'm overjoyed because I can do exactly as I please, without having to worry about anyone else. I go into the apartment, and I eat the food cold, standing up, right out of the pan. I use my fingers, and I don't even take my fur coat off. It tastes much better cold. The heat takes the flavor away.

Then I turn the record-player on full blast and invite Lenka Konovalova over. The two of us take all of Mom's clothes out of the wardrobe and start trying them on and dancing. We dance in long dresses, as the band Blue Bird wails, 'Don't get upset with me, don't get upset, and do not pity me, and do not call, for I won't fall for you, not fall at all.' And the sun beats against the window.

Then Lenka leaves. I sit in the armchair, wrap myself in a blanket and read. I'm reading two books right now: some stories by Julio Cortazar and plays by Aleksandr Vampilov. Mom got these books from her subordinates.

I really like some of Vampilov's lines: for example, 'Dad, a visitor came by, and another visitor.' And the Dad answers, 'Vasenka, one visitor and another visitor, that's two visitors.' I read and see K.K. before me, and I get sad because, after all, he's married and there's a big age difference between us.

Cortazar's story 'The End of the Game' contains the words 'indescribably beautiful'. They affect me so much that I lift my eyes from the page and start thinking. Sometimes just being alive is indescribably beautiful. But sometimes everything becomes boring and I ask Mom: 'Why do people live?' She answers, 'To suffer. Suffering is the norm.' But Dad says, 'That's the norm for fools. Man's created for happiness.' Mom answers, 'You forgot to add "like a bird's created for flying". And you could also add, "pity humiliates man". Dad replies, 'Of course it humiliates, because only fools rely on pity. Clever people rely on themselves.' But Mom says that pity is compassion, empathy for suffering, and the world hinges on it: being compassionate is a talent many lack, even clever people.

But they rarely fight, because they rarely see each other. When Dad's home at night, Mom isn't. And *vice versa*. If Mom's gone, Dad reads the newspaper and watches hockey on TV. (We had a nanny who didn't say 'hockey' but 'phockey'.) After hockey and the newspaper Dad asks me for my school diary and begins to shout at me as if I were deaf or he were at the neighbors' and wanted me to understand him through the wall. For some reason, when Dad shouts at me I'm not at all afraid. I just don't understand him as well. I feel like saying, 'Please don't shout. Just speak normally.' But I say nothing and just blink.

Sometimes Mom gets back pretty late, but still before Dad does. She sees that his leather coat isn't on the coatrack and is absolutely overjoyed. She quickly gets into her pajamas, and we start dancing on the rug, in the middle of the room, kicking our legs like idiots, both in our pajamas and barefoot. Mom's pajamas have a diamond pattern, mine have dots. We have lots of fun, and we pretend to shout with our mouths wide open, but actually only whisper, and it is indescribably beautiful.

When Mom has her days off to go to the library and she spends the time at home preparing the food for the next few days, and Dad isn't home till late, she comes into my room, forgetting that I should sleep and not talk, and she starts draining me, sucking me dry: 'I think he's left us.'

I answer, 'But how about the leather jacket and the jeans? He wouldn't leave without them.'

'But he could pick them up later.'

'That's stupid,' I say. 'He can't hide from me anywhere.'

But I get frightened, and my stomach starts rumbling and my nose begins to itch. I can't imagine life without Dad. I'd sink to only 'C's and 'D's. I'd drop out of school and disintegrate. The only reason I get good grades is because of Dad, so that he'll be pleased. I'd be happy with 'C's. Mom would be, too. She argues like this: a 'C' means satisfactory; it means that the state is satisfied.

'I'm going to get divorced,' Mom says.

'Why?'

'He doesn't help me. I earn money myself. I stand in the lines and I drag home the shopping-bags.'

'Was it different before?'

'No. It was always like that.'

'So why didn't you get divorced before, ten years ago?'

'I wanted to give you a proper childhood.'

'You mean, when I was small and understood nothing, you gave me a proper childhood. But now that I'm grown up you want to deprive me of someone I love. That's unfair!'

'Well, that's how it is.'

'No that's not how it is. In that case, I won't take you into account either.'

'You've got your whole life ahead of you. I just want some happiness.'

I don't understand how a person of thirty-five, married and with a child, could still want some other happiness. But it wouldn't be diplomatic to say that. So I answer, 'And where do you see people who are 100 per cent happy? Aunt Nina is five years younger than you and weighs ten kilos less. But she's unmarried and has to take two kinds of public transportation to get to work – an hour and a half each way. And to make her living she works at some chemical-machine construction outfit. But you work across the street, love what you do, and everybody adores you. You've got your place in life. That's 50 per cent. And I've turned out well. I'm healthy and intelligent. That's another 45 per cent. You aren't ill: that's an additional 1 per cent. Now you've got already 96 per cent happiness – only 4 per cent short. And where have you seen people who are 100 per cent happy? Just name one.'

Mom's silent. She's trying to think of someone. And, indeed, nobody is 100 per cent happy. 'Everybody has his cross to bear.' Or as I read somewhere, 'Everyone has a skeleton in the cupboard.' But that doesn't comfort Mom. She wants the missing 4 per cent, instead of the first 50. She sits on my bed, trembling like an orphan. I tell her, 'Lie down beside me. That'll make you fall asleep.'

She crawls under my blanket. Her feet are cold, and she puts them against my legs, egoist that she is. But I can bear it. One of her tears falls on my eye. I can bear that too. I love her very much. I love her so much that everything inside me aches. But I know that if I start pitying her, she'll let go even more. So I say, 'You should go and look at yourself in the mirror by daylight. Who needs you besides me and Dad? You've got to live for us.'

Actually, I feel that a person has to be an egoist. A careerist and an egoist. So that he'll feel good. Because when he feels good those around him also feel good. If someone feels bad, everyone else gets gloomy. It just doesn't happen that when a person is burning on a stake his friends sing and dance around him.

I hear the scrape of a key in the lock – it's Dad. He always unlocks the door carefully, so that we won't wake up. He tiptoes to the hall and stands there for a while, probably undressing. Then he tiptoes to his room, the floorboards squeaking guiltily. Grandma once said that Dad hasn't found himself. When he tiptoes I think he's looking for himself, glancing in every corner, without turning on the light. And I feel very sorry for him. And suddenly I think that I won't find myself till I'm forty and won't know what to do with myself.

Mom calms down after she's heard Dad's steps and falls asleep on my shoulder, breathing on my cheek. I hug her and hold her like a treasure. I lie there thinking, if only she'd put on weight faster. If only my parents would get older and put on weight, because who would need them then, old and fat? They'd need only each other. And I would need them. But now they walk around like thin sausages stuffed into jeans. Sometimes it seems as though each of them has one leg that's buried, and with the other they're running in opposite directions. But where can you run with a buried leg?

By the way, Lenka's Mom doesn't have a husband at all. She's got three children, all by different fathers, a blind granny, two cats and a puppy. But their place is noisy, messy and jolly. Maybe it's because Lenka's Mom has no time to worry over the next bridge she'll have to cross. When you have free time you start thinking. And, if you start thinking, you'll definitely come up with a reason to worry.

Once, last year, a little boy got run over by a car in front of our house. Everybody ran out to look, but I ran home. I was terribly scared, not for myself but for my parents. Even now I'm worried. What if something happens to me, what if I get run over or grow up and get married? With whom would I leave my parents? What would they do without me?

Zagoruiko went up to Maria Efremovna and handed in his notebook. His happiest day will probably be when the Beatles get back together. Zagoruiko knows all the modern foreign bands: Kiss, Queen, Bony M. All I know is that Beethoven was a plebeian, and I can sightread a serenade by Schumann, and I can do a few things by ear.

I looked at my watch. Sixteen minutes left. There's no more time to think, I told myself, or else I'll get a 'D' and won't be able to stay at school, which means I'll become a lathe-operator with special training or a seamstress. A seamstress with a large vocabulary.

I decided to describe how we planted trees around the school. I read somewhere that everyone, before they die, should plant a tree, give birth to a child and write a book about the times in which he lived.

I remembered how I lugged a bucket full of black soil to the hole so that the tree would take better root. Zagoruiko came up and said, 'Hey, let me help.'

'I'm fine,' I said, refusing, and continued lugging the bucket. Then I poured the soil in the hole and looked at my palms. The bucket handle had left deep purple impressions. My shoulders and even my bowels hurt.

'I'm exhausted,' I said to the others with tragic dignity.

'I knew it!' Zagoruiko said spitefully. 'First she pretends she can't do it, and now she's going to boast.'

Zagoruiko is disgusting. He says exactly what he thinks even though you should be brought up to hide your true feelings when they are out of place.

Despite all this, the tree took root and will be around for future generations. For content, Maria Yefremovna would give me an 'A'. And I hardly ever make mistakes; I'm a born speller.

I looked at my watch again. I had eleven minutes left. I shook my fountain pen – I didn't have a ballpoint pen – and started writing about the day when Dad and I went to the matinee and then visited Grandma. I don't care what grade Maria Yefremovna gives me. I won't become an egoist or a careerist. I'll live without special privileges.

I wrote that the movie, a comedy, was terribly funny. Louis de Funesse played the lead, and we laughed so much that people turned around to look at us, and somebody tapped my back with an index finger, as if it were a door. And at Grandma's it was always like this. We sat in the kitchen and ate delicious fish (although Mom says that Grandma's fish is unsalted and smells of ammonia as if it has been soaked in urine). But the food's not what matters. It's the atmosphere. Everybody liked me and openly admired me, and I liked everybody 100 per cent and this is how I helped others.

I have Dad's eyes, and Dad has Grandma's; they're brown with eyebrows like roofs. We looked at each other with the same eyes and felt the same. And we were like a tree: Grandma the root, Dad the stem, and I the branches reaching to the sun.

And this was indescribably beautiful.

Of course, this was not the happiest day in my life. It was just a happy day. The happiest day hasn't come yet. It is still before me.

Between Heaven and Earth
(1985)

Natasha sat in the airport, waiting for an announcement about her flight. The flight had been postponed repeatedly, first by three and then by four hours. A Bulgarian circus on its way to Baku was waiting for the same plane. The circus people settled down on the floor and in chairs, gipsy-style, and Bolognese dogs, all of the same age and size, freshly washed and combed, kept running circles around them. The circus must have had a music-hall number for dogs on its program.

A tall man walked past Natasha. Something about him reminded her remotely of her first husband. As there was so much time, and she had nothing to do or think about, Natasha recalled her first marriage. Otherwise she wouldn't have thought of it.

They had married when she was eighteen and he twenty-two, and they had separated right away – well, not exactly right away. After all, they had spent eight months together. Their marriage turned out to be unstable. As soon as their passion had subsided, the river of their marriage became shallow, and its bottom, with all sorts of old cans and bottles, with all its trivial trash, became visible. They started arguing with each other, incessantly and over nothing. Their love became frail and ailing, their incompatibilities torturing them like a persistent cough, and finally it died. But, even after they had been separated, they continued to see each other and to argue for a long time. Unable to stay together, they also couldn't manage to be apart. The substance of their fights was that Natasha considered her husband a fool who was no match for her beauty. She felt that beauty entitled a person to additional privileges in life, such as a ticket for a New Year's party. Her husband responded that beauty was an ephemeral phenomenon, gone in twenty years – goodbye, good looks – while his ability to have a lasting emotion, to be faithful, was permanent. It wouldn't devalue with time, so he was a husband who would grow on her. Right now he wasn't quite perfect, but later he'd be just what she wanted. At eighteen, though, it is impossible to think about later. Life seems very long; everything seems to be ahead and available in abundance.

They parted and met again twenty years later. He had married a second time, had a daughter named after her, and lived in another town. Natasha happened to go there on business. Informed that her ex-husband lived somewhere in the vicinity, she phoned 09, gave his name, received his number and dialed. For the first time in twenty years she heard his voice. It was unchanged: the voice is an instrument of the soul, and the soul doesn't age. They spoke with their former voices.

Natasha had said, 'Hello! Don't be surprised.'

And he, guardedly, 'Who's speaking?'

'It's your wife number one.'

After this sentence a pause of such length ensued that Natasha thought they had become disconnected.

'Hello!' she called.

'I'll be there right away,' her ex-husband said. 'Where are you?'

She gave him the name of her hotel and her room number.

After she had hung up, she was overcome with nervousness. Why had she telephoned, why had she invited him there? It was puzzling.

She put on her white French blouse. Then she changed her mind and chose a black one instead, which was more flattering to her figure, but less so to her complexion. It was a choice between figure and complexion.

Sooner than she had expected there was a knock on the door. She opened, and there he was. He had gained some weight in those twenty years, but his expression, his essential self, had remained the same, and this self gazed, unconcealed, out of his big greenish-gray eyes.

'How you've changed . . .,' he said nodding, as if wanting to confirm his prediction. In those twenty years, as he had warned her so honestly, her beauty had vanished like a station seen for a moment from a train.

'And you're the same as ever,' Natasha answered, clearly implying that he was still the fool he had always been.

Natasha had indeed changed. If one were to make a comparison in terms of nature, Natasha's beauty twenty years ago was that of a meadow, while now it was that of a field. But who knows what's better, a meadow or a field?

Something else was surprising: they started arguing at the very point where they had left off twenty years ago, as if all those years had vanished and they had parted only yesterday.

Then they went down to the restaurant for supper. They drank wine. He told her how long it had taken him to get over their separation and how painful it had been. He had married again because he was afraid of becoming an alcoholic.

'Well, you're over it now,' Natasha said soothingly, in an attempt to change the unpleasant topic and emphasize that the pain was behind him, that it was all in the past.

'But I lived through hell . . . .' He stressed 'lived through hell', insisting on the long stretch of life he had wasted in suffering.

'Suffering's good for you,' Natasha said, trying to justify herself. 'It molds the soul.'

'Nonsense,' he disagreed. 'I don't remember who said it, but "happiness is your university". Suffering dries out the soul, and drought doesn't produce any decent growth, just all sorts of weeds – bitterness, for example.'

He certainly had been capable of a lasting emotion. At first he had loved her. Then he had hated her. But there was no forgiving: she was a part of him for ever.

They continued drinking. Natasha told him about her dissertation. She had studied the genetic code of the tiny drosophila flies. Drosophilas were flies that loved fruit. Swarming over fruit, they looked more like dust than living organisms. She interbred them, studied them and came to significant conclusions that affected all mankind.

He told her that after his general medical training he had specialized in dental prosthetics. He had beautiful porcelain from abroad, and he was in such demand that it was physically impossible for him to keep up with it. He said all this to let her know that he had money to burn now and that Natasha had been too impatient twenty years ago. Now he had caught up with her expectations.

'Are you married?'

'Yes,' Natasha lied. She was married, but not legally.

'Do you deceive your husband?'

This was a crucial question. Faithfulness was his main expectation from a woman, and, if Natasha lived up to it, his loss would be immeasurable.

'You should be ashamed!' Natasha said, feigning surprise.

'Well, do you or don't you?'

'Never!'

He became visibly unnerved and dejected. All the emotions that had settled down in the course of his life welled up again from the bottom of his soul, as if someone had stirred the bottom of a pond and dragged its slime to the surface.

Later they said goodbye, for another twenty years, certainly. The town in which he lived and worked was small, and business trips there were rare. But that wasn't the point. The point was that they were of no use to each other.

When Natasha had separated from her husband she had expected to marry soon after, thinking that she only needed to step outside and shout, 'I want to marry!' and instantly crowds would turn up and stand in a long line. But her self-confidence was naïve. Everybody is busy searching for happiness, and only very few – maybe a dozen, maybe even a hundred – find it. But what is a hundred compared to all humanity? In due course, though, Natasha managed to become one of the hundred, or even one of the dozen. She fell in love with Kitaev, a professor of biochemistry who had come up with fourteen brilliant discoveries and hypotheses about the age of the Earth. Instead of brains he seemed to have a high-voltage electric power-station in his head that generated ideas and infected everyone around. A typical genius, he generously scattered his ideas right and left, like the goose that doesn't hover over every golden egg it lays, knowing the next egg will also be of gold.

Kitaev was bald, sallow and shriveled up like an old woman. But Natasha didn't notice. She had already had a handsome man. And she had her own picture of Kitaev. In comparison, all other men seemed pale and indistinct – like a tenth carbon copy.

For a long time Kitaev couldn't believe that Natasha loved him. Later he came around, and over the years he got used to her, just as if she had been his wife, although actually she was not. He already had a wife. But for some reason this other woman was no obstacle and, as Natasha made no demands, nothing needed changing. Kitaev's golden brains were ever changing and shifting, but external changes were anathema to him.

So deeply had they sunk their roots into one another that Natasha sometimes was absolutely certain he'd propose to her the next day. But sometimes she felt it would never happen. She could have stopped the guessing-game and asked directly. But questions – words in general – were so specific and concrete, while love, like music, had to remain in a realm beyond words, and certainly in the realm beyond questions.

This morning Kitaev had telephoned from Baku, where he was attending a symposium of African and Asian nations. When he had asked her to join him for a few days, she didn't ask why; she knew perfectly well that he missed her. He couldn't live through the remaining days without her. But nine hours of these two days had already been stolen. She sat at the airport in Moscow, he at the airport in Baku, condemned to inaction and waiting, and he probably was already regretting that he'd initiated this forced march from Moscow.

A metallic voice announced that the flight was ready for boarding. The acrobats got in motion, and the dogs yapped cheerfully as if they had understood the announcement and were pleased.

Natasha fastened her seatbelt. Fear and the take-off were making her nauseous.

The plane rose unevenly; it kept sinking down, and each time it slumped her heart leapt to her throat in anticipation of the end. It wasn't so much the end she feared as the eternity that came before it, the endless thirty seconds of complete consciousness of what was happening. Natasha had a distant relative by the name of Valik who had been buried alive in the mines. 40 tons of debris had fallen on him, and it took many truckloads to dig him out. When they finally got to him, his eyebrows were white, although he was a young man. For some time – perhaps thirty, perhaps sixty seconds – he must have lived in full awareness of what had happened. His wife Nadka had thrown herself on his coffin with the unfeigned raving of despair, like the great Italian actress Anna Magnani. In the South, funerals are a sort of spectacle, a catharsis, a purification in which you pour out all your despair and your protest against fate. Infected, the other people also wail and pour out their grief to unburden their souls and go on living. Nadka threw herself on the coffin and had to be pulled away; a photographer eternalized these moments. Yet a week later some Petko spent the night with her. It turned out that he had already had a place in her heart when the husband was still alive, and they had barely been able to wait even a week. The neighbors were appalled, and the phrase 'His body wasn't even cold yet', meaning Valik's body, was circulating in the neighborhood. But it was his mother-in-law, Nadka's mother, who was most disturbed by her daughter's betrayal. She came to their home and questioned Nadka's teenage daughter. 'Did he spend the night here?' 'Yes,' the girl answered glumly. 'In the bed?' Nadka's mother asked apprehensively. 'Where else?' the girl replied, puzzled. 'D'you think he was under the bed?' Nadka's mother started crying and wringing her hands. 'But he was here, he *was*, and she acts as if he'd never existed.' Nadka's mother couldn't get over the fact that her daughter behaved as if Valik had never existed, and this instant forgetfulness frightened her more than anything else. It was as if Valik had been buried under the debris twice. Once when he was alive, and once again when he was dead.

Natasha was afraid this would happen to her, too. She knew that people who are alive think about living people. If she were to crash with the plane, Kitaev wouldn't forget her, but would remove her to the far recesses of his memory, and – look into someone else's eyes. Being forgotten was a second death.

The plane had gained its cruising altitude. Natasha let her seat back and closed her eyes. The plane was no longer ascending. Her heart stopped hammering in her throat. She decided to see what was happening below and around her.

Everyone around her was asleep. The large number of sleeping men reminded her of Vereshchagin's painting *The Field after the Battle.**

Next to her sat a young man – a basketball-player, judging by his looks. He was one and a half heads taller than Natasha, who was rather tall herself. She peered outside and saw a fire flaring up from under the wing against the darkness of the sky.

A stupor fell over her, and only one word kept resounding in this stupor as if it were on a tape playing in her empty head: 'unpleasant'. An unfamiliar voice inside her seemed to be repeating apathetically, 'unpleasant'. It said nothing about Kitaev, though. But her body acted independently from her brain, according to its own laws. Natasha clasped the hand of the basketball-player next to her so tightly that her fingers encircled his wrist.

'Whew!' the basketball-player exclaimed, surprised by the pain and the touch.

'We're on fire!' Natasha said rather calmly for such communication.

The basketball-player bent toward the window and looked out attentively.

'No, those are signals,' he said, 'just wing-markings.'

'What are they for?' Natasha countered, in disbelief.

'So that no other plane can crash into us.'

Natasha glued her face to the window again. The lights flashed in regular intervals; they pulsated. A fire would certainly be more spontaneous.

Businesslike and calm, a stewardess walked along the aisle – not at all as she would in the midst of a catastrophe.

The cabin light was turned off. Evidently, the passengers were being invited to sleep. Natasha closed her eyes. The basketball-player also reclined his seat, and their heads were side by side. It seemed as if they were together in a single bed. Warmth radiated from him as if from a stove, and she felt like moving closer, so as to be less lonely and less afraid up here, between heaven and earth. He inched his elbow towards her barely noticeably, half a centimeter, but she felt it, and she did not remove her hand. The energy of a young bio-field flowed from this elbow, enveloping Natasha. They were flying together in a cloud. It was dark and quiet, and in the stillness she heard his heart pounding against his rib-cage like a hammer. As if controlled by some other force, Natasha put her head on his shoulder. He lowered his face so that it touched her hair. Now their hearts were pounding together, and the thought of falling was not terrifying at all, as long as they fell together.

'Are you from Baku?' Natasha asked.

She had to say something. It was too awkward not to.

'Yes, I am.'

'But you're Russian.'

'Well, Russians live there too.'

'Why, have they lost something there?'

'No, really! It's a great city.'

'And what did you do in Moscow?'

'I was at a training-session.'

'You're an athlete, a professional, aren't you?'

'Yes.'

They whispered because passion was choking them. They talked only in order to become distracted and liberated from the insurmountable attraction they felt for each other. It was beyond control, simply insuperable.

The basketball-player bent down to kiss Natasha. His lips were cautious and soft like those of a horse.

Her heart pounded in her throat, as if the plane had fallen into an air pocket.

Never in her entire life had Natasha experienced anything like it. Other serious love relationships she had been fortunate enough to experience had as distant an affinity with the state she was in now as words had with classical music, as a text had with the second Rachmaninov concerto.

'Do you have a boyfriend?' he asked.

'I'm engaged. I'm on my way to see him.'

'Hm . . . . You're still young . . . .'

In the dark, he couldn't see how old she was.

'And do you have a girlfriend?'

'I do. I'm engaged, too. Her name is Snezhana. I worship her.'

'She's a Bulgarian?' Natasha guessed.

'Yes. I just worship her. But what I'm feeling for you right now I've never felt for anyone, and I didn't even know that I could feel this way.'

'What do you feel?'

'I don't know. It's like sunstroke.'

Natasha moved aside and looked at him. She hadn't even seen him yet. Before her was a young face with tightly stretched skin and worried eyes. Seeing him seemed not enough. So she reached over and let her fingers glide over his face, like a blind person trying to memorize features by touch. He wasn't surprised. Everything that happened between them seemed natural, even inevitable. It seemed to her that it wasn't a plane sending off signals at night, but their souls, exchanging signs of recognition.

'What's your life like?' Natasha asked.

'It's rough. I torment myself.'

'What's tormenting you?'

'I want to resurrect my mother. Can you resurrect a person who's dead?'[1]

---

1. The following discussion between the basketball-player and Natasha echoes some of the ideas of N. F. Fyodorov (1828–1903). Formulated in his book *The*

'No, you can't.'

'How do you know?'

'I'm a biologist, and I know it for a fact. It's the only thing that can't be done. Everything else is possible.'

'But they re-created the ancient extinct horses, the tarpans. They were interbred, selected, and restored. Right now a whole herd of them runs around in New Ascania.'*

'A biological species was re-created. But you can't resurrect an individual. A person's unique.'

'But some people believe that it will be possible to resurrect the forefathers from the offspring.'

'Nature is interested in the continued change of generations. People are born, age and die in order to make room for the next generation. You can't turn the wheel of life backwards.'

'But my mother didn't get old. She died young; she didn't get a chance to live.'

'You have to accept it.'

'I can't accept it. I can't live without her. I even wanted to follow her. . . . Do you think I am crazy?'

'No, I don't.

His wish to resurrect his mother didn't surprise Natasha. Or, rather, it did surprise her, but she understood the emotion behind it; she understood what propelled him. Nadka had separated from her husband Valik before he perished, and the fact of his death had changed nothing. The basketball-player had not parted from his mother even after her death; on the contrary, he and she were one person, and he experienced the forced separation as something unnatural. He probably did not experience a separation at all. He was looking for a way out: either to follow his mother, or to bring her back, and he had fixed on the latter.

Philosophy of the Common Task (*Filosofiya obshchego dela*) and influential in the nineteenth century on Dostoevsky, Solovyov, and others, they are quite popular in the Soviet Union now. One of Fyodorov's central concerns is the injustice of death. Mortality, to him, is not primordial: it can be controlled by reason. He defends the idea of an 'immanent raising of the dead', following the model of Christ's resurrection. Preaching a 'scientific-magical' method of 'raising the dead', he speaks of collecting the scattered particles of our ancestors in order to re-create their bodies. His enlightenment faith in the growth of natural science has a strong element of magic.

Even more influential on contemporary Soviet thought is Fyodorov's advocacy of the gospel of love and brotherhood. Civilization, he argues, has fostered non-brotherly life, and is maintained only by fear and violence; all activity only serves war or profiteering. Man is called upon to transform this situation.

'We had no one else in the world; she had me and I had her. My father left us when I was a month old, when she was nineteen. I don't even know whether he existed. I never saw him. We weren't just poor; we were dismal. Sometimes we had only one plate of watery soup all day. One year I couldn't go out all winter because I had no warm shoes.'

Natasha was lying on her reclining seat, her face turned to him. She breathed in every word he said, imbibed his voice.

He told her that his mother had trained at a theatrical institute, but not a single theater was interested in her. She probably was a very poor actress. She earned money by performing illustrations for the lectures of the organization 'Knowledge'. For example, the lecturer would speak on Maxim Gorky's work, and she would step onto the platform in a floor-length dress, a long scarf of gauze draped around her, and recite 'The Stormy Petrel',* embodying ocean and storm with her scarf. His mother could certainly have also performed in regular clothes, in skirt and blouse. But she was an actress in essence possessed by the need to be theatrical and to express herself. But this need did not coincide with reality. Her talent was mediocre, yet she refused to accept it. And it is rare indeed for someone infected with the virus of artistic creativity to be able to admit, 'I lack the talent'. Such an admission would presuppose special insight and courage. Then his mother fell ill and died in a hospital, a year ago. He had been with her day and night. His pockets had been full of crumpled rouble notes to slip to the nurses, but he had done everything himself. At one point the physician in charge had told him, 'Hold out a little longer. There isn't much time left – two or three days only.' And the basketball-player hadn't understood. He was ready to live the rest of his life without eating, sleeping or even sitting down, so long as his mother would breathe and flutter her eyelids. One day he stepped outside to have a cigarette, and when he returned he understood nothing at first. His mother was there, yet she was there no more. She had left for somewhere, leaving behind her body, like people who abandoned their village huts to move to the city.

The other woman in his mother's room pointed at the body, her hand shaking, and whispered, 'She died . . . .' 'Yes,' he had whispered back. 'Tell somebody to take her away.' 'No, no one can touch her.' 'Why?' 'That's the rule.' He hoped that she could be brought back, recalled, from where she had just gone. 'But I can't stand it. I'll go mad.' 'I can't help you.' 'So call somebody.' 'I will, but that won't help.' The woman spoke calmly, in a whisper, and he answered her whispering, trying to explain, he thought. But this was a conversation between two people unhinged by shock – whispered and very logical.

Then he had gone to the doctor, at first to the physician who had treated his mother, then to the head of the division, and he had begged them to resurrect his mother, while constantly apologizing for the trouble he was causing. He was given an injection and sent home. At home he had cut his veins.

'And Snezhana?' Natasha asked.

'She meant nothing. I didn't even give her a thought.'

They fell silent.

'Do you think I'm abnormal?' the basketball-player asked again.

'No, I don't think so. You're just young and can't bear the grief. You haven't had a chance yet to learn endurance.'

'Maybe so. But mother shouldn't have died. It's unfair. Her life was short and terrible. She knew nothing but humiliations, as an actress and also as a woman. Where's the compensation? Death?'

'Every person harvests what he sows. It's cruel, but that's how it is.'

'She sowed gentleness and innocence.'

'That means her soil was poor.'

'What do you mean?' The basketball-player couldn't follow, and he moved his tense face closer to her, looking perplexed.

'She picked the wrong profession. She bore a child for the wrong man.'

'The wrong man, yes. But the child turned out perfect! I loved her and I still love her more than anyone else.'

'It's fate.'

'No!' – he rebelled in a whisper. 'It's unfair.'

Biting on his clenched fist, he hunched over, shaken with sobs.

Natasha had never seen a man cry. Her first husband had come close to crying several times when he was drunk, but these were different tears.

Natasha grasped his clenched fist, unclenched his fingers, and lowered her face into his hand. She wanted him to feel that she was there, right next to him, so that they could support each other up here, between heaven and earth.

'Marry Snezhana,' said Natasha, 'have a daughter and give her your mother's name. What was her name?'

'Aleksandra.'

'So call her Aleksandra. It's a wonderful name. You can abbreviate it in many ways, just as you like: Alya, Sandra, Shura, Sasha. . . . She will look like you, because girls usually look like their fathers and boys like their mothers. Through you, Sandra will resemble your mother, and that's how you can resurrect her.'

'And what's your name?'

'Natasha.'

'The plane has begun its descent,' the official female voice of the stewardess announced 'Put your seats in the upright position and fasten your seatbelts.'

The light was turned on. The passengers came to, fastening their seatbelts. Natasha glanced at the basketball-player, giving him a chance to examine her in bright light. But he didn't notice their age difference. It was as if the sunstroke had affected his brain.

'Shall we see each other?' he asked.

'No,' Natasha answered. 'It's impossible. I'm not alone.'

'Does it matter? Maybe you'll find some time?'

'Maybe. But what for?'

He didn't answer. How could he respond to such a question?

The plane descended with an internal howl. It landed as bumpily as it had taken off. The air under its wings seemed to quiver with nauseating unsteadiness. The pilot, evidently, was not born for this profession, but had only been trained to it.

An iron fence separated the airfield from the city.

Kitaev stood on the other side of the fence, like a noble beast of prey, incessantly staring at the door from which Natasha was to emerge.

Natasha didn't step through the door but stopped by the iron bars looking – literally and figuratively speaking – askance at Kitaev. Then she called in a low voice, 'Kitaev!'

Abruptly he turned around and went up to the fence. Reaching through the bars, he hugged and kissed her firmly and excitedly. His lips were thin and hard, and his kiss didn't move her, but remained on her lips.

While they waited for the luggage Kitaev complained about the delay. An entire night had been lost, followed by a day below par. She could have said, 'It's not my fault. You shouldn't have called me.' But she kept a guilty silence. Kitaev knew nothing of her guilt, yet she knew that she had failed to think of him in her fear of death, and that she had spent the night with someone else. It was double treason.

The luggage arrived. Suitcases, trunks and bags emerged from a dark hole as if from outer space and fell onto a broad, slowly moving conveyor-belt. The passengers – at this point simply overtired people – clustered around and followed the belt spellbound, as if looking at the hand of Santa Claus, although they expected nothing but their own luggage.

At this point Natasha saw the basketball-player. Tall, erect, his beautiful head resting on a strong neck, he looked very impressive on the ground. It was the kind of neck a cartoonist would give to Tsar Ivan or Ivan the Fool figures. With unconcealed consternation he looked at Kitaev and couldn't comprehend why Natasha had left him for this shriveled old man, why he couldn't get the water of life to resurrect his mother, and why he couldn't snatch his frog princess from this wicked, bony old man. His sports bag – you could see by the look of it that it was heavy – went past several times, colliding with other suitcases, causing pile-ups. Similarly the questions in his mind collided and piled up, making his eyes look bigger and darker.

Kitaev picked Natasha's reddish-brown suitcase off the belt. They presented the official with the luggage claim and left the baggage area.

Before leaving the building Natasha turned around. The basket-ball-player had twisted his head like a bird, and his eyes reminded her of a gipsy's from long ago.

Once, when she and her mother spent the summer at a dacha,* a gipsy woman had come by. She had an unusually beautiful but filthy little boy on her arm who held out his dirty little palm. The gipsy begged for food, clothing and money, demanding the maximum because she knew that she had to ask for ten roubles if she wanted to get one. Her mother went into the house and brought out some things she could bear to part with: a meat pie, some money, an old robe. Into the little boy's hand she pressed a baked potato. But she suddenly feared that the potato might not have cooled enough, and she quickly tore it from the boy's hand. Instantly his eyes widened in outrage, filling with tears. He started crying quietly – bitterly, deeply offended, like an adult. He didn't understand that the potato had been taken away for his own good. The basketball-player too didn't understand that Natasha was leaving him for his own good. His eyes, too, seemed to cry out.

People and obligations are like the soil and trees. Like gigantic hands, the tree-roots reach deep into the soil, holding it together, while at the same time they sustain themselves. The soil needs trees, and the trees need soil. Obligations exist not only between the living and the dead, but also between the living. Tearing out one tree, one has to make sure that another tree is planted in its place and will take root and grow. If you tear out one tree without planting another, you will stand above the crater just staring at the damage you have done.

Natasha followed Kitaev, and the basketball-player's gaze burnt into her neck like a ray focused with a convex lens. For an entire week afterwards she could feel this painful point.

Yes. . . . But what did her first husband have to do with all this? Nothing at all. At the beginning of her life it hadn't cost anything to tear out the weak roots, to twist them from the soil and cast them aside. Then she had believed that everything was in the future, that everything was ahead of her.

10

Valentina Sidorenko

Valentina Vasilyevna Sidorenko was born in 1950 in Irkutsk; after finishing school she worked as a conductor on long-distance trains, as a newspaper correspondent and as an administrator of a puppet theater. These experiences are reflected in the stories and novellas of her first book, *Conductresses. The Return (Stories) (Provodnitsy. Vozvrashchenie (Rasskazy)*, 1981). It is a gloomy book, full of the bitterness and resignation of women battered in their encounters with men: deceived, left alone, struggling to work and bring up children and supply them with the bare necessities of life. Her compassion and pain for all those who are unlikely to experience happiness permeates the volume. Sidorenko is a realist, with a keen eye for details, a sensitivity to psychological processes, and a fine ear for the idiosyncrasies of language. Underneath her Chekhovian evocations of ordinary life loom the latent philosophical questions of meaning.

Valentin Rasputin, who had presented one of her first stories to readers in *Literaturnaya Rossiya*, wrote in his laudatory commentary to this volume: 'I know very well how apprehensive readers are about new female rhetoric and heart-rending appeals. Sidorenko, however, has a male hand in this respect. I realize that for a woman, even for a woman writer, having a male hand is a dubious virtue. But if a woman's heart guides this hand, responsive and attentive to what men consider trivia – trivia which few are able to discern – the conjunction of the two principles is fortunate' (*Literaturnaya Uchyoba*, 1981, no. 2, p. 15).

Sidorenko's story 'Marka' was published in 1984. Her work has not previously been translated into English.

Marka
(1984)

There was a sound of chirping and rustling in the grass and something mousy flitted by. Then, suddenly, with a faint sob, a bluish-grey bird with a sharp beak soared up right from under her feet and started circling over her head with loud screeches.

Terrified, Marka sat down, her nose pressed against her knees, her back hunched. She could hear her heart hammering in her chest, and sunny green spots danced before her eyes.

'Maaaarka! Maaaarkaa!' a voice was calling.

Carefully Marka lifted her head and saw her grandma struggling through some reddish willow bushes. Slowly she made her way to Marka.

'What are you sitting there like a frog for? Are you deaf or what? You look like you're glued to the ground and frozen stiff!' She poked her knotty fist into Marka's neck, pulled her roughly by the hair, and stood her on her legs. 'I don't know how you're going to make it. What keeps dragging you out here, for God's sake? Where's the hidden treasure, eh? You show me! I take my eyes off you for just a second, and you're gone. Roaming around from early morning on – and without a bite of bread or nothing. And look at you! Nothing but a bag of bones anyway. . . . Irka from next door, well, she's tough, and strong as a horse, a great sight to look at: just like butter dough. But you, you beanpole, I can even see your veins! I could push you over with my little finger, for God's sake! What drags you over here, eh? All you need is to bump into a stranger, and he'd finish you off and shovel you under, right here, Heaven forbid. Good Lord, forgive a poor sinner; it's wrong to say such things to a child. Don't you want something to eat?'

'Yes.'

'Tummy rumbling, eh?' Grandma said, softening.

'Yes.'

Marka understood perfectly well that her grandmother had had her say and that the worst was over. The girl stepped on a raised squishy tussock and turned around.

Behind her the swamp stretched as far as the eye could see. Clusters of willow bushes and poplar were scattered about, and right on the edge of the swamp stood the three birches that grandmother had planted last summer. Tingling with their tender kopeck-sized leaves, they shone milky white, like little children. And, as usual during the summer months, the light of the early evening sun made the damp grass stand out with special sharpness. Everything around was aflame and flooded with a playful, pliant green that stretched up to the horizon, where the transparent, infinite sky began. But where was the bird that had screeched above their heads? It was out of sight. There was only the grass and the sky. . . .

Marka sighed, listening to the wheezing that accompanied Grandma's breath. Then she asked, 'Granny, who's living in our swamp?'

They had left the willow bushes behind and stepped onto the road, at the spot where Fireman Zuyev's garden began.

'Who do you think lives in our swamp? Snipes and the Wood Spirit,' Grandma answered, after a minute. 'What did you see?'

'A birdie.'

'A snipe, I expect.'

They reached their own garden, Grandma entering through the gate while Marka squeezed through a hole in the fence. Grandma paused a moment by the cucumber patch. With her large reddish hand, she fumbled through the rough foliage and pulled out two fat cucumbers which she stuffed into her apron pockets. They entered the dusky coolness of the house. But for the even ticking of an alarm clock, the house was so quiet that it might have been deserted. Next to the unpainted partition Marka's mother lay stretched on a bed, her face barely visible. All you could make out was her slender pale hand tucked under the head and some cigarette smoke.

'Come here,' she said to Marka in a flat voice.

Marka held on to Grandma and did not respond.

'Come here, my dear . . . .'

Grandma nudged her forward and stepped beyond the partition.

Marka's mother rose listlessly, turned on the light and stepped to the mirror that hung on the wall. Running her hand over her face and her shoulders, she brushed against the knot into which her silky hair had been tied, undid it, and examined the long strands of hair carefully in the light as if looking for something.

'Always staring at yourself,' Grandma said hoarsely from behind the partition. 'Soon you'll be all gray. You'd do better to take care of your daughter.'

The mother sighed, twisted her hair back into a knot so tightly that it stretched the skin on her cheeks. Then she put on a scarf, pulling it well down her forehead.

'And now where are you off to? Where do you want to show off now?' Grandma asked from behind the partition.

'I'll dig up the carrot bed.'

'What for?'

'What's growing there? Three or four roots, that's all.'

'What d'you mean? Till Fall, they're all going to grow roots. But the radishes need putting in. The carrots I'll get myself; I'll dig up the bed.'

In the evening, in her hard bed, a patchwork quilt pulled up to her chin, Marka silently examined the bulging plaster on the ceiling. Slowly the light outside faded. A radiant white star sparkled above. Grandma dropped heavily onto her bed, which, as always, creaked before becoming quiet.

The mother paced up and down the room and smoked. She walked slowly, her face worried and gloomy. It reflected an even, constant sorrow. She was waiting.

For the last couple of days she had combed her hair straight back. She had worn a gray dress and hardly spoken a word. She stood endlessly by the window, staring intently into the darkness. Bony, her face emaciated and sickly, she resembled an uncomely northern bird. Occasionally the lights of a passing car would light up the corner of their house, and she would start and grow tense.

A grayish twilight lingered in the house. Dampness from the swamp crept in through the cracks in the window-frames, and outside the heavy dog-chain clanked. The uneven window-panes reflected a piece of the black, star-studded August sky.

'Don't wait,' Grandma said. 'He ain't coming. He don't need you! He's done horsing around and now he's himself again. But you think about getting him back.'

'You don't have to live my life.'

'I don't give a damn about your life,' Grandma answered evenly. 'Nobody's going to say no evil word about me. And I didn't have no man around to hide behind, but nobody's going to say no evil word about me!'

Marka had become used to Grandma's lecturing long ago. It was something she did as easily as talking about the weather or bewailing the fact that this year's cucumbers hadn't turned out well or that the meat prices had gone up.

'Yesterday Nadka came by and said, how come you don't buy no TV? I says, what do I need a TV for? I've got a daughter – that's like a silent movie. Good Lord – if you knew what a miserable life I had, all alone. All my life I stared out of the window. And you, you're going gray, but you still keep looking in the mirror and staring out of the window. Did I really have any life? Where's it gone? A woman's life is like a spider's web: it sparkles twice, and then it's gone.'

The mother turned her immobile, unseeing face toward Grandma, sighed, and took out the next cigarette.

'I tell you what. All this is just women's nonsense and idiocy. If you've got a man, there's no getting even with him, even after he's dead. . . . Fifteen years I lived with mine, and when he died – may he be in Heaven – in . . .,' Grandma started, licking her lips; 'when he died in . . . I can't remember what year. . . .'

'In '52,' the mother helped.

'Just you watch out that you don't puff away your memory.'

The mother exhaled a breath full of smoke, examining the ceiling indifferently.

'I was left alone just like you. Going to bed was like lying down in a coffin. He was your father, but – I'll make no bones about it – he was no fun to be with. Truly he wasn't. And you picked up all his bad habits. In case I suddenly die, you'd better bury Marka with me. You're no use to her.'

There was a noise outside. Something rumbled and rolled along the hall. The door opened and Pyotr entered.

He had first come over from the factory side of the town two years ago. The early morning haze above the swamp had dispersed, and the fresh November sun, round and crimson, was slowly making its way through the whitish sky without really warming the earth. The ground was hard as iron, because it hadn't snowed yet. If you hit the heel of your boot against it, it seemed that sparks would fly.

Grandma had asked him to kill a six-month-old pig. On that day she bustled and clanked about the farmyard as if preparing for a wedding, alert, bright-eyed, her face hot and excited with the holiday, happy to have found an occasion to call in the neighbors. She wandered around the shed almost crying when she patted the pig's bristles; and she yelled at the mother, who was unusually quiet that day. Her head wrapped in a white scarf, the mother sat resting by the stove.

Then they had a hot lunch. Wide-eyed, Pyotr stared persistently at the mother, deep in thought. Then he whispered to Grandma, 'I'd like to marry your daughter. Can I have her?'

'Just be quiet! Leave her alone, just you stay away!' Grandma punched his shoulder with her reddish fist. 'What are you going to do with your own woman?'

'I'll just throw her out!'

'And your kids, you're going to throw them out, too?'

Pyotr said nothing. He just stared at the mother and gulped down his vodka noisily. Then he rose, walked over to the mother, and sat down next to her. She flinched and glanced at him half-amazed, half-frightened.

Marka had felt alone and sad. After she had eaten her fill she put on her coat and went outside, into the garden. She sat on her log, watching the smoke rise evenly from the neighboring gardens where dry potato plants were being burnt. Looking at the hoarfrost on the gray cabbage stalks and at the ugly black soil, she sighed deeply. Her mother came outside, followed by Pyotr. They stood at the fence. She said nothing, but kept poking the tip of her shoe into the frozen leaves while he talked and talked.

After that he came often. Grandma cursed angrily behind the wood pile so that nobody could hear. She disliked Pyotr. The mother said nothing and did as she pleased. In the morning when it was barely light, she'd walk him to the gate, and Marka, waking up, would see her tired face through the window. It had changed: it shone with a strange, youthful purity.

'Pyotr, where in the world have you been?' the mother said.

Grandma spat in a fit of anger while Pyotr took his coat off, throwing her a furtive glance. The mother quickly led him to her corner behind the stove, as if shielding him with her hands.

Mumbling something about herself, Grandma lay down next to Marka to warm her up and make her fall asleep more quickly.

Marka closed her eyes, and a grayish soft drowsiness enveloped her, in which she drifted away.

A grayish-blue bird penetrated her drowsiness, circling silently and screeching silently; and Marka once more beheld the green, gentle, smoke-colored swamp and the clouds above it.

'Good Lord, have mercy!' Grandma mumbled, sighing deeply. 'You get born – it's a mystery; you die – it's a mystery. But you live, and everything's clear. You know it all: sin and hustle and bustle. Nothing surprising. Like living someone else's life, someone else's messy, good-for-nothing life. Oh Lord . . . . What ain't I seen in my time? Oh Lord . . . . How come I got born for such a life?'

Marka dozed lightly, pressing her nose against Grandma's feather-soft breast, where it smelled of cookies, grass and something sour, familiar, bitter.

Marka knew the truth about Grandma's earlier life. Granny said one can live many lives. If you took the road to Moscow, for instance, that's one kind of life. If, on your way, you felt like stopping in a village, you'd end up with a different sort of life. And, if you turned off elsewhere, you'd have a third kind. Granny was convinced that the road she had taken from her own house had led her to the most miserable and good-for-nothing life. Her real life had got left behind there, in her own village, when she got married to Pavel, who died, having brought her to this little town. And she started to live in misery, day in, day out, hoping it would get better. But, if she suddenly turned around and went through her past, there was nothing in it to make her halt: there was neither real sorrow nor real happiness. And ahead of her she couldn't make out anything.

When she is sound asleep in her wide bed in the cool darkness of the house, Grandma often remembers another house, at the edge of the village. Burning-hot bits of tile are stuck to the mound of earth along the outer walls of the house. The sunset covers half the sky. Women stand by the gates, exchanging remarks while they wait for the return of the herd, whose bells have been ringing loudly from beyond the village. Stomping heavily, the herd plods along the main road; warm dust hangs in the air. The herd passes through the street, filling the air with loud mooing, and with the pungent smell of strong sweat and of sour, rotten soil. Before passing through the wide gates of the inner courtyard, every cow halts a minute by its own entrance to gobble a piece of bread from the hands of its owner.

She also remembers how they used to cut hay, and how they played on holidays. She tosses and turns, telling herself that now it is no longer the same village. She had come too late.

Behind the stove, the mother and Pyotr whispered. The mother hoarsely reproached him: 'I can't take it any longer, Pyotr. I'm worn out. I keep waiting for you, waiting and waiting. You show up, and then you disappear. . . .'

'But I'm not alone, you know,' Pyotr answered her in a hollow voice; 'you've got to understand that. What am I going to do with the two kids? They're no strangers, you know.'

'Well, I'm not saying anything. If you come it's wonderful. If only you could come more often. If only all this waiting didn't drive me mad . . . . Oh, I can't stand it any more, Pyotr; I just can't. Let's decide. Either . . . or . . . .'

In the morning Marka was awakened by a knock against the window. Her bedsprings scraping, Grandma asked in a startled voice, 'Who's there?'

A ray of golden August sun stretched across the floor.

'It's me, Kostya.'

'What Kostya?'

'Kostya Kuliev, from the village.'

'Oh, it's you!' Grandma said, and rose to open the door.

Kostya came inside, put down his suitcase, and, taking off his cap, smoothed down some ash-blond tufts of hair. He was dark-skinned, thin and serious-looking.

'Mother sent me for a visit.'

'It's you,' Grandma repeated, picking up the suitcase with the presents from the village. 'Well, come in! Why stand by the door? Did you come by train?'

'Yes,' Kostya answered, finally looking at Marka.

Kostya came every summer. His mother was the sister of Marka's father, who had died of pneumonia when Marka was a baby. Once Granny had told her that they had been picking blueberries on a hot day, and, after wandering around for a long time, parched by the scorching sun, her father had gulped down lots of cold well water. This did him in in three days, and so he had died.

Kostya would come and help around the house – man's chores – and Grandma and Marka liked it when he came.

After Marka had opened her eyes, she listened calmly to Granny's oohs and ahs, to the groaning and mumbling that sounded like clucking. She watched as the light of the summer morning lazily seeped through the window and spread through the house. Then, following Grandma, she got up, stepped outside, and, stretching and yawning, squinted as she looked toward the swamp. She held on to Grandma's wide skirt with one hand and shielded her eyes with the other, just as Grandma was doing. They called the chickens, fed them some moistened bread, and, when the bright-red rooster from next door flew up on the rosy fence with an unexpected cock-a-doodle-doo, Marka clutched at her chest and angrily hissed through her teeth, 'Stupid rooster! I wish you'd die!'

Behind the garden was a lake of calm black water, thinly covered with water-plants along the shore. Beyond the lake, as far as the eye could see, swamp grass grew all the way up to the factory.

Majestically, beautiful white ducks guided their brood across the lake to the other shore.

For the last few mornings nature had had a transparent and unreal quality about it. Although the yellow heat above gathered force just as slavishly as always, the swamp grass gave off a bitter smell, starting to get dusty from the roots up, and the ducks became more restless and noisy and would not return to their owners. In the evening the women would have to walk along the shore, some with sticks, some with bread, to call in their birds.

After Grandma had fed the chickens, she sat on the cool log next to the mound along the outer wall of the house, and for a long time watched the road across the swamp, making a mental note of who did and who did not go to the factory today.

Her eyes were almost hidden behind her purplish cheekbones. She panted heavily as she closely surveyed her meager vegetable patch.

She liked to work with the soil. Unlike her neighbors' seed-beds, hers were weeded: you couldn't see a single blade of grass. She had planted the onions in a row, one by one; the dill grew strictly along the edges; next to every tomato-bush stood a smooth, ochre-colored peg, hammered in for support; and narrow sandy pathways wound their way through the plot.

Kotsya took a careful look round and picked up the axe.

'Drop that thing! I need a man in here!' Grandma grumbled. 'Come inside!'

Grandma put some fried potatoes on the table, and poured some kvas* over chopped radish, cucumber and onion, and gave Kostya the only wooden spoon they had, which was all chipped.

'Dig in!'

Kostya ate with intent concentration, cutting the bread in big pieces and peeking at Marka.

'You've got eyes like a cow,' he said, convinced.

'Where would she've got other eyes from?' Grandma answered. 'The bean-pole! Better finish up and get going. Come on! Let's get down to it. You came to help, so get busy; take her off my hands. I want to sow the radishes today.'

After lunch, Kostya unexpectedly disappeared. Marka wandered along the fence, and looked in the front yard and the shed. When she went into the vegetable garden she saw some of the boys from town on the road across the swamp. Kostya was walking in front, saying something to Vovka Gurov.

Without a moment's hesitation Marka found the hole in the fence, jumped out onto the road and ran after them. The shoes she had put on her bare feet hurt her left heel badly, and she started limping.

A big puddle stretched across the middle of the road, its sticky warm water flowing around Marka's feet. Catching the sun, the insects sparkled and glinted as they dived into the puddle. Marka slipped, fell hard, and started crying, stuck in the puddle. Disturbed by the noise, the ducks on the lake quacked angrily.

Slowly Marka rose, rubbing her black slimy hands on her dress. When she turned around, she found herself face to face with a hobbled horse. The horse looked at her pensively with its gentle, rose-colored eyes, swished its tail and neighed.

Marka shrugged her shoulders, stepped carefully out of the puddle and continued along the dusty road, leaving a trail of mud.

She had lost sight of the boys and limped along aimlessly. She went on for a long time, until the road ran into the sun-scorched fence of the roofing-felt* factory.

Black soot hovered in the air; scanty hawthorn clung to the fence, its grayish leaves sadly drooping. Not far from the gates she discovered Kostya. He was flat on the ground, peering intently through a slit in the fence that enclosed the factory grounds. Marka went up to him and quietly dropped down alongside.

'I knew it . . .,' Vovka Gurov whispered angrily. Kostya gave Marka a painful punch in the neck.

'Nothing but bad luck all day,' he hissed through his teeth.

'Maybe tomorrow?' whispered a clean, ash-blond boy nicknamed Byashik.

'It won't work tomorrow,' Vovka Gurov answered, gloomily

staring at the sky. He grabbed Marka's ear and pulled it angrily.

Vovka disliked Marka, and Marka was afraid of him. She huddled closer to Kostya. Kostya stroked her hair and said, 'I'd better take her home. She might get into the swamp, and then try and find her!'

A flock of wild ducks merrily flew by overhead. Following them with his gaze, Gurov remarked, 'They're practicing. Soon they'll take off.'

'Yes, if nobody shoots 'em down,' Kostya replied.

'Well, what are we going to do?'

The three of them stood around Marka, staring at her. Marka scowled, breathing heavily through her nose. She knew she wasn't going to budge, even if Kostya wanted to take her home.

'Let her come along.'

'But she's too small.'

'If you make one peep, I'm going to smack you right in the eye!' Gurov said and shook his fist at her.

The roofing-felt factory was much the same as the other factories in town. It was enclosed by a wooden fence, and in the middle of the courtyard stood a sagging old warehouse that stored old paper collected from the whole settlement. It was the warehouse that attracted Vovka and his friends.

Vovka loved medical books. For months he had saved his school breakfast money in order to get himself a physician's reference book; he ransacked the libraries, and he made periodic raids on this warehouse. He burrowed through its dusty piles like a mole.

'Let's go!' Kostya egged them on.

Vovka crawled in first, then Kostya pushed Marka after him. She crept along, scraping her knees on the sun-scorched ground. When she got into the warehouse, the darkness made her squint. It was cool and damp. When she opened her eyes she could make out lots of paper, books and notebooks, all scattered haphazardly and piled into mountains.

Vovka looked around in a business-like fashion and dived into one of the stacks of paper. Kostya gave Marka a shove on the shoulder: pick out what you want. Marka started rummaging slowly, examining the discarded paper with great care. She found some old playing-cards and hid them under her dress.

Vovka never failed to guess correctly in which corner to rummage. Under a heap of foil he hit upon the sharp edges of books. Breathing heavily through his nose, totally absorbed, and frowning at the slight crackle of the foil, he carefully started pulling out the books. Byashik was lucky right away. He found stamps. Noticing a book-cover, Marka crawled over to the neighboring pile.

A velvety spider dashed across the smooth page when Marka opened the book. Calmly she turned page after page, attentively examining the large rows of neat black letters and the long faces of people, and stopping at pictures of heavy carved tables, of brightly luxurious rugs and clothes, and many other things that surrounded these people whom she had never seen.

'Kostya,' she asked, 'do they really live like this?'

'Piss off!', Kostya replied, throwing a furtive glance in her direction.

Marka sighed. She opened another book at random and saw a woman. Semi-reclined, the woman had her pale face turned towards her shoulder. Two elongated fingers of one hand lazily held a smoke-colored scarf. The other hand was hidden in her black hair, the rosy elbow pointed outward. Her gaze was calm and sad, and her eyes sparkled strangely from the deep light that fell upon her through the windows in the picture. She looked at Marka with such quiet and attentive interest that it seemed that at any moment she would raise her rosy hand, wrapped in airy lace, and touch Marka's shoulder. But there was something that made her feel that she had known this woman for a long time, that she remembered her as if she had seen her in a dream, remembered the movement of her hand as it let go of the hair.

'Marka, hey!' Kostya called. Startled, Marka clenched the book and hugged it against her body.

'Look here,' and Kostya showed her an old photograph glued on some heavy cardboard. Framed in two blue hearts, a man with slick, diagonally parted hair sweetly smiled at a woman in a yellow beret.

'Love me as much as I love you': he read her the words at the bottom.

'Kostya, look, who's this?' Marka asked, showing him her book.

'Piss off! It's some woman like all others.'

'You mean, like me? I'm like that?' Marka asked him, petrified. She could not believe that the enchanting, mysterious creature in the picture and she were alike in any way. 'And like Mother?'

'Of course.'

'And Grandma?'

'Yes, yes, yes. Just leave me alone!' Kostya was angry.

Marka turned to the side and sat on a pile of papers. She didn't believe Kostya, but her heart hammered away, and everything seemed unreal.

Rays of light filtered through the chinks in the warehouse wall. A hand-cart screeched in the courtyard, and the voices of two women floated by peacefully. Then everything grew quiet again. The heavy open book slipped out of Marka's hands and disappeared into a brownish heap of paper. Marka tried to reach it, but the book plunged down between various bales and landed smack at the bottom, raising a cloud of dust.

Waving to Kostya, Marka carefully climbed after the book, rolled on a moist bale, sat down and, groping in the darkness, came across the rough back of a heavy book. At this moment the gates of the warehouse were thrown open, and a man shouted, 'There they are!'

Byashik was the first to come to his senses. He shrieked, jumped up and down, and shot out of the warehouse like a bullet. There was a commotion. Someone's heavy boots shuffled behind the gates. Then Marka heard Kostya whimper, 'Uncle, please let me go, I won't come any more!'

Somebody was evidently holding his head down, because his voice came from below, from the ground.

'We've got you now. We've got you!' the man answered. 'I'll take you home for a good thrashing. You boys'll burn down the whole place. It's full of paper, after all!'

Then lots of other loud, angry voices could be heard shouting, and finally the gates were closed.

Nobody had noticed Marka. She had huddled down on the paper and, afraid to stir, had grown absolutely quiet. She heard her breath and tightly closed her lips to stop breathing. But some time went by and nothing happened. Barely soothed and completely worn out from the fear she had experienced, she stretched out her arm and fell asleep.

When she woke up, it was just as quiet and damp in the warehouse as before. The bright cobweb of light that had filtered through the cracks was extinguished. The sun had probably moved to the other side of the warehouse and now stood above the factory roof. Marka did not think of having been left behind. She just lay calmly, waiting for the time when all this would end, when Kostya would come back and they'd go home.

Marka yawned, stretched and wanted to get up, but something

rumbled on the road, the gates of the warehouse opened, and a hand-cart rolled in. The two women who pulled it stopped.

'That's the last load for the day,' the older one said. 'My back hurts like hell.'

Marka rustled. She got up and looked at the women. They sat by the gate where there was hardly any paper, and where the rails flashed brightly on the ground. When she climbed out of her hollow, Marka brushed against a heavy bag, which slid down, pulling some paper with it. Marka froze.

'Rats again,' the older woman said indifferently and looked up. 'They might even feast on it.'

'The rats?'

'Why not? Hunger's no fun,' she answered, her rough hands efficiently adjusting her scarf. 'Are you leaving?'

'I'm off.'

'Do what you like!'

'Well, I'm going,' the younger one repeated. Her checkered scarf covered her head, and the gray, immobile eyes looked straight ahead.

'I'm a human being, too, you know,' she said, hunched over, putting her arms around her legs and pressing her chin to her knees. 'I've thought about it in different ways. I thought maybe it'd pass. He ran off before too, but he came back. There are the kids after all. And he loves 'em. On pay-day he brings 'em pocketfuls of apples. But he's got no word for me, as if I was a stranger. Christ, as if I was just hired to look after his kids. When they get into fights, I stand around at first, waiting for him, just waiting. Raika lives out by the swamp, with her little daughter and the Grandma. I go to the very end of our town and wait. And I think the other women probably aren't waiting. I see him go home along the path. As if I didn't notice anything. Then I went to her workplace and found out who she was. "Good Lord," I thought, "am I really worse than her?" I sewed myself a new dress, got a perm. If he'd only noticed. But now I've decided to forget it. Just forget it. I don't even want anything from him any more. I've got over it. I'll leave. They may as well live together. If he's not sorry for his own kids, at least he can feed someone else's.'

Marka slipped into her hollow and lay down quietly, looking at the black roof with its corners full of cobwebs. The conversation did not surprise her, and the arrival of these women did not destroy that state of dreamy, patient expectation in which she waited to be called and taken home at last.

The book on her chest absorbed her bodyheat, and Marka stroked it, closing her eyes. Out of the darkness, from somewhere above, the clear and wise eyes of the strange woman in the book seemed to look down upon her, like stars.

'I saw her – Raika, I mean,' the older woman replied after a while. 'Compared to her you're weak. The viper's going to latch on for good, till he dies.'

'So let her,' the younger one replied quietly. 'She'll find out: life's no bed of roses with him. He's not a man but a beast. Never has a good word for you. If a pillar's in his way, he'll go around it. But if it's me, he won't; he'll push his way right through.'

'You're a fish,' the older woman sighed. 'Something's missing in you, something . . . well, female. Take Raika, she's thin as a broomstick, but she attracts men. And it's not because she's alone. I'm alone too, but nobody looks at me.'

'And to think that people like her go on living; they just keep on,' hissed the younger woman viciously. 'I won't marry any more. I'll just live without a man.'

'It's already eight,' the older one yawned. 'Let's go.'

It was getting dark and cold. Marka's fear returned. The darkness transformed the piles of paper into monsters.

Marka closed her eyes. Her legs felt weak. She squeezed her lips tightly together so as not to cry.

A warm, gold-colored room appeared before her mind's eye. Grandma slipped a big onion into a nylon stocking and hung it on the hook by the stove. Mother caressed Marka, lifting her above her head with both hands, saying, 'My little sweetheart, my beauty, my little love, my dearest treasure! My sweet berry!' And her eyes shone with joy. Marka flew up and down, got out of breath, held onto her mother's hair, laughing happily, and then flew again.

Suddenly all the events of the day – the road, the horse, the warehouse, the darkness and terror – came to her and, unable to stand it, she began to cry, initially in little sobs, then loudly and incessantly. Suddenly she heard something rustle and crawl toward her from the corner.

'Rats', she thought and let out a wild, piercing shriek.

'What the hell are you yelling for, you idiot!' Somebody hit her on the back, but she kept on screaming, and she came to her senses only when a coarse hand covered her mouth. As Marka raised her head she recognized Vovka. After a brief silence she started crying again, now easily and freely, a happy weakness permeating her body.

Clumsily Vovka stroked her head and said: 'Don't cry, I'll give you a book. Give me your hand and we'll sneak out.'

She clung to the skinny hand of her saviour as if it were a matter of life and death. Vovka sighed, put her on his knees and quietly entreated her to stop crying. Marka buried herself in his hot shoulder and calmed down, listening to his words.

'Don't cry,' Vovka repeated, 'I'll give you a book.'

Remembering her book, Marka got off his knees and quickly found her book in the dark.

'Throw it away.' Vovka hissed menacingly.

Marka scowled and stopped sniffling.

Vovka smacked her in the face, tore the book from her hands and flung it in a corner. Marka started wailing. Vovka took her hand, but she resisted and kept crying.

'You bitch!' Vovka moaned. 'I'll show you once we're out!' He crawled around in the darkness, and finally he found the book.

They crept out of the warehouse, ran ducking past the various buildings, squeezed through the hole in the fence and finally came out by the swamp. There it was dark and quiet, although the silver path of the moon sparkled on the soft water. A pungent odor rose from the damp grass and the water, and their hands and clothes smelled of roofing-felt.

Vovka took Marka to the lake to wash off the persistent odor.

Remembering the conversation of the two women, Marka thought of the rumors about her mother that were circulating in town, of the young woman whose life had been so abruptly shattered.

It was lighter on the shore of the lake than on the road. Vovka threw off his shirt, stepped into the soft, warm water, and swam to the reeds and back. The ducks he had disturbed quacked and took a long time to calm down. While Vovka splashed in the water, Marka sat on the shore and opened her book. In the dim light she couldn't make out the woman. But the yellow reflection of the water made the smoke-colored brightness of the scarf flicker in and out of view.

'Look at her,' she said to Vovka as he climbed out of the water.

Without even throwing her a glance, Vovka walked past, breathing heavily, and dried his hands on his shirt.

'Take your clothes off,' he said to her abruptly. 'Come on, quick.'

Vovka washed her just as thoroughly as he had washed himself, took great pains to wipe her dry, and sniffed to see whether she still smelled of roofing-felt.

'There's such a beautiful woman in here!' Marka repeated, pointing to the book.

'You're all alike,' Vovka growled, pulling on her dress.

'You mean, I'm like that too?' Marka whispered, amazed.

'Well, do you think you're better?'

While Vovka was busy, putting on his shoes and getting the dust off, Marka held the book tightly to her body and looked at the sky. It had changed. It was pitch-black now. The stars shone brightly; the calm water resembled the sky with its frightening illuminated depth. Only from the reeds, where the disturbed ducks were still fussing, tiny swelling circles rolled to the shore. The road across the swamp, barely visible in the dark, quickly disappeared from sight, like a thread emerging from the night-cool space in the distance, full of muffled sounds, shadows, unexpected cries, with an air of restlessness and strangeness.

Today Marka had seen everything in a new light, as if lit by the blinding, sharp glow from an enormous fire ahead: this woman like a mystery from another world, and this swamp that lived its own frightening life hidden from the stranger's eye.

And did Granny or mother know about all this? *Who* did know about all these things?

'Look!' Marka whispered, pointing with her hand.

Vovka turned around and sighed relieved.

'Don't worry,' he said, 'it's a horse.'

The horse walked up to the water and began to drink, neighing softly.

'And the stars, what are the stars?' Marka asked.

'They're suns, lots of them.'

Marka laughed, because even *she* knew that this couldn't be so, yet Vovka had said it.

'Come on! That's a real lie. There's sun when it's day.'

She squeezed her book tightly, and once more she remembered happily that she was just like this marvelous woman in the book. And, most importantly, she would show the picture to her mother and her grandmother and she would tell them that they, too, were like her. Mother and Grandma simply didn't know what kind of women they were! That was the cause of all their grief. And then they'd be happy. They'd find out and they'd be happy. . . .

The children were passing by the haystacks when suddenly someone whistled. Kostya came up to them, and they moved on towards the gardens.

'Listen, about Aunt Raika . . . .' Vovka was silent for a moment. 'Does that fellow – you know, from over there – still come to see her?'

'Do you want me to smack you one?'

'Nooo, I just . . . .'

'Don't you say a thing to anyone. That's none of our business. She's a good person, but she's very unhappy. That's what my mom says, anyway . . . .'

Vovka turned away and fell silent. Marka walked between them and thought that she was going to continue living from morning to night, and again from morning to night, for so long that there would probably be no end to it.

When they reached the backyard Vovka gave Kostya a book.

'I'd better go,' he said. 'I'm going to get it.'

At home Grandma greeted Kostya and Marka, asking, 'Where have you been all day?'

Kostya went right to the attic without eating supper.

Marka huddled against Grandma's shaky knees, smelling the familiar warm odor and sighing happily. 'Do you live for a long time, granny?'

'Long enough . . . . Go to your mother and cuddle her. She's got a present for you.'

Her mother stood by the stove, in a gray dress, her hair combed back tightly, and looked at Marka with sad eyes. 'Here,' she said, 'soon you'll be going to school.' The metal lock of the schoolbag flashed; it smelled of leather.

Marka put the bag and the book under her pillow. As she was falling asleep, she kept thinking through the sweet and heavy drowsiness that she wouldn't be alone any more, that tomorrow she'd look through the book thoroughly, that everybody would love her, and she loved everybody . . . .

The last thing she heard on that day were Grandma's soft steps and her usual mumbling: 'Oh, oh, my useless, good-for-nothing life . . . .'

11

Tatyana Tolstaya

At thirty-seven, Tatyana Nikitichna Tolstaya is the youngest of the authors included in this anthology. Writing is in her genes: her grandfather was Aleksei Nikolaevich Tolstoy, her great grandmother Aleksandra Leontyevna Turgeneva. Born in 1951 in Leningrad, she is a philologist by education. Her first excellent story 'Na zolotom kryl'tse sideli . . .' ('On the Golden Porch . . .'), which appeared in 1983 and is also the title of her first collection of stories (Molodaya Gvardiya, 1988), was barely noticed. But a longer piece, 'Peters' (*Novy mir*, 1986), established her reputation as the most original contemporary writer over night. The best literary journals have printed eighteen of her stories so far. She is presently working on longer narratives. Her literary debut in the USA is scheduled for 1989. A. A. Knopf will publish an English translation of her first collection.

Unlike her contemporary colleagues, she is rooted in the tradition of Gogol and the modernists of the 1920s, especially Olesha and Babel. The most Gogolian trait of her work is her use of one or more unreliable narrative voices which may reveal ignorance and insecurity, and vacillate or even contradict each other. Snatches of conversation, digressions, rhetorical questions and exclamations – some addressed to the reader – create a narrative which is a dialogue with the reader, with characters, with objects or with oneself. The real and the imagined, the lofty and the mundane stand side by side. The reader gets drawn into the story like into a game, having to listen, participate, imagine, remember, guess, shift attention, be alert to changes in tone, gesture, and mimicry, and be able to add and sort out the important from the unimportant.

The authorial stance is, needless to say, playfully ironic and distanced, a manner of narration characteristic of another twentieth-century model of Tolstaya with roots in Gogol: Vladimir Nabokov, widely admired among Russian writers and beginning to be published in the Soviet Union. Thus, she removes the reader from situations which traditionally would evoke compassion, introspection and a sense of personal responsibility or catharsis.

Scoffing at sentimentality, empathy, ethical involvement, she ridicules hallowed assumptions and the clichés of tradition. In fact, most of her stories use parody to undermine old canons.

In addition to the ironic narrative stance and the virtuosity of her narrative voices, strikingly colorful imagery determines the impact of her stories. It is the use of daring, unexpected and often extended metaphors that links her with Babel and Olesha. Often the animate and inanimate are incongruously related, or the spatial or temporal dimensions of the story expanded with the result of an uncanny sense of irreality due to the disappearance of boundaries. At the same time, the abundance of bright colors, shapes, sounds and sights in her imagery creates an airy, poetic atmosphere recalling that of the modernist painters. The use of poetic devices such as assonance, rhyme, etc., enhances this atmosphere.

Tolstaya's protagonists tend to be highly vulnerable. Victims of callousness, misunderstanding, contempt and ridicule, and incapable of self-fulfillment and intimacy, they are frequently elderly people or children. But her implied narrative attitude is not compassion or social pathos, but emotional distance, contemplative objectivity, irony. Her narratives thus often are caricatures of normal living and often debunk, for example, love relationships or other traditionally female concerns – looks, search for a love object, marriage. In the story 'The Poet and the Muse' ('Poet i muza'), for example, a strong-willed female go-getter realizes her romantic dream of passion and poetry by contriving to marry a compliant, weak poet. But she kills his poetic inspiration with her pragmatism, insensitivity, and selfishness. Thus, Tolstaya parodies the image of woman as source of inspiration and as object of adulation, and the myth of the benevolent power of women's love.

Her playfulness and taboo-breaking, however, is at times not only light-hearted and colorful. A note of melancholy sneaks in: what is left when the bubble is popped? Of course, it is the very stuff of life with all its absurdities, seen without rosy glasses and glosses, that delights her and that she wants to communicate. Writing 'is an attempt to overcome my own loneliness, an attempt to get across to others', as she said in an interview with *Literaturnaya gazeta* of July 1986.

'Dear Shura' was published as 'Milaya Shura' in *Oktyabr'*, no. 12 (1985). It is her favorite story, she told me in an interview.

WORKS AND SECONDARY LITERATURE IN ENGLISH

'Sonya' – originally published in *Avrora* in October 1984 – became available in English in Nancy Condee's translation in a newsletter of the *Institute of Current World Affairs* (NPC–17), 1986. It contains an excellent brief characterization of her work. For information about her, see also: Tatyana Tolstaya, 'A Little Man is a Normal Man', *Moscow News*, no. 8 (1987) 10; and Helena Goscilo, 'Tat'iana Tolstaia's "Dome of Many-Coloured Glass": The World Refracted through Multiple Perspectives', *Slavic Review*, 47, no. 2 (Summer 1988) 280–90.

Dear Shura
(1985)

The first time I saw Aleksandra Ernestovna she walked past me bathed in the rosy early-morning sunlight of a Moscow summer. Her legs are crooked, the stockings rolled down, her black suit is worn threadbare and spotted with grease. But the hat! The four seasons – guelder roses, lilies of the valley, cherries, barberries – decorate a disk of bright straw, fastened to her meager hair with a large pin. The cherries had become loose and are knocking about, sounding wooden. She must be ninety, I thought. But I was off by six years. From the roof of a cool-looking ancient house the sunny air slides down along a ray and runs back up, back up to the top where our gaze rarely takes us – where a leaden balcony hung suspended in uninhabitable heights, where the roof slopes off steeply, where a fragile grille juts right into the blue morning sky, where a turret melts away, and a spire, doves, angels, – no, I don't see well. Blissfully smiling, her eyes dazed with happiness, Aleksandra Ernestovna moves along on the sunny side, shifting her pre-revolutionary legs like the arms of a compass. Her shopping-bag, filled with a bottle of heavy cream, a roll and a carrot, weighs down her arm and rubs against the heavy black hem of her skirt. A gentle breeze has strolled in from the south, whispering of sea and roses, promising an easy ascent up heavenly ladders to the blue lands of paradise. Aleksandra Ernestovna smiles at the morning, smiles at me. Then her black attire and the bright hat, its dead fruit clacking, disappear around the corner.

Later I ran into her on the scorched boulevard. She was all

worked up, melting away with pity for a lonely sweaty child stuck in the sweltering city; she had never had any children of her own. A grubby slip is showing under her black skirt. The strange child had trustingly poured its crumbly treasures onto Aleksandra Ernestovna's lap. Don't mess up auntie's clothes! It doesn't matter. Let the child be.

I also saw her in the stuffy air of a movie theater ('Take off your hat, granny! We can't see anything!'). Out of accord with the passions on the screen, Aleksandra Ernestovna breathed heavily, rustled crumpled chocolate foil, gluing her delicate shop-bought dentures with the sticky sweet mass.

Finally, I found her caught in a stream of fire-breathing auto-mobiles at Nikitskie Vorota, frenziedly dashing in different direc-tions, having lost her bearings. She clutched my arm, and made a safe landing on the shore, but she had forever lost the respect of some black diplomat – sprawled behind the green-tinged glass of a shiny sports car – and his handsome curly-haired children. He gave off a roar and a whiff of blue smoke, and sped in the direction of the Conservatory, while Aleksandra Ernestovna, trembling, frightened, eyes agape, hung on my arm and pulled me to her communal refuge – to her knick-knacks, oval frames, dried flowers – trailed by a cloud of validol.*

Two tiny rooms, a high stucco ceiling; on the buckling wallpaper a ravishing beauty, smiling, pensive, or teasing. . . . It is Aleksandra Ernestovna: dear Shura[1] Yes, yes, it's me! The picture with the hat, and without it, and with hair undone. Oh, what a . . .! And this is her second husband, and that her third, not a very good choice. Well, why talk of it now? . . . If perhaps in those days she had decided to run off to Ivan Nikolaevich. . . . Who is this Ivan Nikolaevich? He's not on the wall, he's pressed into the album, stretched into four cardboard slots, squeezed by a lady in a bustle, crushed by some short-lived white dogs dead even before the Japanese War.

Sit down, please. Sit down. What can I offer you? . . . Come by again, of course, please do come again! Aleksandra Ernestovna has no one else in the world, and she'd so much like to chat a little!

. . . Fall. It rains. Aleksandra Ernestovna, do you recognize me? It's me! Remember? Well, it doesn't matter. I've come by to see

---

1. 'Shura' is the endearing diminutive form of 'Aleksandra'.

you. To see me! How wonderful! Come over here, please, I'll put things away right now. I live alone, you see. Survived everyone. Three husbands, you know? And Ivan Nikolaevich begged me to come, but . . . . Maybe I should have made up my mind? Life's so long. That's me, and that's me, too. And that's my second husband. I had three husbands, you know? Though the third one wasn't very . . . .

The first one was a lawyer, very famous. We lived very well. We'd go to Finland in spring, to the Crimea in summer. There were white cookies and black coffee. Hats with lace. Oysters were very expensive. . . . At night – the theater. And so many admirers!

Oh, of course, she had affairs all her life, what else? That's what a woman's heart is like! Three years ago a violinist rented a corner from her. Twenty-six years old, a prize-winner, and what eyes he had! Of course, he kept his feelings hidden in his heart, but his eyes, well, they gave away everything! At night Aleksandra Ernestovna would ask him, 'How about some tea?' and he would just look and say NOTH-ING! Well, you understand? . . . Cun-ning! So he kept his silence while he lived at Aleksandra Ernestovna's. But she could tell that he was on fire, that his heart was virtually seething. The two of them together, alone, in two tiny rooms every evening. . . . You know, there was something in the air – it was obvious to both. . . . He wouldn't be able to stand it and would go for a walk, wander the streets somewhere until late. Aleksandra Ernestovna remained steadfast and gave him no hope. Then he married some woman, quite an ordinary person, out of grief of course, and he moved. One time after his wedding he ran into Aleksandra Ernestovna in the street and gave her such a look – it literally reduced her to ashes! But again he said nothing, buried everything in his soul.

Yes, Aleksandra Ernestovna's heart was never empty. She had had three husbands, incidentally. With her second husband, before the war, she lived in a huge apartment. He was a well-known doctor. They had famous guests. There were always lots of flowers. And always gaiety. And he died gaily too: when the end was in sight, Aleksandra Ernestovna decided to invite gipsies. You know, I think it's easier to die when you look at something beautiful, boisterous and gay, don't you think so? It was impossible to find genuine gipsies. But Aleksandra Ernestovna, imaginative as she was, didn't lose her head. She hired some dark-skinned girls, decked them out in some boisterous, glittering, flowing garments, opened the door to the bedroom of the dying man – and off they went: they started to jingle and wail, to twang, and to form circles and wheels and dance: rosy, golden, golden, rosy flashed the underskirts! Her husband hadn't expected anything like this; he had already turned his gaze to *other* shores. And suddenly this invasion, this swinging of scarves, this squealing; he lifted his body, started gesturing with his hands and wheezed, 'Leave me alone!' But they continued even more gaily, even tap-danced! That's how he died, God rest his soul. The third husband though wasn't very . . . .

But Ivan Nikolaevich. . . . Oh, Ivan Nikolaevich! All that had happened was: the Crimea, 1913, stripes of sun entering through drawn blinds, slicing the planed white floor into small planks. . . . Sixty years had passed, but . . . Ivan Nikolaevich had simply lost his head: leave your husband right away and come to the Crimea, to join him. For good. And she had promised to. Then, in Moscow, she had hesitated: what would they live on? And where? And he had deluged her with letters: 'Dear Shura, please come, please!' Her husband was busy, spent little time at home; and there, under the blue skies of the Crimea, Ivan Nikolaevich paced the gentle sand like a tiger: 'Dear Shura, come for good!' But he was so poor that he didn't have the money for a train ticket to Moscow! Letter after letter arrived, every day, for an entire year. Aleksandra Ernestovna would show them to her.

How he loved her! Should she leave or shouldn't she?

Human life spreads out over four seasons. Spring!!! Summer. Fall. . . . Winter? But even winter is behind Aleksandra Ernestovna. Where is she now? In which direction are her faded, tearful eyes gazing? Tilting her head backwards and lifting her red eyelids, Aleksandra Ernestovna squeezes yellowish drops into her red eyes. Like a rosy balloon, her skull shines through the fine spider's web of her hair. Did that mousy pigtail sixty years ago really cloak her shoulders like a peacock's tail in black? Was it really true that persistent but penniless Ivan Nikolaevich had lost himself once and for all in those eyes? Aleksandra Ernestovna groans as her knotty feet fumble for the slippers.

Now we're going to have tea. I won't let you leave without tea. Certainly not. Don't even think of it.

Yes, I won't go anywhere. That's what I came for: to have some tea. And I brought some pastry. I'm going to put on the kettle right away, don't fret. And meanwhile she will get the velvet album and the old letters.

It is a long way to the kitchen, as if to another town, along an endless shiny hall waxed so well that traces of the mahogany polish cling to your soles for two days. At the end of the tunnel shines the bright spot of the kitchen window, like a faint light in an impenetrable robbers' glen. And twenty-three neighbors hold their breath behind clean white doors. Halfway to the kitchen a telephone hangs on the wall. A note shines white, tacked up long ago by Aleksandra Ernestovna: 'Fire – 01. Ambulance – 03. In case of my death – call Elizaveta Osipovna.' Elizaveta Osipovna passed away long ago. It doesn't matter. Aleksandra Ernestovna forgot.

A pathological, sterile cleanliness reigns in the kitchen. On one of the burners, someone's cabbage soup is babbling to itself. In a corner hovers the curly cone of smoke left by a neighbor's Belomor cigarette. A chicken in a shopping-bag hangs outside the window, as if punished, swaying in the nasty wind. The bare wet tree looks huddled up with grief. Some man in an unbuttoned coat stands, his face pressed against the fence. The sad circumstances of place, time and action. And what if Aleksandra Ernestovna had agreed to drop everything and to run off to the South, to Ivan Nikolaevich? Where would she be now? She had already sent a telegram – 'I'm coming, pick me up' – put her things together, hidden the ticket in a secret section of her wallet, fastened her peacock hair into a tower, and sat in an armchair by the window, to wait. And, far away in the South, Ivan Nikolaevich, disbelieving his luck, burning with excitement, had dashed to the railroad station – to wander about, worry, fret, make arrangements, rent, set up appointments, lose his head, and stare at the horizon hazy from the sweltering heat. And then? She had sat waiting in the armchair until evening, when the first pure stars appeared. And then? She had undone her hair and shaken her head. And then? Well, what then, and then! Life had gone by – that's what happened then.

The kettle boiled. I'll make the tea stronger. The tea xylophone is playing a simple little piece: lid, lid, spoon, lid, rag, lid, rag, rag, spoon, handle, handle. Long is the way back through the dark hall with two teapots. Twenty-three neighbors behind white doors are listening: is she going to spill her rotten tea on our clean floor? She won't, don't worry. I open the wings of the Gothic door with my foot. I was gone for an eternity, but Aleksandra Ernestovna still remembers me.

She has brought out some cracked, raspberry-colored cups, decorated the table with some lace mats, and is rummaging in the dark coffin of a cabinet, setting in motion wafts of air that smell of bread and biscuits and well up from behind its wooden sides. Don't get out, smell! She had to catch it and shut it in with the help of the cut-glass doors. There you go. Now you stay under lock and seal.

Aleksandra Ernestovna brings out some *wonderful* jam; it had been given to her. You just try it – no, no, just try it; oh, oh, words can't describe it. Yes, the jam is really unusual, amazing, don't you think? It's true, absolutely, never in my life did I taste . . . . Well, I'm so happy, I knew you'd like it; take some more, please, do, I beg you! (Damn it, I'll get a toothache again!)

I like you, Aleksandra Ernestovna, I like you very much, especially on this photograph where your face has this beautiful oval, and on this one, where you toss back your head and laugh, showing your dazzling teeth, and on this one, where you act capricious, throwing your arm behind your neck so that the lacy frills are sure to slide off your elbow. I like your life that took its boisterous course somewhere and is of no interest to anyone now, your vanished youth, the solemn succession of your deceased admirers and husbands, everyone who ever called you or whom you invited, all those who passed by and disappeared behind the tall mountain. I'll be seeing you, and I'll be bringing you thick cream and carrots, which are very good for your eyes, and do please open your brown-velvet albums that haven't been aired for so long. Let the pretty high-school girls get some air, and the bearded gentlemen stretch their legs, and gallant Ivan Nikolaevich light up with a smile. It doesn't matter, he won't see you; don't worry Aleksandra Ernestovna! . . . You had to make up your mind then. You had to. Well, and she had made up her mind. Here he is, right here, at arm's length! Here, take him in your hands, hold him; here he is, the flat, cold, glossy, slightly yellowed, gold-edged Ivan Nikolaevich! Eh, do you hear? She had decided, yes, she would come. Pick me up, that was it – she won't vacillate any more. Come and meet me. Where are you? Eh! Hello!

Thousands of years, thousands of days, thousands of transparent, impenetrable curtains fell from the sky, condensed, congealed into solid walls, blocked up roads, and wouldn't let Aleksandra Ernestovna reach her beloved, lost in the centuries. He remained there, on the other side of time, alone, on the dusty southern train station in the South, walking up and down the platform covered with spat-out sunflower shells, looking at his watch, kicking the dusty, bare corncobs with his boots, impatiently plucking bluish cypress-cones. He is waiting, waiting, waiting for the train to emerge from the sweltering morning distance. She didn't come. She won't come. She deceived him. No, that's not true! She wanted to come! She is ready, her baggage packed! White, semi-transparent dresses had their knees tucked in the narrow darkness of the suitcase; the *nécessaire* flashes silvery, its leather squeaking; shameless bathing-suits that barely cover the knees – with arms bared to the shoulder! – are waiting for their hour, squinting in anticipation. . . . The hatbox holds an impossible, exquisite, ethereal hat – oh, words fail to describe it – a white zephyr, a miracle of miracles! At the very bottom, reclining on its back, paws curled up, sleeps a little box with hairpins, combs, silk lace, diamond-powder glued to cardboard palettes for her dainty fingernails; small trifles. There's jasmine gin sealed in a crystal bottle – how it will blaze with a million rainbow colors in the blinding ocean light! She's ready. What has kept her? What's always keeping us from going ahead? Hurry up, time's passing! . . . Time's passing; the years' invisible layers get thicker and thicker; the railroad tracks become rusty, the roads overgrown, and the weeds along the ravines more lush and luxuriant. Time flows, rocking dear Shura's boat, splashing wrinkles on her matchless face.

. . . Some more tea?

And after the war she came back – with a third husband – to these very same tiny rooms. The third husband never stopped complaining. The hallway was too long, the light dim, the windows looked into the courtyard. Everything was behind them. The fancy guests had died; the flowers dried up. Rain is drumming against the windows. He kept complaining and then died; and Aleksandra Ernestovna didn't notice when and of what.

She took Ivan Nikolaevich out of the album and looked at him for a long time. How he had begged her to come! And she had already bought the ticket – here it is, the ticket. Black numbers on a solid piece of cardboard. You may look at it this way, but you can also turn it upside-down, no matter how: forgotten signs of an unknown alphabet, a codified permit for the other shore.

Maybe, if one could find the magic word, if one could guess, if one could sit down and do some thinking or search somewhere. . . . There had to be a door, a crack, an unnoticed secret passage back to that day. They had closed off everything, but maybe at one point they were daydreaming and left a crack; maybe in some old house; or if you bent away some boards in an attic – or maybe in some God-forsaken side street there was a breach in the wall just carelessly covered up with bricks, hastily plastered over, stuffed crosswise helter-skelter. . . . Maybe not here, but in another town. . . . Maybe, in the tangle of railroad tracks, somewhere off to the side, stands a rusty old carriage, its floor collapsed, the very same carriage in which dear Shura failed to take her seat.

'Here's my compartment. Let me pass, please. Excuse me, but here's my ticket; everything's on it!' Over there, at the other end, are the rusty coils of the springs, the reddish, warped ribs of the walls; there's blue sky in the ceiling above, and grass underneath: that's her lawful place, hers! Nobody occupied it, nobody had the right to!

. . . Some more tea? A snowstorm.

. . . Some more tea? The apple-trees are blooming; the dandelions; the lilac. Oh, it's so hot. Away from Moscow – off to the sea. See you, Aleksandra Ernestovna! I'll tell you what it's like there, at the end of the Earth. Hasn't the sea dried up, the Crimea drifted away like a dry leaf, the blue sky faded? Hasn't your exhausted, excited beloved left his voluntary guard-post at the railroad station?

Aleksandra Ernestovna is waiting for me in the stone hell of Moscow. No, everything is as it should be, everything's all right! There, on the Crimea, an invisible, but restless Ivan Nikolaevich strides back and forth over the dusty platform in his white tunic, pulls his watch from his pocket, dries off his shaven neck; back and forth along the latticed, diminutive fence, soiled with white dust, anguished, bewildered. Beautiful heavy-faced young women in slacks, fellows with rolled-up sleeves, enveloped in the impudent badadoo-badadoo of their transistors; old women in white scarves with buckets full of plums; Southern ladies with plastic acanthus clips; old men in stiff synthetic hats – they all walk right through Ivan Nikolaevich, without noticing it; they push their way right through him, stopping at nothing. But he doesn't know anything, doesn't detect anything – he's waiting; time went astray, got stuck halfway, somewhere around Kursk, tripped above the brooks resounding with nightingales and, blind as it is, lost its way on the plains full of sunflowers.

Ivan Nikolaevich, wait a second! I'll tell her, I'll let her know;

don't leave, she'll come, I give you my word, she has decided already, she's agreed; you just stay there for the time being, it's all right, she'll come right away, she's all packed, all set, just needs to pick up her things; and she has her ticket, I know it, I swear, I saw it in the velvet album, she stuck it under a photograph; it's a little worn and torn, that's true, but it doesn't matter – I think they'll let her pass. There, of course . . . you can't get past, something's in the way, I don't remember; well, somehow she'll manage, she'll think of something – she has the ticket, right? – and that's what counts: the ticket; and you know, what's most important, she's made up her mind, that's right – it's true, I tell you!

For Aleksandra Ernestovna you had to ring five times, third button from the top. It's draughty on the landing, and the sections of the dusty stained-glass panel, decorated with frivolous lotuses – the flowers of forgetfulness – are half-open.

Who? She died.

What do you mean? . . . Wait a second . . . Why? . . . But I was just. . . . I just went there and back! What do you mean?

Glaring heat aiming at the eyes falls upon those leaving the crypt of the entry hall. Wait a second. . . .

Behind the corner, in the trash-bins on an asphalt rondelle, the spirals of an earthly existence come to an end. And where did you think they would end? Beyond the clouds perhaps? No, they are over there, those spirals, like the springs dangling from a rotten, gaping sofa. Everything has been dumped there. The oval portrait of dear Shura – glass shattered, her face crumpled. . . . The junk of an old woman – some stockings. . . . the hat with four seasons. Don't you need chipped cherries? No? Why not? . . . A jug with a missing spout. But the velvet album, of course, was stolen. It's going to be handy for cleaning boots. You're idiots, all of you; I won't cry – what for? The garbage turned soft and fluid in the sun; a bunch of letters has been trampled into the goo. 'Dear Shura, when are you finally . . .'; 'Dear Shura, just tell me . . . .'

And one dried-out letter, a yellow striped butterfly, flutters in the air beneath the dusty poplar, not knowing where to settle.

What am I to do with all this? Turn around and leave. It's hot. The wind stirs up the dust. And Aleksandra Ernestovna, dear Shura, real as a mirage, crowned with wooden fruits and cardboard flowers, floats, smiling, along the scintillating lane and around the corner, southward, toward the unthinkably distant glittering South, to the desolate platform; she floats, melts and dissolves in the heat of midday.

12

Sergei Zalygin

Born on 23 September 1913 in Siberia, Sergei Pavlovich Zalygin belongs to the older generation of Soviet writers. After training in agriculture and hydrology (as an engineer) he received the equivalent of a Ph.D. in technical sciences in 1948, became the head of an agricultural land-reclamation department, and took on duties with the Academy of Sciences in Novosibirsk. In the late 1960s he moved to Moscow. In addition to pursing a full career as a scientist, Zalygin has been writing since 1929, utilizing his professional experience in his creative work.

His first stories appeared in 1935, and his first collection in 1941. *Stories of the North* (*Severnye rasskazy*) followed in 1947. Travels in the Siberian countryside resulted in sketches about what he had seen, which were published subsequently in *Novy mir*. They were part of the general boom in essay-writing occasioned by the woeful state of Soviet agriculture and the neglect of cultural monuments.

Zalygin's interest was not confined to an investigation of the Soviet countryside. Professional contacts with the Soviet intellectual elite resulted in a work called *Witnesses* (*Svideteli*, 1956), in which he exposed a new variety of philistinism found in the middle and upper strata of Soviet society. This kind of investigation continued in his first novel, *Paths in the Altai* (*Tropy Altaya*, 1962). The personal values of a group of scholars on an expedition in the Altai Mountains and their attitude to nature and to conservation are its central themes.

In the 1960s Zalygin became one of the leading Soviet writers. His best works are investigations of the fate of the Russian peasant during the Civil War and collectivization. The novel *On the Irtysh* (*Na Irtyshe*, 1964) caused a sensation by the distinction it drew between the genuine revolutionary conscience and revolutionary phrase-making as a cloak for private profiteering and for bureaucratic indifference to people's suffering. This novel helped delineate the moral and aesthetic character of what later became known as 'village prose'.

Salt Ravine (*Solyonaya pad'*, 1967), *The Commission* (*Kommissiya*,

1975) and *After the Storm* (*Posle buri*, 2 vols, 1982 and 1986) continued to deal with the problematic history of Soviet agriculture. In the latter work, which took a long time to write and publish, Zalygin tries to break down preconceptions about the New Economic Policy of the 1920s with its many compromises and major decisions about how socialism should be built. But at the same time Zalygin has been active as an environmentalist and journalist, whose persuasive articles helped prevent the construction of the Lower Ob hydro-electric station in the 1960s and have recently contributed to the demise of the project to reverse the Siberian rivers.

Zalygin's stories of the 1970s continued to reflect his major concerns, but also his vitality as a writer: he experimented with the fantastic – especially in *Oska, the Funny Boy* (*Oska smeshnoi mal'chik*, 1973), an unusual story about the destructive potential of science and progress – and with new themes, among them the theme of this anthology: the situation of women in Soviet society. In 1973 he published the novel *The South American Variant* (*Yuzhno-amerikanski variant*) which analyzes what we would call the midlife crisis of a forty-five-year-old woman and engineer, Irina Mansurova. She commits adultery from frustration, her sense of having lost out as a woman because of technological progress. But Irina's problem is presented as more than just an individual problem. To her, women are either purely feminine or they are desexed, rational 'female eunuchs', who have gender like inanimate objects. Such women are cut off from their biological destiny and hence unfulfilled, constantly searching for inner contentment and personal happiness or for a new spirituality. Irina's affair is disappointing, and she consoles herself with an imaginary companion, 'the Knight', with whom she indulges her longing for alternative lifestyles and adventures. The novel's title symbolises these imaginary journeys to distant places.

Zalygin has a fine ear for dialogue and the idiosyncrasies of Siberian usage. His narrative structure and style are dominantly conventional.

The 'scientific-technological revolution' (abbreviated in Russian as NTR) and the issues of its effect on women and their role in it supply the theme of the story selected for this anthology. 'Women and the NTR' first appeared as 'Zhenshchina i NTR' in *Novy mir*, 1986, no. 6.

WORKS AND SECONDARY LITERATURE IN ENGLISH

The South-American Variant, tr. Kevin Widle (St Lucia, Queensland: University of Queensland Press, 1979).

Gasiarowska, Xenia, 'Two Decades of Love and Marriage in Soviet Fiction', *Russian Review*, 1975, no. 1, pp. 10–21 *(passim)*.

Hughes, Ann, 'Sergey Zalygin and the "Zhenskiy Vopros"', *Journal of Russian Studies*, no. 50 (1986) 38–44.

Nadine Natov, 'Daily Life and Individual Psychology in Soviet-Russian Prose of the 1970s', *Russian Review*, 1974, no. 4, pp. 357–71 *(passim)*.

Shneidman, Norman N., 'Sergei Zalygin: Innovation and Variety', *Soviet Literature in the 1970s* (Toronto: University of Toronto Press, 1979) pp. 61–74.

Cf. also summaries of Soviet discussions of Zalygin's works in *Current Digest of the Soviet Press*, xxv, no. 48 (26 Dec 1973) 8–10; xxvi, no. 45 (4 Dec 1974) 17–18; xxix, no. 2 (9 Feb 1977) 8–10; xxxviii, no. 45 (10 Dec 1986) 13–15, 23–4.

Women and the NTR*
(1986)

It took the Kuzmenkovs almost exactly half an hour to get a taxi. Finally they caught one, squeezed onto the frayed seats and relaxed.

'I'd sew on your button right now,' Nadezhda Vasilyevna said. 'I mean, the button to your leather coat.'

'You've been wanting to do it for half a year.'

'And I might have for three years, but today, right now, I would have sewed it on, honestly! In the subway yesterday I saw a man with a leather coat, and it had only one button. It made me think of you and your coat right away.'

'And I saw a man without coat and hat in the subway today, but I didn't think of you.'

'Well, it just means he was hardy, someone toughened up from childhood on.' Nadezhda Vasilyevna sighed. 'Or he ran away from somewhere. I bet he ran straight from his job! Oh, something else: what's the name and patronymic of the person we're going to see now? I can't remember for the life of me.'

'How often do I have to repeat it to you: Associate Member of the Academy of Sciences of the USSR Anatoly Agafonovich Burlyai! Got it? Do you want me to repeat it?'

'You don't need to tell me it's Burlyai, or that he's an Associate Member of the Academy! I only forgot the patronymic: Aga-fonovich!'

'He's the director of a very important research institute; chairman of the commission – a commission of the Presidium of the Academy of Sciences. And, just think, he gives an interview to obscure little journalist Kuzmenkov. Just get that into your head!'

'Lyovka! How often have I told you? Don't put yourself down! I don't like it, and I won't tolerate it! That's something you must get into your head, and should have long ago.'

'An interview about the most pertinent, topical subject – the NTR – and, if I manage, it'll be even more precise, about *women* and the NTR. It's not going to leave anybody indifferent! It won't pass unnoticed!'

'Maybe so. . . . But what am I supposed to do for your Burlyai? You're hiding something, Lyovka, aren't you?'

'I've already explained it to you more than once! He asked me, "Don't you have a wife?" And I said, "Of course!" And he said, "How about inviting her, too? It would be interesting for such a conversation!" And I said . . . .'

'If he asked me to come, you probably talked about me. Why else would he invite me? He asked you whether your wife was young, didn't he?'

'He did – out of politeness. Everybody knows that the wife isn't older than the husband!'

'And what did you say?'

'That you were young.'

'It's a bad habit to talk about me behind my back. So he's probably going to look me over?'

'Yes, most likely. . . . Nadezhda, just be quiet for a while and let me concentrate. It's a very important, serious interview. A crucial meeting. A very . . . .'

'As if I hadn't seen any Academy members before. Big deal . . . . With us, at the Polytechnic . . . .' Nadezhda Vasilyevna turned away and started looking out of the window.

The panels in Burlyai's office were too glossy and too dark. Bleak to the point of funereal. And the chandelier was too modest, almost domestic. Fine for a bedroom, but not for the office of an Academy member.

Burlyai was over fifty. His nose, though not excessively big, sat too prominently on his face. Well, if a person has small eyes the nose seems bigger. His tie was crude and poorly made, and there was too much red in it.

When Lyovka placed the tape-recorder in front of Burlyai and asked his first question, 'Tell me, Anatoly Agafonovich, what, in your opinion, is the greatest impact of the NTR on simple people like us, and especially on women?' Burlyai looked very attentively at Nadezhda Vasilyevna as if trying to guess what her response to this question might be and what kind of person – or, rather, woman – she was.

'Well? What am I like?' Nadezhda's glance said in response, and, surprisingly, Burlyai became somewhat flustered. Maybe he just acts that way, she thought. Maybe it's his habit to pretend to be flustered at the beginning.

'You see,' Burlyai began, in a rather dull but generally pleasant voice. 'You see, in my opinion the NTR, like any other global phenomenon, affects everything and is manifest in everything, every day. That's why you can't define it exactly, that's why you can't hold it in your fist. The fact is, it has spread everywhere.'

'That's true,' Nadezhda nodded. 'Like sclerosis.'

Burlyai looked at her more intently and would probably have said something, if Lyovka hadn't interrupted: 'Anatoly Agafonovich, you can speak in as much detail as you like, and you don't have to worry about the time. Lots of people were fascinated by your article in *Komsomolskaya pravda*, but there you seemed to be confined by the space a newspaper can allot. Our journal, however, can give you any amount of space you need, a printer's sheet or more. So where did we stop? And, Nadezhda, please don't interrupt Anatoly Agafonovich!'

Burlyai remained silent, and Lyovka encouraged him: 'Anatoly Agafonovich, you aren't a philosopher, or a sociologist, or an economist, or a futurologist, or a . . . . You are a great authority in biology and so you obviously look at the problem with detachment. Of course, you see it from your own independent viewpoint, and that's especially interesting and valuable!'

There was again silence. Nadezhda Vasilyevna decided to divert him.

'May I ask a question? May I turn to you, to begin with?' she said.

'Of course, go ahead!' Burlyai agreed gladly. 'Just join our conversation. Or, even, why don't you start it. Let's have your question guide our talk.'

'My question is: what's going to come after the NTR? Another revolution? I mean, something permanent?[1] Or are we going to have the beginning of a normal evolution?'

'Nadezhda!' Lyovka was seriously upset. 'Nadezhda! What sort of a question is that? Just think a minute: what logic does it have?'

'What do you mean, what logic? A normal logic. Everything that exists has to end sometimes. And what doesn't end, doesn't exist. What's so abnormal?'

'Well, and the universe? Do you think it'll end one day?' asked Burlyai, smiling.

'The universe, well . . .,' Natasha mumbled pensively and then came up with an answer: 'The universe has no beginning! But the NTR began right in front of my own eyes; I witnessed it; that means it must definitely end one day! Everything that has witnesses ends one day.'

'Maybe so . . ., maybe.' Burlyai fell into thought and examined Nadezhda again attentively. 'But the fact is that one epoch is unable to foresee the next. During feudalism nobody anticipated capitalism. And during capitalism nobody foresaw the NTR. So the NTR doesn't know what comes after it.'

'You think so? And when will the NTR find out about it? As you know, as early as the capitalist stage people expected socialism to come. And socialism clearly anticipates communism,' Nadezhda Vasilyevna argued, not giving in.

'We must turn off the tape-recorder,' Lyovka said with a deep sigh. 'Let's just talk in general at first, and we'll turn it on again when we touch on the essence of the question. We've got to save cassettes.'

'Oh yes!' Nadezhda laughed ironically. 'I know your technology:

---

1. 'Permanent' echoes the concept of 'permanent revolution' which Trotsky had advocated originally in 1905. It meant that the socialist and bourgeois revolutions should be telescoped into one. The socialist revolution would begin as soon as the bourgeois revolution had taken place. Nadezhda Vasilyevna has clearly only the vaguest notion of what the original concept meant.

you switch it off, and then it won't turn on. Your economizing is going to get you nothing but ridicule.'

'Let's take the bull by the horns,' said Burlyai. 'I think that it's very important to see the various separate sub-systems of the NTR as some whole. That's the point!'

'Yes, indeed!' Lyovka rejoiced. 'Could you illustrate this interesting idea with a concrete example? Any example, so long as it's concrete.'

'The point is that the NTR needs some precise infrastructure. It is, well, one can also see it as an organization, even a global one, though it is not a closed system yet.'

'Go on, go on, Anatoly Agafonovich! And let's have a concrete example with this thought too, please.' Lyovka virtually trembled with impatience.

'The point is, just imagine how many sub-systems exist in the NTR! The sub-system of the creation of new technology is one; the sub-system, an almost independent one at that, of applying this technology to production is two; the ideological sub-system, its penetration into people's consciousness, is three. The sub-system of education and upbringing, although close to three, is entirely independent, so that's four. The protection of nature, in other words the ecological sub-system, is five. The demographic is . . . which number did we come to? Was it the fifth or the sixth sub-system?'

'The sixth, Anatoly Agafonovich. Let's focus on the next one, the seventh!' Lyovka pressed on.

'All right,' agreed Burlyai. 'Let's take the following problem, the emancipation of women, as the seventh sub-system. That's a phenomenon that started in the last century and looked quite different thirty years ago from the way it looks today. Essential, even fundamental shifts have occurred here too! This sub-system also must be included in the general picture of the NTR. What do you think, Nadezhda . . .'

'Vasilyevna', Lyovka prompted, slightly uncertain.

'Well, what do you think, Nadezhda Vasilyevna? What do you think of this artificial separation?'

'Artificial?' Nadezhda shrugged her shoulders. 'What should I say? It's artificial for scientists and journalists, that's true, but isn't it quite natural as far as the NTR itself is concerned? It probably just can't exist in any way other than split up into various sub-systems?'

'I'm sorry Nadezhda,' Lyovka said, noticeably blushing, 'but only an abnormal intellect – yes, abnormal! – can portray such an unnatural division as normal!'

Nadezhda was about to turn on Lyovka, but Burlyai intercepted. 'Dear Nadezhda Vasilyevna,' he said, 'the point is, we have to begin talking about something more concrete and more interesting for you. Therefore I suggest that we start again at the beginning, and, instead of you asking me, I will ask you the following question: have you noticed that in our contemporary society women increasingly take on the role of men's educators? I'll explain. In nursery schools, almost without exception, the teachers are women; in school they are the majority, and in the lower grades it is almost exclusively women again. If you like, this is also a discovery of the NTR. A dis-co-ve-ry! A boy, after all, should be educated by a man. People understood this perfectly well in the past, when girls were educated by governesses and boys by male tutors.'

'And coaches,' Nadezhda Vasilyevna agreed. 'And teachers of fencing!'

'There you are; so you remember?' Burlyai smiled amiably, even cordially.

'No, I don't remember,' Nadezhda sighed, distressed. 'But I know that it's all the men's fault. Just look at the women! NTR or no NTR, in our century women bring up children just as they always did, for better or worse, and continue to do so. And the men? Did any one of them ever sacrifice himself for the next male generation and volunteer to work in a nursery school? I don't know a single case! And who of them ever became a first grade teacher? Again, I don't know a single example. I just know that men are unhappy with how women bring up boys. I know that they're amazed when women treat adult men the same way. But what's so surprising? Nothing at all! If I got used to rearing a twelve- or fifteen-year-old boy, why shouldn't I rear a forty-year-old man? The difference between them isn't all that great. And, since men bring up neither boys nor girls, they can't possibly have any experience. But women raise both, so they have the experience. Do you understand? You know that men love to dump their responsibilities on somebody else – machines, or women, whatever's around. They dump them and then they call it a "discovery". For example, the NTR.'

Nadezhda Vasilyevna never considered herself a woman with excessive self-confidence, but at this moment she was satisfied with herself. Smiling goodnaturedly at Burlyai, she said, 'When our son Kolya was small he told everybody, "When my mom was little, I didn't even exist at all!" and he was very happy about the . . . dis-co-ve-ry. . . .'

Lyovka asked, 'What's the point of all this, Nadezhda?'

'I think it's about how men, even as children, are happy about their discoveries.'

Lyovka was nervous, but for no good reason. And, since that was the case, it was his personal problem. He'd be nervous for a while and then calm down all by himself.

After some silence Burlyai said, 'The point is: I think it makes sense to return to the beginning of our conversation, which has been quiet interesting so far, and, of course, still is. Dear Nadezhda Vasilyevna, you certainly surprised me from the very outset, when you asked what's going to happen after the NTR. Well, we haven't yet worked out all the ins and outs of the NTR, not yet, mind you, and you want to know already what's going to come afterwards. Dear Nadezhda Vasilyevna you know, I don't recall that anyone has ever posed such a question as yours! We're at a time when tomorrow there might not even be a tomorrow, not to mention the following decade or year. Don't you know that? And don't you take this into consideration when you ask what's going to be "afterwards"? After the NTR?'

'How can I not know? I'm an adult woman! And do you think I, as an adult woman, am only aware of a few of these disgusting and depressing and very unfair things? And what am I to do with all my knowledge? Live disgustingly myself? Or be depressed? Or unfair? No! Whatever the case, I prefer to live decently, and to be as fair as possible and not too depressed. And I still want to know what's going to happen after the end of what's happening now. What will follow it? If nothing follows, what's the point of our conversation today? What do you prefer . . . Anatoly Aga-fonovich?'

His fingers rapping on the table, Burlyai answered, 'I suppose there is some logic . . .'

'In what?' Nadezhda butted in.

'In your answer. To my question.'

'Of course there is!' Nadezhda agreed. 'If you eliminate the logic from my answer, what's left?' And she said these words in the tone of voice she used with Kolya when explaining something to him. This was also the tone she used with Lyovka, and not that infrequently. She knew it was a bad habit, but it wasn't that simple to get rid of habits, the more so if these habits continually got the better of you.

But, before she could decide whether she indeed had offended Burlyai seriously or just a little bit, Lyovka interfered. 'Anatoly Agafonovich!' he exclaimed, clearly in panic. 'Please just forget about her! She's got herself wound up. That happens to her, you know, it does. I've got to admit. But I didn't think, I didn't assume that she'd get so keyed up today, and in your presence! We didn't even get a chance to really get talking, and she's already in a huff!'

'What's wrong with getting keyed up?' Nadezhda Vasilyevna asked, shrugging her shoulders. 'I think you men should thank God that women still get keyed up . . . and all by themselves!' Then she said, 'Lyovka! Go have a smoke, why don't you?'

'Christ! I haven't smoked for a year!' Lyovka got visibly more upset.

'Really? Then just simply take a break, Lyovka.'

Lyovka remained seated, staring at her. Nadezhda Vasilyevna also fixed her eyes upon him, and then she made a decision.

'All right,' she said. 'Let's do it that way: I'll be the first to take a break, right here, by the window.'

She rose and walked over to the window, where a solemn row of decorous chairs had been set up along the entire wall. She quickly powdered her face, arranged her hair, and fixed whatever had become disorderly during the conversation, glancing in the direction of Burlyai to see what he would say next.

'The point is,' Burlyai said pensively, 'we really need some goal in our discussion.'

'Well, I couldn't care less, now!' Nadezhda answered Burlyai with an irreconcilably angry look. 'If you don't ask me to return to the table, you can have ten goals, so far as I'm concerned! Do you want me to leave? For good? Bang the door and leave! Why not?'

But she didn't leave. Instead she started looking out the window attentively.

It was getting dark. The wet snow and slush had increased, the crowd of pedestrians had become even more dense; especially as they crossed the street by the traffic lights. The yellow of the headlights the cars beamed at the crossing masses had darkened, and it was somehow impossible to imagine that there was a single happy person in that crowd, illuminated by the murky yellow rays. But there probably was one, rushing to some happy rendez-vous. For a minute Nadezhda Vasilyevna fought, with all her might, the urge to burst into tears. Suddenly she thought what a nice woman she was! Of course she was nice. They had insulted her, and she had quietly and calmly withdrawn to the window, was looking outside, thinking her own thoughts, and wasn't in anybody's way. And, the longer she stood, the more thoughts came to her. She was unaware of the point at which she had decided to improve even further and sew the button on Lyovka's leather coat, check Kolya's homework and surprise him with a new fountain-pen. Yes, that's what she was going to do. . . . Tonight Lyovka would be in a rage over the way she had thwarted his conversation with Burlyai, but she would smile silently and sew on his button. Yes, tonight she'd start a new life in general and wouldn't ever quarrel with Lyovka again. That was it! That would settle things once and for all. And she also had to understand Lyovka. Forty-two was a critical age. He was either going to be stuck with what he was today, or he was going to make progress in his development. And he should advance; he had what it took, and just needed support. She would have to be a real mainstay to him. She had been in the past, of course, but – why hide it? – not always. Besides, all this wasn't Lyovka's fault. After all, Burlyai, the owner of this office, had invited her, and it was Burlyai who should be civil with his guests, especially if the guest was a woman. 'Women and the NTR?!' What did this Burlyai understand about women? And, if anything, then about what kind of women? She, Nadezhda, would rather be dead than be one of the women Burlyai understood! And what did he understand about the NTR? Everything so far indicated that he understood nothing except maybe some petty details. She sensed it, her instinct told her that this was so, and when had her intuition ever let her down, especially where men were involved? And Lyovka, whatever you could say, was still a nice fellow! He was young and slim, and his nose was normal. Burlyai, surprisingly, had a round face, but a big nose! Served him right! Usually people with round faces had little noses, and people with long faces had big ones. Well, these were such trifles, nothing but trifles. A different matter was the question why, from the very beginning, in their family Nadezhda Vasilyevna had stayed Nadezhda Vasilyevna, and Lev Vladimirovich had become Lyovka. What if it had been the other way around, if Nadezhda Vasilyevna had become Nadka, and Lyovka had remained Lev Vladimirovich? That wasn't so good either, but better than the way things were. . . . And, when Nadezhda earlier had entered Burlyai's office, she had made a much greater impression on him than he had on her. No doubt, much greater. She fitted perfectly into this rather gloomy office in which many of her wrinkles remained hidden, but her slender figure would stand out beautifully, and so would her eyes. 'O these brown eyes', Nadezhda felt like singing. Well, her voice, too, was quite pleasant. In other words, if she were a man, an Academy member over fifty, she would certainly be interested in Nadezhda Vasily-evna, and she'd want to direct the conversation in such a way that her melodious voice could sound even more pleasant, so that . . . . But would Burlyai?! Hardly; he was just a boy, and a boy wasn't terrifying at all. And, to attract the attention of a real woman, a man had to, well, frighten her a little, but just a tiny bit. Unfortunately, Nadezhda Vasilyevna hadn't been terrified in the least by anyone for years. All men had become for her one child's face. That was old age, that's what it was. But so far Nadezhda Vasilyevna hadn't for the life of her been able to imagine herself old. For the sake of her youth she could be enamored of Lyovka and quarrel with him – and fight for this very life, without an audience and applause, somewhere behind the scenes. But for the sake of old age? Good heavens, how absurd! A woman was programmed for youth, and anything else was beyond her personal program, a tax paid to the family, society, the state. That's what should be taped right now! These fellows should be torn away from their NTR to tape this instantly! Afterwards they could go on with their own stuff, what did she care? So what if Lyovka kept glaring at Burlyai and repeating twice in every sentence, puffing audibly. 'Anatoly Agafonovich! Anatoly Agafonovich!' So what if Burlyai started every sentence with 'The point is, that . . .' and less frequently with 'What's the point here?' But first she had to interrupt them, butt in, and tape her demand for youthfulness. That's the kind of revolution they should try to bring about: extending women's youthfulness to the age of seventy! That's what should enter today's interview! But that was impossible for some reason . . . .

A young woman and an old woman were only biologically one species; otherwise they were different beings who didn't understand, anticipate or remember each other. This train of thinking forced another question: although Nadezhda Vasilyevna hadn't turned old yet, wasn't she none the less already living just for her old age, her unknown and unwanted old age? That was very distressing. She could interpret this as having ceased to love Lyovka. There had been love, and now it was gone – it was as simple as that. That explained everything in the world, her entire personal life at any rate. What if she fell in love with somebody just before the curtain came down, and instantly grew younger? What wouldn't she do to feel young again! What if she suddenly experienced a great love? She'd be head over heels – what was the point of talking? It would be terrifying, but, all the same, she'd go for it, head over heels. Even though you might be secretly happy that the years were passing and such a great love hadn't struck you, thank God, but had passed you by, sparing you, if it suddenly appeared she'd, well, go for it, go for it head over heels. . . .

Incidentally, it was to be expected that one or two generations of women would still have to go through this disease of aging, but then the NTR would supply them with some vitamins or some machine or some bio-chamber – and that would do the trick! And then you would read *Anna Karenina* and be overcome with amazement: 'You won't believe it how things were with those barbarians! They threw themselves under trains. And trains went 30 kilometers an hour in those days, and yet they did it.'

Burlyai, behind his desk, said, 'And what's the point? The point is that love and motherhood are the two components which still determine the psychology of the female half of mankind. It is absolutely mandatory that, in our prognoses of the future, we think about evolution and maybe revolution in this area, that we deal with these spiritual spheres and lofty realms.'

'Good Lord, to what heights has Burlyai risen?' Nadezhda wondered. 'And, even at these heights, nothing makes him giddy . . . .'

'Climbing up to his ivory tower,' she whispered so as not to be heard. 'Steeplejacks.'

And again she started ruminating. This time about herself. Lately she had often caught herself looking back at how she had been in the past. Not so long ago she hadn't felt any past in herself; there was nothing to look back to. Not so long ago only the present had existed, the matter of 'life' itself which nature had asked Nadezhda Vasilyevna to embody as figure, form, skin and eyes, voice and movements. It was a mission, in other words, obvious and natural, and impossible to be conscious of and to put into words. But that's certainly how it had been. Well, even then, of course, not only happiness had existed, but the whole range of experience. Yet all this had only been an annoying concomitant of life, not life itself. And only when this feeling of living entirely in the present had begun to disappear had she become conscious of it and begun to live as intently as she could, guessing that it was no sin to think seriously about her looks, her hair-do, the kind of dress and shoes she wore, and which handbag would go with her shoes. As she had had no access to special clothing-shops and couldn't visit expensive hairdressing-salons, she had relied on her own taste and wits. Then she had decided that with her taste and wits she could get married quickly. Now she realised that in those days she had been over-confident, picking a husband on a tourist trip, at a camp-fire, looking at the gentle, moonlit Black Sea. It was so beautiful, so . . . . But soon after, she had felt like writing a proclamation headed 'GIRLS! DON'T CHOSE YOUR HUSBANDS ON TOURIST TRIPS!' with the reasons why in small letters underneath. How much she wanted to warn the young while comforting herself with saying over and over again, 'I acquired experience! Yes, experience.' And with this experience she rather quickly had married the journalist L. Kuzmenkov. Now she knew how not to waste herself, how to guard her youth, though it wasn't in its first bloom, and how to keep herself convinced that she was, yes indeed, still young, and no, certainly not old yet. She knew how ruinous it was to consider herself unhappy, day in, day out. She had to reckon that her sense of youthfulness would gradually diminish, but the end result would still have to be positive. In each new era women had found new methods for such reckoning, but always with the same result. If only once the result had been negative, not only womankind, but all mankind, would have perished – that was certain! Therefore today the task was to give women a method of age-accounting that matched the NTR. Let them have it, and everything would be fine! 'That's the point!' Comrade Burlyai would say, could he have guessed what this brown-eyed, as yet young woman at the window was thinking. But Burlyai wasn't quick-witted. You could tell by his face.

To imagine having fallen in love with such a specialist on women and the NTR! That was almost the same as loving a sexologist who read you lectures on his speciality every night! The only good thing was that the men would do all the talking without her participation. Men talked while she could follow her own train of thought beautifully, perfectly! You never knew in what context you'd find them or lose them.

Lyovka's questions and comments to Burlyai were quite vicious. 'Well, Lyovka, how are you doing?' Nadezhda thought. 'No, he won't fall through the crack; he's still going to grow.'

Burlyai answered Lyovka calmly, from time to time looking in Nadezhda's direction, as if about to call her. But she wouldn't join them. She'd just say, 'No, thank you!' And she wouldn't needle Lyovka with as much as a syllable. Because he was a good man on the whole, even an unusual person; and not every man was able to live with a woman of Nadezhda Vasilyevna's character. What if stupidity made her stop loving Lyovka? Or if Lyovka guessed that she had finally stopped loving him? What then? She'd get the creeps, that's what would happen! She thought herself such a special woman, a woman the likes of whom couldn't be found anywhere on the globe! And neither her husband nor her son could live through a single day without her, she thought. But what if they could? Lyovka had become much more independent and involved in his work over the last few years, and Kolya was able to make his own omelette and hot cereal – of course, if the milk was fresh and didn't curdle and if it didn't burn because he added too much water.

At this very moment Burlyai turned to her: 'Nadezhda Vasily-evna, my dear! How do you, as a woman, notice the NTR in your daily life? What kind of observations have you made?'

And Nadezhda Vasilyevna answered, without further thought, 'The milk's always curdling now. You can't make a normal hot cereal, morning or night. I didn't notice anything like this before the NTR.'

Lyovka jumped up, covering his mouth with his hand like a young lady. Burlyai responded with a rather odd chuckle. Men were simply idiots; they didn't know how to listen to a woman. It wasn't always important what a woman said, but how she said it! But they weren't aware of this 'how', couldn't perceive it. She had spoken jokingly, entirely benevolently, to those boors, those ignoramuses. Well, forget about the dullards. It was a blessing that not all men were as idiotic and dense. For instance, Pokrovsky, the director of the instructional section of the Polytechnic, at which Nadezhda was more or less in charge of the planning-office, had said, 'You can swear as much as you like. I'm always ready to listen to your voice!' On several occasions Nadezhda had told Lyovka about this director. How could she make him grasp that in the Polytechnic she was an important figure, that everybody listened to her, and that someone was constantly asking her about something – students, lecturers, professors and department heads, even deans. Apart from the fact that in the planning-office you encountered computers and the NTR wherever you turned, and that, without Nadezhda Vasilyevna, without her personal participation and her wits, you would be confronted with absolute chaos instead of timetables. The instructional sections, the workshops and the labs would all be mixed up, the night students would be squeezed into the day classes, the correspondence students put together with the regular students, the machine-tool builders with the applied mechanics, the workers servicing automats with the electricians. The specialized classrooms would also be confused, and the entire educational process would go to rack and ruin! She imagined this rack and ruin visually and audibly – something like a Hiroshima without human victims.

Well, and this important figure, who daily saved the Polytechnic from chaos, came home, and her husband Lyovka would be entirely self-absorbed, wouldn't talk because he had trouble at work! But everyone else, of course, had had only pleasant experiences, only he had an upsetting day. That was enough to trigger any fight.

It would start with reproaches, because she didn't have the energy to refrain from nagging Lyovka! Reproaches were her means of self-affirmation, her well-deserved right, and just you try to give up what you consider your well-deserved right! Of course, instead of reproaching Lyovka, she could dig up a piece of fresh meat, fry a hamburger! And she could stroke his head; her hand wouldn't drop off. She could even say a nice word; her tongue wouldn't wither. Anything was possible, but certainly not every day. But she was ready with a reproach at any time.

When she was nagging Lyovka, Nadezhda Vasilyevna would remember that quite only recently she hadn't felt the need to prove herself to anybody. She had been absolutely right by the mere fact of her existence. Then the nagging and reproaching had come all by itself, unrelated to memories, in a chemically pure form.

Now times had changed and she had to prove herself to everyone – to her husband, her son, the educational staff of the Polytechnic and to herself. As to the Polytechnic, she often had imagined leaving. It was terribly nerve-racking work, and she could halve the waste of energy and health. But where would she go? Join some female domain of administrative assistants?

Concentrate entirely on bringing up Lyovka and Kolya? Only the grave could improve Lyovka, and Kolya was normal anyway. So what, if he didn't do too well at school? Lev Tolstoy hadn't either. It was important to get Kolya away from the telephone – that was some task! Maybe he took after his father and was going to be a journalist. The day wasn't long enough for him. No, he had to drag the phone into the bathroom at night, and there you could hear him droning – his voice was getting deeper – and then 'Hee, hee, hee!' You could hear everything, and you wanted to sleep. But in the morning it was impossible to wake up Kolya; you might as well pour cold water over him! How much better it had been when she was his age. There had been lots of girls and boys in the family and not a single telephone. And you couldn't possibly sit in the toilet for any length of time. There were lots of children; you were always under the healthy influence of a healthy collective. Such were the times then! No, she wouldn't leave the Polytechnic. You couldn't find 150 roubles in the street. There were times when the Kuzmenkovs would have had to go begging without those 150 roubles, and who felt like doing that? And such a time could come again; there was no guarantee.

And what else? Nadezhda Vasilyevna could become depressed in an instant, so depressed that Lyovka and Kolya and even the whole Polytechnic would feel wretched, not to mention herself. But she shouldn't. That was the worst, the last thing she could do, and the last thing must always be postponed to later.

At this point Burlyai said, 'Even today we're able to experience love, but how to safeguard this love . . . .'

That was interesting. Nadezhda listened to the conversation, but it had ended; those words had been the last.

As they took leave amiably, Burlyai said, 'Nadezhda Vasilyevna, forgive us for boring you.'

'Boring?' She was amazed. 'What do you mean? I had such a good time sitting and thinking. I looked around, at your dark panels, your chandelier. It's hard to find a place like this for sitting in the epoch of the NTR. And, besides, it's important to be bored a little sometimes. A woman who's never bored is a very boring person!'

In response Burlyai mumbled something about the Polytechnic, about her being the most important and highly regarded controller there and that without her the Polytechnic was like a person without hands.

'Ah, that's interesting!' Nadezhda Vasilyevna thought. 'So Lyovka told him something else about me. So he didn't tell me everything he had said to Burlyai about me. Evidently he very much wanted Burlyai to invite me to this talk. So. . . . Well, watch out Lyovka!'

And Lyovka?

He forgot that even in taking offense you have to keep a sense of proportion. Otherwise you offended your offender with your offense worse than with anything else!

Fate seemed to want to spite them. On the way to Burlyai it had taken them half an hour to flag down a taxi. Now one was standing right at the entrance to Burlyai's Institute, its green light winking, and they hadn't even intended to take one.

Lyovka was the first to get into the taxi, but Nadezhda Vasilyevna didn't feel like getting in. She'd rather have taken the subway and gone home alone, but she decided against it and squeezed into the taxi. Inside, she asked, 'Well, my boy, did you get upset? Just hold on a bit longer and we'll be home. I'll give you some valerian drops, put you to bed and sing you a lullaby.'

Whereupon Lyovka started giving it to her, not minding the driver's presence. The first thing he spat out was that she had so humiliated him before Burlyai that he hadn't known where to sink for shame.

'And do you know now?'

'What?'

'Where to sink! Why don't you sink through the ceiling? Sinking through the floor is too trivial!'

The next item was that Nadezhda was inhuman, vicious, spiteful, psychologically abnormal! Would a normal person tell a famous scientist to his face that he's a steeplejack climbing up to his ivory tower? Tell a member of the Academy of Sciences? Tell the person on whom the fate of her own husband depended?

O Lord! Lyovka had heard what she had said about climbing an ivory tower! That was dreadful!

Through tears Nadezhda Vasilyevna said, 'Well, so what? An abnormal person? A freak? And you think it's normal to make such an issue of this?'

'And have you forgotten "The milk curdles in the epoch of the NTR"? And is it normal to pester a person with "What's after the

NTR?" And to send me out for a smoke, if I don't smoke? And to say, "Take the logic out of my answer and what's left?" Is that normal? Eh?'

Nadezhda Vasilyevna yelled, crying, 'I don't give a damn! I don't care at all any more about who I am! If one person completely misunderstands the other, if that person doesn't comprehend who in reality humiliated whom, and who has been hating whom for a long time, and who got permanently disillusioned today about whom, well, don't you think after all this nothing means a damn thing, that nothing matters?'

After they got home it became generally impossible to understand who said what to whom. Kolya hid in the bathroom, even without his telephone. Everything was a mess, a disgusting mess like never before in their life together, or so it seemed.

Nadezhda Vasilyevna set herself up for the night on the sofa in the dining-room and lay down in her clothes, shaking with sobs. She sobbed and sobbed. Then she undressed, lay down again and continued sobbing. Later she put on an old brown robe, hoping it would warm her knees and her heart, but this time it warmed nothing, and Nadezhda thought, 'All right, it's all decided. But what's going to happen with Kolya?' That was the only undecided problem, everything else was clear. Well, for some reason she thought of Khristina Ulyanovna, the formal head of the planning-office of the Polytechnic. Evidently Khristina suddenly flashed through her mind in connection with the fact that altruism, of course, exists in the world, but always in a strange fashion – namely, at someone's mercy, riding on someone's back. And the person on whose back it is riding doesn't have the strength to topple it. Well, for instance, who needed Khristina as the director of the planning-office? Nobody had needed her for ten years, and she didn't even need the job herself. . . . Khristina lacked nothing; her children had decent salaries and were keeping their mother well-dressed. Nadezhda Vasilyevna wasn't nearly as well-dressed! But these children had apparently rooted their mother firmly and for ever in her job, while she, Nadezhda, always did all the work. And Khristina had nothing else to do but worry about curling her few gray hairs.

Of course in every department, in every small collective, there is always a work-dodger, and everyone knows who it is. It is either the daughter of some higher-up, taking time off regardless of whether it's a workday or not. Or it's someone's son, or maybe just a son who's off on a special assignment, or on a field trip, or gone to a chess-match, whatever the day. With Khristina it was neither. Someone's old mother was going to work regularly as clockwork, taking to heart all matters concerning the planning-office without doing anything about them. And how could she, at her age? If at least she were some higher-up's daughter! Then she would at least bring in some news about what the authorities were saying. That by itself would improve the morale of Nadezhda Vasilyevna, an energetic, imaginative woman whom everyone listened to. It was such a sin not to work the whole day, morning until evening; such a sin to muddle things up; and such a sin to think that she was doing someone else's work.

And every time Nadezhda Vasilyevna felt bad – when she quarreled with Lyovka, or was out of sorts with Kolya or else was ill – she thought of Khristina. She'd come to her mind and wouldn't get out of her head, to prove that it was all Nadezhda's own fault, that she was just paying for her own mistakes: at work she labored for two, and at home it was the same. And now she was supposed to suffer for two! But why? And if she had enough compassion and pity she'd do it for three? For ten? And was it so vile and loathsome to feel sorry for herself? But what did it have to do with her if such a vile arithmetic, if this kind of altruism, existed in the world?

Wasn't egotism much better? Egoism was a common, homely nag which had no room left for further branding. It had been branded, head to tail, long ago. All you had to do was sit on it and it would take you where it smelled roast duck.

Altruism, on the other hand, was a blue-blooded steed, a perfect beauty. But it had one shortcoming: it wouldn't take you anywhere; you had to drag it yourself. You would be the one dragging it, yet it would be the one giving the orders: 'More to the right! Now left! More to the left! Straight ahead and faster!'

Around 4 a.m. Nadezhda distinctly recalled how she had sat by the window in Burlyai's office, gazing outside and thinking about herself. How well, how perfectly well, she had been able to think, and in fact had thought, about herself! It hadn't been so much a sensation of happiness as one of vitality. One really should always live with such a sense of vitality; it wasn't just a mere possibility! If only she could feel it right now, this minute! What wouldn't she give . . .?

At this moment the light went on and Lyovka walked in.

There he was. Feast your eyes! Take delight, wife!

Instead of being self-assured, and instead of nobly apologizing and forgetting about all that had happened, he walked in pathetic, dishevelled, unwanted and unneeded by anybody. The fact that he should and could have been one kind of person, but entered the room an absolutely different one, was in itself enough to make him even more hateful to her!

And it did. Nadezhda Vasilyevna said, 'Leave!' and turned to the wall. She felt nauseated, hearing the familiar breathing of this strange person clad in the colorful pajamas she had bought for him last week. She knew that this man could, yes, could be a real man, but didn't want to, and she thought that this was his own business, his own choice. But what kind of woman was she, Nadezhda Vasilyevna, in the presence of a man who was no man? Had this ever occurred to him?

Lyovka said, 'It's the end', and put the tape-recorder on the magazine table.

Without looking she guessed what he had put down and where he had placed it. Everything became instantly clear to her and she said, 'Serves you right! Absolutely! Just serves you right!'

'It's the end.'

'And who told you? Who warned you? Did the button get stuck – and jam up completely?

'The button too . . . completely. And something else too . . . .'

'Is the tape demagnetized? What's on the tape?'

'I think it's . . . Vysotsky.'

'Vysotsky? Better not be; he was always a rowdy. And who warned you? Serves you right, you and your Burlyai too!'

Lyovka plaintively and quietly, extremely quietly, started talking about how unhappy he was and how he just had no luck. He had no luck, but through dogged work he had been making progress and in the last three years had become a noted specialist on the problems of the NTR. A year ago he had written a book about the NTR, and six months ago he had signed an agreement with a publisher for a second book on the subject. The kingpin in this second book, which would decide his career, was to be Burlyai, the Academy member.

Your kingpin's making my head spin, too! I wish I had never laid eyes on him!' Nadezhda responded.

'Burlyai is very clever, a decent man. Burlyai's our number-one hope – that is, mine and yours.'

'What number?'

'One . . . number one.'

'So what are you going to do with your hope? Hm?' she asked, starting to cry again, quietly, bitterly.

'You know what we're going to do?'

'We?'

'Of course, we. Who else? In difficult moments there's no choice. As soon as you, as soon as we . . . in one word, as soon as you, we, you and I . . . .'

'Speak more clearly! What are you talking about – "you–we" or "we–you"?'

'Good Lord, Nadezhda! What a time to pick on me! Well, I suppose you have nerves of steel. Listen, so . . . . Listen, I, or better you Nadezhda, I think it's better, well, if we call Burlyai later today and ask him to meet us again to repeat the interview. We admit honestly that you didn't check the cassette and therefore we got a double take, and so we ask him . . . I think if you really try hard and phone and explain our situation, we . . . .'

Nadezhda Vasilyevna jumped off the sofa and ran toward Lyovka, her fists raised. Before she got to him she caught herself, turned around and dropped back on the sofa. For a while she lay silently, holding her head in her hands, and then, her brown dressing-gown unbuttoned, she shouted, 'Have you gone mad? To present yourself as an idiot! An absent-minded dodo! An incompetent fool! And to present me as an idiot too? As a dodo and a fool and God knows what else? I tell you: I will never phone Burlyai, and you won't phone him either. You heard me? You will bring him a ready typescript of our interview, no matter how it turned out, understand? And he will sign this interview, no matter how it turned out, understand? Hand me the tape-recorder! Plug it in!'

Nadezhda Vasilyevna held the cold black box in her hands, examining it attentively; after putting it first to one ear, then to the other, she shook it vigorously and hit it first on one side, then on the other. 'And my faithful friend, my wife and mistress of my home . . .' or something like this Vysotsky was singing with his hoarse voice, and after a few measures of guitar-strumming Burlyai's voice said, 'one epoch is um . . . to . . . .'

'This kingpin's making my head spin, too,' Nadezhda sighed heavily. 'A button should be made out of this pin – a number-one button; that wouldn't be bad at all. These people should be made kingpins, and the pins should be made into buttons.'

She wound the cassette back for a few seconds and heard herself: 'My question is: . . . come . . . aft . . . NTR . . . Anoth . . . revolution? I mean, something permanent?' And then Vysotsky sang again.

'Well, for some reason you aren't there at all, Lyovka. . . . Everything else is there, but you aren't. Strange. . . .'

'I am there!' Lyovka said. 'I'll come later, don't worry!'

'Ugh! . . . that pop music! Where's "do", where's "so", where's "do-re-mi"? You just try making it out! Well, then. There's paper on the table, and the fountain-pen must be there too. We'll listen to the tape and we'll be able to put together something from it. Why don't you write and I'll listen and dictate. Do you remember what you said to Burlyai?'

'I don't think so. No, I don't think I can remember. A lapse of memory. Stress. An abberation. Everything's lost. It's all in vain, but you won't see it . . . .'

'But I remember everything Burlyai said. Everything. I sat at the window and didn't listen, but I remember it all. Sit over here on the sofa and write. And spread out the blanket before you sit down.'

'I'm clean! I'm in my pajamas, and they're new,' Lyovka said.

'You've got to stick to the rules; you can't just lie down on someone else's sheets. Well? Let's listen from the beginning! Start!'

The tape-recorder made hoarse sounds, droned, and howled; the neighbors knocked. Nadezhda tried to apologize through the wall, but the neighbors couldn't hear it. The interview was more or less reconstructed. The Kuzmenkovs labored like a clock-work.

Only once did Nadezhda Vasilyevna stop and think for a moment; it was when they noted down the following words of Burlyai: "A woman perceives the phenomenon of the NTR in terms of things, of objects – a new TV, a new machine unit, an unbreakable glass, a new glue that glues any glass and even the heel of her shoe. Women don't think about the idea of the NTR, they even reject the idea, while for men it's the very idea, the general trend of thought that's central.'

'What's the matter?' Lyovka asked Nadezhda. 'You want me to get you some tap water?'

'No, it's nothing. I want to understand what these words about men and women mean in general.'

'It's just a statement of fact, that's all. The establishment of a fact. The fact as such and nothing else.'

'And what are the consequences?'

'Nadezhda? Can you explain to me why you need to know the consequences? Why do you have to know right now, this minute, when it's absolutely inappropriate? If the consequences are so important to you, well, they'll come, don't worry. In about five or ten years. Take it easy and wait. You certainly put strange demands on the facts, very strange!'

'Not at all. I just keep waiting and expecting something from clever people, from clever men. Right now my head's spinning, I even feel nauseated, I can barely sit – not to mention stand – I'd like to lie down this minute and to forget about everything; but I've got to go on, I'm still expecting something . . . .'

'What do you expect?'

'Something from intelligent men. But it's obvious now that it's in vain. Tell me at least what you told Burlyai about me when you arranged your interview.'

'Nothing special.'

'Just remember. Remember what wasn't special.'

'Well, he said, "It would be nice if a woman participated in our conversation, someone contemporary, energetic, who works a lot and is the kind that has a family."'

'What else?'

'And . . . who's emancipated.'

'Was "emancipated" the main thing?'

'I said, "Well, that's my wife!" You want to know the exact words I used? "Honest to God, that's my wife!"'

'You don't know your wife very well.'

'Where was I wrong? Isn't it all true?'

'It's not true, because it's not the only truth. You present your wife much too simply to these people you barely know. It's enough that an Academy member sits in front of you, and you tell him about my character traits. Without my seal and signature, just "Honest to God". Next time please make sure I agree with your character sketch. At least let me read it. You see what happened: I didn't know about my character traits and so I let you down; and I frightened Burlyai. If you had told me in advance who I was, I would have known. And I wouldn't have let anybody down. I'm sorry.'

'For whom are you sorry? Tell me.'

'For myself most of all. Imagine – emancipated from head to toe, and still expecting something from intelligent men. Well, all right,

Lyovka. Right now the point is, we can't go on like this. Soon I've got to get up and wake up Kolya, cook cereal for him and you, and run off to work.'

'You should have cooked the cereal last night! It wouldn't be the first time, eh? We'll postpone the work with the tape-recorder until tonight. I'm also terribly tired. I've got to take a rest and come to my senses.'

'I won't be able to remember anything tonight. Today we are going to fix the exam schedule, and after that ordeal I can't even remember my own name. No, we have to think up something now, something sensible, this minute!'

'Good Lord, when's this all going to be over and done with?' Lyovka implored.

'In the kitchen, on the second shelf, there's a little tape-recorder. Why don't you load it and bring it here? And then we'll do this: we'll listen to the tape together and then we'll speak onto the little recorder what we got from the big one. But we'll divide it up: you will speak for yourself, and I for Burylai.'

'You for Burlyai?'

'Yes, I, since he's absent.'

'And then you know what's going to happen? I'll transcribe our tape on which you speak for Burlyai, I'll type it and take it to Burlyai, and then he won't recognize himself and everything's lost.'

'I bet you anything he'll recognize himself! But be sure to type the inverview very well, without corrections; then he'll recognize himself. I'd do it, but I won't be able to get round to it today. So it's up to you. Make sure: no corrections.'

'Sew on my button, then. You've got to keep your promises, too! But the little tape-recorder hasn't worked for a long time. You've got a strange logic, Nadezhda Vasilyevna. Very strange.'

'If mine is weird, what's yours?'

'You work at the Polytechnic?' Lyovka asked suddenly.

'Yes, and no longer anywhere else!' Nadezhda confirmed.

'You should be used to conversations about the NTR, to thinking about and understanding it.'

'You think so? But, first of all, in the Polytechnic everyone is making the NTR and nobody talks about it. Others do the talking.'

'And secondly?'

'Secondly, you and Burlyai as men don't understand anything about the NTR, and I as a woman don't understand it. And another difference is that you publicize your ignorance while I keep mine to myself. That's the sort of specialists we are. And that's all there is to your interview. So, get the little tape-recorder. In the kitchen, second shelf.'

'It doesn't work. It broke last summer, at the dacha.'

'Just bring it here. We'll give it a few good smacks and it'll work!'

Three days later Burlyai inspected the interview with journalist L. Kuzmenkov and made not a single change. Two months later the article 'Women and the NTR' appeared in a journal and attracted a wide readership. And to this day all kinds of writers are referring to it, not only in our country but also abroad.

Glossary

Abortions. Originally allowed by an edict of 18 November 1920, abortions were forbidden under Stalin by a law of 27 June 1936, in order to raise the birthrate. As this goal was not realized, a decree of 23 November 1955 again legalized abortions. They had to be performed in hospitals before the twelfth week of pregnancy, and only if the last abortion was more than six months ago and there were no medical counter-indications. All clauses that made abortion difficult were dropped in 1968, when it became automatically available to everyone. For an abortion a woman would take an unpaid leave of absence for three days and register for a small fee, five roubles, at a hospital. Thus, in Grekova's story, Lyalka's abortion in the mid-1960s was not a problem.

Böll, Heinrich (1917–85). A German writer famous for his critical portrayals of post-war Germany. His work has been widely translated into Russian.

Borodino Panorama. A round building containing a painting 115 meters long and 15 meters high, painted in 1912 to commemorate the centenary of the Battle of Borodino, in which General Kutuzov failed to prevent Napoleon from entering Moscow. The building also contains other exhibits of documents and portraits.

The Captain's Daughter. A well-known historical novel written by Aleksandr Sergeevich Pushkin in 1836. Shvabrin is the villain of the novel.

Collective farm (*kolkhoz* – abbreviation for *kollektivnoe khozyaistvo*, 'collective economy'). The dominant production unit in Communist agriculture, a rural institution through which the state controls agricultural production. Collective-farm land is owned by the state, and allocated permanently to each collective farm. All assets of such a farm are collective property. Theoretically the collective farm is governed by a general meeting that elects a manager and

239

admits or dismisses members. In practice the Party appoints the manager and directs his activities. In 1974 there were about 30,000 collective farms, averaging 463 households each. Production quotas are determined by central government. Since 1969 a new 'Collective Farm Charter' has allowed peasants to participate in policy-making. Only the details of farm work were organized locally. After state obligations and taxes had been met, part of the farm's annual income was set aside for communal needs (repairs, construction, etc.), a portion was allocated to pay administrative staff, and the remainder – usually very little – was distributed among the members of the collective according to the type of work and number of working-days. Peasants lived at subsistence level, getting their food primarily from their private plots (up to two acres), which they worked in their spare time. A peasant could only leave his farm with the agreement of the farm chairman.

The purpose of collectivization was to increase state income (large-scale farming, using modern agricultural machinery, was expected to be more efficient) and ultimately to raise the rural standard of living, to transform the peasant into an industrial laborer and to eliminate the cultural gap between town and countryside. The abitrary centralized command, low pay of farmers, and their powerlessness and indifference prevented these goals from being achieved. Rural housing, schools, services and utilities are far below the urban standard. Until recently, peasants on collective farms earned less and received fewer benefits from social welfare funds than industrial workers. Drinking and apathy were rampant. In spite of great efforts to modernize and to wean peasants away from old customs and traditions, discipline, efficiency and productivity rose only slightly. Because of the dullness of life and lack of amenities, services and opportunities in the countryside, skilled young personnel have been leaving the villages *en masse*. This has become easier since 1980, as peasants have been granted internal passports.

Communal refuge. A communal apartment in which many individuals or families share one kitchen and one bathroom.

Co-op, Co-operative apartment. Private individuals can obtain an apartment or a summer dacha if they can muster a considerable sum of money (at least 40 per cent of the value of the property) to qualify for a state loan. The payments are higher than the normal rent paid to the state.

Cortazar, Julio (b. 1914). Argentine writer, living in Paris, whose work began to be published in 1949. *The End of the Game* (*Final de juego*) is a collection of stories combining the fantastic with realistic details of daily life.

'Count Nulin'. Aleksandr Pushkin's humorous verse tale of 1826 parodying Shakespeare's 'The Rape of Lucrece' and history; it is a gem of gaiety.

Dacha. Country cottage owned or rented for the summer by city people.

Day of Victory. A holiday to commemorate 9 May 1945, the end of the Second World War for the Soviet Union.

Domostroi (*Household Management*). A sixteenth-century book of rules for the successful regulation of a household. The father, likened to the tsar in power, has supreme authority in the family. Corporal punishment is recommended for transgressions of wives, children and servants. The work's title has become synonymous with patriarchal attitudes and domestic tyranny.

Dormitory. Because of the difficult housing-situation, especially in cities, a former marriage-partner often has difficulties finding a private room or apartment. Therefore he or she moves into a dormitory. Many young workers who want to make the transition from the country to the city also live in dormitories, as it takes five years to qualify for a residence permit.

Exchange. Rooms or apartments for which rent is paid may be exchanged when the need arises: for example, when people get married or divorced. A married couple have a two- or three-room apartment, but the separate partners need a room each after the divorce. Such an exchange can take place slowly through official channels, or more quickly through private advertisements and arrangements. The move then has to be registered with the state housing-authorities. In 'Morning Meetings', Zorin generously moved to a dormitory, leaving the entire apartment to his ex-wife.

Maxim Gorky (pseudonym of A. M. Peshkov, 1868–1936) became the most popular writer and most discussed man in Russia when he was not yet thirty. Ranked with Tolstoy and above Chekhov, he became the champion of Russian literature after 1917. At the turn of the century he came in contact with Marxists and himself became one of the foremost radicals. He wrote for the Marxist review *Life*, which was suppressed for printing his poem 'Song of the Stormy Petrel', an allegory of the coming revolution. The stormy petrel is a seabird.

GUM (Gosudarstvenny Universal'ny Magazin, State General Store). The GUM is the largest shopping-center in Moscow and borders Red Square. The building dates back to the turn of the century and contains dozens of specialized little shops.

Interruption of pregnancy. *See* Abortion.

Karelia. An autonomous republic within the Russian Socialist Soviet Republic. Karelia is located in the far north-west of the Soviet Union, bordering Finland and stretching from the Kola Peninsula to Lakes Ladoga and Onega. It is a flat area with innumerable lakes.

Kefir. Milk thickened and made sour by a special culture of bacteria.

Klin. Town about 80 miles north-west of Moscow.

Kolkhoz. See Collective farm.

Kvas. A slightly sweet, non-alcoholic drink made of hops.

Lithuania. One of the fifteen Soviet republics. Along with the neighboring Baltic states Estonia and Latvia, Lithuania was incorporated into the Soviet Union in 1940, as a result of a deal with Hitler.

May, First of. International workers' day, celebrated with parades. Many factories, collective farms and other enterprises are named in honor of this holiday.

New Ascania ('Askaniya Nova'). A natural reserve of 27,500 acres situated in the Ukraine. One of the last areas of pure untouched steppe left in the world. Exotic animals first brought there in the 1880s and animals rare in Russia breed there successfully.

New Year. The holiday that corresponds to the Western Christmas, though celebrated on 31 January. 'Father Frost' brings gifts to children, and the apartment is decorated with a fir-tree.

NTR. A very common and much-used abbreviation for *nauchno-tekhnicheskaya revolyutsiya* (scientific-technological Revolution). Science and technology have been eulogized in Soviet society because of the role they played in the economic transformation of Russia in the 1920s and 1930s. All science is regarded as an ally of the 'science' of Marxism–Leninism in the building of Communist society. The phrase was used by Bulganin in 1955 at the Central Committee Plenum and entered the new Party Program of 1961. Ever since, the implementation of the NTR has been emphasized as a major precondition for transforming Soviet society.

Patronymic. The middle name of the three names a Russian bears. The patronymic is based on the father's first name, to which *-ovich* for a son and *-ovna* for a daughter is added. 'Agafonovich', for example, means 'son of Agafon'.

Politinformation. A regular subject in Soviet schools is the study of contemporary events, on which students are required to prepare reports. They have to present the 'correct' political interpretation to get a good grade.

Registration. A marriage has to be registered at a state office. This suffices to make it legal.

Roofing-felt. A stiff, pressed material like cardboard, soaked with water-repellent and used for roofing sheds and houses.

Shock worker. Shock workers are also called Stakhanovites, after a worker who exceeded his production quotas. Payments per unit of work are fixed in terms of certain norms which the workers are invited to break. When they succeed, they are praised and rewarded as shock workers, but success causes the norms to be raised for all workers. This program of 'socialist emulation' was launched by the Party in 1929.

'The Song of the Stormy Petrel. *See* Gorky.

Summer or Pioneer camp. An arrangement whereby children spend several weeks of their three-month summer holiday away from home with other children. Usually their parents work, so they would be at home alone. Often it is difficult to arrange for father, mother and children to take their holidays at the same time. The camp serves to ease these problems. Usually each factory or institute has its own camp.

Suvorov, Field-Marshal Alexander (1729–1800). A brilliant commander who won many victories, especially in the Russo–Turkish War (1787–91), and wrote a famous treatise on the training of troops and conduct of warfare. This book has exercised strong influence on Russian military thought.

Taiga. Immense primeval forests in Siberia and the Russian Far East.

Validol. A medication that dilates the arteries.

Vampilov Aleksandr (1937–1972). A well-known playwright whose work began to be published in 1958. His dramas deal with complex moral problems. His most famous work, *The Duck Hunt* (*Utiinaya okhota*, 1970), portrays the tragic degradation of a young man in the context of social callousness, indifference and egotism.

Vereshchagin, Vasily Vasilievich (1842–1904). Russian artist who specialized in painting battle scenes.

Village Council Soviet. Central body of the local administration, elected for a two-year term, consisting of twenty to fifty deputies per village. It meets about six times per year. Party members dominate. 48 per cent are women, 40 per cent workers, 30 per cent under thirty. Most deputies have secondary or higher education. The executive committee of the Village Soviet sets up local government departments (responsible for trade, public welfare, education, culture, library services, women's affairs, housing, etc.).

The three most important members of the executive committee are paid; the rest are volunteers. Most deputies work on one or the other of the standing committees. Local Soviets have power to influence economic growth and public welfare in their areas. The executive committee is held accountable to the next-higher level of administration and to Party organizations. This set-up is being reorganized now under Gorbachev.

Vysotsky, Vladimir. The Soviet Union's most famous and well-loved song-writer, singer and actor. Born on 25 January 1938, he died prematurely at the age of forty-two from a heart-attack. His songs were officially ignored (that is, were not published) because many of the sentiments they expressed were perceived by the authorities as dissident, but they none the less circulated in thousands of taped copies. As a result of Gorbachev's liberalization, Vysotsky's songs have been publicly available since 1986, and a videotape of his life-story has been produced.

Suggestions for Further Reading

Atkinson, Dorothy, *et al.* (eds), *Women in Russia* (Stanford, Calif.: Stanford University Press, 1977).

Buckley, Mary (ed.), *Soviet Social Scientists Talking – An Official Debate about Women* (London: Macmillan, 1986).

Chao, Paul, *Women under Communism: Family in Russian and China* (Bayside, NY: General Hall, 1977).

Corten, Irina, 'Feminism in Russian Literature', in *Modern Encyclopedia of Russian and Soviet Literature* (New York: Academic International Press, 1984) vii, 176–93.

Dunham, Vera, 'The Changing Image of Women in Soviet Literature', in D. R. Brown (ed.), *The Role and Status of Women in the Soviet Union* (New York: Columbia University Press, 1968) pp. 60–97.

Gasiarowske, Xenia, *Women in Soviet Fiction 1917–1964* (Madison: University of Wisconsin Press, 1968).

——, 'On Happiness in Recent Soviet Fiction', *Russian Literature Triquarterly*, 9 (1974) 473–85.

——, 'Two Decades of Love and Marriage in Soviet Fiction', *Russian Review*, xxxii (1975) 10–21.

Hansson, Carola, and Liden, Karin, *Moscow Women* (New York: Pantheon, 1983).

Heldt, Barbara, *Terrible Perfection: Women and Russian Literature* (Bloomington: Indiana University Press, 1987).

——, 'The Burden of Caring', *The Nation*, 243 (13 June 1987) pp. 820–24.

Holland, Barbara, *Soviet Sisterhood* (Bloomington: Indiana University Press, 1985).

Hyman, Tom, *Russian Women* (New York: St Martin's Press, 1983).

Jancar, Barbara Wolfe, 'Women and Soviet Politics', in Henry W. Morton and Rudolf L. Tökés (eds), *Soviet Politics and Society in the 1970s* (New York: Free Press, 1974).

Kollontai, Alexandra, *Selected Writings*, ed. and tr. Alix Holt (Westport, Conn.: Lawrence Hill, 1978).

Lapidus, Gail Warshofsky, *Women in Soviet Society: Equality, Development, and Social Change* (Berkeley, Calif.: University of California Press, 1978).

Lenin, Vladimir I., *On the Emancipation of Women* (Moscow: Progress Publishers, 1977).

Luke, Louise E., 'Marxian Woman: Soviet Variants', in Ernest J. Simmons (ed.), *Through the Glass of Soviet Literature* (New York: Columbia University Press, 1961) pp. 27–109.

Mamonova, Tayana (ed.), *Women in Russia* (Boston, Mass.: Beacon Press, 1983).

Mandel, William N., *Soviet Women* (Garden City, NY: Ramparts Press, 1975).

McAuley, Alastair, *Women's Work and Wages in the Soviet Union* (London: Allen & Unwin, 1981).

Natov, Nadine, 'Daily Life and Individual Psychology in Soviet Russian Prose of the 1970s', *Russian Review*, xxxiii (1976) 357–71.

Pachmuss, Temira, *Women Writers in Russian Modernism: An Anthology* (Urbana: University of Illinois Press, 1978).

Sacks, Michael Paul, *Women's Work in Soviet Russia: Continuity in the Midst of Change* (New York: Praeger, 1976).

Sedugin, P., *New Soviet Legislation on Marriage and the Family* (Moscow: Progress Publishers, 1973).

Shneidman, Norman. N., 'Controversial Prose of the 1970s: Problems of Marriage and Love in Contemporary Soviet Literature', *Canadian Slavonic Papers*, xviii, no. 4 (Dec 1976) 400–14.

Stites, Richard, *The Women's Liberation Movement in Russia: Feminism, Nihilism, and Bolshevism 1860–1930* (Princeton, NJ: Princeton University Press, 1978).

Trotsky, Leon, *Women and the Family*, ed. Max Eastman *et al.* (New York: Pathfinder Press, 1973).

Women in Eastern Europe Group, *Woman and Russia* (London: Sheba Feminist, 1980).

Yedlin, Tova (ed.), *Women in Eastern Europe and the Soviet Union* (New York: Praeger, 1980).